The Defiant

David Lee Corley

Table of Contents

Quote

"A nation can survive its fools, and even the ambitious. But it cannot survive treason from within."

- Marcus Tullius Cicero

Barbarians at the Gate

San Diego, California

Marine Corps Base Camp Pendleton stretched across 125,000 acres of Southern California coastline, its vast expanse a fortress of American military might. Artillery ranges and training grounds sprawled inland toward the mountains. Vehicle pools housed rows of armored trucks and Humvees. The weapons depot - buried in reinforced concrete bunkers - stored enough firepower to equip the 42,000 soldiers in the I Marine Expeditionary Force stationed at the base. Tonight, storm clouds smothered the base in darkness, an unseasonable downpour turning the roads into rivers.

Sergeant Mike Peters rubbed his eyes and sipped burnt coffee that had gone cold hours ago. The rain hammered against the guardhouse roof, each drop another reminder of the endless night ahead. Private

First-Class Andy Chen stared through the rain-streaked window, fighting the monotony of the graveyard shift.

"Three more hours till shift change," Peters muttered. "Man, I hate Echo gate." Chen stretched. "Rather be back in Afghanistan. Remember those village checkpoints?"

"Least we knew everyone wanted to kill us there." Peters spotted headlights cutting through the rain. "Three trucks coming."

Chen checked the manifest schedule and frowned. "No deliveries scheduled till oh-six-hundred."

The lead Freightliner's wipers fought the downpour as it rolled to a stop. A man in a Port of San Diego cap leaned out, rain dripping from the brim as he extended his credentials. The brim of his cap shielded his face from the harsh overhead floodlights.

Chen stepped into the rain. "Nothing on the schedule for this hour."

"Special delivery for the armory," the driver said. "Called in late."

Peters reached for the phone. His hand never made it.

A suppressed Glock emerged from the shadows inside the truck's cab. The first shot whispered through the rain. The silenced round pierced the side of Peters's head, his body slumping forward onto the desk. Chen spun toward the sound, his hand moving to his sidearm. The suppressed Glock coughed again. Chen crumpled against the rain-streaked window, crimson streaking the glass. Another shot in each corpse assured their continued silence.

A black-clad figure wearing body armor moved with practiced efficiency through the rain, entered the gatehouse, and pressed the gate control. The gate opened. The black-clad figure jumped on the truck's driver side steps and rode into the base followed by two more trucks. On the back of each truck was a steel cargo container for overseas shipping.

Somewhere in the storm, a single shell casing lay forgotten in the mud. Its headstamp matched no known manufacturer.

As the truck convoy moved deeper into the base, it rolled to a stop. Six figures emerged from the back of the lead truck and moved off into their darkness. Their gear marked them as professionals - ceramic plates, encrypted comms, night vision goggles, suppressed MK18 carbines. Each man flowed to his assigned position without hesitation or confusion, their movements honed through endless rehearsal until every step became muscle memory. The trucks continued on in the rain.

Colonel James Morrison woke to cold steel pressed against his temple. A gloved hand covered his wife's mouth before she could scream. Black-clad figures filled their bedroom, faces hidden behind tactical masks, weapons pointed. The team leader's whispered orders carried deadly certainty: "Call the armory. Tell them to open up for an emergency weapons inspection."

Morrison's hand shook as he dialed. His wife's muffled sobs pierced the darkness. "This is Colonel Morrison. Prepare for an emergency inspection at the armory."

"Move," said the team leader handing Morrison his robe.

Slipping on his robe, Morrison left with five of the black-clad figures leaving his wife with the sixth. The sixth waited until the front door closed, then pumped three rounds into Mrs. Morrison. Checking to make sure she was dead, he moved to join his comrades.

The three trucks pulled in front of the armory's loading

dock gate ready to back in the containers. His robe sopping wet, Morrison stood in front of the fence surrounding the armory. A marine inside the armory peered through a window in the door and the saw the Colonel waiting outside the reinforced gate. He buzzed Morrison in. Morrison pushed open the gate and entered the armory compound followed by five figures now dressed in marine uniforms with their faces hidden in the shadows from their caps.

As the Colonel approached the front door, the marine inside opened the thick steel door sounding a loud buzzer and triggering red flashing lights. Morrison and the five shadowy figures entered the armory. The five shadowy figures moved closer to the other marines on guard inside the armory.

The marine at the door said, "Sir, what's—"

Suppressed weapons coughed. The real Marines dropped. Morrison spun toward his captors. A single round pierced his forehead. He fell to the concrete floor. A second bullet in the heart insured he was dead.

The team leader pressed the loading dock gate release.

The compound's perimeter gate opened and the three trucks backed up to the loading dock. The loading dock roll up doors opened. The team leader opened each of the container doors. More black-clad figures poured out, some entered the armory, others took up defensive positions around the armory. The raiders moved through the armory. Each man knew his role.

The armory sprawled beneath Camp Pendleton like a concrete labyrinth - three subterranean levels of reinforced bunkers designed to survive a direct missile strike. Each vault housed enough firepower to equip an entire Marine Expeditionary Unit. Row upon row of weapons filled the climate-controlled chambers: latest generation M27 Infantry Assault Rifle with advanced optics, Barrett M107A1 .50 caliber sniper rifles, M240G medium machine guns, AT4 anti-tank launchers, FIM92F Stinger air defense systems, and high-rate of fire M134 Miniguns with their six Gatling-style rotating barrels.

The ammunition bunkers stretched deeper - millions of rounds of match-grade ammunition, specialized breaching charges, grenades, mortars, missiles, and explosives. This wasn't just an armory - it represented the cutting edge of American military technology, each weapon incorporating classified improvements in materials, electronics, and targeting systems.

The team leader moved through the vaults, selecting specific weapon crates from a map. The kind of firepower that could pierce any armor, knock helicopters from the sky, reduce buildings to rubble. In the wrong hands, these weapons could devastate a city, bring down airliners, or equip an army of mercenaries with capabilities matching any special forces unit, but with enough firepower to take out an entire division.

Six men untethered the power cables to a line of the forklifts. They climbed behind the controls and drove the forklifts into the alleys of shelves where pickers were waiting in front of selected crates of weapons and ammunition. They knew exactly what they wanted and where they were located. The forklifts lifted the heavy crates of weapons and ammunition, drove them to the loading dock, and dropped them in the cargo containers.

A security expert sat down behind a console of camera monitors showing different views of the interior and exterior of the armory. He reached down and pulled out the hard drives recording the views of the security cameras. He loaded the drives into a rucksack. They would be leaving with him.

Outside the armory, men armed with submachine

guns watched for potential threats. There were none. The soldiers were asleep and the guards were unaware of any enemy inside the base.

When the last of the crates were loaded into the cargo containers and all but six professional operators were once again back inside the containers, the doors were shut. The six operators climbed on to the trucks' steps one riding on each side as the trucks headed for Echo gate.

Twenty-six minutes after entering, they emerged into the storm. No alarms pierced the rain's steady drumming. No emergency lights painted the clouds red. The base slept as the trucks vanished into the California night, leaving behind a trail of dead and questions about who possessed the skills, intelligence, and access to breach one of America's largest Marine bases.

Portland, Oregon

Fog rolled off the Willamette River, shrouding Portland's industrial waterfront in gray murk. Giant cranes loomed like prehistoric creatures above Terminal 6, their steel arms swinging cargo containers from the depths of a Korean freighter. The port sprawled across 800 acres of concrete and asphalt - a maze of warehouses, rail yards, and storage facilities where thousands of containers arrived weekly from across the Pacific.

Three unmarked containers slid onto waiting flatbeds. No customs agents approached. No dogs sniffed for contraband. The paperwork listed machine parts from Seoul. The crane operator noted nothing unusual about the weights.

The trucks rumbled through the port's security gate, diesel engines grinding as they merged onto Marine Drive. They crossed the Columbia River into

Washington state, then cut east on I-84. The highway climbed into the Cascade Mountains where Douglas firs stretched toward cloud-wrapped peaks. Spring snow still capped Mount Hood's summit to the south.

The convoy turned south back into Oregon onto smaller roads, deeper into the mountains where logging trucks outnumbered cars. Mile by mile, the trucks left civilization behind. They vanished into the vast green wilderness where thousands of square miles of forest concealed whatever secrets men wished to hide.

Culper

A rental car's engine echoed across the water. Frank looked down from his perch near the top of the lighthouse. A man in a worn sport coat stepped out of the car. His shoulders were broad beneath the jacket as he walked the weathered boards of the pier. His gait had a military rhythm. At the end, he stopped and stood facing the lighthouse.

Frank returned to his work, trowel scraping against old brick as he repointed another section. The man could wait. Or leave. Frank didn't care which. He wasn't in the mood for visitors.

Hours passed. The sun sank into the ocean, painting the waves copper and gold. Still the man stood, motionless as the granite blocks that formed the breakwater. His shadow stretched longer until it merged with evening darkness.

Climbing the newly rebuilt stairs, Frank checked the

light, wound the clockwork mechanism that would keep it turning through the night. He flipped the switch turning the light on. It began to turn sending its beam across the waves. When he looked again, the man was a silhouette against the pier.

Dawn broke grey and cool. Frank's boots echoed on the stairs as he climbed to check the light in the lighthouse cupola. His fingers found the switch, mechanical and certain. He turned the light off. It spun to a stop.

He looked toward shore through salt-streaked glass. The man still stood at the pier's edge. His sport coat rippled in the morning breeze. He might have been a statue, might have been there forever. Might never have moved at all.

Curiosity gnawed at Frank like an old wound. The boat's engine growled as he guided it toward the pier, salt spray stinging his scars. He cut power, letting momentum carry him to the weathered pilings. The man hadn't moved. Frank tied off the boat, his huge hands making the rope look like thread.

"Who are you?" Frank's voice scraped through his ruined throat.

"My name is Culper."

Frank went still. The name settled in his mind like a stone in deep water. "You're Culper?" The man nodded once.

"What do you want?" Frank's words carried caution.

"You," Culper said simply.

The waves lapped at wooden pilings. Seabirds wheeled overhead. And somewhere in the depths of Frank's memory, doors long sealed began to open.

Burnt coffee stains ran down the side of the ancient percolator. Frank measured grounds into the metal basket. Years of violence had left his hands scarred and twisted, but they still remembered gentler work. Behind him Culper studied the lighthouse walls. New mortar between old stones. The rebuilt spiral staircase leading to the cupola. Fresh paint over salt-weathered wood. The work of careful hands.

A shadow moved. Culper turned. Yellow eyes watched from beneath the stairs. The cat's scarred face matched Frank's own. Battle-marked survivors recognizing their own kind.

"Friend of yours?" said Culper.

Frank grunted, then poured coffee in two mugs and set them on the weathered table.

Culper took the offered mug. The liquid black as pitch. He sipped. Eyes widened. Spat it back into the mug.

"Jesus, Frank. Whoever taught you to make coffee should be drawn and quartered."

Frank grunted. Drained his mug in three swallows. Reached for Culper's mug and poured the rejected coffee in with his own. Drank that too.

"Most men dream of this. Peace. Purpose. The satisfaction of creating rather than destroying." Culper moved to the window. Stared out at grey waves. "But we're not most men, are we?"

Frank's grunt carried decades of understanding.

"America's changing, Frank. Change brings chaos. Chaos brings vultures." Culper's reflection watched Frank in the salt-streaked glass. "Our enemies see a nation divided. Left against right. Rich against poor. Urban against rural. They watch us tear ourselves apart over pronouns and statues while they gather strength."

Frank turned back to the coffee pot. Started another batch. Less potent.

"Five days ago Camp Pendleton was raided." Culper

pulled a folder from his coat. Set it on the table. Crime scene photos spilled out. Dead marines in a guardhouse. Blood on rain-soaked concrete. "Professional team breached the armory. Killed seven marines, the camp commander and his wife. They stole enough hardware to outfit a brigade."

"Not my problem," said Frank without making eye contact.

Culper continued ignoring Frank's comment, "Everything they took was chosen with purpose. M27 assault rifles. Stingers. AT4s. Barrett sniper rifles, even M134 Miniguns. The kind of weapons that could turn militias into armies. Citizens into insurgents." Frank grunted. At least he was listening.

"The night of the raid three cargo containers were stolen from the Port of San Diego. Those same containers surfaced at Portland's Terminal Six three days later. Forged manifests listed them as containing machine parts from Korea. No customs inspection. No dogs. Clean as spring water. Highway Patrol traffic cameras tracked the three containers going east on I-84, until the disappeared in Oregon's backcountry somewhere near Mount Hood. FBI sent helicopters and search planes to find the containers. So far, nothing, except millions of trees that can hide just about anything. Whoever took those weapons is planning something serious while America argues with itself."

The percolator bubbled. Frank poured two fresh cups. This time Culper drank without complaint.

"I direct an unauthorized agency. We're not CIA. Not FBI. Not military." Culper's words carried weight. "Those agencies are bound by laws. Oversight. Politics. They see threats but can't act. Their hands are tied by the very democracy they're trying to protect. We operate in the shadows between agencies. No official sanction. No oversight. No records." Culper's eyes met Frank's. "Just results. Sometimes protecting democracy requires working outside its rules."

Culper set his cup down. "The title Culper comes from Washington's first spy ring. Patriots who served in secret. Who died unknown. Who saved America before there was an America."

Frank's grumble might have been acknowledgement.

"America is in danger. China probes our defenses. Russia tests our resolve. But they're not the real threat." Culper leaned forward. "It's the ones who claim to love America most. Who'd burn down the Constitution to save it. Who'd destroy democracy to preserve their version of it."

Frank turned to the window.

"You took the same oath I did." Culper's words carried weight. "To protect America from all enemies, foreign or domestic. Not left or right. Not red or blue. America." He paused. "That oath doesn't expire just because you're tired. Because you want to stack stones instead of standing watch."

Frank's massive shoulders tensed.

"While good men hide in lighthouses, patriots-turned terrorists plan our destruction. They count on our exhaustion. Our desire to look away and mind our own business. That oath we took. It wasn't to any political party. Any president. It was to an idea. That democracy, for all its flaws, deserves protection. Even from itself. We need operatives like you, Frank."

"No," said Frank simply as his damaged throat made the word sound like gravel.

"No is not acceptable. Not this time. Look around you. Cities burn while politicians point fingers. Parents fight over schoolbooks while China builds carriers. Citizens calling other citizens traitors. Everyone so busy screaming about their rights, they forget about their duties."

Frank, seemingly disinterested, stared at the sea.

"Remember Kosovo?" Culper waited. "Neighbors who'd lived together for generations. Shared meals. Watched each other's children. Then some men with guns came. Told them they had to choose sides. Those that chose wrong were executed."

Frank's huge hands gripped the windowsill. "Others can fight." Frank's voice scraped out.

"Who? The regular agencies? They're hamstrung by rules written for simpler times. By oversight committees more interested in scoring political points than stopping threats. We need men like you, Frank. Men who understand that sometimes protecting democracy means working outside its rules. Men willing to stand in darkness so others can live in light."

Culper was frustrated. He knew Frank Kane would be tough to recruit, but he seemed unmovable. Culper had one more card and it was time to play it.

"NSA picked up an encrypted text message two days before the Pendleton weapons heist. It was a weapons shopping list from a militia leader in Nevada just outside of Elko. Analysts believe the recipient of the encrypted message was Mitchel Walker."

Frank went still. The name settled in Frank's bones like an old pain. Images flashed through his mind. Firefights in Tunisia. Midnight raids in Sudan. Covert assassinations in Libya. Frank fighting side-by-side with Walker. Both fearless veterans that had perfected the art of war.

Culper said nothing. He let the name of Walker do its magic. It was his ace-in-the-hole and his last hope.

"Walker's a patriot," said Frank after a long moment.

"Yes," said Culper. "The worst kind. An idealist

caught in the past. He loves America so much he's willing to destroy it to save it."

Frank gripped his coffee mug. Ceramic creaked under the pressure.

"Frank, we need men who'll protect America as it is.

Messy. Divided. Imperfect. But worth dying for." "I served my country."

"So, did I. But the threats facing America haven't gone away. They've increased."

"You must have others."

"There is no plan B, Frank. You're the only person that can get close enough to penetrate Walker's organization. The only person that understands his way of thinking… his strategy… his next move."

Deep in thought, Frank stared out the window. Waves crashed against granite below. The cat joined him on the sill, both of them staring out at slate-grey waters.

"The day is coming when Americans will have to choose," Culper said. "Between comfort and duty. Between looking away and standing fast." He stepped closer. "Walker's smart. Some say brilliant. He's planning something bigger than stolen weapons. Something that will shatter this country while foreign powers watch and wait. We need to stop him before it's too late. It's your mission if you will take it. And for God's sake take it, Frank."

Culper rested his case. He had said all that should have been said. It was time to shut up.

Frank focused on the waves beyond his window. The lighthouse had been his attempt at redemption. At building something instead of destroying. At finding peace.

But some men weren't meant for peace.

"When do I go?" said Frank.

"Now," said Culper.

Frank nodded once. Mission accepted.

Cover

Frank stood in the sporting goods store, his bulk casting shadows across aisles of fishing tackle. A place small enough that strangers drew notice. The clerk watched him through glass counters, uncertain of the maimed giant inspecting rod cases.

He selected one long enough for his Barret sniper rifle's barrel and added a tackle box to his pile. Large enough for the scope, stock, and extra magazines. The plastic latches would break before revealing their true cargo.

He paid cash. No receipt. No words exchanged beyond the clerk's nervous greeting and final total.

Back at the lighthouse he laid his weapons across the table. Light from a single bulb caught the worn steel of the matched Ruger Redhawks. Not showpieces. Tools used hard and maintained better. He checked each cylinder, the mechanisms clicking with certainty in the quiet room.

The smaller revolver - a Colt Cobra .38 followed. Then the concealed weapon for his boot – a Remington Model 95 Derringer, small but with two cartridges of real stopping power. Last chances given physical form.

His KA-BAR rested in its sheath, the blade that had opened men from Kandahar to Mogadishu. He tested its edge with his thumb, leaving a thin red line. Still sharp enough.

The Barrett 82 sniper rifle lay disassembled on the table along with its ammunition - .50 caliber bullets some shells coated in Teflon for piercing armor. Each piece found its measured place in the fishing rod case and tackle box. A weapon that could kill from a mile away disguised as a tourist's pastime. The rifle's components disappeared into harmless shapes.

His rucksack held his armored vest with its ceramic plates. Weight that would stop multiple bullets as the dozen patched holes in the vest's fabric verified.

The tools of his trade assembled without excess or shortage. Only what necessity demanded.

Before leaving, he sliced open a bag of cat food with the KA-BAR. Let it spill across the floor. Lifted the toilet lid for water. The scarred Tom watched from the stairs, yellow eyes understanding the goodbye that wasn't spoken. The tall, ugly human always came back before the food ran out. That was all that mattered.

The Imperial's engine caught on the second try. Frank pointed it west as Maine disappeared in the rearview.

Interstate miles blurred under tires, states passing beneath his wheels. Towns where people lived in ignorance of men like him. Frank didn't care that they didn't appreciate the sacrifices he made. He didn't like them anyway. He didn't like anyone.

Nights spent in roadside motels with flickering signs

or pulled off forest roads where no eyes would find him. He slept on ground harder than any mattress, stars his only cover. No tent between him and whatever watched from the darkness.

Utah's salt flats shimmered like broken glass. The Imperial's temperature gauge climbed past warning, needle trembling toward disaster. Steam hissed from beneath the hood. Frank nursed the car to the side of the highway, waited as the radiator cooled enough to refill. The desert passed the time without patience or mercy.

Oregon greeted him with walls of green. Forests dense enough to swallow civilization. Rivers cutting through rock that stood before humans walked upright. Rain followed him across the highway, mountains looming like slumbering giants. Out there somewhere Walker lingered beyond the treeline, unknowing that his old comrade in arms had come to fulfil an oath.

Frank found a motel in a town whose economy had collapsed with the timber industry. Boarded storefronts. Peeling paint. Men with nowhere to go lingering outside liquor stores with eyes that had forgotten hope.

Frank rented a room with cash. Carried his gear inside without drawing attention. His size and scars were a curiosity only worth a brief glance. There were more important things on the minds of the downtrodden.

Frank sat in a booth at a local diner, watching through the window as fishing boats returned with the early morning's catch. Rust-streaked trawlers cut through harbor fog, decks crowded with men in yellow slickers. Gulls swarmed above, white shapes against gray sky screaming for entrails and headless fish.

His massive frame overcrowded the vinyl seat, springs complaining beneath his weight. The laminated menu lay untouched. Waitresses moved around him like water around a boulder, keeping distance from the stranger filling their usual space. Their eyes found him then slid away, instinct warning against closer study. A man built to absorb violence and return it multiplied.

His coffee remained black. No sugar or cream to soften its bitterness. The Formica tabletop bore decades of cigarette burns and carved initials, history of smaller lives passing through. His hands dwarfed the mug, scarred knuckles telling stories of men whose faces he'd reconstructed.

Steam from the kitchen carried smells of frying bacon and burned toast. Local men in flannel and work boots occupied the counter stools, conversation hushed when they caught his reflection in the diner's pie display case.

Frank cut his hotcakes. Fork and knife moving like instruments in surgery, each bite identical to the last. His eyes never stopped tracking movement outside. The harbor master inspecting docks. Delivery trucks dropping supplies. A police cruiser making its morning rounds, slow and predictable.

Frank signaled for his check with a raised finger. Paid cash including a tip that was neither generous nor insulting. Calculated to avoid memory either way. The bell above the door announced his exit.

Frank walked to the Imperial. Its weathered paint matched the town's faded prosperity. The engine caught, coughing once before settling into rhythm.

He drove out to the abandoned lighthouse on the point. The road narrowed, pavement surrendering to gravel then dirt. Salt air corroded metal signs warning trespassers away. The structure stood alone on its rocky outcrop, paint stripped by decades of coastal storms.

Frank circled the building. Foundation stones had shifted, cracked by time and neglect. Metal stairs coiled up the tower's interior, groaning under his weight. Empty window frames gaped where local teenagers had shattered all glass. Beer cans and graffiti marked their territorial claims.

Despite its decay, Frank's eyes registered tactical advantages. Clear lines of sight in all directions. Multiple escape routes down weathered paths to the shoreline. Thick stone walls that would stop most small arms fire. The isolation provided cover for a man who didn't want to be found.

In the basement he discovered access to old storm drains, tunnels leading toward town. A secondary exit if things went wrong. Always have a back door.

Frank stood in line at the county records office, his mass dwarfing the local residents with their property disputes and permit applications. Fluorescent lights buzzed overhead, washing color from already pallid faces. Government efficiency moved at the pace of erosion.

The clerk flinched when she looked up to find him looming at her window. His disfigured face prompted her to speak louder as if he were deaf rather than damaged.

"Can I help you?" Voice pitched high with unease.

"Lighthouse blueprints." The words scraped from his ruined throat.

She fumbled with her keyboard, glancing up between keystrokes to ensure the mountain hadn't moved. "The one on North Point?"

Frank nodded once.

"Purpose of inquiry?" Her pen hovered above a form.

"Renovation."

"I'll need to see some ID."

Frank placed his driver's license on the counter. She studied it longer than necessary, uncertainty battling with fear of offending him.

"Out of state?" she said.

Frank nodded once.

The clerk assigned Frank a table number where the blueprints would arrive. He waited in a plastic chair designed for smaller frames, its legs creaking when he shifted.

A file cart squeaked across linoleum. The blueprints arrived in a cardboard tube older than the clerk who delivered it. Frank unrolled the sheets, weighted their corners with brass paperweights worn smooth by decades of use.

The lighthouse revealed itself in faded blue lines and architectural notations. Foundation extending deeper than visible stonework suggested. Sublevels marked in handwritten annotations.

Frank moved methodically through the documents as if evaluating repair costs, making notes in a spiral binder.

At the counter he requested copies. Paid cash.

Outside, rain started again. Drops tapping Frank's shoulders as he secured the blueprint tube in the Imperial's trunk, then drove away.

Frank returned to the motel, blueprint tube tucked under his arm like a rifle. The room smelled of industrial cleaner failing to mask decades of cigarettes and sweat. He locked the door, dropped his key on the particleboard nightstand.

Rain hammered the window with Oregon persistence. Not a storm. Just the constant weeping of Pacific sky that locals stopped noticing. Water streaking glass distorted the view of empty parking spaces and the neon VACANCY sign flickering its invitation to nonexistent travelers.

He cleared the small table of lamp base and telephone.

Unrolled the blueprints, weighting corners with his Ruger Redhawks. The six-pack from the corner market sweated rings into the fake wood veneer. He snapped the first can open, drank half before turning his attention to the lighthouse schematics.

The drawings revealed more than just structure. They showed history layered in pencil notes and amendments. Original construction from 1887. Reinforcement during World War II when coastal defenses feared Japanese invasion. Later modifications when the Coast Guard maintained actual presence instead of automated beacons.

Frank's eyes lingered on the foundation specifications. Thick walls that had withstood a century of Pacific storms. Rooms large enough for equipment but small enough to secure. The tunnel system connecting to storm drains provided secondary egress.

He finished the first beer, opened a second. His thoughts returned to Maine, to the lighthouse the renovation was near completion. Stone and mortar he'd restored with his own hands. Work that built instead of destroyed. Purpose measured in something other than blood and bodies.

This Oregon lighthouse offered similar possibilities. A restoration project for after Walker. After the killing stopped. If it stopped. Another beer disappeared.

The rain continued its assault on glass and asphalt. Three hundred days a year according to the gas station attendant. Season irrelevant to the mechanics of ocean air hitting coastal mountains. A sobering climate for men who couldn't afford illusions.

Frank pulled out his map as darkness claimed the parking lot. Spread it beside the blueprints, trading one tactical assessment for another. Tillamook sat on the coast, commercial fishing and dairy operations keeping its economy from complete collapse. Walker's sawmill operation lay inland near Government Camp at Mount

Hood's base. Not close. Sixty miles of winding roads cutting through national forest.

Distance a sportsman would travel for salmon runs. Steelhead and Chinook in rivers that drained snowmelt from ancient volcanic slopes. A cover identity solid enough for frequent trips without raising suspicion.

He traced potential routes with his finger. Logging roads that might bypass highway checkpoints if things went wrong. Forest service fire breaks that could accommodate the Imperial in emergency evacuation. Alternative approaches for when direct routes became compromised.

Another beer. Frank's eyes moved between blueprints and maps. Structures and terrain. Defense and offense. The board taking shape in his mind—not just pieces but potential moves stretching ten steps ahead. Walker's sawmill operation. The lighthouse fortress. Rivers connecting both. The perfect cover of a man with time and fishing rods.

He finished the six-pack as midnight approached. Rolled the blueprints back into their tube. Folded the map along established creases. Preparations complete but for tomorrow.

The bed squeaked under his weight. Springs fighting a battle they'd already lost. Frank stared at the ceiling, listening to rain drumming its percussion against the roof. Sleep came in tactical intervals. Twenty minutes awake. Forty asleep. Training impossible to unlearn. A predator's rest even in supposed safety.

Frank rose before dawn. Made his own coffee in the room. He considered his weapons and decided to only carry the Derringer in his boot and his KA-BAR. He doubted anyone would take a shot at him... not yet anyway. He packed his rucksack and carried it along with his fishing gear through the doorway.

Outside, He slipped the room key into the drop box outside the motel's office.

The Imperial's windshield reflected silver dawn through rain droplets. He scraped condensation from the inside glass with his sleeve, cranked the defroster to its anemic maximum.

The engine caught on the second try. A Detroit dinosaur whose maintenance he trusted to no mechanic. Its bulk crawled through Tillamook's empty streets, past shuttered storefronts where economic collapse hung perpetual "closed" signs. The town sighed behind him, another victim of timber's decline.

He turned eastward, leaving behind the walls of Sitka spruce and fog-shrouded cliffs. Road signs warned of elk crossings and coastline viewpoints. Frank passed them all. The road cut through forests thick enough to hide armies. Douglas firs 200 feet tall stood sentinel, their trunks wider than the motel room he'd left behind.

The highway curved inland through dairy country where black and white Holsteins dotted green pastures like chess pieces abandoned mid-game.

Near the city of Banks the sun appeared, transforming raindrops on windshield into prisms. The Imperial's wipers cleared the last of morning mist. Frank turned on to Highway 26, leaving coastal weather patterns behind.

Logging trucks passed in opposite direction, their loads of fresh-cut timber larger than the buildings they would become. The road narrowed through valleys carved by river systems ancient when humans first crossed the land bridge. Farmland appeared in pockets, red barns standing against backdrops of evergreen mountains.

Frank's stomach grumbled. He stopped at Shari's diner in Beaverton. After scarfing down his breakfast, he ordered a slice of marionberry pie. It was gone in three bites.

Portland announced itself through increasing density. The city grew from suburbs to urban landscape with transitions marked by bridges spanning the Willamette River. Downtown rose in glass towers reflecting clouds back at their source. Mount Hood loomed eastward, its snow-covered peak visible between buildings when alignments permitted.

Frank navigated streets crowded with bicyclists wearing rain gear in bright colors. Coffee shops occupied every corner, lines forming outside despite the returning drizzle. Food trucks clustered in parking lots offering cuisine from Thailand to Nigeria. Tattoo shops displayed flash art in windows between vintage clothing stores and marijuana dispensaries. A city comfortable with contradiction.

He crossed the Willamette on the Burnside Bridge, steel girders humming beneath the Imperial's tires. The east side presented industrial warehouses being converted to loft apartments. Gentrification pushing against established neighborhoods where families had lived for generations. Decay and renewal locked in uneasy partnership.

Frank joined Interstate 84 eastbound, following the Columbia River Gorge. The highway clung to basalt cliffs carved by ice-age floods powerful enough to reshape continents. The Columbia stretched wide as an inland sea, its surface rippled by wind carrying hints of ocean four hours westward.

Waterfalls appeared without warning on the southern cliffside. Multnomah Falls dropped 620 feet in two-tiered descent, its upper portion visible from the highway. Others cascaded from heights where clouds met rock, water that had fallen as snow on hidden peaks now returning to the river system.

The gorge widened near Hood River. Windsurfers braved whitecaps, their colorful sails darting like dragonflies across water turned white by pressure systems funneling through the mountain pass. Orchards covered hillsides south of the river, pear and apple blossoms turning entire valleys pink in spring. Now they stood laden with summer fruit.

The Imperial's engine worked harder as Highway 35 climbed toward Mount Hood. The temperature dropped with each mile, air thinning as elevation increased. Pine forests replaced deciduous trees. Clearings revealed meadows thick with wildflowers – purple lupine and orange paintbrush pushing through soil only recently freed from snow.

The mountains held snow until August, landscapes permanently shaped by winter's dominance. The road passed ski resorts closed for summer, chair lifts hanging empty above slopes where grass now grew through retreating snowpack. Cabins built to withstand twenty foot accumulations huddled beneath trees that had survived centuries of alpine conditions.

Government Camp appeared around a curve, a cluster of lodges and equipment rental shops servicing the winter tourism economy. Its streets lay quiet in offseason stillness. Only a few restaurants showed open signs, catering to hikers exploring Pacific Crest Trail segments and climbers testing themselves against Hood's permanent glaciers.

The Imperial growled down Highway 26, its tires humming against wet asphalt as Frank followed the Sandy River's course. The waterway ran beside the road like a companion, sometimes visible through breaks in the treeline, other times announcing itself through sound alone. Glacier melt from Mount Hood's slopes turned river water cloudy with sediment, perpetually cold even in summer months.

Walls of Douglas fir and western hemlock rose on both sides of the highway, trees two centuries old standing like cathedral columns. Their branches filtered sunlight into scattered patterns across the forest floor where sword ferns and salal bushes fought for remaining light. The air smelled of pine resin and river moss, scents impossible to find in cities.

Frank turned onto a rutted access road leading to the river. Posted signs indicated a public fishing area. The Imperial's suspension absorbed punishment from potholes deep enough to swallow smaller vehicles. He parked beside a red pickup with three fly rods mounted on its rack.

River Rapids Bait & Tackle occupied a log cabin structure that had seen better decades. Smoke curled from a stone chimney despite summer warmth. The porch boards creaked under Frank's weight as he approached. Wind chimes made from fishing lures clinked hollow greetings.

Inside smelled of coffee and wood heat. Shelves displayed hand-tied flies and spinner lures alongside deer antler mounts and faded photographs of men holding trophy steelhead. The floor had been swept that morning but permanent stains from minnow buckets and wader boots marked high-traffic paths.

Behind the counter stood a man shaped by six decades of river life. White beard reaching mid-chest, skin tanned leather-dark by sun reflected off water. Eyes that measured each customer against some internal standard only he understood.

"Help you?" The question carrying enough gravel to match Frank's own voice.

"License with salmon tags."

The man produced forms, pushed them across worn wood. Frank filled out minimal information.

"Earl Mackey." The man extended a hand gnarled by decades of tying flies and handling fishing line. "Welcome to God's country."

Frank accepted Earl's handshake. "Frank Kane."

"Staying long, Frank?" Earl reached for a stamp to validate the paperwork.

Frank shrugged. "Good fishing?"

"Best in the Northwest when the Chinook are running." Earl nodded toward the window.

"Walker's Mill?"

"Yeah. Fishing's good there. Chinook and Coho with the occasional Steelhead. Couple hundred yards up river's best. Too much sawdust downriver. Salmon don't like that."

"Owner okay with that?"

"Yeah." Earl stamped the license. "Walker loves this river about as much as anybody. Used to take my grandson fishing on his private stretch before the boy moved to Seattle. Walker actually funded riverbank restoration downstream. Replaced culverts to help salmon migration."

"Unusual."

"Walker's not your usual anything." Earl leaned forward confidentially. "Military background. Special forces they say, though he never talks about it. Moved here when the timber industry was on its knees. Saved a hundred jobs when he bought that operation for pennies on the dollar. Locals were grateful."

Frank examined spoons and spinner lures in a display case, his reflection ghosting across dusty glass. "Bait for Chinook?"

"This time of year?" Earl pulled open a refrigerated case behind the counter. "Salmon eggs cured in this." He produced a jar of red liquid. "My own secret recipe. Borax and anise oil base with a few additions I keep to myself. Walker's men swear by it. Half those boys stop here for coffee and gossip."

Frank nodded. "Okay. One."

Earl packaged the eggs and cure. "Walker runs a tight operation, but he's good to the community. Sponsors Little League, helped rebuild the school after the flood three years back."

Frank grunted, paid, and left.

The car door groaned open and shut. He drove down the rutted road towards the mill.

Inside the bait shop, Earl watched the Imperial disappear in the woods. He picked up the phone and dialed. "Mitchel, it's Earl. Strange visitor asking questions about fishing around the mill. Big guy, lots of scars," Earl picked up the fishing license paperwork. "Name's Frank Kane. Yeah, I'm sure."

Late afternoon found Frank thigh-deep in the Sandy River, cold water numbing his legs through his waders. Overhead, clouds gathered. Another Oregon rain. He cast, the rod extension of his arm. He spun the spinner's handle snapping the basket closed. He saw the line sweep downstream right where he wanted it.

His eyes tracked movement along the river's bank hidden by the treeline. Frank appeared focused on the water's surface. He imagined Walker's security was nibbling at the bait… himself.

The river moved like cold mercury beneath a colorless sky. The first watcher appeared and kept his distance on the bank. Militia-trained but lacking refinement. Too obvious in his observation. Frank cast his line. Let it drift. The watcher spoke into his handheld radio twice then departed.

An hour later, the second appeared. Different man. Same purpose. This one positioned himself upstream. Pretended to photograph birds while his lens captured Frank. The camera's shutter sound carried across water. Frank reeled in. Changed bait. Cast again. Gave the man nothing beyond the image of a fisherman consumed by his task.

The third arrived as shadows lengthened. Black jacket. Military boots beneath civilian pants. He crossed the shallows fifty yards upstream. Approached with practiced casualness. Fishing rod in hand though he carried it wrong. Grip too high. Frank studied the water.

"Any luck today?" The man's voice carried forced friendliness.

Frank grunted. Shifted weight. "Water's running higher than normal." "Hmm." Frank's throat grinded.

"You staying around here?" The question too direct. Amateur mistake.

Frank lifted his rod. Pointed to a flash of silver beneath the surface.

The man looked. Saw nothing. "I know most locals. Don't recall seeing you before."

"Earl." The name scraped from Frank's damaged vocal cords.

"Earl?"

Frank kept his eyes on his line. "Said fishing good here."

"Earl Mackey from the bait shack?" Frank nodded once.

"What're you fishing for?"

"Chinook." Frank's massive hands worked the line. Adjusted the tension.

"I'm Mike Pierce. I didn't catch your name?" Frank ignored the question.

"Just making conversation."

"Fish don't like talk." Frank's words fell like stones.

Pierce nodded. The conversation had delivered what was needed. Description confirmed. Basic assessment made. He'd report back – large male, scarred, minimal speech, claimed connection to Earl Mackey, focused on fishing with no apparent secondary objectives. He remained five minutes more, then departed upstream.

Frank continued to fish. The shadows lengthened across the water. Walker's security now knew of his presence. The bait was set. He only needed to wait for the hook to be taken.

Thirty minutes later, his line went taut. The rod bent double, nearly pulled from his grip. A large Chinook had taken the bait – Earl's salmon eggs and cure.

Frank braced against the current, feet finding purchase on river stones slick with algae. The fish thrashed against capture, its forty-pound mass surging downstream with desperate power. Even with Frank's immense strength, the battle stretched beyond expectation. Each time he gained line, the salmon would run again, stripping the reel with sounds like mechanical protest.

Ten minutes of combat passed, man and fish locked in ancient struggle. Finally, the Chinook tired. Frank guided it toward shore, massive hands gentle as he removed the hook from silver-scaled jaw. Blood from the puncture stained the water momentarily before dispersing in current.

He held the fish briefly, feeling its life force against his palms. Considered smoking it as he'd done in Alaska years before. But time was a resource more precious than meat. With careful movements, he lowered the Chinook back to the river. It hung suspended for three seconds, gathering strength, then kicked powerfully against his hands and disappeared downstream.

Frank watched its path until the silver flash vanished around a bend. Predator recognizing predator, both continuing their hunts in separate worlds.

The sun slipped behind the mountains, taking daylight with it. Frank reeled in his final cast, the line cutting a dark path through water turned to brass by sunset's last stand. He worked with efficiency born from decades of practice. The hooks cleaned of bait. The rod disassembled with swift movements.

The Imperial waited in a gravel turnout, chrome dulled by road dust. The massive car a relic from times when American steel ruled highways. He placed the fishing gear in the trunk. He started the engine and drove the Imperial down the dirt road. After a half mile he spotted what he was looking for and pulled the car to a stop along the road and turned off the engine. The car's engine ticked as it cooled in the mountain air. He stepped from the car and checked his surroundings. Nothing but wilderness. No cameras. No observers. No trails except game paths worn by deer and elk.

He hiked up an incline. A hundred yards from the car, he found what he sought. A massive Douglas fir, its core hollowed by lightning strike years earlier, facing away from the road. The charred opening at its base formed a natural vault. Frank knelt. Swept aside fallen needles. The hollow extended four feet upward into the trunk. Dry. Protected. Invisible to casual observers. Satisfied, he walked back to the car.

The trunk opened with a groan of aged hinges. He removed the Barret's barrel hidden in the fishing rod case, the tacklebox holding the other components of the sniper rifle, and his rucksack. He also retrieved several pieces of oilcloth, and a waterproof tarpaulin camouflaged with the same colors in the forest.

Carrying the heavy load, he hiked back to the tree. He

wrapped the fishing rod case and tacklebox in pieces of oilcloth, then placed them inside the burned-out tree trunk. In his rucksack lay the other tools of his trade. The matched Redhawk revolvers with 7.5-inch barrels rested in custom shoulder holsters. The Colt Cobra .38 in an ankle holster. Speedloaders and extra ammunition for both weapons. He removed each piece. Checked actions. Verified loads. Confirmed function with hands that knew each weapon better than most men knew their own fingers. He wrapped them in oil cloth and set them inside the tree trunk next to the Barret's components. Lastly, he removed his armored vest with its ceramic plates from the rucksack wrapped it in oil cloth. He covered everything with the camouflaged tarpaulin and covered the opening with forest debris arranged to appear undisturbed. The camouflage wasn't perfect, but it would do.

He kept the Remington Derringer in his boot. Small enough to escape notice. Powerful enough to matter when distance collapsed to inches. And, he kept the KABAR in its worn leather sheath around his waist. He doubted they would raise any suspicion in these parts.

Memorized four landmarks to triangulate the position. As he headed back down hill, he covered his tracks dug deep into the loose soil.

He drove a few hundred yards and pulled over once again. He retrieved the spotting scope from beneath the seat. Military grade. Twenty-power magnification. Thermal capabilities. He tucked it into his jacket and began the ascent toward the ridgeline overlooking the sawmill. He moved through the forest with surprising silence for a man his size. Found a position - a natural depression offering concealment and clear sightlines.

Below, Walker's sawmill sprawled across thirty acres of cleared forest. Four massive buildings constructed of corrugated metal and timber. The main mill dominated the complex—a cavernous structure where logs entered whole and emerged as dimensional lumber. Its roof peaked like a steel mountain. Conveyor systems connected it to the three smaller outbuildings. Stacks of raw logs waited in neat rows, each trunk tagged with colored markers denoting species and grade. Cedar. Douglas fir. Hemlock. Pines of various types. The inventory of a legitimate operation.

Frank settled. Adjusted the scope's focus. The day shift was ending. Men streamed from the main building toward the parking lot. Forty-three workers. Most carried lunchboxes. Some smoked. Their movements matched their profession—the tired shuffle of physical laborers ending a day of honest work. Nothing in their behavior suggested military training or clandestine purpose.

Floodlights clicked on as darkness claimed the valley. Their harsh illumination created islands of daylight amid growing shadow. The night shift arrived in pickup trucks and older sedans. Twenty-eight workers. They entered the mill in groups of three and four. Their clothing appropriate for sawmill work—heavy boots, Carhartt jackets, some with reflective striping for safety.

Inside the illuminated mill, machinery rumbled back to life. Debarkers stripped raw logs of outer layers. The massive bandsaw blade—eight feet in diameter—began its relentless cycle through fresh-cut timber. Planers smoothed rough-cut boards into finished products. Chippers converted waste wood into mulch and particleboard material. Through the open bay doors, Frank watched the coordinated dance of industrial forestry.

Movement near the mill's side entrance caught his attention. A woman emerged from what appeared to be an office building. She carried a large stainless steel coffee urn and a box balanced precariously beneath it. Long dark hair tied back. Practical work clothes that did nothing to hide an athletic frame. She moved with purpose across the yard toward the active mill floor.

Frank adjusted the scope's focus. Her face came into sharp relief. Early-thirties. Features that stopped short of conventional beauty but carried striking intelligence. High cheekbones. Green eyes that missed nothing. A small scar above her right eyebrow. She navigated between machinery with the confidence of someone who knew the space intimately.

Workers greeted her with obvious familiarity. She set up the coffee urn on a break table, arranged cups from the box. Steam rose as she poured the first cup and handed it to a man operating the planer. Their brief conversation included laughter. Her smile transformed her face. Made her beautiful in ways catalogs never captured.

Frank scanned her interactions with each worker. Looking for hierarchy. For deference that might indicate her position. The men treated her with respect tinged with something else. Not fear. Not quite deference. Recognition of authority carried lightly. She moved among them, distributing coffee, exchanging words, noting something in a small notebook she pulled from her pocket. More manager than servant despite the coffee service.

A radio call pulled her attention. She spoke into a device clipped to her belt. Nodded at whatever response came. Finished her coffee distribution and headed back toward the office building. Frank tracked her movement. Noted how she paused to inspect a lumber stack, checking something against her notebook.

The lumber stacks surrounding the mill contained standard dimensional cuts. Two-by-fours. Two-by-sixes.

Four-by-fours. Pressure-treated timbers. Cabinet-grade hardwoods. Everything a legitimate sawmill would produce.

Frank shifted position. Adjusted the thermal settings. The heat signatures matched expectations. Machinery ran hot. Workers moved between stations. The boiler building pumped steam through kilns for drying green lumber. Nothing triggered his instincts for deception.

Security seemed minimal. Guard at the gatehouse checking trucks in and out. Two men patrolled the perimeter. Standard procedure for protecting valuable equipment, not excessive. Their routes predictable. Their attention focused outward, watching for timber thieves, not protecting interior secrets.

Frank's brow furrowed. He scanned again. The operation appeared legitimate in every visible aspect. Men cut trees into boards. Trucks took finished products to market. Waste material became secondary products. The cycle of timber processing continued as it had for generations in these mountains.

He returned his scope to the office building where the woman had disappeared. Light glowed from a second floor window. Her silhouette moved behind blinds. She spoke with someone unseen. The conversation appeared animated. Then a second figure joined her at the window. Taller. Male. The distinctive profile of Walker, unmistakable even in shadow.

Frank watched their interaction. The body language. The proximity. The casual touch of Walker's hand on her shoulder. Professional relationship but something more. Trust. Shared purpose. Walker pulled the blinds shut.

He thought of Culper standing on that Maine pier. His certainty about Walker. The stolen weapons. The threat assessment. Watching the sawmill's honest labor, doubt crept in. Perhaps Walker had changed. Perhaps Culper was wrong.

The scope revealed only the surface. What lay beneath remained hidden. The night shift continued their work, oblivious to his surveillance. Frank packed the scope away. Descended the ridge with the same silence with which he'd climbed it. The Imperial's door groaned as he slid behind the wheel. The engine came to life with a deep-throated rumble.

He'd seen nothing that confirmed Culper's suspicions. Nothing that triggered his own instincts for danger. Yet experience had taught him threat assessment required patience. Surface appearances often concealed deeper truths. He'd continue watching. Walker would reveal himself eventually. Men like him always did.

The Imperial's headlights cut through gathering darkness as Frank drove back toward town. His mind filtering what he'd seen against what he knew of Walker. The contradiction would resolve itself in time. It always did. Until then, he'd watch. And wait. And keep his weapons close.

Gray fluorescent light buzzed overhead. The diner smelled of fried onions and burgers. Frank occupied the corner booth, back to the wall, eyes on the door. Old habits. His plate held meatloaf swimming in brown gravy. Double portion. Mashed potatoes mounded beside it like pale foothills. More brown gravy. A mound of coleslaw barely fit on the overfilled plate. A separate plate for a stack of bread. The waitress had raised eyebrows at his order but said nothing.

He ate with mechanical efficiency. Cut the meat into precise squares. Forked each bite without looking down. His attention remained on the entrance. The Coke sat without ice, just as he'd requested. He drank it black and warm.

The bell above the door jingled. Frank's hand moved beneath the table, fingers brushing the Cobra holstered at his ankle. Then stopped.

Walker entered. Older now. Gray at the temples. Smile lines engraved around eyes that missed nothing. His tailored flannel shirt and quality jeans marked him as management, not labor. The leather jacket spoke of money but not flash. He scanned the diner with practiced casualness, eyes registering each patron, each exit. Military habits embedded in civilian life. He froze when he spotted Frank. Disbelief crossed his features, replaced quickly by recognition. Then something unexpected— genuine pleasure.

Walker approached the booth. Stood looking down at Frank. "Son of a bitch," he said softly. "Frank Kane. I thought you were dead."

"Hello, Mitchel." Frank croaked. "It's been a long time."

"Sure as hell has been. I heard you caught a Russian PKM round in Karbala. Full magazine, center mass. No way to survive that." Walker's eyes flickered to Frank's chest, as if searching for evidence of those wounds. "Yet here you sit, eating meatloaf like you didn't die."

Frank shrugged. The gesture dismissive of both death and explanation. Forked another bite of meatloaf.

Walker slid into the booth uninvited. Called to the waitress. "Coffee. Black. And whatever pie's freshest, Donna." The waitress nodded. Walker clearly a regular. His eyes never left Frank's face. Searching for confirmation of shared history. For the man he'd once known. "Been what... nine years? Tunisia? That cluster with the rebel faction?"

Frank nodded once. Continued eating.

"You disappeared after Karbala. Word came down you were KIA. Anderson took it hard." Walker leaned forward, voice dropping. "Remember Anderson? Skinny guy from Georgia? Sniper. He said no way anyone survived that much lead. Told everyone who'd listen that he saw you go down with his own eyes."

Frank's damaged throat produced something between grunt and laugh. He pointed to his neck, the scar tissue visible above his collar. "They missed."

Walker's eyes narrowed. Understanding dawning.

"That why you don't talk much anymore? Vocal cords?" Frank nodded. Pushed away his empty plate.

"So, the big man finally ran out of luck." Walker shook his head. "Though not completely, I guess. You're still breathing."

"Barely," Frank managed, the word scraping from his throat.

Walker's eyebrows rose at the rare speech. "That's more than most get in our line of work."

Donna arrived with Walker's coffee and a slice of cherry pie. "Here you go, Mr. Walker. Fresh this morning."

"Thanks, Donna. How's your boy doing at the community college?"

"Dean's list this semester." Pride straightened her tired shoulders. "That scholarship from the mill made all the difference."

"Hard work should be rewarded. He earned it." Walker's smile seemed genuine. Donna beamed as she left.

When she was out of earshot, Walker leaned forward. "What brings you to nowhere, Oregon? Bit far from wherever rock you've been hiding under."

Frank lifted his right hand. Made a casting motion.

"Fishing? You came all this way for fish?" Walker's laugh carried genuine amusement, revealing white teeth against tanned skin. "The same Frank Kane who couldn't sit still long enough to complete a surveillance op without getting twitchy? The man who shot up a Libyan marketplace because the waiting made him

'uncomfortable'? A fisherman now?"

Frank tapped his temple. Made the sign for silence, then peace.

"Quiet. Peaceful. I get it." Walker nodded, studying him with new interest. "We all look for somewhere to lay our ghosts to rest." He took a bite of pie, chewed thoughtfully. "Serious question, though. Anyone follow you here? Any chance this miracle resurrection has an audience?"

Frank shook his head. "Ghost."

"And a good one too." Walker sipped his coffee. Considered this. "Coincidence us meeting again?" His tone carried calculated skepticism.

"Chinook." Frank's damaged voice forced the words. "Best run."

"Clackamas is better. Willamette ain't bad either. But our Sandy gives 'em a run for their money."

Walker studied him. Eyes calculating distances, possibilities, probabilities. Weighing truth against suspicion like ammunition on a scale. "Where you staying?"

"Motel." Frank's scarred hand indicated vaguely eastward. "Fish early."

Walker set down his fork. "That fleabag motel off

Route 20? The one with the flickering vacancy sign?" Frank nodded once.

"Nonsense. You'll stay with me." Walker's tone brooked no argument. "Got plenty of room at the house next to the mill property. Just me and Sarah my housekeeper these days." He leaned forward, enthusiasm seemingly genuine. "We should fish together tomorrow. I know holes tourists never find. Places where fortypounders hide under cutbanks. Spots the locals keep secret from outsiders."

Frank's hesitation lasted exactly three seconds. Each one calculated. Each one necessary to make the acceptance appear reluctant rather than planned. He nodded once.

"Excellent." Walker finished his coffee with a satisfied expression. "Follow me in your car. Ten minutes up the valley road, past the mill entrance. Private drive marked with carved wooden sign." He dropped cash on the table. Enough to cover both meals plus generous tip. "Like old times, eh? You remember Fallujah? That safe house near the market where we holed up for three days? When Rodriguez took that shrapnel?"

Frank nodded. Remembered the mission. The firefight. Walker dragging a wounded teammate through machine gun fire without hesitation. The blood that had soaked into sand-colored concrete. Rodriguez had lived. Barely.

Walker stood. Adjusted his leather jacket with the unconscious precision of a man accustomed to checking his weapon placement. "Different war now, but still worth fighting." Something in his tone changed. Darkened. Hints of zealotry beneath the affable exterior. Then brightened artificially. "But tomorrow—just fishing between old friends. No talk of wars past or present. Deal?"

Frank rose from the booth. His massive frame dwarfed Walker despite the other man's considerable height. He extended a scarred hand. Walker clasped it. Their grip spoke of shared battles, of trust earned in blood, of bonds that transcended years of separation.

"Never thought I'd see you again," Walker said, genuine emotion breaking through his controlled facade. "World's been poorer without men like you in it."

Frank said nothing. The compliment hung between them, neither accepted nor declined.

They exited together into the cool mountain evening. The diner's neon cast red shadows across their faces. Walker climbed into a new Ford F-350 Limited, its black paint pristine under the streetlight. Custom wheels. Tinted windows. A vehicle that announced success without shouting it.

Frank folded himself into the Imperial. The ancient car groaned under his weight, suspension long past its prime. The leather seat cracked beneath him, worn smooth by years of use. His fingers found the ignition.

Both engines started—one a modern purr, the other a throaty rumble from decades past. Walker flashed headlights once, then pulled onto the empty main street. Frank followed, maintaining precise distance.

Professional habit.

The road wound through dark forest. Occasional houses appeared, then disappeared. The valley narrowed. Trees pressed closer to the asphalt. Frank checked his mirrors. Nothing followed.

The sawmill lights appeared ahead, industrial illumination cutting through darkness like searchlights. The complex loomed larger than it had appeared from his surveillance position. More substantial. More permanent.

Walker's brake lights flashed as he slowed, then turned onto a gravel access road that bypassed the main entrance. Frank followed. The Imperial's suspension protested each pothole. The gravel road climbed away from the mill, curving through dense forest until it emerged at a clearing.

A house stood there. Two stories of cedar and stone, its architecture blending with the surrounding wilderness while suggesting strength. Like Walker himself. Windows glowed amber against the night. A wraparound porch faced the valley below, offering commanding views of the mill, the town, the approaches. No position could reach this house unseen. Frank noted defensive sight lines, cover options, potential fatal funnels. Old habits.

Walker parked under a timber-framed carport next to two other vehicles—a Range Rover and an older Jeep Wrangler. Frank pulled alongside. Killed the engine.

The Imperial ticked as it cooled. Walker approached, hands visible. Friend, not threat. Not yet.

"Welcome to my humble mountain retreat," he said, gesturing toward the house with a hint of irony. Nothing humble about it. "Tomorrow, we fish. Tonight, we drink. And you listen while I talk enough for both of us." His smile revealed no hint of the darkness Frank had glimpsed earlier. "Like old times. Except you were never much of a talker anyway."

Frank emerged from the car. The night air carried pine scent and sawdust. Somewhere an owl called. Tomorrow would bring whatever it brought. Tonight was for gathering intelligence. For watching. For waiting.

He followed Walker toward the house, noting each security camera disguised as landscape lighting. Each motion sensor hidden in ornamental shrubs. The casual visitor would see a successful businessman's mountain retreat. Frank saw a fortress pretending to be a home.

Walker opened the front door. Light spilled across the porch. "After you, old friend. We've got a lot of catching up to do."

Lion's Den

The den's walls wore cedar paneling like a second skin. Trophy heads watched from above—elk, moose, bear. Their glass eyes reflected firelight. A gun case displayed rifles that had never been fired at game. Walker crossed to a cabinet of burnished walnut. Crystal decanters caught the fireplace's glow.

"Still drink Laphroaig?" Walker asked, hand poised over a bottle.

Frank nodded once.

Walker poured amber liquid into matching glasses. The bottle's label announced twenty-five-year aging. Success measured in distilled form. He handed one glass to Frank. Their fingers brushed. Both scarred from the same wars. The same operations. Different paths since.

"How's the neck?" Walker asked, settling into a leather chair. "Bad as it looks?"

Frank's hand touched the scar tissue briefly, but said nothing.

"PKM rounds?" Walker sipped his scotch. Savored

the smoke and peat.

Frank nodded.

"You always did have the devil's own luck." Walker raised his glass in salute. "Tried to find you after. Even sent Anderson looking. Trail went cold in Germany."

"Wanted it that way. Done."

Walker nodded. Understanding professional ghosts. "You remember that villa outside Fallujah? When

Reynolds stepped on that pressure plate?" Frank grunted. Memory stirring.

"You tackled him. Took the blast yourself. Two months in Landstuhl Medical Center with shrapnel in your back and legs." Walker's eyes searched Frank's face. "You always put the team first. Loyalty. That's what I remember most."

Frank drank. Said nothing.

"A man who understood sacrifice. Who saw the bigger picture." Walker leaned forward. "Country's lost its way, Frank. Forgotten what made it great. It needs men like you."

Frank's expression revealed nothing. Listened. Evaluated.

A phone vibrated. Walker checked the screen. "Need to take this. Business." He rose. "Make yourself comfortable. I'll just be a minute."

Walker stepped into the hallway. Closed the den's door. Pressed the phone to his ear.

"It's Pierce." The voice carried tension beneath control. "You sure about having him here? So close to everything?"

"Frank Kane is exactly where he needs to be."

Walker's voice dropped. "Where I can see him."

"He was watching the mill today."

"I would expect nothing less."

"And that doesn't concern you?"

Walker's laugh held no humor. "Frank always did his homework. It's why he survived this long." A pause. "Question is, why show himself now? After all these years?"

"Maybe fishing is just fishing."

"Nothing is ever just anything with Frank Kane." Walker checked the hallway. Empty. "Wait until after midnight. Search his car. Tell me what you find."

Walker ended the call. Stood motionless for ten seconds. Recalibrating. Then returned to the den.

Frank hadn't moved. The fire popped. Threw shadows across scarred hands holding crystal.

"Lumber futures," Walker explained, settling back into his chair. "Markets never sleep." He refilled both glasses. "So, what have you been doing all these years?"

"Restoring a lighthouse in Maine." "Sounds peaceful." Frank nodded.

"Peace has its place." Walker swirled his scotch. "But men like us... action's in our blood. Can't wash it out." He studied Frank's impassive face. "Some wars never end, they just change battlefields."

Frank sipped his drink. The liquor traced fire down his damaged throat.

"Tomorrow we'll hit Eagle Creek." Walker drained his glass. Set it on a side table of polished pine. "Twenty pound Steelhead there on a good day. Need to be on the water before dawn."

Frank finished his scotch in a single swallow. Nodded.

"Guest room's upstairs. Second door on the right." Walker rose. "Bathroom's stocked. Maria keeps things ready for visitors."

Frank stood. His massive frame towered over Walker. "Like old times," Walker said. "Team back together." Frank's grunt carried no confirmation.

They climbed stairs side by side. Men who'd once

trusted each other with their lives. Men who now calculated distances, angles, vulnerabilities. Each step measured. Each word weighed. The night settled around Walker's fortress house. Somewhere in the darkness, Pierce prepared to search the Imperial. The game advancing one move at a time.

Walker paused at the top of the stairs. "Sleep well, old friend."

Frank nodded. Entered the guest room. Closed the door. Listened to Walker's retreating footsteps.

The window offered clear view of the approach road. The Imperial sat in the driveway, chrome gleaming under security lights. Frank watched it from darkness for the next move in a game where neither player acknowledged they were playing.

Moonlight painted the Imperial silver. Pierce approached it from shadow, his movements economical. tested the driver's door. Unlocked. Careless for a man with Frank's background. Or deliberate. Pierce hesitated, then opened it.

The interior smelled of old leather and gun oil. Pierce swept the beam of a penlight across seats worn smooth by decades of use. Nothing in plain sight. He searched methodically. Checked under seats and found the spotting scope. Studied it. Military specification. Thermal capability. Night vision. The kind used by sniper teams and professional hunters. He put it back. Checked behind sun visors. Inside the glove compartment. Found fishing permits. Road maps. A receipt for tackle from a Maine sporting goods store. Nothing that didn't belong to a serious fisherman.

Moved to the rear of the car and picked the trunk lock, careful not to scratch the chrome. The lid opened. The vast trunk contained fishing gear. Rod cases. Tackle boxes. Waders still damp from the river. A small canvas duffle with clothes. A toiletry kit. A cardboard tube. He opened it and found the blueprints. Multiple views. Construction details. Interior layouts. The title block identified it as "Point Beacon Lighthouse." Curious, but nothing damning. He put the drawings back and closed the tube. Nothing hidden in the wheel well. Nothing beneath the spare tire.

He closed the trunk. Left the car showing no signs of search. Walked fifty yards into the forest before making the call.

Walker answered on the first ring. "Report."

"Car's clean." Pierce's voice barely above whisper. "No weapons. No surveillance equipment except a highend spotting scope."

"Spotting scope?" Walker's voice sharpened. "What kind?"

"Military grade. Thermal. Night vision. Twenty-power magnification minimum."

Silence on the line, then a grunt from Walker.

Pierce scanned the darkness. Ensured he remained alone. "Found blueprints too. Lighthouse on the Oregon coast. Recent date."

"I wonder what that's about?"

"I think it's that lighthouse on the point near Tillamook," Pierce continued. "Place looks like it's about to fall down."

"Maybe he's thinking of renovating it," said Walker wondering outload.

"Why would he do that?"

"Keeping himself busy, I guess."

"Sounds boring."

"Leave everything exactly as you found it." Walker's voice hardened. "Kane would notice. He always notices."

The call ended. Pierce pocketed his phone. Looked back toward the Imperial. The old car revealed nothing new in moonlight. A relic holding secrets. Like its owner. He faded into forest shadows.

The night deepened around Walker's mountain compound. Security cameras tracked movement. Guards maintained perimeter watch. And somewhere inside, Frank Kane either slept or waited. The dangerous uncertainty of a predator in another predator's territory.

Frank lay in darkness. Walker's guest room held nothing of its owner. Clean sheets. Empty drawers. A deliberate absence that spoke volumes. The clock showed 1:17 AM.

He rose without sound. Boots in hand, he moved to the door. Listened. The house settled around him. Floorboards murmured beneath carpet. Heat cycled through ducts. Walker's compound breathed in sleep. The hallway stretched empty. Frank placed each foot with care. Found the dead spots between joists where noise wouldn't betray him. The stairs presented greater challenge. He descended along the outside edge where nails held tighter to frame. Years of practice guided his movements. The front door lock yielded to practiced fingers.

He slipped outside. Night air carried pine scent and sawdust. Distant shapes of mountains against starfield. The Imperial waited in the driveway but would make too much noise. This excursion required stealth not horsepower. Frank pulled on his boots at the porch steps. The Derringer nestled against his ankle provided minimal comfort. The KA-BAR more certain weight against his hip.

He moved across the gravel without sound. The road to the mill wound downhill. Moonlight cast enough illumination to navigate. Frank kept to the treeline. His massive frame improbable in shadow. Each footfall carefully placed. Ten minutes of descent brought him to the mill perimeter. Security proved minimal. Twelve-foot chain-link fence. Padlocked gate. Guards patrolled in predictable patterns. Frank timed their rounds. Found the gap. Scaled the fence between camera sweeps. Dropped to the other side without sound.

Machinery hummed from the main building. The night shift at work. Frank moved through shadow, staying beyond the floodlights' reach and out of the sight of patrolling guards. He approached the loading dock where lumber waited in stacks. Inventory lists attached to clipboards revealed nothing suspicious. Simple description of board size and grade. Total volume. Destination.

Frank made his way toward the main mill floor. The building's wall offered windows at eye level for someone his height. He peered through. Inside men operated machinery in practiced symphony. Logs fed into debarkers. Planer tables smoothed rough-cut lumber. The massive bandsaw blade sliced through the wood without resistance. Nothing unexpected. Nothing that suggested Walker's operation held darker purpose.

He worked his way around the building. Checked each outbuilding in turn. The tool shed contained only what belonged. The chemical storage held wood preservatives, stains, and lumber treatments. All legitimate.

Frank worked his way toward the administrative building. A stack of cedar two-by-fours provided cover as headlights swept the yard. A security truck made its rounds. Gravel crunched under tires. The vehicle parked thirty yards away. Driver's door opened. A guard stepped out, flashlight beam cutting darkness. His boots scraped concrete as he approached the lumber stacks.

Frank pressed against the wood. Cedar scent filled his nostrils. The guard passed within arm's reach. Radio crackled at his belt. "Perimeter check complete," came a voice through static. "All clear." The guard stopped. Swept his light across the lumber. The beam passed inches above Frank's head. "Something wrong?" the radio asked. The guard hesitated. Frank didn't breathe. His hand found the KA-BAR's handle. Steel whispered against leather. "Thought I saw something," the guard said. "Probably just a critter." He took another step. His boot heel landed beside Frank's hand. The flashlight beam dropped lower. Would find him in seconds.

A crash came from the main building. Metal against concrete. The guard's head turned toward the sound. "What was that?" the radio squawked. "Sounds like a forklift dropped a log where it didn't belong. I'll check now." The guard moved away, flashlight swinging toward the noise.

Frank remained motionless until the guard entered the main building. Only then did he release his grip on the KA-BAR. His heart maintained its steady rhythm. Professional discipline overriding natural response. He waited three minutes before continuing his reconnaissance. The guard's nearness confirmed security remained human. Fallible. Exploitable when needed.

The administrative building stood dark except security lights. Through windows Frank saw desks. Computers. Filing cabinets. Normal office landscape. Sarah's workstation identifiable by a family photo. The image showed younger Sarah beside an older woman whose face mapped future lines in her daughter's. Nothing hidden in plain sight.

Frank spent two hours examining the mill. Every corner. Every shadow. Everything appeared legitimate. A successful lumber operation running night shift to meet demand. Men earning honest pay for honest work. No weapons crates. No suspicious shipments. Nothing to confirm Culper's intelligence.

The floodlights cast hard shadows across the yard. Frank moved through them like liquid. The fence presented no greater challenge on exit than entrance. He gained the treeline and began the climb back toward Walker's house.

Dawn would break soon. Time enough to return unseen. His mind worked against what his eyes had witnessed. The mill's legitimacy challenged Culper's certainty that Walker planned something requiring stolen weapons. Either Culper was wrong or Walker concealed his operation better than most military installations Frank had breached.

The house emerged from forest shadow. Light burned in a second-floor window. Sarah's room. Frank froze. Her silhouette moved behind curtains. Too early for normal rising. Too late for insomnia. She spoke to someone unseen. The shadow of a phone held to her ear. Frank waited until her light extinguished. Continued to the house. Re-entered through the door he'd left unlocked. Made his way upstairs without sound. Returned to the guest room. The clock showed 3:38 AM. First light would soon break across the mountains. Frank removed his boots. Lay atop the covers. Closed his eyes. The floorboards outside his door creaked. Someone paused. Listening. Then continued past.

Cold woke him. Always did. Old bones broken too many times protesting. The dark still owned the sky. Frank lay still, ears tuned to the house's breathing. Boards settling. Heat ducts murmuring. Whispers of a place where he didn't belong. He reached for his boot and found it. The Derringer still nested in his boot by the bedside. Small comfort. A clock face showed 4:37. From below came a mix of smells. Coffee. Bacon. Someone else awake in this mountain tomb.

He dressed in silence, blue jeans and flannel. The cold floor took his feet as he moved toward the door. The old house creaked beneath him. Each tread announced his weight to whoever waited below. He didn't try for stealth. Stealth meant intent. He wanted no one to suspect.

The staircase spilled into a hallway the color of weak tea. Light from the kitchen cut a yellow rectangle against the dark wood floor. He moved toward it, following scent like a compass.

She stood at the stove. Back to him. Long dark hair pulled back with something red. Her shape outlined against the white cabinets. The woman from the mill. Her hands moved with practiced certainty across skillet and coffeepot. She hadn't heard him yet. Few did. Then she turned. Something in her stillness told him she'd known he was there all along.

Her green eyes found him in the doorway, seized him. Working eyes. The kind that measured supply against demand and came up right every time. "You move quiet for somebody who takes up that much doorway," she said.

Frank said nothing. She gestured with a spatula. "Coffee's ready. Help yourself." He crossed to the pot. Took the mug she'd set out. Plain white ceramic, chipped where some prior hand had gripped too tight. He measured this against the perfection of everything else in Walker's house. Noted the dissonance. "Mitchel said you don't talk much."

Frank poured. Black liquid steamed. Grunted.

"He didn't say why."

Frank touched his throat with scarred fingers.

"Injury?"

He nodded. Sipped. The coffee held its own with the Maine brew he'd left behind. Almost.

"I'm Sarah." She cracked eggs with one hand into the skillet like a short order cook. Their whites crawled across hot iron with small protesting sounds.

"You're Frank." A statement. Not a question.

He nodded anyway.

"Mitchel told me last night. Said you were some kind of legend." She pushed bacon with the spatula. Cast iron hissed.

Frank watched her hands. The way they never stopped. The way they knew their business. Same hands he'd seen passing coffee to millworkers. Same certainty of movement.

"Hungry?" she asked.

"Yes." His voice cut the word to pieces. Made it sound like gravel underfoot. Something moved behind her eyes when she heard it. Not pity. Recognition maybe. She pushed a plate across the butcherblock island. Three eggs. Bacon in a pile. Toast already buttered. He took it without thanks, sat at the pine table overlooking Walker's domain.

The sky outside showed first suggestion of dawn. The mill far below. Just outlines still. No detail. Like memory. Sarah brought her own plate. Set it across from him. Two eggs. One slice of bacon. Wheat toast dry. "Mind company?" she asked.

Frank chewed. Shook his head once. She sat. Rolled her sleeves showing forearms tanned despite the Oregon winter. A scar on her left wrist. Old and white. Defensive wound. Someone had come at her with something sharp once and she'd thrown up her arm to protect her face.

Frank knew such calculations. Had made them himself.

"How long have you known Mitchel?" she asked.

"Tunisia."

"The war?"

Frank nodded. Cut egg precise. Watched her eat. The practiced movements of someone used to taking only what was needed. Discipline in small things that spoke to larger control.

"He thinks the world of you," she said. He chewed.

Waited. "Says nobody better in a fight."

He drank coffee. The house's heat came up through vents. Stirred the air. Made the curtains dance.

"That true?"

"Once."

Her fork played with the eggs. Appetite lost to some thought that worked behind her face.

"How long you staying?"

Frank shrugged. Neither of them believed the gesture.

"Been here five years now," she said. "Started at the mill checking lumber grades. Still do that. But Mitchel trusts me with the books too. And the crew."

Frank counted the words she gave. The careful assembly of a story any stranger might hear. He wondered what lived beneath the easy talk. What history hid under that smooth skin. What bones.

"The mill's his life," she went on. "Everyone from town works there. Nothing else for fifty miles pays this well. Mitchel built it from nothing. It was a wreck when he bought it."

Frank nodded. The eggs went down in mechanical bites.

"Most folks around here think he's some kind of savior. Tells you something about how bad things were." Floorboards in the hallway announced weight. Walker's tread. Not trying for silence like Frank. A man without reasons to hide his coming. Frank registered the sound before Sarah. Noted that too. Walker filled the doorway. His smile too wide for so early an hour.

"I see you two found each other."

Sarah stood. The movement smooth and practiced as everything about her. "Breakfast is ready." Walker crossed to the coffee. Poured while looking at Frank with eyes too sharp for the friendly voice he wore. "I hope Sarah's been making you welcome."

"She has." The ruined voice made Walker's smile tighten, but he pressed on.

"Good. I want you comfortable here."

He brought his mug to the table. "Sarah's the best thing that ever happened to me." Frank registered the words beneath the ones Walker spoke. The claim of ownership. The warning.

"Sarah. This is Frank Kane. Finest operator I ever worked with. We were in Tunisia together. Fallujah too. Went through Hell and came out the other side."

Sarah nodded. "So, I've heard." Her voice flatter now. Something between them. A current Frank couldn't see. Just feel. Walker cut into his eggs. "If the Steelhead are running. Eagle Creek will be the place. But we need to get going."

Frank nodded. Walker stuffed his mouth with bacon and washed it down with coffee. They both rose and headed through the doorway into the hall. Frank stopped and turned back. "Thanks," he croaked.

Sarah nodded with a smile.

Dawn greyed the river. Frank stood thigh-deep in cold current, water numbing his legs through waders. Walker worked twenty yards upstream, his casts precise arcs against mountain shadows.

The steelhead struck Frank's line with violence. Rod bent double. Reel screamed. The fish broke water, sunlight catching silver scales. "You got one," Walker called. "Big one too." Frank fought the steelhead with patience. Let it run. Gathered line when it tired. The battle lasted nine minutes. The fish weighed eighteen pounds when Frank finally lifted it from the river.

Walker waded over. Studied the catch. "Beautiful specimen." Frank reached for the hook in the fish's mouth, then knelt down to release it back to the current.

Walker's hand stopped him.

"Hold on. Sarah makes the best steelhead you've ever tasted. Secret recipe her mother taught her."

Frank hesitated. The fish thrashed weakly in his grip.

"Unless you're still sentimental about these river rats," Walker added with a half-smile. Frank grunted. Slid the fish into the creel hanging at his side.

"That's more like it." Walker cast again. His line arced through morning light. "Been too long since we had fresh catch for dinner." They fished until noon. Walker landed two more steelhead. Smaller than Frank's but respectable.

The sun climbed higher. Heat replaced morning chill. Walker reeled in his final cast. "Sarah will be pleased. Nothing she likes better than cooking fresh fish." They loaded gear into Walker's truck. Walker wrapped the fish in wet burlap. They climbed into the cab and headed back toward the house.

Frank woke in Walker's guest room. Light slanted golden through windows. The late-night recon and early morning on the river had taken more from him than expected. Clock showed 5:48 PM. He'd slept three hours. Water ran downstairs. Kitchen sounds drifted up. Frank pulled on his boots and followed the noise.

Sarah stood at the sink, sleeves rolled to elbows. The steelhead lay split and seasoned on cedar planks. The oven hummed behind her. She turned when his boot hit the last step.

"Sleeping beauty awakes." Her voice carried no edge despite the words.

Frank grunted. Kitchen smelled of herbs and wood smoke.

"Mitchel called. He's running late. Business in Portland."

She gestured toward the counter. "Drink?"

Frank nodded. She poured whiskey into two glasses. Set one before him. "Fish needs forty minutes. Low and slow like ribs. That's the trick." She took her glass toward the door. "Porch is better than watching an oven."

The porch wrapped around three sides of the house. Views stretched across valley to distant mountains. Frank settled into an Adirondack chair. Sarah took the adjacent one. Her hair hung loose tonight.

"Your fish will do fine. Mom's recipe never fails." She sipped her whiskey. "One of the few things I kept after she died."

Frank waited. Let silence work for him.

"Pancreatic cancer. Five years ago." Her voice flattened. "Six months from diagnosis to funeral."

Frank studied her profile against fading light. Her face revealed more than her words. "Medical bills bankrupted us. Insurance denied experimental treatments. Mitchel stepped in. Flew in a specialist from Cedar Sinai." "Didn't help?" rasped Frank.

Sarah shook her head. "Nothing would have. But Mitchel tried. Paid for hospice. The funeral. Said Mom wouldn't want me worrying about bills while grieving." Frank sipped his whiskey. The damaged throat made each swallow a negotiation.

"He gave me the job at the mill afterward. Said Mom would have wanted me taken care of." Her fingers traced the glass rim. "Been working there ever since."

"She knew him before?"

"Mom went to high school with him. Class of '86." She looked toward the darkening valley. "He takes care of his people. Always has."

Frank absorbed it. The obligation Sarah carried. The debt to Walker.

She drained her glass. "The mill's the closest thing to family now. The crew. Danny." The name hung between them. Walker's absence suddenly pronounced.

"The fish needs turning." Sarah rose. Her hand touched his shoulder briefly. An unexpected gesture.

Frank stiffened beneath it.

"Relax. Mitchel won't be back for at least an hour." She disappeared inside. Frank remained on the porch. Her touch lingered on his shoulder. Warmth not from whiskey spread through his chest. The valley stretched before him. Shadows gathered in folds of land. Lights from the mill punctured growing darkness.

Inside, the kitchen timer buzzed. Sarah moved between counter and oven. Her efficiency belonged to someone accustomed to managing alone. Walker's obligations bound them both. Different chains. Same keeper. Frank finished his whiskey.

The mission clarified then blurred. Culper's certainty about Walker weighed against Sarah's experience. The debt she carried. The loyalty it purchased. Night claimed the mountains. Stars appeared overhead like bullet holes in black fabric. The fish cooked. The house settled around them. The phone rang inside. Sarah answered it. She had a short conversation that Frank couldn't hear, then hung up.

The oven door opened. Cedar smoke and fish scent drifted to the porch. Sarah's voice called, "Dinner's ready."

Frank rose. Carried the empty glass following her voice inside. The porch light flicked on automatically behind him. Illuminating space he'd vacated. Warning of night's arrival and all its hidden movements.

The kitchen glowed amber with lamplight. Frank entered from the porch. Sarah worked at the counter, her movements precise. The steelhead glistened on cedar planks. Skin crackled golden over pink flesh.

"Just us tonight," she said without turning. "Mitchel called. Won't make it back."

Frank nodded though she couldn't see. Watched her hands as they arranged wild rice on plates. Grilled asparagus. The steelhead sectioned with practiced skill.

"Sit."

She pointed with her chin toward the table. Two places set at the corner rather than across. Proximity not distance. Frank sat. The chair complained beneath his weight. Sarah brought their plates, set them down with care. Returned with the whiskey bottle. Refilled their glasses.

"To fish worth catching," she said, raising her glass. Frank touched his to hers. The crystal sang briefly. They drank. She settled beside him. Their elbows nearly touched. The fish steamed between them. Frank cut into his portion. The flesh separated easily. Melted against his tongue. Flavors he couldn't name danced through the damage in his throat.

"Good," he managed.

Sarah smiled. "Mom would be pleased. She was particular about cooking fish right." They ate in shared silence. Not the strained quiet of strangers, but something older. More familiar. The comfort of those accustomed to keeping their own counsel.

"How's your lighthouse coming along?" she asked finally. Frank looked up. Her question carried knowledge she shouldn't have.

"Mitchel told me you're restoring a lighthouse in Maine," she said clarifying.

"Good. Almost finished," he croaked.

"What happens when you're finished?"

"I find a new home."

"Another lighthouse to restore?" Frank nodded.

"We've still got a few of those on the Oregon coast. Most have been turned in bed and breakfast inns. I guess folks think it's romantic staying in a lighthouse for a couple of nights. I've thought about it. You know, opening up an inn. Cooking vanilla waffles for tourists.

It wouldn't be a bad life. Peaceful." "Too many people."

"For you maybe. But I get it. Still, it's a nice dream. Everybody needs a dream, Frank. What's your's?"

Frank considered for a long moment. How much to share.

"Peace," Frank said, the words scraping through his damaged throat.

"That's it? Just peace?"

Frank cut another piece of fish. "It's enough."

"Peace is the absence of something, not the presence." Sarah refilled their glasses. "What would you do with all that quiet?"

"Listen."

"To what?"

"Waves. Wind. Anything that isn't screaming."

Sarah studied him. The lamplight caught shadows beneath her eyes that makeup didn't quite hide.

"Screaming follows us. Even into silence."

Frank met her gaze. "Yes."

"How long were you in the same line of work as Mitchel?"

"Too long."

"And now lighthouses."

"Stone doesn't lie. Doesn't betray." "Unlike people," Sarah said softly.

Frank nodded.

"Is that why you don't trust me?" she asked.

"Should I?"

Her laugh held no humor. "Probably not."

She pushed rice around her plate. "We all wear masks here."

"You too?"

"Especially me." She drank deeply. "Everyone has secrets, Frank. Some are just... smaller than others."

"And yours?"

Her fork stopped moving. "Too numerous to count."

"Walker holds them?"

"Some." She drank deeply. "Others I keep for myself."

Frank watched her over the rim of his glass. "Why stay?"

"Where would I go?" She gestured toward the valley beyond the window. "This town, these mountains.

They're in my blood."

"But Walker—"

"Mitchel is complicated." She cut him off. "He believes in something bigger than himself. That's rare these days."

"What does he believe in?"

Sarah's expression closed. "You should ask him yourself."

"I'm asking you." Their eyes locked. The kitchen seemed to shrink around them.

"America," she said finally. "The idea of it. Not what it's become."

"And what's that?"

"Weak. Divided. Rotten from within." Her words carried cadence that wasn't her own. Walker's rhetoric in her mouth.

"You believe that?"

Sarah hesitated. "Parts. Not all." "Which parts?"

"That people have forgotten what matters.

Community. Purpose. Something beyond themselves."

She pushed her plate away. "But his methods..."

Frank waited. Let the silence work again.

Sarah leaned back. "Why are you really here, Frank? And don't say fishing."

The directness surprised him. Frank considered his next words carefully. "Old debts." "To Mitchel?" He nodded.

"What kind?"

"The kind that don't wash off."

Sarah studied him. "Blood?" Frank said nothing.

"He saved your life."

"Once."

"And now you're returning the favor?" Her tone sharpened. "Or something else?"

Frank set down his fork. "You ask a lot of questions." "So do you." She stood, collected their plates.

"Difference is, I've answered some of mine."

"What do you want to know?"

She turned from the sink. "The truth. Just once from someone."

"Truth is complicated."

"So are we." She crossed back to the table. Stood beside him, her hip against the wood. "I've seen things at the mill Mitchel doesn't show visitors. I know what's beneath the surface."

Frank's muscles tensed. "And?"

"And I wonder which side you're really on."

"There are sides?"

"There always are." She touched his shoulder again. This time her hand lingered. "Sometimes we don't choose them. They choose us."

Frank looked up at her. The kitchen light cast half her face in shadow. "Why tell me this?"

"Because when you visit the mill, you'll see what

Mitchel wants you to see. And I want you to know there's more."

"Why?"

Her hand moved from his shoulder to his face. Fingertips traced the edge of scar tissue along his jaw. "I'm tired of masks."

Frank didn't move. Her touch mapped damage even as it offered something he'd forgotten existed. "What's beneath the surface, Sarah?"

Her hand withdrew. "Ask me again when you've seen the operation."

"Why not now?"

"Because I need to know which side you're on first."

Frank stood. His massive frame towered over her. "And how will you know?"

"I'll watch your eyes when you see what Mitchel's building. They'll tell me everything."

"Eyes lie too."

"Not yours." She stepped closer. Their bodies nearly touching. "Not to me."

The space between them charged with something dangerous. Something neither had planned.

"I should go," Frank said.

"Probably." But she didn't move away.

Frank studied her face. The question formed in his mind like a splinter working through skin. Why him? What could this woman want with a scarred giant? His massive frame, ravaged throat, and scarred face belonged on battlefield fringes, not with someone like her. He'd caught his reflection in glass enough to know what others saw—a broken machine designed for violence, not tenderness. Sarah could choose any man from miles around. Someone whole. Someone with a future instead of just a past.

His eyes moved over her—the copper hair, green eyes

that missed nothing, the graceful hands. And then she spoke softly as if she read his mind, "Most men want things from me. Information. Access to Mitchel. Or just..." she gestured vaguely at herself. "A trophy to display."

She stepped closer, her hand finding the scar tissue at his neck. "But you—you don't want anything. Or need anything."

Her fingers traced the damaged flesh without flinching. "Do you know how rare that is? Someone who sees me, not what I represent?"

Frank realized the truth in her words. He'd watched her without agenda beyond understanding. Had seen her movements, her efficiency, her careful navigation of Walker's world.

"We recognize our own kind, Frank," she said softly.

"People who've survived what should have killed them."

The house creaked around them. Wind pressed against windows. The valley sprawled dark beyond glass.

"I've had my fill of handsome men with easy smiles and rehearsed lines." Her fingers traced his scarred knuckles. "I prefer honest damage to pretty lies. I know what I'm getting with you."

"And what's that?"

"A man who can't hide what he is. Even if he tried. I need honesty." Her eyes held his. "We're both broken, Frank. Just in different ways." He absorbed this. Found truth in it he hadn't expected. The house creaked around them. Wind pressed against windows. The valley sprawled dark beyond glass.

"This is a mistake," Frank said.

"Probably." Sarah's hand found his. Cool fingers against scarred palm. "But I'm tired of making only safe choices."

Frank didn't move. The mission parameters blurred further. Culper's orders. Walker's secrets. Sarah's touch pulling him toward something that complicated everything.

"You think too much," she said.

"Occupational hazard."

"What does instinct tell you?"

Frank looked down at their joined hands. "That some traps are worth springing."

Her smile reached her eyes this time. "Then spring it." She tugged gently. Led him toward the stairs. Each step away from the kitchen moved them into deeper shadow. Into territory unmarked on any map Frank carried. Whatever waited in the darkness above, whatever it cost him, he followed. Some choices weren't really choices at all.

The morning hung gray through the kitchen windows. Frank stood watching Sarah clean breakfast plates, her movements economical and practiced. He'd said nothing through the meal. Just eaten the eggs and bacon she'd set before him.

Sarah wiped her hands on a dishtowel and caught him watching. "What?" she said.

"Payphone." The word tumbled from his damaged throat.

She tilted her head, brow furrowed. "In town you mean?"

Frank nodded once.

"There's a phone right here." She pointed to the wall unit near the refrigerator. "You can use it anytime. Mitchel won't mind."

Frank's massive hand brushed the air between them. Dismissal. "Private."

The word hung between them like smoke. Sarah's

hands stilled on the plate she was drying. Her knuckles whitened around the dishcloth. "Private," she repeated, the word harder now. "After last night, you're still keeping secrets?"

Frank shifted his weight, floorboards complaining beneath him. She set the plate down with deliberate care. "You're a weird duck, Frank Kane. We share a bed, but you can't share a phone call?"

The muscles in his jaw tightened. He offered nothing. Sarah turned back to the sink, her movements now sharp, precise with anger. "Must be nice, having compartments for everything. People too, I guess."

"Lighthouse business," he managed, the lie sounding hollow even to him.

"Sure. Lighthouse business." She didn't look at him. "Because that's urgent enough to drive into town at nine

in the morning. Must be life or death." He still said nothing.

She dropped a plate in the sink. It shattered. "Shit!"

She realized she was making a fool of herself. She calmed and said, "The pharmacy on Cedar Street has a pay phone outside. Probably the last working payphone in three counties. Most folks don't even notice it anymore. Like a fossil nobody bothered to excavate."

Frank reached into his pocket, withdrew a worn leather wallet. Checked for bills.

"You need quarters?" she asked.

"Got some."

She threw the broken plate pieces in the trash and hung the dishtowel on a hook. "Pharmacy's next to the hardware store. Can't miss it. I don't suppose you want company?"

"No."

Frank moved toward the door, boots heavy against the hardwood. Sarah watched him go, arms folded across her chest.

"Frank?" He stopped, hand on the doorknob. "Nobody uses payphones for good news," she said. "Whatever it is, I hope it works out." Her words carried weight beyond their surface.

He grunted acknowledgment. The door closed behind him with finality.

The Imperial waited in the gravel drive, frost melting from its chrome in the morning sun. The starter was strained in the cold air. The engine caught on the second try. Frank guided it down the mountain road, switchbacks uncoiling beneath tires that had crossed a continent to bring him here.

The town appeared below, small against the vastness of Oregon wilderness. Buildings huddled like survivors. The pharmacy sign visible even from this distance, its red lettering a wound against gray sky. Frank pressed the accelerator, metal responding beneath his foot. Whatever waited at the end of a payphone call couldn't be worse than the silence that followed him down the mountain.

The pharmacy stood like a forgotten monument to smalltown commerce. Red brick weathered by decades of winter storms. Windows clouded with age. The payphone hung on the exterior wall beneath a metal awning streaked with rust. Frank fed quarters into the slot. Each coin dropped with finality. A sound from another era. He dialed from memory.

The connection clicked three times before going through. Security protocols unchanged. Culper always careful. "New England Historic Society." The voice answering belonged to no such organization. "Zero-fourseven-dash-echo-nine." Frank's damaged throat made the code sound like wheat grinding. The line went silent. Then Culper's voice replaced the receptionist.

"Good to hear from you, Frank."

"Walker's operation is clean." Frank kept his back to the street. Eyes scanning for watchers. "Logging. Employment. Nothing suspicious."

"Are you certain?" Culper's tone carried concern, not accusation. "Our information suggested otherwise."

"Mill's legitimate."

"I believe you. But Walker's history suggests there's more. Perhaps something not visible on first inspection." Frank watched an elderly woman exit the pharmacy. She glanced at him then away. "Staff devoted. No military presence."

"What about Walker himself?"

"Same man. Different cause."

"His causes have always been concerning." Culper paused. "How's your position?"

"Getting closer to him. Need time."

"Take what you need." No pressure in Culper's voice. "But be careful, Frank. Walker inspires loyalty in good people. Makes them believe in his vision."

"I remember."

"Keep up your infiltration. Walker wouldn't risk exposing whatever he's planning to just anyone."

Frank shifted the receiver to his other ear. "Got his trust. Working on others."

"Check in when you can. Good hunting." The line went dead. Frank replaced the receiver. The metal cool against his scarred hand. He stood motionless for ten seconds. Processing. Planning.

Thirty feet away, through the pharmacy's back storeroom wall, Mike Pierce and a technician had been listening and recording the conversation on the payphone. "Got it all?" Pierce said.

The technician nodded. His fingers touched the recording device. "Every word."

"Who the hell is Culper?"

"Don't know. But he's asking about Walker's operation. Kane is looking for something."

"Walker needs to hear this. Now."

"What about Kane?"

Pierce peered through a gap in the blinds. Frank still stood at the payphone, staring at mountains as if they might offer answers. "He's not going anywhere we can't find him."

The technician packed equipment into an innocent looking duffle bag. Pharmaceutical logos stenciled on canvas. "You think he suspects?"

"Kane's good. But not that good."

Pierce and the technician slipped out the back. The alley narrow and damp between buildings. "Get this to Walker. I'll keep an eye on Kane."

The Imperial's engine growled to life five minutes later. Frank guided it toward the mountain road. He glanced in the rear-view mirror and saw Pierce's truck following at a distance. The watchers watched.

The Request

Morning fog clung to the valley floor like smoke from distant fires. Walker's truck rumbled through the mill's main gate, tires crunching gravel. Frank sat silent in the passenger seat, watchful. The facility sprawled across acres, aluminum roofs gleaming wet with dew.

"Started with just the main building." Walker gestured toward the largest structure. "Previous owner went bankrupt during the spotted owl restrictions. Town was dying. Two hundred families without income."

Workers looked up as the truck passed, nodded at Walker. He waved back, knew names. Called greetings through his open window. "We'll start with the sorting yard."

The yard stretched beyond vision. Logs stacked in rows higher than men. Each stamped with colored markings indicating species and grade. Forklifts arranged them according to some system Walker understood instinctively.

"Douglas fir. Cedar. Hemlock. Pine. Each suited for different purposes." Walker pointed to sections of the yard. "Cedar brings premium these days. Decay resistant. Natural oils protect it. Like nature's own preservative."

Frank watched machinery sort fresh-cut logs. The rough bark. The exposed pale wood beneath. The scent of sap still strong. His eyes scanned for something he had missed at night during his recon.

"Quality control happens here." Walker led him to a station where workers examined boards coming off the planer. "Grade affects price. Highest grade goes to furniture makers. Lower grades to construction."

The main mill floor roared with mechanized accuracy. The massive bandsaw screamed through a log thick as a man's torso. Sawdust filled the air like mist. Workers moved with practiced efficiency, their hearing protected by muffs, their eyes alert to danger.

"Three shifts. Twenty-four hours. The logs never stop." Pride filled Walker's voice. "Providing good jobs. Fair wages. Purpose."

Frank studied each station. Each process. Each worker. Nothing hidden. Nothing suspicious. Just lumber conversion on industrial scale.

"Shipping happens there." Walker pointed to loading docks where finished boards were bundled, wrapped, tagged. "Most stays in the Northwest. Some goes east. Specialty cuts go overseas."

They climbed back into the truck. Walker steered toward another gate leading deeper into forest. "Got a cutting crew working a cedar stand up in the hills. Worth seeing."

The road narrowed, pitched upward. Potholes forced Walker to slow. Trees pressed close on both sides, branches scraping metal. Twenty minutes passed in mountain silence punctuated only by engine noise and Walker's occasional comment about the territory.

"Old growth here." Walker broke the silence. "State

protects most of it now. We work selected stands approved for sustainable harvest."

The logging camp appeared in a natural clearing. Six men worked with chainsaws and heavy equipment. The screaming steel teeth cutting through cedar trunks older than any living person. The smell stronger here. Fresh wood exposed to air for the first time in centuries.

"Biggest cedar stand in three counties." Walker stopped the truck. "Taking only what's approved. Leaving seed trees. Coming back in fifty years when they've regrown."

Frank watched men guide a falling giant. Measuring its length before limbing began. The efficiency of their movements spoke of years doing the same work.

"Most of these guys are second, third generation loggers." Walker leaned against his truck. "Families worked these forests since the 1800s. Their grandfathers cleared land with crosscut saws and oxen."

Frank studied the operation. The cutting. The loading. Equipment that cost more than most houses. All of it legitimate. "Good business," he rasped.

"The best." Walker watched his men work. "Giving people dignity through labor that matters."

They ate lunch with the crew. Sandwiches from a cooler. Coffee from thermoses. Talk of board feet and seasonal restrictions. Weather forecasts that determined work schedules. Nothing about politics. Nothing about guns. Nothing about anything beyond trees and the cutting of them.

The drive back carried different weight. Walker watched the road with eyes seeing beyond it. Thoughts gathering behind his face like storm clouds. "You ever wonder what happens to men when their purpose gets taken away?" Walker asked finally.

Frank said nothing.

"They find new purpose. Or they die inside." Walker's hands tightened on the wheel. "Men need meaning. Something beyond themselves." The Imperial waited in Walker's driveway.

"How about a drink?" Walker asked.

Frank nodded.

Walker led him to the den. Poured whiskey neat into matching glasses. The fire in the stone hearth threw heat against the mountain chill. Walker settled into his chair. Something in his posture had changed. Decision made. Cards to be shown. "You ever heard of constitutional militias, Frank?"

Frank sipped whiskey. Revealed nothing.

"Second Amendment. Right of citizens to form regulated militias for common defense." Walker leaned forward. "Perfectly legal. Protected by the highest law in the land."

Frank watched him over the rim of his glass.

"I lead one. Here in Oregon." Walker studied Frank's face for reaction. Found none. "Three hundred members. Most veterans. All patriots who remember their oath to protect against enemies foreign and domestic."

Walker paused as if considering one last time.

"I need your help with something. Something important." Frank set down his glass, listening.

Walker rose. Stood with his back to the fire. "The federal government hates state militias. Sees them as threat rather than resource. Been trying to eliminate them for decades."

Frank waited. Let silence pull more words from Walker.

"There's a man. Goes by 'Culper.' Runs some kind of unauthorized agency. No oversight. No accountability. He's been making noise about weapons stolen from

Camp Pendleton. Trying to pin it on militias."

Walker's eyes narrowed. "On my militia specifically."

"Why?"

"To discredit us. To justify shutting us down." Walker refilled their glasses. "But I think it goes deeper. I think Culper's operation stole those weapons themselves.

Creating false flag to justify crackdown." Frank kept his expression neutral.

"Evidence?"

"Circumstantial but compelling. Culper's group took over an abandoned NSA communication facility in Idaho. Remote location. Pahsimeroi Valley. Been retrofitting it for months. Strange equipment going in. Military-grade security."

Frank drank. Considered his words carefully. "What do you need?"

"Reconnaissance. See if you can find those stolen weapons at Culper's facility. Discover what he's really doing out there."

"Why me?" Frank rasped.

"Because you're not me." Walker leaned closer.

"You have the skills to get past that security. You'll know where to look and recognize what you're seeing. You're the only one I trust beyond seeing it with my own eyes. You're the best recon operative I've ever worked with." Walker's voice carried genuine respect. "And because America needs men like you now more than ever."

The fire popped. Threw sparks against the grate. Frank stared into his whiskey as if it might contain answers.

"Pay would be substantial. Enough to get you started on that lighthouse you've eyeing on the Oregon coast." Walker smiled thinly. "All expenses covered. Equipment provided. Support on call."

Outside, twilight claimed the mountains. Shadows stretched across the valley toward the distant mill.

Frank set down his empty glass with finality. "No."

The word fell between them like a stone. Walker's smile froze. Died slowly. "No? Just like that?" Frank nodded once.

"You haven't even asked about details. About security parameters. About extraction plans."

"Don't need to."

Walker's stance shifted subtly. The friendly host replaced by something harder. "After everything we've been through? All those operations together?"

"Different time." Frank rose. His massive frame dominating the space between them. "Different war."

"This is the same war, Frank. Just different battlefield." Walker's voice tightened. "America's being hollowed out from within. By people who claim to protect it while stripping away everything that made it worth protecting."

Frank turned to walk away as if ending the conversation. Walker's hand caught his arm. Not threatening. Pleading. "At least think about it. Give me that much."

Frank looked down at the hand on his arm. Then at Walker's face. "Already have."

Walker released him. Stepped back. "You've changed."

"Yes," Frank said with a nod.

The fire consumed another log. Outside, an owl called across darkening forest. Frank stepped into the hallway. Left Walker standing in the den, firelight throwing his shadow against the far wall. Elongated. Distorted. A darkness growing beyond its source.

The Imperial's hood gaped like a mouth swallowing

Frank whole. His massive shoulders disappeared beneath metal aged by decades and miles. Only his legs remained visible, worn boots planted against gravel. Tools scattered in precise arrangement beside him on the fender. The old radiator had been leaking again. The mountain grades punishing metal never designed for such abuse. The crunch of boots on gravel announced her arrival. Frank recognized the cadence. Weight and rhythm as distinct as fingerprints. He didn't emerge from beneath the hood.

"Radiator trouble again?" Sarah's voice carried across the distance between them. Frank grunted affirmation. His hands stayed buried in engine compartment. Knuckles scraped against metal corners never designed for fingers his size.

"That old dinosaur's determined to die in these mountains." Her voice closer now. Standing beside the car's quarter panel, just beyond his vision.

Frank worked a bolt loose. Felt coolant trickle across his wrist. The liquid warm against his skin.

"I brought coffee. Figured you might need it." A mug appeared on the fender near his elbow. Steam rising from black surface. "No cream. No sugar. Black as the oil in this beast."

Frank's hand emerged, found the mug. His fingers brushed hers during the transfer. Brief contact that neither acknowledged. The coffee tasted of mountain water and careful brewing. Not the industrial sludge served in diners.

Sarah leaned against the car. Blue jeans and work shirt making her look more like the mill workers than Walker's personal assistant. Her dark hair pulled back from her face. "I was wrong this morning."

Frank twisted another bolt free. Said nothing.

"After what happened, I figured I had some claim on

you. Truth is, I don't." Her fingers traced patterns in the Imperial's dust. "One night doesn't make me keeper of your secrets."

The radiator cap came loose with a hiss of pressure. Frank set it on the edge of the engine bay. Inspected the neck for cracks.

"Walker told me about your conversation. About Idaho." She waited, received no response. "About you turning him down. Sounds like he thinks he owes you too."

Frank reached for a rag tucked in his back pocket. Wiped his hands, leaving dark streaks across the cloth. His eyes finally met hers. Waited.

"I'm not here to change your mind. Not about that." She sipped from her own mug. "Just wanted to clear the air between us."

Frank straightened to his full height. Towered over her though she wasn't small. The engine's heat radiated against his chest. "Appreciated."

"You talk even less when you're upset." Sarah's mouth quirked at one corner. "Most men can't shut up when they're angry. You go the other direction."

Frank drank coffee. His eyes never left hers.

"Walker's militia isn't what you think. These aren't weekend warriors playing soldier in the woods." Her voice dropped. "They're mostly local men trying to protect what little they have left. Loggers. Mechanics. Men who watched their jobs disappear and their towns die."

"Not my concern." His damaged throat made the words sound harsher than intended.

"I know. And that's okay." Sarah set her mug on the car's roof. "I didn't come to talk about Walker or militias or abandoned government facilities."

"Why then?"

Her hand found his forearm. The touch light against scarred skin. "Because I miss you. Because I'm sorry about this morning." Frank studied her face. Looked for manipulation beneath the surface. Found only the same directness he'd first noticed at the mill. The same efficiency of movement that wasted nothing. "Nothing to be sorry for." His voice softened to the extent his damaged throat allowed.

"There is. I pushed too hard. Expected too much." Her hand slid up his arm, leaving warmth in its wake. "We both have secrets. Things we can't share. That takes trust and time. I forgot that this morning."

The evening gathered around them. The forest beyond the house growing darker with each passing minute. Birds called last warnings before night claimed the canopy. Frank set down his mug. His scarred hands finding her waist. A question in the touch. Permission sought without words. Sarah answered by stepping closer. The space between them collapsing.

"I have nightmares sometimes." Her voice barely audible. "Dreams about being trapped. About losing control."

Frank nodded once. Understanding beyond words.

"Last night was the first time in years I slept through until dawn." Her hands found his chest. "No dreams. No waking in cold sweat."

Frank's massive arms encircled her. Held her against him despite the engine grease and sweat. Her head rested against his chest, ear pressed to his heart. Its steady rhythm keeping time with the evening's descent.

"I don't expect you to stay." Sarah's words muffled against his shirt. "I don't expect anything from you. Just tonight. Just now."

Frank's hand moved to her chin. Tilted it upward. Their eyes locked in silent communication more precise than any language. Then his scarred lips found hers. The contact electric despite its gentleness. Her arms slid around his neck, pulling him closer. When they separated, her eyes held both invitation and understanding.

"We can finish the radiator later." Her hand found his. Fingers interlacing with surprising strength. "If you want."

Frank's response came in the form of a single step toward the house. Their hands remained joined as Sarah led him through gathering darkness toward the porch. Light spilled from windows, cutting gold rectangles across the approach. Neither spoke as they climbed the steps together. The door closed behind them with finality.

The Imperial waited in the driveway, its hood still open. Tools laid out that would remain untouched until morning. The mountains watched without judgment as darkness claimed everything but the windows where warm light burned against the night.

Steam rose from the claw-foot tub, misting the bathroom mirror. Frank sat wedged in porcelain never meant to hold a man his size. Knees jutted like islands. Water barely covered his chest. His huge hands gripped the tub's edges. The door opened without a knock. Sarah entered carrying two glasses of whiskey.

"Thought you might want this." She set one on the tub's edge within his reach. Drank from the other.

Frank nodded. Made no move to cover himself. She settled on the closed toilet lid. Watched him over the rim of her glass.

"Looks uncomfortable."

"Been worse places."

Her eyes traveled his exposed torso. The lattice of scar

tissue. Entry wounds puckered and white. Exit wounds larger, angrier. A roadmap of violence etched in flesh.

"So I see."

rank sipped the whiskey. The amber liquid burned less than her scrutiny. "Mind if I help?"

She set down her glass. Removed her flannel overshirt, leaving the tank top beneath. Before he could answer, she knelt beside the tub. Found the washcloth floating in the water. Applied soap in slow circles. "These from Tunisia?" Her finger hovered above three round scars beneath his collarbone.

"Mogadishu."

She continued washing his back. Her touch firm yet gentle against damaged skin. "And these?" Fingers traced a series of thin white lines crossing his shoulders like latitude markers.

"Glass. Baghdad."

"Jesus."

"Wasn't there."

Her laugh came unexpected. Genuine. Frank's mouth twitched in response. She worked in silence for minutes. Her hands following the contours of old injuries. The knife wound near his kidney. The burn across his left shoulder blade. The exit wound where a bullet had somehow missed his heart.

"You've died a thousand times," she whispered.

Frank's voice emerged low. "Feels that way some mornings."

"Does it hurt? When the weather changes?"

"Always."

She poured water over his back, rinsing soap away.

"Roll forward."

Frank complied. Her hands continued their work across his chest. More scars revealed. More stories written in scar tissue.

"Walker says you're the best he ever worked with." Her voice casual. Conversational.

"Long time ago."

"He's worried about this Idaho situation. Says Culper is building something dangerous." Her hands never stopped moving. The washcloth circling old wounds.

Frank said nothing.

"I don't trust Walker's judgment sometimes." She reached for the whiskey. Drank. "He sees enemies where there might be none."

Frank watched her face. Waited.

"But I've learned to trust his instincts. When he's truly worried, there's usually cause." She set the glass down with deliberate care. "He's worried now."

Frank closed his eyes. Let water lap against his chest. "Not my fight."

"Maybe not." Sarah wrung out the washcloth. "But what if he's right? What if this Culper is building something dangerous at that facility? Using those stolen weapons for something worse than self-defense?"

"If."

"Yes. If." She handed him the soap again. "I grew up here, Frank. This valley's the only home I've known. These people matter to me."

Frank washed his arms. Machine movements. Mechanical.

"I hate the idea of militias. Men playing soldier in the woods." Her voice harder now. "Violence never fixed anything worth keeping."

Frank's eyebrows rose slightly.

"Yes, I see the irony. Given what you are. What you do." Her hand found his. Rested atop. "But what if checking this place is the way to prevent violence rather than cause it?"

Frank drained his whiskey.

"Walker has men. Doesn't need me."

"He thinks you'll recognize things they wouldn't. See patterns they'd miss." She stood. Found a towel from the rack. Held it open. "I'd go with you."

rank's head turned sharply. "What?"

"Road trip to Idaho. You and me. A cover story that makes sense." She shrugged. "I know the area. My uncle had a cabin near Challis."

Frank rose from the tub. Water cascaded from his massive frame. Sarah didn't look away from his nakedness or his scars. Held the towel steady. He stepped into it. Her arms wrapped the cotton around him. "Two people traveling look less suspicious than one. We could be a couple taking a fishing trip." Her hands worked the towel across his back. "The Pahsimeroi has good trout runs this time of year. We could tell folks we're on our honeymoon."

"Walker's idea?"

"No. Mine." She stepped back. Met his gaze. "Walker wants to send a team. Four men with military background. They'd stick out like blood on snow."

Frank considered this. Found truth in her assessment.

"You don't have to decide tonight." She gathered her flannel shirt. "But if you do this, I want to help. Not for Walker. For the truth."

Frank wrapped the towel around his waist. "Why?"

"Because I'm tired of living in shadows. Tired of not knowing what's real." She leaned against the doorframe. "If this Culper is building something dangerous, we should know. If Walker's paranoia is unjustified, I need to know that too."

"Dangerous for you."

"Maybe. But no more dangerous than staying here wondering." She studied him. "Besides, I suspect being with you is the safest place within five hundred miles."

Frank grunted. Not confirmation. Not denial.

"Think about it." She turned to leave. "Walker's leaving for Portland tomorrow. Three-day business trip. We could be in Idaho and back before he returns. No one would question my taking time off."

The door closed behind her. Frank stood dripping on the bathroom tile. The mirror had cleared enough to show his reflection. The same scarred face that had stared back at him through decades of violence. But something different in the eyes now. Something that hadn't been there on the Maine coast. He wrapped the towel tighter. His decision already forming like sediment settling in still water.

Dawn broke cold across the mountains. Frank guided the Imperial down dirt roads unmarked on maps. The car's suspension protested each rut.

He stopped where forest crowded the narrow track. Killed the engine. Silence settled like dust. He scanned the treeline. Searched for disturbance. For boot prints not his own. For broken branches signaling visitors. Nothing. The forest kept its promises better than men.

Frank moved uphill. His boots left minimal impression in the soft earth. Habit more than necessity now. Decades of training embedded in muscle memory that wouldn't die before he did. The great Douglas fir appeared around a bend. Lightning-struck. Hollowed. Dead but standing. Nature's perfect vault. Frank approached from the blind side, circled twice ensuring no one watched. Checked for trail cameras. For disturbed undergrowth. For anything suggesting discovery.

He knelt at the opening. Swept aside forest debris arranged to appear random. The camouflaged tarp beneath matched pine needles and soil. Frank pulled it back. The hollowed tree revealed its secrets. The oilcloth packages lay undisturbed. First the fishing rod case containing the Barrett's barrel. Then the tackle box holding the scope, stock, firing mechanism, and bipod. Frank unwrapped each component. Checked for moisture. For damage. The metal remained clean. The matched Ruger Redhawks came next. Six-shot revolvers with 7.5-inch barrels. Their weight familiar. He checked each cylinder, spun each action.

The Colt Cobra .38 received the same inspection. Each weapon cleaned before storage. Each still ready.

Frank rewrapped the arsenal in fresh oilcloth. The old pieces tucked into his pocket for burning later. Nothing left to trace. Nothing left to find.

The armored vest came last. Ceramic plates shifting inside tactical fabric. He traced a finger across old bullet impacts. The vest had saved him in Karbala. In Fallujah. In places government documents would never name. He gathered everything. Made one final scan of the area. Erased what little sign his presence had left.

The burned tree looked untouched when he finished.

Its secrets once again hidden beneath natural camouflage.

The Imperial's trunk opened with protest from aged hinges. Frank arranged the weapons on the floor of the trunk. The vest folded to minimize profile. Everything placed for quick retrieval if needed. The tarp came last. Military surplus. Desert tan on one side. Woodland pattern on the other. He spread it over the arsenal. Arranged fishing gear atop it. Rod case. Tackle box. Waders. The props of a cover identity layered over tools of his true profession.

Sarah would ride in the car. Would place her bag in the trunk beside his. Would never know what lay beneath the tarp unless everything went wrong. Frank preferred it that way. He closed the trunk. The metal latched with finality.

Frank stood watching sunrise paint mountains gold and crimson. The day would bring preparation. Maps studied. Routes memorized. The business of violence approached with the same cold precision he'd always brought to it. The mission parameters had changed but the essentials remained constant. Observe. Report. Avoid engagement unless necessary. The old rhythms returned like flood waters to familiar channels.

Culper would get his intelligence. Walker would get his answer. And Frank would get...what? Peace seemed further away with each mile driving him from that Maine lighthouse.

The Imperial's engine caught on the first try today. Frank guided it back toward the main road. Whatever waited in Idaho would not find him unprepared. Some habits never died. Some skills never faded. The car disappeared around the bend, leaving forest undisturbed.

Recon

Walker spread the maps across the desk in his study. Outside rain hammered the roof. The kind that came sideways in the mountains. Frank stood looking down at the satellite images. At the topographic lines that marked elevation. At the red circle Walker had drawn around a complex of buildings nestled in the Pahsimeroi Valley.

"NSA installation. Built in the eighties to monitor Soviet communications over the pole." Walker pointed to the main building. A concrete structure half-buried in the hillside. "Four sublevels. Hardened against nuclear strike. Self-contained power and water systems."

Frank studied the approach routes. The valleys that funneled toward the facility. The ridgelines offering observation posts.

"Government abandoned it officially in 2002. Budget cuts after 9/11 shifted resources elsewhere." Walker flipped to another image. Ground-level photographs showing a chain-link fence topped with razor wire. Security cameras mounted at intervals. "But there's been activity. Last six months. Unmarked trucks. Night deliveries. New security systems installed."

Frank grunted. His eyes never leaving the images.

"Culper's operation moves different than government agencies. No official vehicles. No uniforms. No identifying markings." Walker pointed to a grainy image of men unloading crates from a panel truck. "These aren't Bureau. Aren't Agency. Private contractors with military bearing."

Walker pulled out another sheet. A schematic of the facility's interior. The lines faded from decades of storage.

"Source inside the Defense Department got me these. Not complete, but shows the basic layout." His finger traced hallways. Communication centers. Power distribution nodes. "What I need is confirmation of what they're doing there. Why Culper chose this place specifically. Why now."

Frank studied the plans. Noting emergency exits. Blind spots in the security camera coverage. Places where the earth had been disturbed along the perimeter fence.

"If they've got the weapons from Pendleton, they'll be stored here." Walker indicated a sublevel marked SECURE STORAGE. "Or possibly here." A room labeled COMMUNICATIONS EQUIPMENT.

Sarah entered with a tray. Three coffee mugs steaming. She set them on the desk edge and stayed, listening. Her eyes flicked between the men and the maps.

"What I need most is proof of Culper's real intentions. Evidence of the stolen weapons. Signs of whatever operation he's planning." Walker sipped his coffee. Watched Frank over the rim. "Get in. Document what you find. Get out. No contact with Culper's people. No engagement unless absolutely necessary."

Frank nodded. A single downward motion conveying understanding.

"The facility's remote nature works for us. Nearest town is May. Population less than 200. You and Sarah can base operations there without drawing attention. Couple on a fishing trip. Nobody looks twice at tourists in those parts."

Walker rolled up the maps. Secured them with rubber bands. Handed them to Frank.

"Memorize these, then burn them. Nothing written down. Nothing that connects back to us."

Frank took the rolled maps. His enormous hand engulfing the tube.

"Sarah knows the area. Has family history there. Her cover story is solid. Let her handle the talking. The social interactions."

Frank looked at Sarah. She nodded once. Her face unreadable.

Walker checked his watch. "I need to make some calls before we leave for Portland tomorrow. Sarah, got a minute?" He gestured toward the door.

Sarah followed Walker into the hallway. Frank watched them through the gap in the door frame. Their voices low. Bodies angled away from the study. Walker's hand on Sarah's shoulder. The kind of touch that suggested ownership more than affection. Sarah nodded at whatever instructions he gave. Her shoulders straightening under the weight of his words.

Frank turned back to the maps. Spread them once more across the desk. His eyes moved methodically over the terrain. Cataloging approaches. Extraction routes. Defensive positions. The work of a professional measuring killing ground. Weighing advantages against liabilities.

Behind him the door opened. Sarah entered alone. Her face composed again into careful neutrality.

"Anything else you need?" Frank shook his head.

"Walker wants us to leave tomorrow. Dawn. He'll be in Portland by then." She gathered the empty coffee mugs onto her tray. "You should pack tonight. We'll take

my Jeep. Less conspicuous than your car." Frank rolled the maps.

"No," he said.

Sarah paused at the door. "No?"

"Imperial."

She studied him. Weighing arguments against his immovable mass. Then nodded once. "Alright. The Imperial. But I'm driving part way."

Frank almost smiled. The motion so small it barely registered at the corners of his eyes.

"Maybe," he said.

Sarah left with the coffee mugs. Frank listened to her footsteps receding down the hallway. In the other direction Walker's voice carried from his office. Words indistinct but tone clear. Commands being given over the phone. A general marshaling forces.

Frank returned to the maps. Committing each detail to memory not because Walker ordered it but because survival depended on knowing terrain better than those who would kill you for crossing it. Old habits from older wars. The same calculations whether the ground was desert, jungle, or abandoned government buildings in remote valleys.

Outside the rain continued its assault. The Imperial sat in the driveway taking the worst of it. Water finding the pinhole in its radiator. Seeking weakness. Frank rolled the maps tight and bound them. The mission parameters clear enough. What Walker didn't say mattered more than what he did.

Every recon had secondary objectives unspoken. The kind that changed operation parameters without warning. Frank knew this dance from previous experience. The truth hiding under official briefings like the facility buried in that Idaho hillside.

He would go. Would look. Would report what he found to Walker or Culper depending on what he discovered. Both men spoke of peace while planning violence. Men using words like "country" and "loyalty" to conceal blood already spilled and blood yet to be drawn. Frank had played this game before. Had the scars to prove it. This time would be different only in the uniform his enemies wore. If they wore uniforms at all.

He tucked the maps under his arm and left the room. Behind him the lights clicked off automatically. Darkness settling.

The clock on the nightstand showed 2:17. Frank lay still listening to the house settle. Floorboards contracting in the cold. Wind finding gaps in century-old construction. Sarah's breathing next to him barely audible.

He sat up without sound. Pulled on his clothes in darkness. Boots last. The Derringer already tucked inside left one. His fingers checked the KA-BAR at his waist. Cold steel reassurance.

The hallway stretched empty. Frank placed each foot with care. Found the dead spots between joists where noise wouldn't betray movement. The third stair always creaked. He avoided it. The front door lock yielded. Cold mountain air rushed in carrying pine scent and distant water.

Outside stars punctured the dark where clouds had finally broken. Frank stood motionless. Letting his eyes adjust. Scanning for security cameras Walker had mounted in trees. For infrared sensors disguised as landscape lighting. For the guards who sometimes patrolled the perimeter.

Nothing moved. Just night creatures following ancient patterns beneath an indifferent sky.

The gravel would announce his departure. Frank moved to the Imperial. His hands finding the door handle. He released the parking brake. Put his weight against the driver's door. The car resisted then surrendered to his mass. Metal groaning faintly as it began to roll.

He guided it down the slope. Gravity doing the work engines normally handled. The night cold enough to see his breath. Fifty yards down the drive he pulled the door closed. Let momentum carry the car further before turning the key. The engine caught without hesitation. Low rumble that carried less than the gravel would have. Frank guided the Imperial down the mountain road. Headlights off. The car descended through forest shadow onto valley floor. Town lights visible as dim glow beyond the next ridge. He turned on the headlights.

Main Street lay abandoned at this hour. Businesses closed. Streetlights casting pools of sickly yellow at corners where nothing moved. Frank guided the Imperial past darkened storefronts. Past the hardware store. Past the diner where waitresses had already set tables for tomorrow's breakfast.

The payphone stood outside the pharmacy. Illuminated by a single bulb above that attracted moth battalions. Frank parked the Imperial across the street. Watched the phone booth for five minutes. Checked for surveillance cameras. For watchers in darkened buildings. For anything electronic that didn't belong.

Nothing. Just small-town midnight abandonment. He crossed the empty street. The payphone waited like a relic from another century. Frank dropped quarters into the slot. The coins falling with hollow finality. He dialed from memory. Three digits in. Four. Five. His finger hovered above the sixth.

If Walker spoke truth. If Culper had stolen those weapons. If the government man built something in that mountain requiring guns and ammunition and military expertise. If the country Frank had bled for now turned weapons against its own.

Frank's hand stilled on the receiver. The night pressed closer. Years of service weighed against him. Years of following orders while political machinery ground good men to paste beneath its treads. Years watching agencies claim defense of principles they violated in the claiming.

He replaced the handset. The connection never completed. The quarters clattered into the return slot. Frank collected them. Returned them to his pocket and walked back to the Imperial.

Two blocks away a parked Ford truck. Inside Pierce watched through night vision monocular as Frank climbed into the ancient car. Watched the engine start. Watched the Imperial pull away from the curb and head back toward Walker's compound.

Pierce reached for his phone. Sent a one-word text. "Aborted."

He set the phone down. Continued watching the street where Frank had stood. The empty payphone beneath its corona of moth-light.

Pierce started his truck. Let it idle as he considered options. For now he would watch. Would follow the Imperial at a distance back to Walker's place. Would observe and report without intervention. Walker's instructions clear on that point.

On the mountain road Frank guided the Imperial uphill. The V8 working against gravity now. His choice to withhold information from Culper settling like stone in his chest. Not commitment to Walker's cause. Just hesitation born of too many missions where all was not as it seemed. Too many operations justified by lies. Too many dead who never knew which side had truly killed them.

He would go to Idaho. Would look for himself. Would determine truth or falsehood with his own eyes. Then decide where loyalty belonged. If it belonged anywhere at all.

The Imperial's headlights caught Walker's house through the trees. Dark now except security lights. He killed the headlights and cut the engine at the top of the drive. Let momentum carry him to the parking spot. The car settling into silence as if it had never left.

He slipped inside the house. Retraced his path up stairs designed when men stood shorter. The door to his room closed without sound behind him. Opening the door, he saw Sarah sleeping quietly. Frank removed his boots. Set the KA-BAR within reach. Lay back on sheets gone cold in his absence. Decision postponed but not abandoned. Trust suspended between men who dealt in violence and called it patriotism.

Frank closed his eyes. Sleep would not come easy. The ghosts of wars past and wars to come crowded the darkness behind his eyelids. Making promises neither could keep.

Morning fog hung in the valleys as the Imperial crested another mountain pass. Oregon falling behind, Idaho waiting ahead. The engine roared against the grade. Frank's hands rested light on the wheel despite the car's weight.

The highway unspooled before them, empty this early. Dawn still just a promise beyond eastern ridgelines.

Sarah's boots rested on the dashboard. Position Walker would never have permitted in his vehicles. Her window cracked despite the chill, hair dancing in the slipstream. Some pop song played low on the radio. Her fingers tapped against denim-covered thigh, keeping time. "You hungry?" she asked, voice bright against the engine's bass rumble.

Frank shook his head. Last diner's eggs still with him.

"I know a place in Baker City. Best huckleberry pancakes in the Northwest." She stretched, spine popping against the seat. "My dad used to take me there on fishing trips. Before..." The sentence disappeared into memory.

Frank glanced sideways. Caught her smile. Different from those at Walker's compound. Less guarded. More genuine. As if crossing the state line had removed some invisible burden. "What?" she asked, catching his look.

He shrugged. Returned eyes to the road. "You're thinking something. Spill it." "You seem different," he managed.

"Different good or different bad?" Her eyebrow arched. Challenge in the question.

"Good."

Sarah rolled down her window further. Cold mountain air flooded the car's interior. She thrust her hand into the slipstream, letting wind catch her fingers. "Nobody watching. Nobody expecting anything. Just the road." She closed her eyes. "Freedom."

The Imperial rounded a curve. Valley opening below. Fog clinging to the river course like a ghost of ancient water. Trees crowding slopes. Sarah leaned forward. Pointed toward a distant ridge where light caught something metallic. "Fire lookout tower. Manned in summer. Empty now." Her finger traced the horizon. "My grandfather worked one summer there. Said the silence drove men mad by August."

Frank grunted. Understood such solitude.

"Drove me from Boise to Oregon when I was fourteen. After my dad left." Her voice carried no selfpity. Just fact offered without weight. "No stops except gas and bathroom. Said women traveling alone shouldn't linger."

Frank downshifted. The transmission growled acknowledgment. The highway steepened into Idaho.

"Ever been married, Frank?" The question came sideways. Unexpected.

"No."

"Not once in all those years? No one waiting while you traveled the world?" Her hand made a circular motion. Encompassing violence left unnamed.

"Wouldn't be fair."

"To her or to you?"

Frank considered. "Either."

Sarah reached for her bag on the rear seat. Rummaged until finding venison jerky wrapped in wax paper. Broke off a piece. Offered the rest to Frank. He accepted with scarred fingers. The dried meat tough enough to keep conversation at bay while he chewed. A sign announced the Idaho border.

Sarah rolled her window completely down despite forty-degree morning air. Thrust her arm out. Middle finger extended toward Oregon. "See ya, wouldn't wanna be ya!" she shouted into the wind.

Frank's eyebrows shot up.

Sarah caught his expression. Laughed. Sound bright as shattered glass. "Something Walker and I do every time we cross back to Oregon. Tradition." Her smile faltered, then steadied. "Guess some habits stick."

Frank nodded. Understanding rituals of transition. He'd had his own between combat tours. Between identities. The Imperial's gas gauge dipped toward empty. Frank pulled into a station on the outskirts of Baker City.

While the attendant filled the tank, Sarah disappeared into the convenience store. Returned with coffee in paper cups and a plastic bag. "Got us road snacks." She settled back into the passenger seat. Opened the bag to reveal packets of sunflower seeds, chocolate bars, gummy worms in lurid colors. "Essential supplies."

Frank eyed the assortment with skepticism.

"Don't tell me you've never had proper road trip food." His silence answered. "Oh my God. You're such a..." Words failed her. She tore open the gummy worms. Selected a green one. Held it before his face. "Open."

Frank stared at the candy. At Sarah's expectant expression. Opened his mouth slightly. She pushed the gummy worm between his lips. Watched as he chewed experimentally. "Verdict?"

"Sweet," he managed, the artificial flavor strange against his tongue.

"That's the point." She ate a red one herself. "Road trips need sugar. It's scientific fact."

The station attendant tapped the window. Frank paid cash. No credit card trail. No electronic signature. Sarah noticed but said nothing. Just sipped her coffee as they returned to the highway.

They crossed into the high desert of wester Idaho. Landscape changing from forest to scrubland. Basalt cliffs rising from beige earth. Sagebrush and juniper replacing pine and fir. The Imperial's shadow stretched long beside them, companion on empty asphalt.

"Can I try?" Sarah asked after an hour of comfortable silence. Frank glanced at her. Confusion in the small movement. She gestured toward the wheel. "Driving.

This beast looks like it has stories to tell."

Frank hesitated. The Imperial was extension of

himself. Private domain no one entered. Then slowly nodded. Pulled onto the shoulder. Dust rising behind them. Killed the engine. They switched places. Sarah settled behind the wheel. Adjusted the seat forward to reach pedals. Her hands looked small against the massive steering wheel. She turned the key. The V8 responded instantly. Her smile widened. "Sweet Jesus, listen to that." She revved the engine once. The car shuddered with contained power. "How old is this thing anyway?"

"Sixty-two." His hand rested on the door panel. Protective. Watchful. Sarah guided the Imperial back onto the highway. Her driving surprised him. Smooth. Confident. Respectful of the car's age and weight. "My first boyfriend had a '71 Chevelle. Not as nice as this, but same era. Big block. Heavy metal." Her laugh came quick. "Car outlasted the relationship by a decade until he wrapped it around a telephone pole pull doing eightyfive. Broke his back."

Frank watched the desert passing. Let another person control his direction. Strange surrender from a man who'd navigated his own course through darker territories. The Imperial responded to her touch. Accepted her command.

"Tell me about the lighthouse." Her request came gentle as the hand on the wheel. "The one in Maine. The one you're fixing." Frank studied her profile as she drove. Found no agenda in the question. Just genuine curiosity. He considered how much to share. What parts belonged only to him. "Stone. 1887. Built after three ships wrecked on the rocks." His damaged voice gained strength through the telling. "Foundation needed work. Sea air eats mortar. Replaced 200 blocks." "With your hands? All of it?"

He nodded. Remembered the weight of the stones. Satisfaction of something rebuilt rather than destroyed.

"I'd like to see it someday." The words slipped out. Surprised them both. She focused harder on the road after saying it. As if the admission required concentration.

Frank said nothing. The invitation hung between them. Possibility neither examined too closely. The Imperial continued eastward. The sun climbed higher.

The desert rolled past unending.

Sarah hummed along with the radio. Some old country tune Frank vaguely recognized. Her fingers tapped the wheel in rhythm. No sign of the careful woman who navigated Walker's domain with such care. This Sarah laughed easier. Took up more space. Claimed the world rather than fitting herself to its corners.

A gas station appeared on the horizon. Sarah pulled in without asking. Parked with care. "Bathroom break and driver switch. Your car's amazing, but my arms are getting tired. That steering's no joke."

Frank reclaimed the driver's seat. Settled into familiar space. Sarah returned from the convenience store with more coffee and a paper bag. She waited until they were back on the highway to reveal its contents. "Surprise."

She produced two ice cream sandwiches. Passed one to Frank. "Eat fast before they melt."

Frank stared at the wrapped rectangle. At Sarah's expectant face. Accepted the offering. The last time someone had bought him ice cream, Reagan had been president. The vanilla sweet and cold. Simple pleasure nearly forgotten.

"Good?" she asked, her own ice cream half gone.

Frank nodded. The dessert disappeared in three bites. Sarah laughed at his efficiency. The sound carried no mockery. Just delight in the shared moment.

The Imperial ate miles. The landscape shifted again. Mountains reappeared on the horizon. The Pahsimeroi

Valley waited beyond them. Sarah's boots back on the dashboard. Her face turned toward sun streaming through glass. And Frank allowing himself to exist in this moment uncomplicated by past or future.

The Imperial's tires hummed against cracked asphalt as they descended into Pahsimeroi Valley. The sign announcing MAY, IDAHO - POP. 127 leaned at an angle, rusted bullet holes puncturing the metal like asterisks correcting an outdated count.

The town materialized in the valley bottom like debris washed up after a flood. Buildings weathered to the same gray as the sagebrush surrounding them. Single-street settlement with telephone poles serving as its spine. One gas pump outside the general store. A post office no larger than a shed. A bar called simply DRINKS with windows too dirty to see through.

Frank guided the car past a boarded-up church to a gravel lot where the general store, bar, and post office shared parking. The engine ticked as it cooled. Heat rising off the hood into mountain air.

"Metropolis," Sarah said. "Just like I remembered."

Inside the general store smelled of dust, coffee grounds, and beef jerky hanging in plastic bags near the register. The floorboards had been worn pale by decades of boots. A potbelly stove occupied the center of the room, cold now but ready for winter that always came early to these elevations.

Behind the counter, a woman in her seventies watched them enter. Hair pulled back in a severe bun that matched the line of her mouth. A name tag pinned to her flannel shirt read ELEANOR in faded letters.

"Help you?" The question contained no warmth.

Sarah approached the counter, smile brightening her face like she'd flipped a switch. "Just passing through. Thought we'd stay a day or two. Do some fishing."

Eleanor's eyes flicked between Sarah and Frank, who stood examining a display of pocketknives in a scratched glass case. "River's been low. Not much catching."

"Still, it's beautiful country." Sarah leaned on the counter with practiced casualness. "Any recommendations for spots a local might know?"

"Guidebooks cover most of it." Eleanor's attention shifted to Frank, who'd moved to examine the store's small selection of ammunition. "Your husband interested in hunting?"

"No ma'am. Just protection." Sarah followed her gaze. "Remote places, you know how it is."

Eleanor grunted acknowledgment. Sarah purchased beef jerky, trail mix, and two bottles of water. The transaction completed without further conversation.

As they left, a man entered. Denim worn white at stress points. Beard streaked with gray though his face suggested forty, not sixty. He nodded at Eleanor and eyed the strangers with the careful blankness of rural people assessing outsiders.

Outside, the sun hammered the valley with indifferent brightness. Across the street, three pickups were parked at the bar despite the early hour. Frank checked his watch. 11:17. Time stretched differently in places where occupation rarely changed with the clock's movement.

"Friendly bunch," Sarah said, climbing into the passenger seat.

Frank grunted. Started the Imperial. The car drew little attention in a town where vehicle models rarely post-dated the Reagan administration.

They drove the single road to its end where it intersected with a narrower county route. A diner occupied the corner. Concrete block construction with a sun-faded Coca-Cola sign. Windows tinted with decades of grease. A metal chimney emerging from the flat roof.

Inside, five booths lined the wall opposite a counter with fixed stools. Three were occupied. Men in work clothes. A young waitress moved between them refilling coffee cups. She couldn't have been more than nineteen. Blond hair escaping a hasty ponytail. Eyes too old for her face.

Frank and Sarah took a booth by the window. The vinyl seats had been repaired with duct tape that matched the gray theme of the valley. The waitress approached.

Her name tag read BETH.

"Coffee?"

Sarah nodded. "Please. And whatever's good today."

"Meatloaf's fresh. Comes with potatoes. Real ones, not instant." The girl delivered this with pride as if defending family honor.

"Sounds perfect," Sarah said. "For both of us."

"Double for me," rasped Frank.

"You're gonna get fat," said Sarah with a sly grin.

Frank grunted.

Beth poured coffee and disappeared into the kitchen. The men at the counter observed the newcomers with peripheral vision, conversation continuing in low tones.

"I haven't been back here since I was fourteen." Sarah stirred sugar into her coffee. "Nothing changes. Like the whole place is suspended in amber."

Frank scanned the diner. Exit points. Defensive positions. Occupants who might pose a threat. Old habits.

"My uncle used to bring me fishing up here. Had a cabin about twenty miles out. Near where the NSA facility sits now." Sarah's voice dropped. She leaned forward. "People didn't like it when the government moved in. Fenced off good hunting land."

The three men at the counter paid their bills and left, work boots clomping on warped linoleum. Only one booth remained occupied. An elderly couple who ate in synchronized movements without speaking.

Beth returned with plates of meatloaf, mashed potatoes, and green beans that had surrendered their color to the cooking process. "Anything else?"

Sarah smiled up at her. "Lived around here long?"

"All my life." Beth tucked the order pad into her apron pocket. "Not much choice."

"I remember there used to be a government facility up north. Big place with fences. Good fishing in a nearby stream."

Beth's expression closed like a gate. "Don't know about that. More coffee?"

"Please."

The girl refilled their cups and retreated. Sarah cut into her meatloaf. "Well, that went nowhere."

Frank ate without speaking. The food better than the surroundings suggested. Seasoned with herbs that didn't come from industrial suppliers.

"People clam up about that place," Sarah continued. "Even more than when I was a kid. Used to at least acknowledge it existed."

They finished eating. Paid cash. Left a tip that matched the bill. Outside the light had begun its slow surrender to afternoon. The air cooled with altitude's promise of night.

The Pine Valley Motel sat at the edge of town. Six units arranged in an L-shape. Concrete construction with wood veneer attempt at mountain aesthetic. A neon sign buzzed with indifferent promise of VACANCY.

The manager emerged from unit one when Frank knocked. A man shaped by decades of cigarettes and minimal movement. Skin like leather left in the sun. Eyes watery behind thick glasses.

"Need a room," Frank said.

"Got five." The manager jerked his thumb toward the empty parking lot. "Take your pick." "Two rooms," Frank clarified.

Sarah stepped forward. "One's fine." She placed her hand on Frank's arm. The gesture possessive. "We're on our honeymoon."

The manager's eyes moved between them, question forming then abandoned. "Forty cash. Check-out's eleven."

Frank paid. Received a key attached to a plastic tag marked 4. The manager retreated to his office without further interaction.

Unit four smelled of industrial cleaner failing to disguise cigarette smoke embedded in curtains and carpet. A queen bed dominated the room. Beside it a particleboard nightstand supported a lamp with shade askew. A television bolted to the wall. Remote control chained to the bed frame.

Frank set his bag on the dresser. Checked the bathroom. Shower with vinyl curtain. Toilet that ran unless the handle was jiggled. Towels thin as promises.

"Honeymoon suite," Sarah said behind him. "Just like I imagined."

Frank turned. "Why one room?"

"People talk less about married couples." She sat on the bed. Tested its firmness with her palm. "Fewer questions."

"That why you picked me at the diner? Fewer questions?"

Sarah looked up at him. Her expression unreadable. "Mitchel encouraged it. Thought I'd learn more about your intentions. But that's not why I stayed." Frank waited. Let silence draw her out.

"Why do men always think they know what women are thinking? What women want? They have no idea."

She stretched back on the bed, arms extended above her head. "Women are as different as the colors in a crayon box. Some want muscle and a nice smile. Some want wealth and control. And still others want stability and protection. It's impossible to predict what a woman wants unless you're a woman."

Frank considered this. "What do you want?"

Sarah sat up. "Right now? A shower that doesn't give tetanus." She gathered her bag. "Then sleep… maybe a little fooling around."

She disappeared into the bathroom. Water pipes groaned in the walls. Frank moved to the window. Parted the curtains with two fingers. The parking lot remained empty except for the Imperial. Down the streetlights had come on at the bar. Moths already gathering.

Beyond the town the mountains waited. Somewhere in those peaks an abandoned NSA facility held answers neither Walker nor Culper had shared. Frank released the curtain. The room returned to shadow. Outside, May continued its isolated existence. A town that asked nothing, expected less, and kept its secrets as close as the mountains kept theirs.

Dawn broke over the Pahsimeroi Valley, light spilling across sage flats in slow golden waves. Frank and Sarah lay belly-down on the ridgeline. Juniper provided minimal cover, twisted trunks shaped by decades of wind coming down from the mountains. Frank wore his shoulder harness with the matching Redhawks. Sarah wore a Civil War era 1860 Colt revolver in a holster strapped her hips. The cap and ball pistol fired a .36 Caliber paper cartridge and had been handed down through her family for generations. The spotting scope's lens caught occasional glint of sunrise despite Frank's careful positioning.

Below them the facility sprawled across twenty-three acres of fenced compound. A concrete bunker complex partially buried in the hillside. Three satellite dishes aimed skyward, their massive white parabolas motionless against the landscape. The largest spanned forty feet in diameter, designed to capture the faintest signals from passing satellites. The dish's supporting struts showed orange streaks of rust. Two geodesic domes stood at the facility's north end, their white honeycomb surfaces stained by years of weather. Protective coverings for more sensitive equipment. Windows black and empty in the dawn light.

"Looks abandoned," Sarah whispered, passing binoculars back to Frank. "No guards. No vehicles. No activity at all."

Frank adjusted the spotting scope. The viewfinder revealed chainlink fence sections fallen in places. Tumbleweeds caught against the perimeter. The guard booth at the main gate sat empty, its window broken. No lights showed anywhere in the compound. No generators hummed. No radio traffic on the frequencies Walker had provided.

"Mitchel said Culper's people moved in six months ago." Sarah kept her voice low despite the distance.

"Where's the security? The trucks? The stolen weapons?"

Frank scanned methodically. The loading dock where supplies would arrive stood empty. Concrete stairs leading to the main entrance untraveled. Weeds grew between the cracks. The parking lot contained only windblown debris. A raven landed on one of the smaller satellite dishes. Preened itself with no concern for human disturbance.

"Something's wrong," Sarah said. "Mitchel's not usually wrong about stuff like this. He gets his intel from reliable sources."

Frank nodded once. He shifted the scope to the facility's communication tower. One hundred feet of steel lattice rising from the center of the compound. No blinking lights marked its presence for aircraft. No transmission equipment appeared attached to its upper sections. The tower stood abandoned as an industrial fossil.

"Could they have moved everything inside? Kept the outside looking abandoned?" Sarah shifted position, keeping her profile low against the ridgeline.

Frank studied the access road leading to the main gate. Dirt track showing no recent tire marks. No indication of heavy equipment transport. No sign that anything had moved through this valley for months, perhaps years. Only mountain wind and occasional wildlife.

"Let's get closer," Sarah suggested. "Check the fence line."

Frank considered. Possible trap. Possible misdirection. Possible intelligence failure. Only one way to find out. The sun climbed higher. Shadows shrinking as morning advanced across the valley floor. He packed the spotting scope. Nodded once.

They descended the ridge using natural features for cover. Sagebrush. Rock outcroppings. Dry creek beds carved by spring runoff. The approach took forty minutes. Deliberate movement sacrificing speed for stealth despite the apparent absence of observers.

The fence rose twelve feet, topped with rusted barbed wire that sagged between posts. A metal sign hung crooked from the links: PROPERTY OF UNITED STATES GOVERNMENT - AUTHORIZED PERSONNEL ONLY. The paint faded to ghost lettering. Bullet holes marked one corner where local teenagers had used it for target practice.

Frank examined the lock on the main gate. Heavy-duty padlock showing weather damage but no tampering. The chain threaded through fence links had worn grooves into the metal over decades of wind-driven movement. He studied the ground near the entryway. Boot prints would show in the dust. Tire tracks would mark the hardpack. Nothing. Only animal tracks and insect trails marred the valley soil.

Sarah circled west along the perimeter. Returned ten minutes later. "Fence is down in two places. Looks like wind damage, not cutting. Found an old coyote den under the northwest corner."

Frank made short order of the lock with his pick set. They entered the facility's perimeter. Frank moved to the nearest geodesic dome. The white panels had yellowed with age. Several sections missing entirely. He pulled two flashlights from his rucksack handing one to Sarah. Through the gaps he could see electronic equipment inside. Outdated consoles with analog displays. Reel-to-reel tape systems from the early digital era. Everything covered in dust. Everything untouched for what appeared to be years.

"This doesn't make sense," Sarah said. She pointed to the satellite dishes. "Those are still intact. Valuable copper wiring. Metals. Parts that scrappers would have stripped first."

Frank nodded. Government abandonment usually meant methodical removal of classified systems followed by contractor salvage of anything valuable. This place looked simply walked away from. Left to the elements with equipment still installed.

"Maybe the NSA thought they might use the facility again," said Sarah.

Frank grunted at the possible explanation.

They approached the main building. Concrete

brutalism given form. Windowless lower sections. Narrow apertures on upper floors allowing minimal light for human operators while maintaining structural integrity against potential nuclear shock waves. The entrance doors, thick steel with reinforced frames, hung partially open. One off its hinge entirely.

Sarah unholstered the Colt revolver she'd brought. Frank's hand moved to his waist where the KA-BAR waited. They entered the shadowed interior. Dust motes swirled in light shafts penetrating from damaged ceiling sections. The lobby contained a security desk abandoned mid-shift. Papers still stacked in wire baskets. Ancient computer monitors with screens gray and lifeless. A coffee mug positioned as if set down temporarily thirty years ago, contents long evaporated to stain.

"What did Walker think was happening here?" Sarah's whisper echoed slightly in the dead space.

They moved deeper. Hallways branched in efficient angles. Government design prioritizing function over comfort. The walls institutional gray. Floor tiles cracked and buckling from freeze-thaw cycles. No electricity. No emergency lighting. Only the sun's determined intrusion through damaged sections revealed the facility's interior.

The communication center occupied the building's heart. Banks of equipment arranged in concentric circles. Receivers, analyzers, decoders. Technology that had once represented cutting edge now obsolete as stone tools. Chair cushions dry-rotted. Ceiling panels collapsed onto workstations below. A clipboard hung from a nail beside the main door, sign-out sheet still attached. Last entry dated August 18, 1993.

"Mitchel had intel. Surveillance photos. Delivery schedules." Sarah turned slowly, taking in the abandoned operation center. "How could he be this wrong?"

Frank moved to a wall map still hanging. Pushpins

marked coverage areas where satellites had once passed over Soviet territories. Red markers indicating transmission stations across the mountain west. Everything historical. Nothing current. Nothing that explained Walker's certainty about Culper's operation.

They descended stairs to the sublevels. Concrete corridors leading to storage areas. Equipment rooms. Living quarters for personnel during cold war drills when isolation might stretch weeks. Everything emptied of valued materials but organizational debris remained. Furniture too bulky to justify removal costs. Papers deemed unimportant enough to leave behind. The detritus of government operation abandoned when budgets shifted priorities to the Middle East.

The lower level contained server rooms. Racks emptied of hardware. Cable runs hanging like technological moss from ceiling mounts. The power distribution center sat dark, circuit breakers thrown to their OFF positions. Dust lay undisturbed on every surface. No footprints. No indication anyone had visited in decades.

They found the weapons storage room behind a reinforced door hanging open on broken hinges. Empty weapons racks bolted to walls. Shell casings scattered across the floor from some long-ago inventory reduction. Gun oil stains marking concrete where armaments had once been maintained. Nothing remained that would fire. Nothing waited for recovery or discovery.

"There's nothing here," Sarah said. Her voice had dropped the whisper, resignation replacing caution. "Hasn't been for years."

Frank examined the facility's structural aspects. The construction solid despite cosmetic deterioration. The basic infrastructure intact beneath the abandonment. The concrete walls eighteen inches thick. The air circulation system designed for positive pressure to resist nuclear fallout. The water tanks still in place below ground though likely empty or contaminated now.

They emerged from the main building into afternoon light. The sun had crossed zenith during their exploration. Shadow patterns reversing across the compound. The satellite dishes stood as monuments to obsolete purpose. The domes as relics from a war grown cold then hot then forgotten by the citizens who funded their construction. They squinted against the harsh afternoon light as their eyes readjusted.

"Why would Mitchel send us here?" Sarah replaced her weapon. Scanned the compound one final time. "What did he think we'd find?"

As if following a thought, Frank moved toward the rear of the facility where the main building met earth. He crouched near the foundation wall, brushed away decades of dust and scrub. Sarah followed, watched him uncover what lay beneath the neglect. A concrete junction box. Six steel pipes arranged in precise formation, each holding filaments thinner than human hair. Fiber optic lines still intact after years of abandonment. The pipes extended beyond the perimeter fence then vanished beneath soil as if the earth had swallowed them. She knelt beside him. Her fingertips traced one of the steel housings.

"I don't get it. Where are they going?"

Frank said nothing. His face hardened into something remote and cold. Something that recognized danger without requiring explanation.

"Go to the motel," he said finally tossing her the keys to the Imperial.

"I'm not going anywhere without you."

"Need to move fast."

"I can keep up if that's what concerns you."

"No, you can't." He adjusted the rucksack on his shoulders, checked the matched Redhawks at his sides.

Without another word he turned northward following the direction of one of the pipes before it disappeared below the ground. Exiting the main gate he began to run. Not the measured pace of a man covering distance. Something else entirely. Something inhuman in its speed and purpose. His massive frame moved with impossible efficiency across the valley floor toward Montana.

Sarah took two steps to follow then stopped. Watched his form diminish against the landscape. He'd been right. She could never maintain that pace. Whatever drove him now belonged to a world she couldn't enter. She stood alone in the shadow of abandoned government architecture with dust devils spinning across empty concrete. The fiber optic lines continued their silent journey beneath miles of wilderness. Carrying signals or nothing at all.

Days and nights bled into one another as Frank followed the buried line. Running. Always running. His breath measured against miles rather than minutes. The pipe occasionally showed itself where wind or water had stripped away earth's concealment. Rusted steel housing catching sunlight like an industrial fossil partially exhumed.

He stopped only when absolute necessity demanded. Drank from streams that crossed his path. Consumed jerky from his rucksack without slowing. Slept in thirty minute increments when his body threatened collapse, then rose and continued before dew had settled on his clothes.

The terrain shifted beneath his boots. Sage flats giving way to rockier ground. Juniper and scrub pine dotting hillsides that had watched civilizations rise and vanish with geological indifference. The fiber optic line maintained its unswerving course. The shortest path leading to somewhere. Something. Proceeding with mathematical certainty while nature arranged itself haphazardly.

Frank followed the trench line on foot. The soil disturbed where machines had buried the fiber optic cable years before. A ruler-straight path cutting through wilderness toward something important enough to connect.

The cable reached a two-lane highway where the trench disappeared beneath asphalt. Frank stood at roadside, his massive frame unmistakable against barren landscape. He extended his thumb. Three vehicles passed. The fourth slowed.

A pickup truck with Montana plates pulled onto the shoulder. Engine knocking from years of hard use. The driver rolled down his window manually, glass disappearing into the door. "Where you headed?"

"North."

"I'm going up to Great Falls. That help?"

Frank nodded once. Climbed in. The man wore a John Deere cap worn colorless by sun and sweat. Asked no questions that would require answers. Just handed over a thermos. Coffee black as the coming night.

They drove in silence. The road following the same heading as the buried cable. Frank watched out the window where the ground showed subtle differences in color. The cable's path visible like a vein beneath skin to those who knew what to seek.

"Here," Frank said when the highway turned eastward away from the pipe's northward route.

The driver pulled over, studying Frank with eyes that had seen enough to know when not to press. "Sure you don't want to go further? Nothing out this way."

"Sure."

The truck disappeared eastward, leaving Frank standing at the intersection. The fiber line continuing straight toward whatever waited miles ahead across uneven ground. He walked once again. The land opening beneath a sky gone endless with Montana in the distance. Moving steadily toward the revelation of steel and concrete that would explain what Walker truly hunted beneath that Idaho mountain.

On the fourth day the land opened before him. A vast depression in the earth where government engineers had carved away Montana soil decades prior. At its center stood a concrete monolith no casual traveler would recognize for what it contained. Missile silo. ICBM. Cold War architecture designed to deliver apocalypse from belowground.

Frank dropped to a prone position on the ridge overlooking the complex. Observed through the spotting scope what was no abandoned facility but active military infrastructure. Air Force Security Forces. Men in digital camouflage with patches identifying them as Malmstrom AFB personnel. Their movements carried the discipline of active-duty military, not private contractors. Standard issue M4 carbines. Radio communication at regular intervals. Practiced patrol patterns around a perimeter the government acknowledged on no public map.

The fiber optic line descended straight into the facility's heart. Now its purpose revealed itself with cold clarity. The abandoned NSA station—a communications hub. Hardwired connections to missile silos across the western states. Montana. Wyoming. North Dakota. The hardwire network had been abandoned when it was replaced by highly encrypted KIV-7 satellite and microwave feeds.

Frank studied the security setup. Military-grade

motion sensors. Infrared cameras mounted at precise intervals. Guard rotations timed to standard Air Force protocol. He recognized the lieutenant overseeing the detail—career military with the bearing that came from a decade in uniform. Everything about the operation spoke of legitimate government activity rather than Walker's feared insurgency or Culper's shadowy counteroperation.

He remained motionless on the ridge like another feature of the landscape. The giant had found not conspiracy but continuity. The machinery of national defense operating exactly as designed, hidden from public view not through malice but through the practical requirements of security. The question remained whether Walker knew this truth or whether his fears of Culper had blinded him to it. Or maybe there was some other reason that Frank had not discovered yet.

Night had almost vanished when Frank withdrew from the ridge. Left no trace of his vigil overlooking government men guarding government weapons. He cut east before turning south. Away from established roads where military patrols might question solitary figures in restricted territory.

By dawn he reached the interstate. Stood on the shoulder with thumb extended as eighteen-wheelers hauled the commerce of a nation past. The third truck stopped. Air brakes hissing judgment against the driver's decision to welcome a giant with a ruined face into his cab.

"Where you headed?" The trucker had the look of a man who'd measured his life in white lines down black asphalt. "Idaho." The single word scraping from Frank's throat. "I can get you as far as Butte. Climb in."

The cab smelled of cigarettes and spilled coffee. The trucker talked without requiring response. Stories of ex-wives and dispatcher incompetence filling miles that unwound beneath massive tires. Frank stared through the windshield at mountains. His search for answers had only provided more questions.

Why target a communications hub that served nuclear silos? The ICBMs themselves remained secure. Launch codes stored in safes that required multiple authorized personnel to access. The warheads useless without the complex sequence of commands that converted dormant metal into apocalypse.

In Butte another truck. Different driver. Same need for company across vast stretches of American emptiness. This one hauled refrigerated produce from Washington orchards to Midwest supermarkets. Had theories about government surveillance that would have seemed paranoid before Frank had seen that buried fiber network with his own eyes.

He slept in the passenger seat. First real rest since leaving Sarah at the abandoned NSA facility. His body collapsed into unconsciousness that dreams couldn't penetrate. Woke when the truck stopped for fuel outside Pocatello. The Idaho border crossed while his eyes had been closed.

Frank stepped down from the cab. Nodded thanks to the driver. Watched the truck diminish down the highway toward places he wouldn't follow.

He ate at the truck stop's diner. Eggs and toast that meant nothing to his body except continuation. The waitress avoided looking at his scars. He paid cash and moved on.

His mind returned to the fiber optic lines. To Walker's interest in an abandoned communications facility. To Culper's concern about a group with weapons powerful enough to defend against government intrusion.

The most dangerous possibility formed in his thoughts like frost on glass. Control of communications without control of warheads. The missiles themselves beyond reach but the commands that directed them potentially vulnerable. A man with access to those fiber lines could perhaps intercept, perhaps even replace legitimate signals with his own. Could create confusion in a system where confusion meant death multiplied beyond mathematics.

Frank caught a final ride in a pickup driven by a rancher headed to May. The man asked no questions of his passenger. Had the weathered look of someone who'd long since stopped expecting explanations from the world or the people who inhabited it.

Twilight painted the Pahsimeroi Valley in colors no human hand could reproduce. The Pine Valley Motel appeared like a concrete afterthought against mountains that had witnessed ice ages come and go. Frank stepped from the truck. His body exhausted but his mind clear with terrible understanding of what might be at stake.

The stakes weren't just high. They were final. The kind where miscalculation meant cities reduced to radioactive ash. The kind where being right brought no satisfaction because the alternative left no one alive to recognize the accuracy.

The road had carried him through places without names. Lands where only wind spoke. Days of other men's vehicles. The gratitude of strangers burning away beneath his silence. Montana falling behind like something shed.

Frank stood in the motel parking lot where the Imperial should have been. Gravel marked by absent tires. His massive frame casting shadow across emptiness that hadn't been there before. The key turned in the lock. The door opened to vacant space. No duffle on the bed. No boots beside nightstand. No scent of her on sheets gone cold.

The clock showed 2:17. Same numbers that had faced him when he'd left. As if time had stopped while mountains passed beneath his feet. He checked the bathroom. Towels hung. No hair in the drain. No cosmetics arranged by height on the sink's edge. Nothing to say she'd been there at all except memory and that could lie.

The motel owner appeared in the doorway. Face creased like something folded too many times. "You're back."

Frank grunted.

"Woman left this morning. Didn't check out."

"Car?"

"Gone with her."

"Where?"

The owner shrugged. Indifference his natural state. "Didn't ask. Don't care. Room's paid through tomorrow."

Frank stood at the window. The glass showing only his reflection. Something hardening behind his eyes.

"Need a ride," he managed.

"Got a bus comes through at four."

"Now."

The owner studied him. Calculated risk against the weight of bills Frank withdrew from his pocket. A stack that suggested urgency rather than request.

"My truck. Fifty."

Frank peeled off bills. Placed them on the dresser.

"Where to?"

"East road."

The truck smelled of tobacco and something older. Oil and sweat worked into vinyl over decades. The heater rattled like bones in a can. The owner drove with one hand. "That woman your wife?"

Frank stared through windshield glass, remained

silent.

"Girlfriend then. Bad business trusting women these days."

Frank's silence continued to fill the cab. The owner stopped talking.

The land opened toward mountains. The owner slowed at a curve where the road climbed. "How far?"

"Here," Frank said.

The truck halted. Idled against stillness. Frank opened the door. The ground took his weight without complaint.

"You want a ride back?"

"No."

The truck disappeared around the bend. Gravel dust lingering like gunsmoke. Frank stood on road's edge where darkness had begun gathering in creases between hills. The way ahead unmarked and empty. The silence perfect except for wind singing through sage.

He walked. Each stride eating distance as he'd done heading to Montana.

The ridge rose against sky made silver by approaching night. Frank climbed. His body mechanical in its purpose. Reaching the crest he saw what waited beyond. The NSA facility. Still. Empty. No Imperial. Something inside his head told him not to enter. Something was wrong.

He moved to the ridgeline overlooking the facility. He would wait. Would watch. The scope brought everything closer. Everything the same as he had left it but no Sarah.

Night settled across the valley. Frank remained motionless as stars wheeled overhead. The watcher becoming stone. The hunter becoming shadow. Hoping dawn would bring answers.

Dawn broke over the ridgeline. Light spilled across the valley floor in thin yellow streams that pushed against darkness like fingers through closed blinds. Frank watched the NSA facility through his scope one final time. Nothing moved. No vehicles approached. No personnel patrolled the fence line. The buildings remained silent as graves beneath the growing light.

He slid the scope into his rucksack and began his descent. Each footfall calculated against loose shale that would announce his approach. His weight pressed into earth that held a thousand years of silence. The Derringer nestled in his boot. The KA-BAR rode his hip like an old friend. The matched Redhawks hung in their shoulder harness balanced against his massive frame.

Frank paused at the bottom of the slope where juniper provided final cover. The facility's fence stood as he'd left it. Chain link rusting in the morning dew. Gates hanging open on aged hinges. He watched for five minutes. Counted heartbeats against seconds. Studied shadows for inconsistencies. For movement that didn't match wind patterns. For anything that suggested human presence where abandonment should rule.

Frank moved across open ground with the cautious efficiency of a predator entering another's territory. His eyes swept the perimeter. The satellite dishes stood motionless against the brightening sky. Their massive white parabolas collecting nothing but dust and bird droppings.

At the main gate he stopped. Crouched. The hardpack dirt showed tracks that hadn't been there before. Boot prints pressed into soil still damp from the night's offering. Not his own massive footprints. These belonged to someone smaller but still substantial. Larger than Sarah's delicate impressions would leave. A man's boots. Military tread. Recent.

One of his Redhawks slid from its holster. Five out of six chambers loaded. Hammer resting on an empty cylinder as his training had demanded across decades of violence. His finger rested alongside the trigger guard rather than on the trigger itself.

Frank followed the tracks. They led through the main gate toward the primary building. Showed no hesitation in their direction. No exploratory patterns suggesting unfamiliarity. Whoever had entered knew where they were going.

He circled the facility's perimeter before approaching the main structure. The boot prints were in a straight line toward the building's entrance. Purposeful. No companion tracks suggesting multiple visitors.

The facility stood as abandoned as before. Wind sang through broken windows. Dust devils spun across concrete expanses where government employees had once parked vehicles with security clearance designations on windshields. Nothing else disturbed the desolation of official abandonment.

Frank approached the main building. The entrance doors remained as he'd left them. One partially ajar. One hanging from a single hinge like a broken jaw. The concrete façade showed decades of weather damage. Cracks where water had frozen and thawed a hundred times. Stains from minerals leaching through imperfections in the structure.

He entered with the Redhawk by his side. Darkness greeted him. Shafts of morning light penetrated through gaps in the structure where time had defeated engineering. Dust particles hung suspended in beams like microscopic galaxies. He stood motionless allowing his eyes to adjust. Allowing his other senses to catalog the environment.

The air smelled of limestone and rust. Of concrete slowly surrendering to entropy. Of metal oxidizing in the absence of human touch. Of electrical components growing cold after decades of generated heat.

But beneath these expected scents lay something else. Something human. Sweat. Gun oil. The faint trace of tobacco that clung to clothing long after smoking ceased. Someone had been here. Recently.

Frank moved deeper into the facility. His boots made no sound against the tile floor. His massive frame somehow defying expectation by moving with absolute silence.

The security desk still encased in grime. Computer monitors filmed with dust. Wire baskets containing papers held down with weights whose importance had expired with the Soviet Union. Coffee mugs positioned as if their owners expected to return after brief absence rather than decades.

The boot prints continued down the main corridor. Past offices where forgotten technology perched on desks like mechanical fossils. Past break rooms where vending machines stood hollow as obsidian monoliths. Past bulletin boards where papers hung by single pins, their messages faded beyond legibility.

Frank checked each room systematically. Clearing corners with practiced economy. Confirming empty spaces with glances that missed nothing. The facility remained as abandoned as government records claimed.

No lights operated. No generators hummed. No radio signals transmitted.

Only the boot prints suggested otherwise.

He descended concrete stairs to the facility's bowels. Each step measured against potential ambush. Each landing cleared before proceeding deeper. The basement levels spread in brutalist architecture rendered invisible by darkness that his flashlight cut like a surgical tool.

The communication center waited at the complex's heart. Banks of equipment arranged in concentric circles.

Stations where intelligence personnel had once monitored signals from space. Had transcribed transmissions from enemy territories. Had tracked satellites that observed without permission.

The boot prints led directly here. Stopped at the central control station. Resumed their path toward a door Frank hadn't fully explored in previous reconnaissance. Steel reinforced. Hinges designed to withstand explosive force. The words SECURE ACCESS stenciled across its surface in government typography that brooked no argument.

The door stood open a hand's width.

Frank approached with predator's patience. One step. Pause. Listen. Another step. The Redhawk steady in his grip. His body coiled against the violent possibilities that might wait beyond that threshold of steel and authorization.

He adjusted his grip on the Redhawk. Steadied his mind driving out any hint of fear or anxiety. Neither served him in moments like these - facing the unknown. Moved through the doorway to confront whatever secrets government had buried beneath Idaho mountains and whatever intruder had arrived to claim them.

The server room stood like a technological mausoleum. Banks of equipment disconnected from power sources years before when the last government technician had thrown circuit breakers and walked away. Metal racks filled with defunct hardware. Cable runs extending from floor to ceiling then disappearing into wall conduits leading nowhere. The fiber optic line remained the room's only active component, its glass filaments carrying signals to places Frank had tracked across mountain wilderness.

His boots made no sound on concrete flooring. He checked each row methodically. Each corner. Each shadow where threats might wait. Morning light penetrated through a single high window, casting weak illumination that barely pushed against the room's darkness. Dust particles hung suspended in the beam like cosmic debris.

Frank moved between the silent machines. Checked behind each server rack. Each cabinet. Found nothing but quiet permanence. The military-grade equipment sat untouched since decommissioning. No signs of tampering. No evidence of reactivation. The Cold War relics stood like petrified skeletons of extinct digital species.

The fiber optic junction box remained the only modern element. The connection point where buried communication lines met original infrastructure. The dust was disturbed. Someone had accessed this nexus. Had examined what government believed secure through obsolescence.

Frank's back prickled. The sensation familiar from a hundred combat situations. From moments when instinct outran conscious thought. From times when being wrong meant being dead.

Someone behind him.

"Easy." The voice came low and controlled. Professional. "You don't want to do anything rash."

Frank didn't turn. The voice belonged to a stranger. A man whose inflection carried military bearing.

"Put your pistol back in its holster slowly. Keep your finger away from the trigger."

Frank calculated angles. Distances. Possibilities that all ended with someone bleeding onto government concrete. His finger slid from the Redhawk's trigger guard. The revolver found its holster. The man wouldn't fire unless provoked. Not yet. Information had value that bullets discarded.

"You can turn around slowly. No sudden moves." Frank complied. Mike Pierce stood ten feet away. Brown hair cut short at the sides. Face weathered by outdoor operations. Standard military stance. Glock 9mm held in proper grip. Both hands. Elbows slightly bent. Weight balanced on both feet. The posture of someone who'd conducted firearms training beyond civilian requirements.

"I've been looking for you for three days. Where have you been?"

Frank said nothing. His damaged vocal cords a convenient excuse for silence.

The man's eyes narrowed. The gun remained steady.

"Where's the woman? Where's Sarah?" "Behind you," said a voice from the darkness.

The man's body tensed. His eyes tightened. Muscles coiled for action born of professional reflex. He whipped around with the fluid economy of someone who'd survived situations where hesitation equaled death. Frank drew both his revolvers.

Thunder filled the room. The ancient Colt revolver in Sarah's hand discharged its nineteenth-century certainty. Smoke billowed from the barrel. The bullet found the man where neck met shoulder. Tore through flesh and artery and bone with the indifference of lead traveling at lethal velocity.

The man's body crumpled to the floor. His pistol clattered against concrete. Blood spread beneath him in slow expansion. His eyes registered surprise, then confusion, then nothing at all as consciousness surrendered.

Sarah stood where the man had been looking just moments before. The 1860 Colt trembled slightly in her grip. Smoke curling from the barrel in lazy tendrils. Her face drained of color. Eyes wide with realization of what she'd done. Her breathing came rapid and shallow.

"Oh God," she whispered. The Colt lowered as if suddenly too heavy for her grasp. "I killed him."

Her legs buckled. She caught herself against a server rack. The ancient metal groaned beneath her weight. The Colt clattered to the floor beside her. Her hands shook with adrenaline aftermath. With the reality of taking human life.

Frank moved to the fallen man. Checked the neck for pulse. Found none. Death had claimed the intruder. Frank bent to retrieve the man's weapon. Tucked it into his waistband at the small of his back.

"He was going to kill you," Sarah managed, her voice barely audible over her own ragged breathing.

Frank looked at her. Studied her reaction. The trembling. The shock. The pallor that accompanies first blood spilled by those unaccustomed to violence's reality.

"Why?" The question scraped from his damaged throat.

Sarah hugged herself as if suddenly cold in the facility's subterranean stillness. "I don't know. But Mike Pierce is Mitchel's assassin. Probably watching us the entire time." She drew a shaky breath. "Maybe he figured you found something you weren't supposed to when you disappeared."

Frank's gaze returned to the dead man. Pierce. The name meant nothing to him. Just another player in a game whose rules remained obscured. Another body added to countless others that had fallen in Frank's proximity.

"Maybe," he managed, the word carrying weight beyond its simplicity.

Blood continued spreading across the concrete floor. Morning light caught the edges of Pierce's still form, transforming death into something almost artistic against the facility's industrial backdrop. Sarah remained against the server rack, her body still processing shock's chemical cocktail. Frank knelt beside the corpse, searching pockets for identification. For answers that bullets had made permanently inaccessible.

They buried Pierce's body in the dry soil beyond the facility's eastern fence. Frank dug, the shovel rising and falling in steady rhythm. The earth surrendered to his strength. Rock and clay and sand. Sarah stood nearby, arms wrapped around herself, gaze shifting between the lengthening grave and the surrounding landscape.

The morning heat pressed against them like a physical presence. No birds sang. No insects hummed. Only the shovel's bite into earth broke the silence. A natural order disturbed by human necessity.

Frank paused to wipe sweat from his brow. The hole now deep enough to conceal evidence of their encounter. His muscles worked beneath sweat-darkened fabric with inhuman endurance. When the grave satisfied his assessment, he climbed out and approached Pierce's body.

Sarah averted her eyes as Frank dragged the corpse toward the opening. Death had stiffened Pierce's limbs into unnatural angles. His face had settled into an expression neither peaceful nor particularly troubled. Just absent. The final mask everyone eventually wears.

"Should we say something?" Sarah asked, her voice small against the valley's emptiness.

Frank grunted. Lowered the body into earth's embrace. The dead man's blood had dried to rust-colored patterns on his clothing. Final artwork never meant for exhibition.

They filled the grave together. Sarah's hands blistered on the shovel's wooden handle. Frank worked with the steady determination of someone who'd performed this duty before. Too many times to count. Too many to remember individually. The shovel rose and fell. Soil covered Pierce's face. His chest. His military boots. Until nothing remained visible of the man who'd threatened them.

When the ground lay flat again, Frank scattered rocks and plant debris across the disturbed soil. Made the grave indistinguishable from surrounding terrain. Nature would complete the concealment within days. Would reclaim the site as if nothing had happened there at all.

Sarah placed a small stone at the grave's head. Not a marker. Just acknowledgment. Her hands still trembled slightly. Her face remained pale beneath the morning sun.

"What did you find after you left?" she asked, her eyes still on the freshly covered ground.

Frank considered. The buried communication lines. The missile silo in Montana. Active military personnel guarding infrastructure that connected to the NSA facility through glass threads running beneath wilderness. The scale of what Walker might be planning if he controlled those connections. The apocalyptic potential.

"Nothing," he said finally. "Lost the pipe's route."

"Too bad." Sarah brushed dirt from her palms. "It could have answered a lot of questions."

Frank studied her face. Looked for recognition of her lie beneath the shock of recent violence. Found nothing but exhaustion and residual trauma. Whatever game they played extended beyond this valley. Beyond the dead man beneath their feet. Beyond the facility with its technological fossils and secrets.

He collected the shovel. Wiped the blade clean on sparse vegetation. An old habit that left no evidence where evidence might later speak. Sarah watched him with eyes that had seen something fundamental change within herself. The transition that violence forces upon those who employ it. The invisible boundary crossed when taking life.

They walked back toward the facility without speaking. The grave silent behind them. The valley indifferent to human concerns about mortality and consequence. About truth and deception. About whatever waited at the end of fiber optic lines buried beneath miles of American wilderness.

Deception

The Imperial growled through Walker's residence main gate, tires crunching gravel beneath its considerable weight. Frank guided the ancient car toward the house on the ridge. Sarah sat silent beside him, eyes fixed on the approaching structure. The sawmill complex sprawled below, its industrial rhythm uninterrupted by their absence.

Walker appeared on the porch before they'd fully stopped. His stance reflected something between welcome and military readiness. Expectations held tight against his chest like concealed weapons. He watched Frank shut off the engine, the V8 ticking as metal cooled.

"You're back sooner than I expected," Walker said as they approached the steps. His gaze moved between them, cataloging details professional habits wouldn't let him ignore.

Sarah answered with a smile that didn't reach her eyes. "Not much to see."

The house accepted them with creaking floorboards. Walker led them to his study where maps still covered the heavy oak desk. Their edges curled from multiple handlings. Pins marked locations their recent travels had rendered either significant or meaningless depending on perspective.

"Bourbon?" Walker gestured toward the crystal decanter.

Sarah nodded. Frank remained standing, his massive frame refusing the comfort of offered chairs.

Walker poured three fingers into matching glasses. Passed them around like communion. "Tell me everything."

Sarah sipped her drink before beginning. Set the glass on a coaster with deliberate care. "The facility's abandoned. Completely. Has been for decades by the look of it."

"That's impossible," Walker said. "My intelligence—"

"Your intelligence was wrong, Mitchel," Sarah interrupted. "The place is a tomb. Everything stripped or left to rot. No personnel. No activity. No sign anyone's been there in years except local teenagers breaking windows."

Walker's face tightened. He turned to Frank. "You confirm this assessment?"

Frank nodded once. A single downward motion carrying weight of absolute certainty.

"What about the equipment deliveries?" Walker pressed. "The unmarked trucks my sources observed?"

"If that happened, they weren't bringing anything to that facility," Sarah said. "The satellite dishes are rusting in place. The communication center's dead. The power's been off so long the backup generators wouldn't start if Christ himself threw the switch."

Frank grunted agreement. His glass remained untouched.

Walker moved to the window. Stared out at his domain below where the mill continued its lumber production. His reflection in the glass showed confusion fighting with his natural certainty. "I don't understand. The intelligence was solid. Multiple confirmations of Culper's operation."

"Culper's either working somewhere else or your sources have been compromised," Sarah said. She stood and approached the maps on Walker's desk. Traced the outline of the facility with her finger. "We went through every room. Every sublevel. Nothing but dust and forgotten technology."

"What about the fiber optic lines?" Walker turned from the window. "Did you find the junction box where they enter the facility?"

Sarah's expression remained neutral. "Yes. Still intact but inactive. No sign they're being used for anything."

Frank shifted his weight. Floorboards complained beneath him.

"You went there directly from the highway, covered the entire complex, and returned without incident?" Walker's tone carried subtle accusation beneath factual inquiry.

"We took our time," Sarah said. "Did proper reconnaissance. Observed the facility for several hours before entering." The lie falling from her lips with practiced ease. "Frank's very thorough."

Walker nodded slowly. Acceptance battling disappointment. "I see."

He crossed to the desk. Collected satellite images showing the NSA facility from above. Filed them in a drawer with finality. As he moved papers across the desk Frank's eyes caught on an invoice half-buried beneath maps. Moore Warehousing LLC. Junction City. Monthly rental for Building 17. The amount substantial for rural Oregon. Walker noticed Frank's gaze and slid the invoice beneath a folder. His movement casual but deliberate. "Well, it seems I've wasted your time. And exposed you to unnecessary risk."

"We learned the truth," Sarah offered. "That's never wasted effort."

Walker's smile returned though diminished. "Always the optimist." He refilled his own glass. Left the others untouched. "By the way, you haven't seen Mike Pierce, have you? He was supposed to check some equipment at our eastern property line but hasn't reported back."

"Pierce?" Sarah's voice remained perfectly controlled. "No. Haven't seen him since before we left."

"Strange," Walker said. "He's usually so reliable. Military punctuality hammered into him through three combat tours." He studied Sarah's face. "Not answering his phone either."

"Maybe he found better employment," Sarah suggested. "Or a woman worth disappearing for."

Walker laughed without humor. "Not Pierce. Too dedicated for either distraction." He glanced at Frank who remained impassive as stone. "I'm sure he'll turn up. Men like him always do."

Frank finally raised his glass. Drank the bourbon in a single swallow. The movement drawing Walker's attention away from Sarah whose fingers had tightened around her own drink.

"Well," Walker said, setting down his empty glass, "I appreciate your thoroughness. Even if the results weren't what we expected."

"What happens now?" Sarah asked.

Walker moved to a filing cabinet. Withdrew an envelope thick with what could only be cash. "Now you get paid for your time and professional assessment." He extended the envelope toward Frank. "As agreed."

Frank took it without counting the contents. Trusted Walker's business practices if nothing else.

"And what about Culper and his crew?" Sarah pressed. "If they're not at the facility, where are they?"

"That's my problem now," Walker said. His tone suggested the conversation had reached its conclusion. "You two have done enough. Take some time off. Sarah, the mill will manage without you for another few days."

They left Walker standing among his maps and certainties. The study door closed behind them with quiet finality. The hallway stretched toward the front entrance. Toward the Imperial waiting in the driveway. Toward whatever lay beyond the deception they'd constructed together.

"He knows something's not right," Sarah whispered as they reached the porch.

Frank's expression revealed nothing.

The Imperial's door groaned open. The envelope of cash disappeared into his pocket. Payment for confirmation of absence where Walker had expected presence.

They drove away. The mill diminished in the rearview mirror.

The diner smelled of burgers and french fries. Midmorning light cut through windows filmed with grease. Three locals hunched at the counter. Weathered faces. Calloused hands. Men who'd watched timber jobs vanish like mist off the mountain.

Sarah slid into the booth. Frank lowering his mass onto vinyl seats. The waitress came. Coffee pot in one hand. Order pad in the other. Named Doris according to the tag pinned to her uniform.

"Coffee?" she asked.

Frank nodded.

"For me too," Sarah said.

Doris poured black coffee into thick mugs. Set the coffee pot down on the table and pulled a pencil from her ear. "What can I get, ya?"

"Two bacon cheeseburgers. Double fries. Double coleslaw. Coke, no ice," said Frank.

"How is it you're not dead from clogged arteries?" said Sarah, then turned to Doris. "One burger. No bacon. No cheese. Coleslaw. No fries. Coffee's fine." "Got it," said Doris and left.

Frank stared through the window at the Imperial parked outside. The ancient car coated with road dust.

"Mitchel seem pretty upset about the NSA facility when we told him it was empty," Sarah said.

Frank turned his eyes to her. Studied her face the way he'd study terrain before crossing.

She sipped her coffee. "What?"

Frank shook his head. Returned to watching the street. A logging truck passed. License plate caked with mud.

"Frank, I'm a woman. You need to talk with me. Or at least grunt more." Frank grunted.

"Wonderful. At least you're making an effort. What do you think Mitchel is going to do?" Frank shook his head.

"This Culper guy is out there somewhere making his next move. He sounds like a serious threat. At least Mitchel thinks so."

Frank grunted, giving nothing away.

"Drives me crazy not knowing," said Sarah folding her napkin into small squares like a nervous habit. "I was thinking we could go up to Astoria, maybe spend the night in one of those spas. Relax and unwind a bit. The town's beautiful. By the ocean. Maybe get some fried clams for supper. It's not that far from here."

Doris returned with their food. Burgers on plates chipped at the edges. Steam rising from meat. Frank's portion dwarfing Sarah's like everything else about him.

She pushed a bottle of ketchup toward him. He poured half the bottle by the fries creating a large pool of red.

"So, what do you think of my Astoria idea?" Sarah said. "Get away from the mill. From Mitchel. Just for one night. I think we need it. I know I do." "No," said Frank.

Her burger paused halfway to her mouth. "No?"

"Need to check something… alone."

Sarah set her burger down. "Alone?"

Frank chewed. Swallowed. His eyes moved to the men at the counter. Back to Sarah. "Yes… alone."

"Something you don't want me to see?"

"Yes. I need to think."

"Well, at least you're honest about it."

She stewed as she watched him eat. Doris refilled their coffee cups. She could feel the tension and moved away quickly. Sarah traced the rim of her mug with one finger. "Funny thing about trust. Works both ways. Gotta give some to get some."

Frank grunted as he picked up a handful of fries. Dipped them in ketchup. Woofed them down.

"I'll drop you at the mill," said Frank his mouth filled with food.

"Big of you," she said. "I suppose I should be grateful."

Frank shook his head.

"Honestly, Frank. I don't get it," she said moving closer and lowering her voice. "I sleep with you. I keep your secrets. Hell, I've even killed for you. And you still don't trust me?"

"Somethings are private," said Frank meeting her eyes. Unapologetic.

"This is bullshit."

Frank took another bite of his burger. Chewed methodically. The silence between them hardened like concrete setting. Frank stared at her. His eyes revealed nothing. Just flat assessment like terrain being mapped for strategic value.

She pushed her half-eaten food away. "You're impossible, Frank Kane."

Frank reached for his second burger. Demolished it in four mechanical bites. Washed it down with the Coke. Not a word spoken.

Sarah's fingers tightened around her mug. Knuckles whitening. "When you decide I'm worth trusting, you know where to find me."

Sarah got up and stormed out. The bell above the door chimed.

Frank finished the last of his fries and coleslaw. Dipped his paper napkin in his water glass. Wiped his mouth and hands. Set cash on the table. More than enough to cover both meals plus tip. His weight shifted the booth as he rose. The vinyl exhaled beneath him like something deflating.

The bell jingled as he left. The Imperial waited outside like an extension of his will. Engine growled to life. Tires crunching gravel as the ancient car pulled away.

Junction City revealed itself through the Imperial's windshield. Buildings weathered by decades of indifference. The kind of place bypassed when interstate highways redrew America's circulatory system. Main Street businesses closed more days than open. FOR

LEASE signs bleached by sun until barely legible. A place where hope went to expire.

Frank guided the Imperial through streets laid out on perfect grid. The ancient car moved with surprising grace despite its bulk. Its engine whispering power in low gear as he navigated past abandoned storefronts. Fourth street turned to Moore Avenue. Industrial zone where commerce had once mattered enough to construct warehouses. Now they stood mostly empty. Monuments to prosperity's migration.

Building 17 occupied the corner lot. Corrugated metal sides gone to rust along lower edges. Loading bay large enough for semi-trucks. Chain link fence topped with razor wire that had lost its gleam to rain and neglect. Security that announced value inside despite exterior decay.

Frank parked the Imperial two blocks away. Left it facing outward for quick departure if necessary. The V8 cooled in evening air.

He walked the building's perimeter studying approach options. No human guards visible. No vehicles suggesting security presence. Just cameras mounted at corners. Red lights indicating active recording. Motion sensors disguised as utility boxes. Standard equipment for protecting valuable assets without drawing attention.

The fence stood twelve feet. Only one gate accessible from street side. Padlocked with a thick chain. Frank circled to rear where a neighboring lot had been abandoned. Found a metal drainage pipe that had eroded soil beneath fence. Created gap just wide enough for a man.

He slid beneath. Moved in crouch along a wall staying beneath camera angles. The security system's control box mounted beside rear entrance. Standard installation. Frank produced tools from coat pocket. Popped cover exposing circuit board and wiring configuration he'd seen in facilities with higher priorities than abandoned warehouses.

Red display counted seconds toward alarm trigger. Frank stripped two wires. Crossed them. Bypassed authorization protocol. Light shifted from red to yellow. System disabled but still capable of recording. He moved to door. Lock yielded to picks with minimum resistance.

The corrugated metal door rolled opened. He moved through the doorway and closed the door.

Inside smelled of machine oil and cold concrete. Darkness held shape without detail. Frank produced small penlight. The beam cutting narrow path through interior gloom. Three shipping containers arranged in a perfect row. Each painted standard commercial green. Each bearing padlocks beyond normal shipping requirements.

No markings identifying contents. No shipping manifests attached. Just containers that shouldn't be stored in a building Walker paid substantial monthly rent to maintain. The kind of anonymous arrangement favored by those with resources and reasons for discretion.

Frank approached first container. The padlock heavy gauge steel. Not impossible. Not simple either. He worked pins with practiced patience. Metal surrendered to skill with minimum protest. The hasp swung free. Frank removed the lock. Set it aside for later replacement.

The container doors opened with hinges needing oil. Interior darker than warehouse itself. Frank swept penlight beam across contents. Crates stacked. Markings identifying contents in alphanumeric code recognizable to those who spoke Defense Department inventory taxonomy.

He opened nearest crate. M27 Infantry Automatic Rifles. Each weapon in perfect condition. Frank used his phone to take photos of the weapons and close ups of the serial numbers. Next crate contained Barrett M107A1 sniper rifles. .50 caliber antipersonnel weapons capable of engaging targets beyond a mile distance. Capable of penetrating light armor.

Frank moved to next container. Picked the lock with same methodical approach. Same result. Door swinging open to reveal crew-served weapons. M240 machine guns with tripods. M249 light machine guns. Ammunition cans stacked to ceiling. Enough firepower to engage company-sized element with reasonable expectation of success.

The third container required more time. Lock newer. Pins more resistant. Still surrendered eventually. Inside waited anti-armor capability. AT4 anti-tank rocket launcher. Stinger surface-to-air missiles. The kind of weapons that transformed militia from nuisance to genuine military threat. That elevated confrontation from law enforcement problem to national security crisis.

Frank photographed everything. Each crate. Each weapon type. Each serial number visible. Documentation against denial should evidence become necessary. Against possibility that the containers might move before actions could be taken.

The warehouse held stolen arsenal sufficient to equip brigade combat team. To hold territory against conventional response force. To provide asymmetric advantage against law enforcement agencies unprepared for military-grade resistance. The kind of weapons Walker had described as necessary for defending against Culper. That instead waited deployment for purposes Frank now understood with perfect clarity.

He closed container doors. Replaced locks in reverse

order of removal. He closed the rolling outer door and replaced the lock. Left no evidence of entry beyond knowledge now carried in memory and digital storage. The warehouse returned to apparent abandonment.

The security system reactivated with reversed sequence of disabling. Lights shifted from yellow to red. Monitoring resumed without record of interruption. Frank erased evidence of his presence with practiced efficiency. Tools disappeared into pockets. Footprints eliminated where soil might hold impression.

He slid beneath fence at the same point of entry. Rose on street side within camera blind spot. Walked unhurried toward the Imperial. Gave appearance of legitimate purpose that discouraged question or memory.

From second-floor window of abandoned office building across street, binoculars tracked Frank's movement. Steady hands held lenses with practiced stability. Professional assessment made without emotion. Without hesitation. The kind of surveillance that betrayed military background. That spoke of patience developed through operations where discovery meant failure at minimum. Death at worst.

Frank reached the Imperial. Door hinges protested age and rust as he slid behind wheel. The engine caught first try. Headlights illuminated the empty street as ancient car pulled away from curb.

The slam of a car door outside broke the evening quiet. Walker glanced at the grandfather clock in the corner of his study—just past nine. He'd been on the phone for the better part of an hour, his voice low and measured despite the urgency of the conversation. At the sound of heavy footsteps on the porch, he quickly wrapped up.

"He's back. I'll call you tomorrow." Walker hung up just as the front door swung open.

Frank stood in the doorway, grimy and weary. The wind had carved lines into his face that hadn't been there this morning. His presence seemed to fill the room with something unsettled.

Walker leaned back in his leather chair, affecting casualness. "Bit late coming back. Where've you been?"

Frank's eyes swept the room, lingering briefly on the phone, before he grunted, "Checking on lighthouse."

"Find anything interesting?" Walker asked, rising to his feet and moving toward the bar cart in the corner. He lifted a crystal decanter. "Scotch? Might take the edge off."

Frank shook his head, already turning toward the stairs.

Walker watched him go, noting the slight drag in his step, the way his hand gripped the banister a little too tightly. "Sarah was looking for you earlier," he called after him, but Frank didn't respond, just continued his heavy ascent.

The guest bedroom was exactly as Frank had left it that morning—bed made, his few possessions arranged on the dresser in neat rows. He didn't bother turning on the light. Moonlight spilled through the windows, painting silver rectangles across the hardwood floor. Frank removed his boots and jacket before lying down fully clothed on top of the covers, one arm flung across his eyes.

He was halfway to sleep when the door hinges creaked. The soft padding of bare feet crossed the room, and then the mattress dipped slightly. Sarah's familiar scent—lavender and something earthy—reached him before her voice did.

"I thought you'd left for good this time," she whispered, curling up beside him, careful not to touch him directly. Her presence was a warmth beside him, tentative but determined.

Frank didn't open his eyes. "No."

A long silence stretched between them, filled only with the distant sound of wind in the trees and the house settling.

"I'm sorry," Sarah finally said, her voice small. "About this morning. About... everything. I don't know what's gotten into me lately. I'm usually not this emotional."

Frank's breathing remained steady, but his arm slid from his face. In the moonlight, their eyes met—a long look that carried years of history, both shared and separate.

"It's been a long time since I've been with someone I cared about. It's kinda scary. The feeling that I have something to lose."

"Not lost. Still here," said Frank.

Frank didn't pull away. The weight of the day pressed him deeper into the mattress, and exhaustion finally began to win over vigilance. Sarah's breathing gradually synchronized with his, deepening as they both drifted toward sleep, questions unanswered but temporarily set aside. Outside, clouds moved across the moon, darkening the room.

The digital alarm clock by the bed read 3:14 AM when Frank opened his eyes. He'd never actually fallen asleep—just a state of half-consciousness, alert to every creak of the old house. Beside him, Sarah's breathing was deep and even. He studied her face in the dim light, the curve of her cheek, the slight frown that remained even in sleep.

Carefully, he extracted himself from the bed. Sarah stirred but didn't wake. Frank slipped on his boots silently. He moved to the door. The house was silent except for the distant ticking of Walker's grandfather clock downstairs. Frank paused at the top of the staircase, listening for any sign of movement from Walker's room at the end of the hall. Nothing.

He descended the stairs with practiced care, avoiding the third step that always announced visitors. At the bottom, he glanced toward Walker's study—door closed, no light visible beneath it. He let himself out of the house.

The Imperial was parked next to the pharmacy. Frank was already on the payphone waiting for Culper to come on the line.

"Where the hell have you been, Frank? We thought you were dead."

"Recon," said Frank.

"Alright, fine. But you need to report in more often. You are not the only one working reconnaissance. What did you find?"

"Stolen weapons."

"You found them?"

"Warehouse in Junction City."

"I assume Walker's connected?"

"Yes."

"Do you have evidence?"

"Not enough. There's more."

"What else?"

"NSA facility. Pahsimeroi Valley."

"I know it. It's shutdown. What about it?"

"Walker wants it. Sent me to recon."

"Why would Walker want it? All the equipment is obsolete."

"Fiber optic cables."

"Yeah. So? To what end?"

"Hardwired to ICBM silos."

"Yeah, but without the launch codes they're useless.

Besides, the cables were disconnected from the network over a decade ago."

"Don't know."

"Can you find out what Walker is up to?"

"Maybe."

"Any idea when he might make his move?"

"No. But soon."

"Keep digging, Frank. Get me something concrete—proof of what he's after and why."

"Understood."

Frank hung up without waiting for a response. The night air felt suddenly colder as he walked back to the Imperial, mind racing through possibilities, none of them good.

The drive back to Walker's was quick and dark. He approached Walker's house. Killed the engine. Coasted to a stop. Only the crunch of gravel beneath the tires disturbing the surrounding forest. He parked exactly where he'd been before and reentered the house as silently as he'd left. Back in the guest room, he slipped into bed beside Sarah, who stirred at his return.

"Where'd you go?" she murmured, half-asleep.

"Just getting some air," he lied smoothly, settling beside her.

She moved closer, fitting herself against him. "I'm glad you came back," she whispered, her voice trailing off as she drifted back to sleep.

Frank lay awake, one arm around her, eyes fixed on the ceiling. The ease with which the lies came back disturbed him almost as much as what he'd found at the warehouse. Some things, it seemed, you never really left behind.

Frank was finally asleep. Sarah curled up beside him.

Arms intertwined.

Darkness still owned the room when they came. No footfalls on the stairs. No whisper of clothing. The door eased open and they flowed in like black water.

Six shapes materialized from shadow, their faces set with grim purpose. Walker stood at the foot of the bed. Pistol hanging at his side. Moonlight caught the steel.

Frank woke to the weight of men upon him. Arms pinned. Legs immobilized. Hands pushing his chest into the bed.

Sarah woke. "What the hell are you doing, Mitchel?"

"Shut up and keep still, you traitorous bitch," said Walker.

Frank surged upward. Muscles coiled with violent intent. He heaved sideways, taking one man with him. The attacker sailed through darkness and hit the wall with a sound like wet laundry dropped from height. Plaster cracked. The man folded to the floor and lay still.

The others doubled their efforts. Hands like iron bands. Walker stepped forward, something glinting in his left hand. Needle. Frank bucked again but they held him fast. The needle plunged into his neck. Cold spreading beneath skin.

"Hold him still," Walker said. Quiet and certain.

The cold turned to lead in Frank's veins. Muscles refused command. His body betrayed him limb by limb.

Sarah sat up, sheet pulled to her chest. Her eyes wide with confusion turned to terror. Walker placed the pistol against Frank's temple. Metal cold on skin.

"No!" said Sarah panicked.

"Where is Mike Pierce?" His voice quiet as falling snow.

Sarah's mouth opened. Closed. "I don't know."

"Wrong answer." Walker pressed harder with the gun barrel.

"Okay. Wait." Words tumbled now. "Pierce was going to kill Frank. I shot him."

"Is he dead?"

"Yes."

"Where's his body?"

"Outside the NSA facility. We buried him."

Walker's arm moved in a blur of motion. The pistol connected with Sarah's cheekbone. Sound of impact flat and final. Blood beaded along her brow.

Frank could only watch. His body useless as a fallen tree. Mind trapped inside unresponsive flesh. Forced to witness what followed.

Walker nodded to his men. One yanked Sarah from the bed. Zip-tied her wrists.

The remaining four men lifted Frank, almost 400 pounds of dead weight. The paralytic rendered Frank unable to feel his own body.

Walker leaned close. Whispered in Frank's ear. "You're not so smart, Frank. You never were."

They carried them out into mountain darkness. The night taking them like it had taken so many others before. It was Walker's kingdom and he ruled it with absolute power.

Sedition

The Eastern sky greyed behind gathering clouds as Walker stepped from the small regional jet. Wind cut across the tarmac. He carried nothing but a leather portfolio and a single hard-sided suitcase. Men like him traveled light. Possessions anchored those without purpose to places without meaning.

The rental car waited beyond security where promised. Keys tucked above visor like civilization still operated on faith not deserved. He drove with one hand. The other checking the Glock secured beneath his jacket. The highway empty this early. Towns passing indistinguishable from those he'd seen across a nation that looked the same everywhere men sought comfort in recognizable shapes. Gas stations. Fast food. Storage units holding overflow from houses representing lives worth abandoning at the first opportunity.

Snow lay in frozen patches where shade had denied the sun. Winter still holding ground in this part of

Virginia where the Air Force had built a base that looked like all others. Fences topped with razor wire. Concrete barriers designed to stop vehicles driven by men with purpose clearer than his. The base itself invisible beyond a rise where trees still stood despite military's general preference to clear anything that might provide cover for approach.

The cafe squatted beside the highway like something that had grown from asphalt rather than been placed upon it. The sign missing letters. Coffee Shop now read C ff e Sh p. The windows filthy beneath neon beer signs. The lot held four cars. None newer than a decade.

Walker parked between a rusted Ford missing its rear bumper and a Buick with mismatched doors. The kind of cars owned by men who believed their fortunes temporary. Their struggle permanent. He checked his watch. Precision mattered in meetings concerning dark things. Deadly things. The colonel would be inside. Third booth from the window. Alone with coffee he wouldn't drink and regret he couldn't hide.

The bell above the door announced Walker's arrival. The cafe smelled of grease and cigarettes though smoking had been banned in such establishments for years. The waitress looked up. Assessed Walker with a glance that had measured men accurately since before he'd been born. Her eyes moved to the suitcase. Then returned to the crossword puzzle folded beside the register.

Colonel Wilson sat where expected. His hair cut military short though he wore civilian clothes that looked new enough to seem unfamiliar. A costume rather than wardrobe. The coffee before him untouched. His eyes tracking Walker's movement across the cafe with recognition that needed no prior acquaintance. Some men identified their own kind without introduction.

"Mind if I sit?" Walker asked.

"Does it matter?" The colonel's voice carried East Coast refinement dulled by years shouting orders across the drone of engines. "You'll sit regardless."

Walker settled across from Wilson. The suitcase placed on the empty seat beside him. The booth's vinyl squeaked beneath his weight as if protesting proximity to the transaction about to occur. "How's Martha? Any better?"

Wilson's eyes hardened. Something like hatred flickered behind them. "Worse. The doctors say she has three months. Maybe less."

"The treatment in Switzerland?"

"Still possible. If I can get her there." Wilson's jaw tightened. "Insurance won't cover experimental

procedures. Military looks after its own until it doesn't."

"Two million will buy a lot of treatment," Walker said.

Wilson stared at the untouched coffee. "She doesn't know. About this. About you. About any of it." His voice cracked. A man accustomed to command now reduced to supplicant. "Twenty-six years in uniform. Never thought I'd sell my honor."

"You're not selling honor," Walker said. "You're buying time for someone who matters."

Wilson looked up. The self-loathing in his eyes replaced by something harder. "Let's just do this. You have my payment?"

Walker smiled. His hand on the case but not opening it. "I'd like confirmation of what's being purchased first."

Wilson reached into his jacket. Produced a thumb drive smaller than the last joint of his index finger. "Everything we discussed. Backdoor access to the verification network. Launch protocols. Authentication sequences that will let you into the missile defense grid."

"And control? Once we're inside?"

"Full command authority. You'll have access to the same console and tactical display that the commander of NORAD would see in a launch situation. Complete with targeting maps."

Walker nodded. "Lockout provisions?"

Wilson leaned closer. Voice dropping to hear his own treason. "Once inside, you'll have command authority that supersedes every failsafe in the system. The override was designed for continuity of government scenarios. If Washington gets wiped off the map, someone still needs to be able to launch so the rest of the nation will survive."

"And we can't be traced?"

Wilson shook his head. "The system was built before modern security protocols. No blockchain. No biometric authentication. Just codes and confirmation sequences. The Air Force has been meaning to update it for a decade. Budget constraints keep pushing it back."

"Convenient."

"For you." Wilson's eyes moved to the suitcase again. Watching it like medicine that might save or poison depending on dosage. "My payment?"

Walker placed the case on the table. Spun it toward Wilson. "Half now. Half when we confirm it works."

Wilson's hand moved toward the case. Stopped when Walker's finger tapped its surface. "Not here."

"There's an alley on the side of the building," said Wilson as he placed a couple of bucks on the table for the coffee.

The two men stood. Walker moved toward the door. Wilson following a step behind. The waitress watched without expression as they left. The bell above the door marking their exit with same indifference it had announced their arrival.

The alley beside the cafe smelled of rotting vegetables and urine. Snow piled against the wall in dirty mounds.

Their breath visible in morning air that carried industrial scent from the base three miles distant. Walker opened the case. Wilson's eyes fixed on the stacks within. Not greed. Something closer to desperation. The amount enough to keep Martha alive another year. Another chance at remission. At life beyond hospital walls and machines that measured what remained in beeps and numbers falling.

Wilson held out the thumb drive. "This wasn't easy to get. Had to access three separate terminals. Create a ghost account with admin privileges."

"The effort noted and appreciated." Walker took the drive. Tucked it into jacket pocket next to the Glock's reassuring weight. "I am sure she'll get the best care in Zurich."

Wilson's hand hovered over the open case. "Why these codes? What are you planning?"

"You're a smart man, Colonel. Smart enough not to ask questions that might complicate saving your wife."

"Martha would rather die than have me—" Wilson stopped himself. The weight of what he'd already done settling across shoulders that had carried stars and stripes without bending. "The instructions for accessing the system are on the drive. Requires physical connection to a machine with appropriate security clearance."

Wilson closed the case. Clutched it like life itself. "I've already arranged compassionate leave. Flight to Zurich leaves tomorrow night."

"Good timing." Walker's voice softened with what might have been genuine sympathy in another man. "Give Martha my best. Tell her she's got at least one fighter in her corner."

"I will." Wilson's face showed momentary relief. The burden of his betrayal balanced against possibility that some good might come of it. "The backdoor will work as promised. I am a man of my word."

"I believe you."

The Glock's suppressor made the shot sound like foot stamping snow. The subsonic round struck Wilson's sternum. His eyes registered surprise then understanding. The second round ensured silence made permanent. He fell backward. The case hitting concrete without spilling its contents. Walker knelt beside the body. Checked for pulse where none could exist. Took back the case. The entire exchange completed in the span of heartbeats.

Walker wiped the pistol with a handkerchief. Placed it in his jacket. He could not allow a man as unstable as Wilson to interfere with the militias plans. His secrets were dangerous. He might fold under pressure. Better to eliminate any chance of a leak.

He walked back to his car. The thumb drive in his pocket smaller than a man's finger but representing the nation's throat. He thought of Wilson's eyes in that final moment. The recognition that had come too late. The understanding that idealism died with same indifference whether wrapped in patriotism or love. That a wife waiting for miracle would receive instead news of husband found dead behind cafe where he had no reason to be.

Walker drove back toward the airport where a plane waited to carry him west. His mind already calculating next steps. The operation's stages unfolding like a battle plan prepared with accuracy and purpose no Pentagon strategist could match.

The abandoned factory stood like a monument to American industrial collapse. Broken windows. Machinery rusted in place. Concrete floors stained with chemicals long since banned.

They gathered on the factory floor, thirty-seven men

encircling Walker who stood upon a wooden platform surrounded by maps and charts. The air smelled of motor oil and dead ambition. Wind whistled through vacant spaces where glass used to be. Cold Denver air seeping in like unwelcome memory. Walker's men armed with some of the stolen weapons provided security.

Walker surveyed the assembled men. Each led militias across western states. Each commanded loyalty from men trained for insurgency. Each carried firearms beneath civilian clothing. The collective firepower in the room could easily have taken a small town. But to take on a nation they need a man like Walker.

"Gentlemen," Walker began. Voice steady and measured. "Please thank your donors for their financial support. The money will be well spent. We've entered the final phase." The men shifted. Some nodded. Others checked doorways from habit.

"Constitutional amendment requires two-thirds majority in both chambers of Congress to propose it. Then three-quarters of states must ratify." Walker's hands moved through air as if shaping invisible clay. "The President has no role. No veto power. The Founders, God bless them designed it this way."

A man with a beard like steel wool raised his hand. Sleeves rolled to expose forearms mapped with prison ink. "What about states wanting to join later? After we've made our stand?"

Walker nodded as if expecting the question. "Not initially. The seceding states form our alliance first. Others may apply for membership afterward. We vote on their admission. Majority rules." Murmurs rippled through the gathered men. Some disapproving. Others calculating advantage.

"What about California?" said another militia leader. "They have substantial armed forces in our rear and flank."

"Which is why we will leave the golden state alone. Once they find themselves cutoff from the rest of the United States, my guess is they will also secede and form their own country. But no matter what they do, they are not our concern unless they threaten us. We will leave them be. No need to poke a bear that doesn't need poking." There was nervous laughter in the audience.

"The NSA facility status," Walker continued. "Our recon team has determined that the structure remains intact. Equipment obsolete but functional. Capable of issuing commands once fiber optic networks are restored." He moved to blueprints pinned to a map board. The schematics showed underground tunnels. Communication networks spreading like arteries from the facility heart.

"The fiber lines have been severed at strategic junctions between the facility and missile silos. Once we secure the installation, our technicians will locate and repair these breaks." Walker's finger traced paths across the blueprint. "When reconnected, the facility communicates directly with ICBM silos in all seceding states."

A man in a hunting jacket spat on the concrete floor. "Those government boys will hit back hard once they figure what we're doing."

"Which is why the weapons acquisition was necessary." Walker gestured to a man by the wall who stepped forward with photographs. "Defensive positions here, here, and here. The stolen arms give us holdout capability against initial response forces."

The photographs circulated. Men studied them with professional scrutiny. A militia leader from Idaho – face weathered like drought-cracked earth – cleared his throat. "Those M240s and Stingers might handle ground forces.

Maybe helicopters and drones. But high-altitude bombers? Air Force will turn that facility to dust once they understand what's at stake."

Silence settled across the room. The question that had haunted planning sessions for months. Walker didn't flinch. "I'm aware of the threat assessment. Provisions are in motion." He paused. Let the words land with their full weight. "I need six men from each of your organizations. Your best. For a covert acquisition of ground-to-air defense systems."

No one asked where such systems would come from. Some questions better left unspoken.

"None of this matters without launch codes," said a voice from the back. Former Air Force. The group's only member with missile system experience. "Silos stay locked without valid authorization."

Walker's smile never reached his eyes. "In the event that Washington gets vaporized and no one's left to give the order to defend our nation, the Pentagon and NORAD maintain backdoor launch protocols."

His hand went to his pocket. Withdrew a thumb drive secured on a chain around his neck. "My operative at the Pentagon delivered this last week. The override sequence." The room went still. Men who had handled weapons their entire lives suddenly conscious of mortality's frailty. Of atoms splitting. Of fire that could cleanse cities from maps.

"If Congress or the states refuse our amendment, an ICBM targets Washington. Or any state capital opposing secession." Walker tucked the drive away. "Total destruction. No rebuilding."

A militia leader with a face like weathered granite leaned forward. "With respect, they won't believe the threat. Pentagon's spent decades convincing everyone only the President can authorize launch."

Walker's eyes narrowed. "Which is why we will demonstrate our capability first." The room went still.

A man near the back – former Navy, hands steady as stone – broke the silence. "Demonstrate how exactly?"

"We launch an ICBM at Desecheo Island." Walker's voice remained calm as if discussing weather. "Small.

Uninhabited. Wildlife refuge off Puerto Rico."

Murmurs erupted. A balding man with wire-rimmed glasses shook his head. "A nuclear detonation in the Caribbean—"

"Will be visible from San Juan," Walker cut him off. "Precisely the point."

He revealed a map on one of the stands. A small speck marked in red. "Thirteen miles offshore. No radiation reaching populated areas. Nothing there but birds and lizards." His finger tapped the location. "The blast creates no human casualties, but everyone from Miami to Caracas sees it. The seismic signature registers worldwide."

"Jesus Christ," someone whispered.

Walker continued, unmoved. "We give them thirty minutes advance notice. Just enough time to confirm it's real, scramble their response systems, get satellites in position." He surveyed the room. "They'll watch, helpless, as the detonation proves our control of nuclear launch systems. One demonstration – bloodless but undeniable."

"The environmental damage—" began a former state senator.

"Is irrelevant compared to what follows if they refuse our demands," Walker finished. "One small island against the potential destruction of Washington D.C." His eyes hardened. "After the demonstration, no one will doubt our resolve or our control of the system. The amendment will pass. The states will ratify."

Walker surveyed the room. Saw the weight of understanding settle across their faces. Men who had discussed revolution in hunting cabins and backroom meetings for years now confronted with its atomic reality. "Gentlemen, we've talked in theory and planned for three years. It's now become a reality because of you and your commitment to freedom." His gaze moved from face to face, challenging each man to meet his eyes. "It's time to strap on your big boy pants. This is the real deal."

The factory's emptiness amplified his words. Dust particles hung suspended in weak light cutting through broken windows. No one spoke. "Some of you joined because you lost jobs. Some because the government took your land. Some because you watched your towns die." Walker straightened. "Well, now we're past talking. Past training in the woods with ARs and surplus gear. This is when we find out who's serious and who's been playing soldier."

"The panic—" began a former state senator. "Will be manageable and brief," Walker finished. "And afterward, no one will doubt our resolve or our control of the system. The amendment will pass. The states will ratify. All without a single American life lost."

The men exchanged glances. Some troubled. Others resolute. None speaking the fear that settled in their guts like cold stone. Walker raised his hand, remembering something important. "Your shadow governments must be prepared to assume immediate control in each state. The moment secession is announced, functioning administrations need to step in. Power grids. Water systems. Law enforcement. No gaps that invite federal intervention or chaos."

A militia leader from Montana – retired judge with eyes like flint – spoke up. "My people are positioned throughout state offices. Ready to maintain continuity."

Others nodded. Similar preparations in place.

Walker's expression softened slightly. "I want to be clear about something. This isn't about bloodshed or revenge. It's about freedom from a system that abandoned its founding principles." He looked each man in the eye. "I don't want a single American to die in this transition. Not one." He let that sink in before continuing. "But understand this – if Washington forces violence upon us, we will respond in kind. If they leave us no choice, the responsibility for what follows rests with them, not us."

The hardness returned to his face. "We're simply reclaiming what the Founders intended before the federal government grew into this monstrous thing that devours liberty." Nods circled the room. Men who had waited decades for this moment.

"Secession Day is scheduled for April fifteenth. Tax Day. Fitting, I think." Walker stepped down from his platform. "Your communication networks will alert you to any changes. Questions?" None came. The men understood.

They had crossed the line between insurgency and revolution. Between protest and war. Their cause now measured in megatons.

Outside, Denver traffic continued unaware. People shopping. Working. Living. None suspecting the conversation that had just redrawn the nation's future in an abandoned factory where Americans once built machines for a shared prosperity.

Walker shook hands with each man as they departed. Different exit times. Different routes. Security protocols followed. The factory returned to emptiness when they departed. Just concrete and rust and broken glass. And the echo of plans that would reshape a continent.

The room held no windows. Just concrete walls gone gray with age and a steel door that wouldn't yield to anything less than explosives. Frank tested every inch, fingers probing for weakness in the seams where wall met floor, where ceiling connected to vertical surface. Nothing gave. The table anchored to concrete by steel bolts thicker than his thumb. Two chairs, metal frames with plastic seats, the kind found in government buildings where comfort ranks below durability.

He heard the lock mechanism engage. Stepped back from the door measured and ready. The steel swung outward revealing Walker, expression cold as winter stone. Frank took one stride forward.

Walker's pistol appeared in practiced motion, barrel steady at Frank's forehead. "One more step and I'll blow your head off and you know I can do it. So, sit the fuck down."

Frank measured the distance. Calculated odds. Walker's finger already tight against the trigger. Not enough space to cross before the bullet would find him. He lowered himself to the chair, movements slow and deliberate.

Walker kept the gun trained while producing a smartphone from his jacket pocket. Tapped the screen without taking eyes off Frank. Turned it to face him.

The screen showed another room. Same concrete construction. Same institutional emptiness. Sarah strapped to a chair, leather restraints at wrists and ankles. A man in coveralls worked methodically, attaching electrodes to her temples. Her eyes wide but chin set firm. The man placed a wooden stick between her teeth, positioned crosswise.

The man stepped back. Adjusted dials on a metal case. Sarah's body convulsed. Back arched against restraints.

The wooden stick cracked between her teeth.

"Enough," Frank said.

"Stop," Walker commanded into the phone. The man's hand pulled back from the controls. Sarah slumped forward, breath coming in ragged gasps. Sweat plastered hair against her face. Blood running from her mouth where her teeth had dug further into her gums and jaw.

Walker slipped the phone into his pocket but kept the pistol aimed. "Next are her nipples, then genitals, and after that... we'll get creative." His voice carried the certainty of someone who'd witnessed such progression before. "Betrayal deserves the very best I have to offer."

Frank's hands rested on the table. Palms flat against metal surface. No sudden movements. Nothing to provoke the bullet waiting behind Walker's trigger finger. "What do you want?"

"You, of course." Walker's smile carried no warmth. "There is a Patriot missile system being delivered from the assembly installation in Florida to Edwards Air Force Base in California in one week. I need it. You are going to get it for me."

"Then what?" Frank kept his voice level despite the rage building behind his ribs.

"If you deliver the Patriot system, Sarah and you go free. No harm. You have my word." Walker's gun didn't waver.

"I don't believe you." Frank's eyes held Walker's. Two predators recognizing each other across artificial distance.

"You don't have a choice... and neither does Sarah." Walker tapped the phone in his pocket, reminder of leverage that existed in another concrete room.

"I want to see her." The words pushed through Frank's damaged throat with effort that cost something physical.

"No." Walker's refusal came quick as gunshot. "Not

until you deliver a plan that I approve, then I will give you two minutes with her."

Walker's confidence suggested a man who held all advantages. Who calculated risks and found them acceptable. "Deal?"

"Deal." Frank knew his word meant nothing in this room. Just as Walker's promises carried weight only as long as utility remained. The real negotiation would come later in blood and brass.

Walker backed toward the door, gun never lowering until steel separated them again. The lock engaged. Frank sat motionless, listening to footsteps recede down concrete hallway. His mind already working through angles and approaches. Ways to secure both Sarah and himself while denying Walker the weapon that would turn militia into genuine military threat.

Frank entered the war room as the others stood aside. A living fortress of muscle and scar tissue moving with surprising grace for a man his size. Several armed guards stood against the walls just in case Frank misbehaved. The fluorescent lights washed color from everything, making the maps spread across steel tables appear bloodless despite the violence they represented.

Walker waited at the far end, arms crossed over chest, face unreadable as the giant who'd once fought beside him now planned to steal a weapons system worth more than everything else in the militia's arsenal combined.

Frank settled his bulk before the maps, massive hands hovering over topographical contours like a pianist preparing for complicated sonata. The room fell silent around him. Even those who'd questioned his loyalty went quiet in the presence of focused competence that required no explanation or defense. He studied the rail routes between states without expression, measuring the spaces between civilization where eighty-six tons of military hardware might pass unnoticed if guided by the right hand. His own.

Frank spread the satellite photos across the metal table. Images taken at different angles, showing length of track cutting through Colorado landscape. Walker stood across from him, hands resting on table edge.

"Rail junctions." Frank's damaged voice barely carried across the table.

Walker frowned. "We've selected the ideal ambush point. Why concern yourself with junctions?"

Frank's finger traced the winding route where tracks cut through mountain terrain. His eyes found what he sought—places where commercial lines connected to secondary tracks. Service spurs abandoned after mining operations ceased. Maintenance access points used by railroad crews.

"Show full route," he demanded.

Heller unrolled a larger map. The entire Colorado transit marked in red. Frank studied it with practiced efficiency, mind calculating distances and timing. His finger stopped at a particular junction where the main line began a steady uphill grade, then connected to a secondary track five miles later.

"Grade percentage?" Frank asked.

Heller consulted the topographic overlay. "Twopoint-six percent incline for three miles, then levels briefly before junction."

Frank nodded. His finger moved to where an abandoned mining spur connected to the main line after the grade flattened.

"This junction operational?"

Walker leaned closer. "Maintenance access. Used monthly for track inspection vehicles."

"Switch controls?"

"Manual. Not electronically monitored." Walker's eyes narrowed. "What are you thinking?"

"Separate troops from cargo."

"How are you going to do that?" said Heller.

"Release troop car on grade. Switch to maintenance spur."

Walker and Heller exchange a look. "Are you sure that will work?" said Walker.

"No," said Frank. "But I will be sure."

"The air brakes," Heller interjected. "When you disconnect cars, the system automatically engages brakes. They won't roll freely."

Frank coughed heavily. His throat dry and soar from talking too much. He opened and emptied a water bottle, then said, "Brake release valve."

Heller looked skeptical. "You'd need to manually override each car's system before disconnecting. That's at least—"

"Know procedure." Frank cut him off. "Four-man team. Bleed brake system before incline." "Who uncouples the cars?" said Walker.

"I will," said Frank.

The room fell silent as Walker and his lieutenants processed the audacity of Frank's plan. Not just the physics of moving train cars, but the technical knowledge required to manipulate railway braking systems without alerting security personnel.

"You know how to operate train brakes?" Walker couldn't hide his surprise.

Frank's expression remained unchanged as he said, "YouTube."

"This is insane," Heller shook his head. "The timing would be impossible."

"You want easy?" said Frank. "Stay home."

"Fuck you. I'm going," said Heller trying to save face.

Walker exchanged glances with his lieutenants. The technical complexity concerned him, but the reduction in operational signature was significant. The plan's elegance remained. He smiled and said, "Gotta give it to you, Frank. It's a bold plan. No firefight. No casualties. No evidence trail. They'll never see it coming."

"Once we have control of the flatbed cars, then what?" said Heller.

"We ride them back to flat. Offload."

"We have Chinooks ready," Heller offered. "Two CH-47s could—"

"Not enough lift." Frank cut him off. "We need cranes."

"The Chinooks can manage the individual components if we disassemble the systems."

"No time."

"He's right. Once we grab the Patriots, the entire US military will be on our asses."

"Twenty-two minutes," said Frank having already calculated the response time.

"That's not much time," said Heller.

"No. It's not," said Frank.

"You want to transport the Patriots by road? Aircraft will spot them," said Walker.

"And what about roadblocks?" said Heller.

"I have plan," said Frank tired of talking.

"I bet you do," said Walker, impressed.

Walker led Frank down the concrete corridor, boots echoing against the cold floor. Frank's hands bound before him in steel cuffs that bit into his wrists. Two guards trailed ten paces behind, rifles at ready position.

"Two minutes," Walker said. "No touching. No passing notes. No coded messages." Frank stared ahead, measured his breath against the distance. The hallway smelled of bleach and something else. Something like fear.

Walker stopped at a metal door marked only with a number. He turned the key in the lock, pushed it open. "Clock's ticking."

Frank stepped inside. Sarah sat in a metal chair bolted to the floor, her wrists secured to armrests with leather straps. Dried blood darkened the corner of her mouth. Purple bruise bloomed across her left cheekbone. Her eyes found his, widened with recognition.

"Frank," she whispered.

He moved toward her, stopping when one of the guards raised his rifle. Frank stood five feet away, close enough to see the tiny cuts across her knuckles.

"You okay?" Voice like gravel pushed through his damaged throat.

Sarah smiled, split lip reopening. Fresh blood beaded. "Been better."

Frank's eyes cataloged her injuries. The burn marks at her temples where electrodes had been. The tremor in her left hand. The torn fingernail on her thumb. "They want the missile system," she said.

Frank nodded once.

"Don't give it to them." Her voice stronger now, urgent. "Whatever they do to me."

Frank didn't move, but something shifted behind his eyes. Something cold and certain.

"They'll kill us anyway," she continued. "You know that."

"Yes."

Walker checked his watch from the doorway. "One minute left."

Sarah leaned forward as far as the restraints allowed. "Listen carefully. The fiber optic lines. I overheard them. Something about nuclear launch codes. Override protocols."

Frank's massive frame went still as stone.

"Mitchel is obsessed. He's planning something with those missile silos in Montana." Her words rushed now, feeling the seconds slip away. "That's why he needs the

Patriot system. Air defense."

"Enough," Walker said. "Time's up."

Frank didn't move. His eyes held Sarah's like a lifeline across drowning water.

"I'll find you," he said.

"I know." She straightened in the chair, chin lifting.

Something passed between them. Something the guards couldn't see or touch. Walker stepped into the room. "Let's go."

Frank turned, knowing exactly how many steps separated him from the door. From the guards. From Walker. Calculations. As he passed Walker, Frank paused. Their eyes met for one second. Walker's hand moved imperceptibly toward his holstered pistol, muscle memory responding to the promise in Frank's gaze.

"Soon," Frank said. Walker's mouth tightened.

"Clock's ticking on your mission, not just your girlfriend."

Frank walked out, back straight despite the cuffs. Behind him, Sarah watched through the closing door, her face set with the same determination that had once killed a man to save him. The lock turned with mechanical finality. In the corridor, Frank walked ahead of Walker, measuring distances. Mapping exits. Counting guards. Planning.

Dawn broke cold across the two-lane highway winding through mountain passes where vehicles passed seldom enough for men to conduct business beyond law's reach.

Heller and twenty-one of his men lay concealed among pines that crowded road's edge. Each dressed in civilian clothes beneath tactical vests that would remain hidden until their purpose required their revelation. Each carrying sidearms with suppressors attached. Each understanding that blood must not stain uniforms they would claim from men who had worn them last.

Heller checked his watch. The convoy would arrive in seven minutes if intelligence held. The drone overhead had confirmed twenty-two men. Three blades requiring three separate transport vehicles. Each specialized trailer designed for loads that seemed to defy physical possibility. Each requiring lead driver and rear driver to navigate curves that normal trucks could manage without consideration. Each worth millions to companies that built them and priceless to Walker for purpose that transcended commercial value.

"Comms check," Heller said into radio clipped to vest hidden beneath a hunting jacket chosen to match region and season and operation requiring precision that left no room for error.

Five acknowledgments returned through earpiece. Team leaders confirming readiness. Men positioned where highway curved sharply enough that convoy would slow to speed that made intervention possible. The false patrol car waited at curve's apex. Light bar genuine. Uniform on Dalton recovered from deputy who would not report for duty again. The trap laid with attention to detail born of professional understanding that men died from small oversights more often than grand miscalculations.

The first transport appeared around the bend. Its diesel engine laboring against grade that challenged even vehicles designed for extraordinary burden. Warning flags fluttered from the blade's extensions that hung beyond the trailer's edge like an appendage from a mechanical creature beyond nature's imagination. The convoy moved with careful certainty of men who transported cargo valuable enough to warrant security beyond ordinary consideration.

Dalton stepped from the patrol car. Hand raised in universal signal requiring compliance from all who recognized uniform and badge and duty it represented. The lead truck with a "WIDE LOAD" sign on top of the cab slowed.

The driver's window descended. A man leaned out. Face composed in professional concern rather than suspicion that events had transcended ordinary into terminal. Dalton approached with practiced gait of men authorized to interrupt journeys of those who crossed territories they protected.

"Morning, Officer. Problem?"

"Permit check." Dalton's voice carrying just the right mixture of authority and routine. "Had reports of oversized loads without proper documentation."

"Everything's in order." The driver reached toward glovebox where paperwork would confirm legitimacy now irrelevant to conclusion already determined. "Blade shipment for the wind farm project outside—"

"Step out of the vehicle, please."

"Is that necessary? We're on a tight schedule."

"Won't take but a minute." Dalton's hand moved toward his sidearm not yet drawn. The implied threat understood by men who operated vehicles requiring authorization beyond standard licensing. "Your personnel too."

The driver sighed with resignation born of experience with uniforms and schedules and bureaucracy that interfered with deliveries and paychecks and lives built upon all three. He opened the door. Stepped down from cab to asphalt still cool from night's recent departure. Called over shoulder to men behind him. "Hold up. Permit check."

Transport crew complied. Twenty-two men emerging from vehicles stretched along the highway's curve like mechanical vertebrae of a creature now stilled. Each wearing company uniform colored industrial blue with logo across breast pocket.

Heller gave signal through the radio that required no verbal confirmation. His men emerged from treeline like shadows breaking from larger darkness. Their movements coordinated through training and repetition that allowed no hesitation once decision had been reached. Weapons appeared from concealment. Faces now hidden behind masks that would prevent identification.

The driver recognized truth too late to alert men still complying with instructions that seemed legitimate until sudden appearance of operators who moved with purpose beyond traffic regulation or permit verification.

His hand moved toward his pocket where communication device would prove useless against weapons already aimed. Dalton's pistol made soft coughing sound. The man fell without a cry that might have warned others still emerging from vehicles unaware that lives built upon schedules and paychecks had already ended regardless of what actions followed.

"Nobody moves," Heller announced, voice pitched to carry exact distance required but no further. "Hands where we can see them."

The transport crew froze. Understanding arriving simultaneously across twenty-one faces with expressions ranging from incomprehension to resignation. They stood along the highway with hands raised. Each calculating odds against armed men whose number and purpose and capacity now revealed left no uncertainty regarding outcome should resistance be offered.

"On your knees. Hands behind your head."

The men complied. Asphalt cold against limbs unaccustomed to such positioning. Heller moved among them with efficiency born of training that had included scenarios much like this one. His men securing weapons from security personnel stationed throughout the convoy. Removing communication devices from all who might have reached for them. Ensuring compliance through presence that required no elaboration regarding consequences of refusal.

"You're making a mistake," said a man with captain's insignia on uniform collar. "This shipment is tracked by satellite. Response team will deploy within thirty minutes of communication failure."

"We're aware of your protocol," Heller replied without breaking stride or purpose. He approached the captain. Studied him with cold assessment of man who recognized authority regardless of uniform worn or absence of it.

The captain's face revealed calculation behind words meant to dissuade through deception now revealed. "What do you want with wind turbine blades? You'll never be able to sell them."

"You don't need to concern yourself with that." Heller nodded to men who had segregated the transport crew into smaller groups more easily controlled through division that denied strength through numbers. "Remove their uniforms. Collect credentials and personal effects. Maintain condition of the clothing."

The militia worked with practiced efficiency. The transport crew stripped with methodical dispassion that denied humanity beyond necessity required for immediate purpose. The uniforms collected with attention to detail. Twenty-one men soon knelt in their underwear upon asphalt gone warm with sun now risen above mountains.

"What are you going to do with us?" asked the captain.

Heller studied the man. Noted the defiance that remained despite circumstance that rendered it meaningless. "We are going to let you go. Into the forest. All of you."

The twenty-one men exchanged glances.

"Move," Heller ordered. His men positioning themselves behind the crew. Weapons visible now.

The transport workers stood. Bodies pale against mountain air gone suddenly colder against skin no longer protected by clothing. They moved toward the treeline.

Some requiring encouragement delivered through rifle barrels pressed against flesh.

Pines swallowed them. Shadows falling across skin gone gray with understanding that had arrived too late to alter outcome. The forest floor soft beneath feet accustomed to truck pedals and highway asphalt. Birds continued singing. Insects moved through undergrowth.

Nature indifferent.

"Here," Heller said.

The men stopped. Twenty-one bodies arranged in a rough semicircle within a clearing that sun dappled through branches. The captain stood straighter. His eyes finding Heller's with a last attempt at connection that might transcend circumstance now undeniable.

"You don't have to do this," he said.

Heller's face betrayed nothing. Not satisfaction or regret or recognition of moment that separated men like him from those who stood waiting for conclusion they still hoped might be avoided.

"On your knees."

The men complied. Some requiring assistance

delivered with rifle butts against limbs gone weak with fear that body recognized before mind admitted. They knelt upon forest floor carpeted with pine needles fallen through natural cycle.

The militia moved with coordinated purpose that required no verbal direction. Each positioning himself behind a kneeling man. Distance maintained through training that ensured maximum efficiency and minimum evidence scattered beyond necessary radius. Weapons raised with synchronized precision.

"Close your eyes," Heller instructed.

Some obeyed. Others stared forward with last defiance that would change nothing but meant something to those who offered it. The captain among them. His gaze fixed on Heller with judgment that would outlast his physical body.

"Do it," Heller ordered.

Twenty-one muzzle flashes. Twenty-one bodies toppling forward. The sound diminished through suppressors but still carrying through the trees.

The captain fell last. His body collapsing across pine.

"Make one grave seven feet deep. Three feet of soil, then lime, then the rest." Heller surveyed the bodies arranged in death. "I want nothing left if this site is discovered."

His men worked with efficiency. Shovels appearing from vehicles parked along the roadside. The earth opened. Bodies arranged within the depression that would hold evidence until decomposition rendered it indistinguishable from surrounding matter.

Heller watched without emotion. He turned away as first layer of dirt covered faces already gone vacant.

Forty-three minutes later the convoy reassembled. Heller's men now wearing uniforms taken from men whose bodies would nourish soil.

Heller took a position in lead vehicle. His attention focused on the road ahead and mission still unfolding across multiple fronts. The dead left behind no longer factored into his calculation. The highway carrying them east toward rendezvous where the blades would serve purpose beyond anything their manufacturers had intended.

The convoy halted at the abandoned quarry thirty miles from the ambush site. Stone walls rising around them like sentinels. Heller stepped from the lead truck, boots grinding against gravel.

"Phillips. Moore. With me."

Two men approached carrying a tablet with schematics and a duffle of specialized tools. Heller walked to the first turbine blade, white surface gleaming under afternoon sun.

"GPS is embedded in the structural support. Nineteen feet from the base," Phillips said, consulting the tablet.

Moore ran detection equipment along the composite surface. "Here. Strong signal."

Heller pulled on gloves. "Cut here."

Phillips used a modified rotary saw that whined against the composite skin. He cut a square section eighteen inches across. Moore reached into the cavity and extracted a device smaller than a cigarette pack.

"Got it."

Heller examined the tracking unit, then placed it in a shielded bag. "Now the others."

They repeated the procedure on the remaining blades with the same method.

"Seal them," Heller instructed. "Factory finish. No evidence."

Phillips applied composite patches that matched the

surrounding material perfectly. Moore held up the three extracted devices. "What about these?"

"Separate vehicles. Keep moving east on the original route. When you reach Falls Creek, attach them to logging trucks headed north."

The men nodded, understanding the deception would send monitoring systems on a false trail, buying hours their operation required.

"Ten minutes," Heller announced to the waiting convoy. "Then we move. Walker's waiting."

The massive blades, now silent participants in the deception.

Machinations

The summer heat shimmered off the tarmac at Eglin Air Force Base, distorting the air above four massive components of the MIM-104 Patriot system. Radar. Engagement Control Station. Power plant. Launcher. Each piece waiting like patient sentinels, their combined worth over one billion dollars.

Lieutenant Torres wiped sweat from his brow, checking his manifest against the physical inventory. Twelve Patriot missiles in their transport containers stood on special pallets, each missile capable of intercepting aircraft or ballistic threats at ranges exceeding forty miles.

"Containers secured?" Torres asked Master Sergeant Reeves.

"Affirmative, sir. Impact monitors installed on each one."

Along the rail spur that cut into the base, four reinforced flatbed cars waited. The diesel locomotive idled at the head of the formation, its engine sending vibrations through the steel rails. Two troop carriers—one positioned at the front of the flatbed cars, one at the rear—stood ready to receive the security detail.

Four M1070 Heavy Equipment Transporters stood alongside the Patriot components, their massive eight axle frames soon to be secured to the same flatbeds, providing immediate mobility once the system reached its destination, each transporter capable of hauling seventy tons across terrain no civilian truck could navigate.

The massive crane swung into position above the Patriot radar set. Even powered down and sealed for transport, the radar assembly weighed over ten tons. The crane's steel cables tensed as the radar lifted from its transport vehicle.

"Steady," called the loadmaster. "That's the eyes of the whole system you're dancing with."

The radar settled onto the first flatbed with a groan of metal and springs. Airmen swarmed the car, securing heavy chains and tensioners to specialized anchor points. The Engagement Control Station—heart of the Patriot system—came next, its exterior sealed against dust and weather. Inside, millions in sophisticated electronics waited in dormant silence.

Staff Sergeant Willis stood before the assembled security platoon. Thirty-six soldiers in battle rattle, plus himself and Lieutenant Torres. Their faces streaked with sweat beneath Kevlar helmets despite the morning hour.

"First squad takes the front car," Willis said. "Second squad in the rear. Two fire teams with Stingers in each car. Two teams with AT4s. I don't expect trouble, but we prepare for it."

The men nodded. They had drilled this operation multiple times. The Patriot system represented critical infrastructure, its movement planned with the secrecy of a nuclear transport.

"Rotation schedule is in your briefing packets," Willis continued. "Eight-hour shifts. No sleeping outside designated rest periods. Full gear at all times."

Torres watched as the power plant component was secured to the third flatbed. The diesel generator system that would feed electricity to the Patriot's hungry systems during operation now sat dormant, its fuel tanks emptied for transport.

"Status on the launcher?" Torres asked.

"Loading now, sir," Reeves replied.

The last flatbed received the missile launcher assembly. Without its complement of interceptors, the launcher resembled an empty steel frame, its hydraulics locked for transit. The missile containers were secured to specially designed racks on the same car, their contents cushioned against the jolts of rail travel.

Inside the front troop car, First Squad stowed their gear in overhead compartments. Each man carried his M4 carbine plus sidearm. The designated Stinger teams checked their launch tubes. The AT4 operators secured their anti-tank weapons in special brackets designed to prevent accidental discharge.

"Comms check," Willis called from the center of the car.

Each fire team leader responded in sequence, confirming operational readiness of their radios and satellite phones. No dead zones allowed on this transport.

In the rear car, Second Squad mirrored the preparations. Sergeant Dixon arranged his men by fire teams, positioning the Stinger operators near the back of the car for rapid deployment if needed.

"Remember your sectors," Dixon said. "Front team watches forward for threats. Rear team watches our six.

Side teams have 180-degree coverage each."

The loadmaster made a final inspection of the four flatbeds. Each Patriot component secured with redundant systems. Each tie-down checked twice. GPS trackers mounted discreetly in twelve different locations across the consist.

"All components secured," he reported to Torres. "Train is ready to roll."

Torres gave the signal to the locomotive engineer. The diesel engine increased its rumble, the couplings between cars tensing as slack disappeared from the line. Metal wheels began their slow turn against steel rails, the distinctive clacking rhythm marking the beginning of the journey.

"Junction Control, this is Patriot Transport," Torres spoke into the secure radio. "Package is moving. I say again, package is moving. Authorization code Sierra-Whiskey-Three-Four-Delta."

The radio crackled with acknowledgment.

Somewhere above, surveillance satellites adjusted their focus, tracking the valuable cargo now beginning its cross-country journey.

Inside the troop cars, the security detail settled in for the long haul. Weapons within arm's reach, body armor creating uncomfortable heat but necessary protection. The men checked watches, calculated rotation schedules, mentally prepared for days of constant vigilance.

The Patriot system rolled westward under guard, unaware that its course had already been plotted on maps other than those carried by its official escorts. Unaware that its journey would be interrupted long before reaching its intended destination.

The white Ford F-350 rolled through pre-dawn darkness, Oregon plates mud-splattered to obscure identification.

Three men rode inside, rifles secured behind the seats, provisions packed for two weeks' deployment. They weren't alone on the highway.

Miles back, a convoy of ten pickups crossed the Montana border, gun racks visible through rear windows, men who spoke little and checked mirrors often. Their leaders had received coordinates three days prior. Instructions to travel separately. To maintain radio silence. To avoid patterns that might trigger attention.

Curtis Malden gripped his Dodge Ram's steering wheel, knuckles white against the leather. Former Delta Force. Eighteen years in service before discharge. The three men with him had similar backgrounds. Special forces. Combat experience. Men who understood violence as language and weapon both.

"How many you figure will actually show?" asked his passenger. "Five hundred minimum," Malden replied. "Thirty from each militia, plus Walker's core group."

From Washington came forty-six vehicles carrying communications specialists—former NSA technicians and military signal corps—men who could resurrect dormant networks with improvised parts if necessary. Their equipment cases held sophisticated tech hidden beneath camping gear, their cover story maintained through detailed backstopping.

Wyoming sent sixty-two former military engineers with expertise in hardening facilities against both conventional and nuclear strikes. Nevada contributed fifty-eight ex-Air Force missile technicians who understood the interface protocols between command systems and launch hardware. Arizona delivered forty-three snipers trained on government ranges, now turned against former employers.

Twenty-seven former Navy SEALs led the Colorado contingent, their trucks loaded with specialized diving equipment for accessing underground water systems. New Mexico sent forty-four men with backgrounds in nuclear security protocols from the national laboratories, their knowledge of failsafe mechanisms crucial to Walker's endgame.

An Alaska National Guard captain—discharged for extremist views—brought thirty-five men with arctic warfare training and communications expertise suited for isolated conditions. Their vehicles carried cold-weather gear despite the season, preparation for the facility's underground levels where temperature remained constant year-round.

Walker's own militia contributed 120 men—his core force of true believers who had trained together for years.

Not weekend warriors playing at combat, but professionals who maintained physical standards matching active military units. Men who had sacrificed careers, relationships, normal lives to prepare for this moment.

Two hundred miles south, Walker supervised the loading operation at Junction City. Men worked methodically in the warehouse, connecting diesel trucks to the stolen weapons containers. The weapons from Camp Pendleton now sealed in transport configuration.

"Secure those chains properly," Walker ordered. "If we lose a container on some mountain pass, the whole operation fails."

The men nodded, tightening connection points, checking brake lines and hydraulics. Each truck would travel a different route. Each container would arrive at staggered intervals. No convoy to draw attention. No pattern for satellite analysis to detect.

Inside the containers, weapons that would transform civilian militias into legitimate military threat waited in organized silence. Five hundred M27 rifles stored in wooden crates. Forty-eight Barrett sniper systems packed in custom foam. Seventy-six Stinger missiles in transport configuration. One hundred twenty AT4 anti-tank weapons secured against movement. The arsenal capable of holding territory against initial government response until the nuclear option forced capitulation.

Miles away, Frank sat in the passenger seat of a nondescript panel van. Six men behind him checked equipment with quiet efficiency. Former military all of them. Men chosen for specific skills. For ability to follow instructions without question. For competence under pressure.

The van contained specialized equipment. Brake release tools. Railway switch equipment. Communication devices operating on frequencies that wouldn't trigger normal transportation monitoring systems. Everything needed to stop eighty-six tons of military hardware without firing a single shot.

Frank studied the satellite photos, committing every contour to memory. The railway grade. The junction points. The maintenance access road that would allow their approach without detection. Years of operational planning compressed into one mission that would determine whether Walker's insanity could be contained or would spiral into a national catastrophe.

Across the western states, a force of over 500 militia members converged on the Pahsimeroi Valley. Not weekend warriors playing soldier. Not untrained civilians with grievances. These were men with professional military backgrounds, technical expertise, specialized knowledge of government systems. A shadow army capable of executing complex operations under strict operational security.

Idaho militias provided the advance teams, establishing perimeter security around the NSA facility, placing motion sensors and thermal cameras to detect approach. Former border patrol agents among them created layered defensive positions using the same tactics they'd once employed to secure America's boundaries. Claymore mines lined the perimeter fence.

The combined force represented something unprecedented—a militia movement transformed into professional insurgency. Men with combat deployments. Officers with command experience. Intelligence analysts familiar with government response protocols. Communications specialists capable of intercepting and decrypting official channels.

Frank turned the envelope in his massive hands. Inside, the detailed operational plan for the train heist. Timetables. Contingencies. Extraction routes. Everything precisely calculated except the one variable that mattered most—his own intentions. His own plan forming beneath the surface like tectonic pressure before an earthquake.

The men behind him checked equipment one final time. Railway tools. Communication devices. Weapons kept minimal but effective. Men chosen because Walker trusted their loyalty more than their judgment. Men who would follow orders without questioning wider implications.

"First checkpoint," the driver announced as they passed a highway marker.

Across America, the movement converged. Pickups and panel vans. SUVs with tinted windows. Rental trucks with false documentation. The invisible infrastructure of insurgency flowing toward Idaho's mountains like water seeking the lowest point. Men with training, equipment, and determination built over years of preparation. Men capable of holding territory against conventional military response long enough for Walker's nuclear leverage to force government capitulation.

The stolen weapons traveled hidden within commercial shipping containers.

And between these forces moved Frank Kane, massive and inevitable as a continental drift, his purpose single and absolute. Walker's plan, stopped. America, preserved from madness wrapped in patriot's garb.

Everything else negotiable.

The old man on the porch of May's general store lowered his coffee cup as the first trucks appeared. Lifted his chin toward the road running through town. "Feels like something wicked is coming," he said to no one in particular.

The woman behind the counter stepped out, wiping hands on her apron. Stood beside him as vehicle after vehicle passed. Pickups with mud-caked tires. SUVs with darkened windows. Panel vans bearing commercial logos that didn't match their movements. They kept coming, a river of metal and purpose flowing through the town that had seen nothing like it since logging operations shut down decades before.

"What you reckon that is?" she asked.

The old man shook his head. "Nothing good."

By noon, the residents of May had counted over two hundred vehicles passing through. Men in the vehicles stared straight ahead, faces set with determination or something harder. Gun racks visible through rear windows. Antennas mounted to some vehicles suggesting communications beyond normal civilian requirements. License plates from ten western states, some obscured with mud that seemed deliberately applied.

Eleanor locked the general store early. Called her sister in Challis. Told her something strange was happening. Then, the line went dead.

They worked in broad daylight, trucks bearing utility company logos that wouldn't raise questions. Militia in reflective vests and hard hats moved with bureaucratic confidence no local would challenge. The first team parked beside the telephone junction box at the town's edge, orange cones establishing perimeter that kept curious eyes at distance. They severed main lines with industrial cutters while one man spoke into a radio that transmitted nothing, pantomiming official communication. The second team disabled the cell tower on Wilson Ridge, climbing with safety harnesses and toolboxes containing small charges they placed at critical junctures. The third team blocked the access road to the backup tower with signs announcing scheduled maintenance, methodically removing transmission components residents wouldn't recognize as vital. Locals drove past with casual glances, witnessing invisible siege conducted through infrastructure's quiet dismantling, the deliberate creation of silence disguised as routine work.

The town of May found itself suddenly isolated from outside communication. Unable to call authorities if help was needed.

Ten miles north, the convoy approached the NSA facility. Vehicles dispersed into predetermined formations. Advance teams moved ahead on foot, securing the perimeter. Armed men in civilian clothes but military posture swept the area with practiced efficiency. Hand signals and radio clicks guiding movement where voices might attract attention.

The main gate fell without resistance. The chain-link

fence, rusted from decades of weather, yielded to bolt cutters applied at precisely measured intervals. Twenty men converged on the entrance, clearing the way for vehicles that followed. All-terrain forklifts. Backhoes. Construction equipment painted in non-military colors began digging defensive trenches and forming dirt berms to give fire teams height advantage against any approaching intruders.

Walker's truck stopped at the administration building. He stepped out, surveyed the operation unfolding around him. Five hundred men now deployed across the facility grounds. Men with purpose. Men with training. Men with belief solid as the mountains surrounding them.

"Begin Phase Two," Walker said into his radio.

The first container trucks arrived at 1430 hours. Massive diesels pulling commercial shipping containers on flatbed trailers identical to millions moving across American highways daily. The drivers backed them into position with exactness born of rehearsal. Container doors opened to reveal not commercial goods but the arsenal stolen from Camp Pendleton weeks before.

Men swarmed the containers like worker ants, unloading weapons with practiced efficiency. M27 rifles passed hand to hand, each finding designated owner who immediately checked function, loaded magazine, chambered a round. Barrett sniper rifles distributed to men who moved toward high points surrounding the facility, some climbing to shooting platforms built in trees. Their movements revealing training beyond civilian shooting ranges.

"Defensive positions," Walker ordered.

The backhoes began digging. Three concentric rings around the facility. Men with shovels widened the trenches, created fighting positions at calculated intervals. Pallet after pallet of sandbags—9,000 in total—materialized from trucks. The triple-layer barriers rose under practiced hands. Interlocking fields of fire established. Killing zones measured in yards by men who understood such calculations intimately. Men replaced the dilapidated gates and perimeter fence with new chain link capped with razor wire.

Scout teams deployed into surrounding territory. Four-man fire teams moving in grid patterns through forest and scrubland. Former Army Rangers and reconnaissance specialists establishing observation posts on ridgelines within a five-mile radius. Men who understood terrain. Who knew how to become invisible within it. Who could provide early warning of approaching threat from any direction.

"Alpha Team in position," crackled a radio from the northern ridge. "Clear lines of sight to highway approach."

"Bravo Team established on eastern saddle," reported another. "No movement."

Walker studied the tactical display where each team's position appeared as blue dot on topographical rendering. Multiple observation posts creating security bubble beyond the facility's immediate perimeter. Men with thermal imaging equipment, encrypted radios, and supply caches sufficient for seventy-two hours without resupply.

Stinger missile teams established positions at compass points. The shoulder-fired anti-aircraft systems capable of denying airspace to anything below 20,000 feet. AT4 anti-tank weapons positioned to cover approach roads. Demolition teams planted shaped charges at strategic points—not to destroy but to channel any attacking force into prepared kill zones.

Inside the main building, technicians attacked the

electrical systems. Dust cleared from panels. Specialized equipment brought online. Generators humming as they restored power to systems dormant for decades. The NSA facility awakening under new management.

By dusk, the NSA facility had transformed from abandoned government relic to fortified compound. Sandbag emplacements three layers thick surrounding critical positions. Fighting holes occupied by men with military-grade weapons and communications. Power systems humming with renewed purpose as generators fed electricity to dormant systems.

Snipers in ghillie suits blended with the surrounding landscape, their Barrett rifles capable of engaging targets beyond a mile's distance. Stinger teams maintained watch rotations, their missile systems ready to transform approaching aircraft into falling debris. The defensive perimeter established with overlapping fields of fire that would make conventional assault prohibitively costly.

The outer security perimeter extended miles beyond the facility itself. Fire teams positioned at natural choke points. Men with night vision equipment watching access routes. Special operations veterans who understood surveillance. Who knew how to remain undetected while observing. Who could disappear into mountain terrain at moment's notice if necessary.

"Ridgeline teams reporting status green," the operations officer informed Walker. "IR sensors emplaced at all approach vectors."

Walker nodded. "Seismic?"

"Grid established. Anything larger than coyote triggers alert."

Inside the main command center, Walker gathered his lieutenants. Maps spread across tables once used by government technicians. Satellite imagery showing the facility and surrounding terrain. Defense positions marked in red. Fallback points in blue. Everything calculated with professional military planning.

"Communications blackout extends thirty miles in all directions," reported the signals officer. "Any attempt to report our presence will fail. Landlines cut. Cell towers disabled. Radio frequencies jammed."

Walker nodded. "Satellite coverage?"

"Next pass in forty-seven minutes. We'll be visible then."

Militia leaders from ten western states stood around the table. Men who had planned this moment for years. Who had recruited and trained with this specific objective. Who believed themselves patriots even as they prepared acts that any government would classify as highest treason.

The NSA facility—designed during an earlier era of existential threat—now served new masters with the same apocalyptic potential. The compound glowed with renewed purpose, its lights visible for miles across the Pahsimeroi Valley.

In May, residents watched the glow on the northern horizon. Gathered on porches and street corners, speaking in hushed voices about the convoy that had passed through. About the sudden silence of phones and internet. About the helicopters they'd seen flying northward.

"Government will come," said the old man on the general store porch, still nursing his coffee gone cold hours before.

The woman beside him nodded slowly. "Question is, what happens when they do?"

The answer waited thirteen miles north, where Walker's men had transformed an abandoned communications facility into an armed compound. Where sandbags rose three layers thick in defensive rings. Where weapons stolen from military arsenal now pointed outward, ready to receive whatever force might come to challenge their presence.

Walker stood on the facility roof, surveying the perimeter now secured beneath pools of generator powered light. Hundreds of men with military training guarding the perimeter. Security teams watching from surrounding ridgelines and forests. Communications equipment capable of monitoring government response. The second phase completed.

The secession of the western states was no longer theoretical. It had taken physical form in concrete and steel, in sandbags and defensive positions, in men willing to die for a belief wrapped in patriotism's flag. The die had been cast. The first moves made. The response would come soon enough.

The Georgetown townhouse sat quiet beneath the afternoon rain, red brick darkened by steady drops, windows revealing nothing of activity within. Culper's office occupied the second floor, walls insulated against electronic surveillance, zero-emission protocols in place. The kind of room where government business occurred without government acknowledgment.

The encrypted phone rang once. Culper lifted it without checking the display. Only three people possessed this number. All with information that couldn't wait.

"Speak," he said.

"Transmission incoming. Priority Alpha." The voice belonged to his deputy director of operations. Tone suggesting urgency beyond standard parameters.

Culper's computer chimed, indicating secure transfer

initiated. He entered sixteen-digit authorization code, watched encryption barriers dissolve, file transfer percentage climbing across screen.

"Source?" he asked.

"KH-11 satellite. Routine pass over western U.S. Nothing routine about what it found."

The download completed. Culper opened image files, each bearing a time-stamp from two hours previous. Aerial photographs showing the abandoned NSA facility in Idaho's Pahsimeroi Valley. No longer abandoned.

"Jesus Christ," he whispered.

The facility perimeter showed concentric rings of defensive positions. Sandbags arranged in military configuration. Armed men visible at established intervals. Vehicles parked in tactical formation around the compound. The unmistakable signature of professional operation.

"Asset count?" Culper asked, scrolling through subsequent images showing wider perimeter.

"Preliminary estimate 400 plus. Thermal imaging of surrounding terrain suggests closer to 500. Defensive posture consistent with former military personnel."

Culper enhanced sections of the photographs. Observation posts on surrounding ridgelines. Patrol patterns establishing security perimeter extending miles beyond the facility itself. Not random. Not amateur. Methodical security implemented by men who understood the principles.

"Weapons assessment?"

"Matches inventory stolen from Camp Pendleton. Small arms. Crew-served. Anti-aircraft capability in the form of Stinger systems at compass points. They're prepared to deny airspace to conventional response."

Culper stared at the screen for precisely ten seconds. Reached decision with the same clarity that had kept him alive through three decades of shadows and violence. "Get me the White House. Slattery's direct line."

Eight minutes later, the White House Chief of Staff's voice filled his secure office. No pleasantries exchanged. Time belonged to national security now, not protocol.

"I'm looking at the images now," Slattery said.

"Assessment?"

"Five hundred personnel minimum. Former military from multiple branches. Defensive posture suggesting expectation of armed response." Culper's voice carried the dispassion of professional analysis. "They've established three perimeter rings with overlapping fields of fire. Observation posts on surrounding high ground. Tactical positioning indicating leadership with combat command experience."

Silence on the line as the Chief of Staff digested information. Then: "Walker?"

"Almost certainly. We've been tracking his movements for months. The formation matches his known tactical preferences."

Slattery exhaled slowly. The sound of a man recognizing weight descending that couldn't be avoided or redistributed. "Options?"

"FBI Hostage Rescue Team could deploy within four hours. Delta Force within six." Culper laid out standard protocol. "Full military response would require presidential authorization under Posse Comitatus exceptions."

"No." Slattery's voice hardened. "The President is adamant we're not creating another Waco. Not another Ruby Ridge. No massive federal response that turns these people into martyrs."

"With respect, this is significantly beyond those incidents in scale and capability."

"Which is precisely why we need surgical approach,

not sledgehammers." Keyboard clicks audible as Slattery reviewed additional imagery. "Those media vultures would swarm before the first shot. Every militia group in the country would see it as vindication of federal overreach. Recruitment would spike. We'd be creating the very threat we're trying to prevent."

Culper waited. Let the Chief of Staff reach the conclusion already forming in both their minds.

"The President wants you to handle this directly," Slattery said finally. "Your team. Your methods. Off the books."

"Sir, the legal—"

"He'll worry about the legal framework when we succeed. No official agencies. No paper trail. If these people have the weapons stolen from Pendleton, they could inflict significant casualties on conventional response forces. That's not acceptable."

Culper nodded though no one could see it.

"Understood."

"Do you have assets inside?" Slattery asked.

Culper hesitated, the fraction of a second that spoke volumes about operational security. "I have resources deployed," he said, the calculated vagueness deliberate. "No contact in seventy-two hours."

Slattery didn't press. Understood the unwritten rule of their relationship – Culper's operational methods remained his own domain, results the only currency that mattered. "Whatever, Walker's planning goes beyond armed standoff. The NSA facility suggests communication capability as primary objective rather than defensive position."

"Agreed," Culper said. "The strategic value lies in what the facility connects to, not the structure itself."

"Handle it," Slattery said. "Quietly. Effectively. Keep me informed through this channel only. No paper. No briefing books. No interagency communication until resolved. The President needs this contained before it becomes impossible to manage discreetly."

"Yes, sir."

The line went dead. Culper sat motionless for precisely thirty seconds, rain still tapping against windows like nature's own countdown timer. Then lifted his secure phone again, dialed the number only four people on earth possessed.

"Standby for operational alert," he said when his deputy director answered. "Begin personnel recall. Full discretionary parameters."

"Timeline?"

"Immediate. Assemble at Site Three. No electronic communications beyond initial contact." "Understood," came the reply.

"I need deeper intelligence before full briefing," Culper added. "Have Anderson prep aerial reconnaissance package. Low observable platform. I want eyes inside that compound within twelve hours."

The call ended. Culper turned again to the satellite imagery showing 500 men who believed themselves patriots transforming government property into an armed compound. Men with training. With weapons. With belief toxic as radiation when concentrated beyond safety parameters.

His mind shifted to his operative inside Walker's organization. A man whose existence remained unknown even to Slattery. A weapon deployed when normal channels proved insufficient. A last resort who operated beyond official accountability. Whatever had prevented communication created another variable in an equation already overwrought with unknowns.

The rain continued falling on Georgetown streets. On Idaho mountains. On a nation whose history had just found a new chapter being written in an abandoned facility where old ghosts and new grievances now danced together, their movements visible only from space and from the watchful eyes of men like Culper who lived in shadows between official existence and necessary deniability.

Shadows grew long as the sunset. The troop car swayed beneath the soldiers' boots, the monotonous clack of steel wheels against rail joinings marking time like a metronome. PFC Miller pressed his forehead against the window, watching sagebrush and scattered pine trees slide past. Nothing moved out there except occasional clusters of cattle, their heads lifting briefly to watch the train before returning to the serious business of chewing. "How much longer?" he asked nobody in particular.

"Twenty-one hours give or take," replied Corporal Diaz without looking up from his paperback. "Unless we derail, then it's forever."

"Jesus, man. Don't even joke about that," said Specialist Sanchez, rubbing the silver crucifix hanging from his neck.

Master Sergeant Reeves moved down the center aisle, his shadow falling across each soldier in turn. His voice carried above the train's constant rumble. "Eyes up, gentlemen. Just because we're in the middle of nowhere doesn't mean we're alone. Stinger teams rotating in thirty. AT4s check your gear."

A few soldiers straightened in their seats, adjusting body armor that had been loosened against the boxcar's stifling heat. Most continued their slumped vigil, eyes fighting the hypnotic rhythm of motion and boredom.

"Reeves thinks Taliban's gonna pop out behind a tumbleweed," whispered Rivera to Chen. "Man needs to switch to decaf."

"I heard that, Rivera. Two extra watches for you," Reeves called without turning. "Anybody else feeling chatty?"

Silence answered him except for the train's mechanical breathing.

Twenty miles ahead, Heller positioned the second crane beside the railroad tracks, hydraulic stabilizers extending outward like mechanical talons biting into gravel. Behind him, six men unloaded steel plates from flatbed trucks, laying them across soft ground where the crane treads would need to maneuver.

"Hurry up with those plates," he ordered. "Train's on schedule."

"Plates are down. Stabilizers secure," a voice called back. "Radio check with all positions."

His radio crackled with confirmations. Eight teams spread along five miles of track, each with assigned tasks that would unfold in sequence once the train appeared.

Twelve miles up the rail line, Frank crouched behind granite boulders overlooking the switch point where main track met abandoned mining spur. Three men waited with him, their breathing controlled despite the elevation and anticipation. The fourth man lay fifty yards distant, ghillie suit blending with scrub brush, eye pressed to rifle scope watching the empty track disappearing around a distant curve.

A fifth team member worked silently atop the cliff face, positioning the communication jammer where its signal would blanket the entire valley. The black metal box hummed to life, its antennas extending like insect feelers seeking frequencies to disrupt.

"Jammer active," came the whispered confirmation

through their earpieces. "Military bands blocked in five mile radius."

Below the ridge, pressed against earth in a natural depression, the switch operator waited. His hands steady despite adrenaline coursing through his veins. The manual switch lever lay beside him, oiled hours earlier to ensure silent operation when the moment came.

The spotter's hand raised. Three fingers. Train approaching.

Frank checked his watch. Right on time. His massive frame unfolded from behind the boulder, moving with unexpected grace for a man his size. As per Walker's orders, he was unarmed except for his fists. They were more than enough in most cases.

"Switch after separation," he rasped to the communications officer beside him.

"Message relayed," came the whispered response.

The distant horn sounded, mournful across the empty landscape.

Frank's team moved into position, bodies pressed against the cliff where the track cut through hillside, a natural blind spot for both engineer and security detail.

The locomotive's rumble grew, vibrations traveling through rock and soil before the engine itself appeared. Black diesel behemoth pulling steel cargo with industrial determination. The engineer's cab passed, followed by the diesel tender, then the front troop car where armed guards maintained watch. The sentry posted on its roof gazed forward, searching the horizon for threats from that direction, never thinking to look behind.

Behind the front troop car rolled four flatbeds, each carrying components of the Patriot missile system under canvas covers. The train slowed as it began the grade, diesel engine laboring against combined weight and incline. Next came the rear troop car carrying the remainder of the security detail. The caboose with Lieutenant Torres monitoring operations from inside formed the final car, a single guard patrolling its roof.

At the switch point, the operator saw his moment. As the caboose cleared the junction, he threw the lever with practiced motion. Steel rails shifted position, main line now disconnected, spur line engaged.

Frank signaled. The four men moved as one, cliff in a coordinated surge. They cleared the lip just as the rear troop car passed beneath.

The guard on the caboose never saw what hit him. Frank's boots connected with the man's chest, sending him tumbling from the roof into trackside brush. The guard's rifle clattered against the caboose's metal roof before following its owner into the underbrush.

Frank landed in a crouch, absorbing impact through bent knees. The other team members landed seconds later, each finding balance despite the train's motion. The guard's unconscious body disappeared behind them as the train continued its uphill journey.

Inside the caboose Torres heard the boots landing on the roof. He listened and heard nothing more. He ignored it thinking it was the clumsy guard.

Without pausing, Frank swung down from the caboose roof to its side ladder. The brake tool already in hand, he found the manual release valve. Twisted it with precise quarter turns. Air escaped in a steady stream, pressure dropping below threshold needed for mechanical engagement. The caboose's braking system went silent, hydraulics rendered mute against steel wheels. Frank moved beneath the coupled cars, body suspended inches above gravel that would tear flesh from bone at this speed. He reached the rear troop car's undercarriage, scarred hands finding the main pressure tank. The brake tool connected to release valve with machinist's meticulousness. Air bled from the system in controlled hemorrhage, making sound like final breath escaping dead lungs.

Above, his team crawled across the troop car's roof. Four men moving with silence born of practice and necessity.

The soldiers inside continued card games and half slept, unaware of death's passage just feet above their heads. Radio chatter and engine rumble masked any sound the men might have made.

Frank reached the coupling between the rear troop car and flatbed. His hands found the release mechanism. Applied pressure that should have separated steel from steel. The lever resisted, jammed between positions by weight and momentum working against mechanical design. He pushed harder. Metal groaned but held. "Problem?" The whispered question came through the earpiece.

"Coupling jammed," he replied, words barely audible above rushing wind.

Footsteps approached along the flatbed's edge. Militia man appeared at coupling, face questioned without words. Frank motioned to the stuck mechanism. The militia man nodded. Frank braced one foot against troop car, the other against flatbed. His massive hands gripped both cars, muscles bunching beneath his shirt. He pulled them together, slightly narrowing the gap that stressed coupling mechanism beyond tolerance. Weight momentarily equalized between cars. The militia man seized opportunity. Hands worked release lever now freed from pressure. Metal surrendered with mechanical reluctance. The coupling separated with sound like bones breaking. Air hose between cars disconnected, final pressure escaping in serpent's angry hiss. The militia man was still on the flatbed car as the two cars separated.

The gap appeared. First inches. Then feet. Distance expanding between rear troop car and flatbed.

Frank pushed away from the troop car, body suspended momentarily above racing ground. He pulled himself over to the flatbed car.

"Brakes disabled on all flatbeds," came confirmation through radio.

The rear troop car fell behind, soldiers inside still unaware of what transpired. Distance widened like a wound between severed things.

Frank rose to crouching position, watched as night swallowed their security detail. So far, so good.

The troop car and caboose continued forward briefly, momentum carrying them up the incline. Then physics asserted itself against steel and men. The cars slowed, momentum lost without engine's pull. They paused, seeming to hesitate, then began rolling backward down the grade.

Inside the troop car, confusion erupted. Master Sergeant Reeves felt the deceleration before understanding its cause. His hand grabbed for radio that wouldn't respond, jammer on the cliff face ensuring communication blackout.

"We're uncoupled!" he shouted above the soldiers' confused voices. "Emergency brake! Now!"

But the emergency brake yielded nothing when activated, air system bled dry by Frank's earlier work. The cars gathered speed moving backward, rails singing beneath steel wheels spinning in reverse.

Frank and his team crouched low on the flatbed, watching as the troop car and caboose receded down the grade, distance expanding with each second.

The caboose hit the switch at speed, wheels finding new direction along the spur's path. The troop car followed, both cars disappearing into the abandoned mining branch, soldier's confused shouts fading with distance.

"Switch reset," the switch operator confirmed through his radio, throwing the lever back to reconnect the main line for the eventual return journey. The rails shifted again, ensuring the train's forward path remained clear.

Reeves grabbed the manual brake wheel at the troop car's end, muscles straining against mechanical resistance. The wheel turned grudgingly, brake shoes pressing against wheels. Sparks erupted beneath the car. The deceleration threw men against seats and walls, curses filling the closed space.

The cars slowed, then stopped, two miles down the mining spur. Outside lay nothing but empty landscape and rust-colored hills. Reeves tried the radio again. Static answered.

"Comms are down," he announced. "We've been separated and diverted."

Lieutenant Torres appeared from the caboose, face flushed with anger and confusion. "What the hell happened?"

"Sabotage, sir. Someone cut us loose," Reeves replied. "We need to get back to the main track. Find out what's happening with the Patriot system."

Torres assessed the situation with quick efficiency. "Gear up. Full combat load. We're double-timing back to the main line."

Soldiers grabbed weapons, checked magazines, secured equipment against their bodies. The car door opened to empty wilderness, no signs of civilization visible except the rusted rails beneath them.

"Move out!" Torres ordered. "Two-by-two formation. Security perimeter as we advance."

Eighteen men leapt from the stranded cars, boots hitting gravel beside the tracks. They formed up, weapons ready, eyes scanning surrounding terrain for threats. Reeves checked his watch, calculated distance versus speed.

"Two miles back to the junction, sir," he reported. "Twelve minutes at double-time."

Torres nodded grimly. "Then we've got no time to waste. Forward march!"

The security detail began their run along the abandoned spur, boots crunching against gravel and rotting ties. Behind them, the empty cars sat like beached whales, useless and immobile on tracks that led nowhere.

Frank climbed forward along the train's underside, body suspended in darkness between steel and rushing earth. His hands found purchase where none should exist.

Every muscle working against gravity and momentum with mechanical disregard for human limitation.

He reached the coupling between front troop car and first flatbed. The space where forward security element met cargo they were sworn to protect.

The door above him swung outward. Metal against metal. Light spilled from troop car interior across small platform where soldiers sometimes stood for air when claustrophobia claimed them. Boots appeared. Then uniform pants. A soldier stepped out, unlit cigarette dangling from lips, cupped hand sheltering lighter from wind that tore through mountain pass. The soldier never saw what waited below.

Frank's hand shot upward. Found uniform fabric.

Closed like a vise around material never designed to bear such weight. The soldier had time only for confusion before the cigarette fell from his mouth. Frank yanked sideways with force that spoke of purpose rather than rage. The soldier left the platform as if gravity had suddenly shifted orientation. His body suspended briefly in night air before disappearing into trackside darkness without sound to mark his passing.

"Coupling," Frank grunted into radio.

One militia man appeared, having traversed the flatbed with practiced stealth. He nodded to Frank that he was ready.

Frank positioned himself against both cars. Legs spread to brace against opposing forces. His hands gripped metal never meant for human contact. He pulled inward, massive frame becoming piston working against mechanical design. The cars drew together, pressure on coupling mechanism momentarily relieved. The militia man worked quickly. Hands finding release lever now yielded to human intervention. The mechanism surrendered with sound like metal fatigue given voice.

Coupling separated. Air hose between cars disconnected with final angry exhalation.

The forward troop car maintained speed, still connected to the locomotive that pulled it westward with industrial indifference. The flatbeds hesitated. Momentum carrying them forward briefly before physics asserted primary claim. They slowed. Stopped. Then began its backward journey.

The grade beneath rails became ally rather than obstacle. Gravity pulled steel wheels into rotation opposite their intended direction. The flatbeds gathered speed, rails singing beneath them as velocity increased beyond safety's recommendation.

Frank and his four-man team rode the accelerating

cars. Bodies pressed low against steel that vibrated with gathering momentum. Wind tore at clothing, at exposed skin, at anything not secured. Their speed increased with each passing second, controlled fall down mountain grade that had taken locomotive's full power to climb.

Around the final curve they came. The junction to the mining spur appeared ahead. And with it, security detail just arrived from diverted cars. Soldiers who had run two miles along the abandoned mining spur, weapons ready, faces set with purpose undermined by timing's cruel mathematics.

The flatbeds flashed past the junction. Steel wheels striking rail seams with percussive certainty. The soldiers could only watch as Patriot missile system components rode gravity's insistence toward valley floor where Heller waited with cranes already deployed. Some raised weapons instinctively. Lowered them with realization that bullets meant nothing against physics now fully engaged. They did not want to miss and hit the Patriot system.

The last flatbed cleared the junction. Distance opened between soldiers and mission now beyond their reach.

The men stood motionless. Breath visible in cold mountain air. Rifles useless against disaster already concluded. Lieutenant Torres spoke into the radio that returned only static, jammer on ridgeline ensuring their isolation remained complete.

The flatbeds continued their descent. Speed regulated only by grade's gradual relaxation as they approached valley floor. Frank's plan executed. The calculations made prior now proven accurate against reality's unforgiving test. The cars slowed as grade leveled. Momentum bleeding away without engine's push. Frank grabbed the manual brake wheel and engaged the brake shoes. They rolled to stop exactly where predicted, where cranes waited to receive government property now claimed by men with different purpose.

Behind them, the security detail began their renewed descent. Boots striking wooden ties with rhythmic futility. Their charge already lost to shadow force that had calculated their response with mathematical certainty. The operation continued, time counting down until wider forces mobilized against the theft already complete.

The cranes stood like primordial beasts in moon shadow, steel arms extended toward the flatbeds on the track. Heller checked his watch. Three minutes ahead of schedule.

Frank appeared from lead flatbed car, massive frame descending.

"Begin offload," Heller ordered through radio.

Men swarmed the flatbeds. Some secured lifting straps beneath canvas coverings. Others connected chains to reinforced anchor points designed for precisely this purpose. The first crane operator extended his boom and lowered the tackle block.

"Radar assembly first," Heller directed. "Cable tension at forty percent until clear of mounting brackets."

The canvas fell away, revealing the Patriot system's electronic eye. Ten tons of technology designed to see death approaching from beyond the horizon. The crane cables tightened. Metal groaned against sudden weight. The radar assembly rose from the flatbed car.

Heller watched Frank directing placement with hand signals that required no verbal elaboration. The giant's fingers indicating adjustments measured in inches not feet. The radar component and its trailer settled onto a reinforced semi-truck trailer. Local plates. Mud strategically applied to obscure identification numbers. A dozen men covered the radar and its military green trailer with tarps, then strapped it down securing the load. The truck and its stolen cargo sped off toward a nearby forest that would hide the equipment as it traveled.

"Engagement control station next," Heller commanded.

The second crane positioned above flatbed carrying the system's brain. The component that made radar information useful rather than abstract. That translated electronic signature into targeting data.

Men secured lifting straps and chains. The crane lifted, cables strained against resistance then surrendered. The multi-million-dollar component and trailer swung over to a waiting truck trailer. Same process. Tarps. Straps. The truck and cargo took off for the forest.

The two remaining components – the generator and the launcher were loaded onto trailers as the time clicked down before the military response arrived. The trucks sped off. The final truck trailer accepted the missiles in their containers. More tarps and straps. Secured, the driver took off for the forest.

It all had happened in less than twenty minutes. A well-planned and audacious heist. The stolen cranes were abandoned.

The men loaded up in civilian pickup trucks along with Frank and Heller. When the last man climbed in, the drivers took off for the forest. All that was left were the empty flatbed cars and the wind.

The stolen Patriots headed toward rendezvous point twenty-four miles distant where final concealment would occur.

An abandoned steelworks waited in an industrial zone forgotten when manufacturing fled overseas. Red brick fortress with rusted sign still proclaiming WESTERN

MOUNTAIN STEEL AND IRON. A single massive roll-up door stood central in main building facade, thirty feet high and twenty wide, designed for rail cars that once delivered raw materials.

The first giant turbine blade on its transport trailers already waited in position. Its specialized trailer bearing the blade's hollow composite shell extending through factory door and into yard beyond. Two drivers coordinated movement – one in the truck cab, another in the steering station on the rear trailer designed for navigating oversized loads through difficult terrain. Frank directed operations from the factory floor. His eyes missing nothing as technicians prepared the blade's interior according to specifications measured against Patriot system components.

"First transport approaching," announced the lookout. The truck carrying radar assembly entered through secondary gate, navigating concrete expanse once used for cooling steel, now cracked from winters without maintenance. It backed toward the waiting blade inside the factory, positioning precisely where overhead crane could transfer its cargo. Men swarmed removing the straps and tarps freeing the cargo.

The crane lifted the radar assembly from the truck's flatbed. Swung its massive hook toward the blade opening like a surgical patient awaiting implantation. Inside the blade, metal rails had been attached to the interior. The radar descended into the composite cavity with just millimeters of clearance. A large forklift carefully pushed the radar system on the interior rails sliding it deep within the blade. Technicians inside the blade, secured the radar component with quick-setting foam and customized brackets designed for perfect fit despite transportation's inevitable movement.

"Missiles," Frank said, the word barely audible above

machinery's noise.

Heller nodded. Spoke into the radio clipped to vest. "Bring in the missile containers."

As the first truck and trailer backed out of the factory door, another truck and trailer backed in. The straps and tarps were removed to reveal twelve missile containers arranged in precise rows. Each sealed in military transport configuration. Each capable of delivering death to aircraft or incoming projectiles with equal efficiency.

"Careful," Heller commanded as the overhead crane engaged the first container. The missiles represented the system's actual offensive capability. The radar found targets. The control station processed information. The launcher aimed. But these sleek containers delivered the promise all other components merely supported.

Frank directed placement of the missile containers behind the radar assembly inside the turbine blade. His hands indicating exact position where weight distribution would maintain the blade's expected balance while concealing the deadly cargo. The containers slid into reinforced mounting cradles.

Technicians secured each container with locking brackets and stabilizing foam. The weight arranged precisely along blade's central axis that would pass casual inspection. Nothing that would trigger deeper investigation during transport.

"All missiles secured," announced the lead technician. Frank checked his watch. Schedule maintained. The blade would still appear as nothing more than renewable energy component to any observer without reason to cut through composite shell.

"Seal it," he commanded.

The giant metal cap was lowered into place on back of the blade. Welders sealed the cap to the blade preventing spying eyes. A militia man with a spray gun painted the welding seams white to hide the recent welding. Once Frank was satisfied, he ordered the truck and two trailers on their way to the NSA facility.

As the first blade left the steelworks, the second turbine blade was backed into place inside the building and the loading process continued.

When the final blade was sealed with the components inside, Heller ordered his men to close up shop leaving no evidence behind. The militia men obeyed. Nobody fucked Heller.

"Air assets mobilizing," came report from a communication technician monitoring the radio waves. "Helicopter lifting from eastern base. ETA fifteen minutes."

Heller turned to Frank and said, "Good timing." Frank grunted in response.

The militia men and their equipment piled into pickup trucks for the journey back to the NSA facility.

Frank piled into the backseat of a four-door truck with a "Wide Load" sign that would follow the last turbine blade. Heller followed and climbed in next to him. Walker had obviously order Heller to keep an eye on Frank. The driver drove off in pursuit of the last turbine blade already several miles up the highway.

Lead by a front truck with "wide load" sign on the roof, the convoy inched forward on the paved road—massive flatbeds and back trailers carrying the three wind turbines followed by the rear truck with its "wide load" sign mounted on the roof. The afternoon sun cast long shadows across the valley as they rounded a bend, a river glittering below.

"Roadblock ahead," the driver announced.

Two Humvees with machine gun turrets were positioned across the road, creating a checkpoint. Four soldiers in full combat gear stood on the road, their M4 carbines held at the ready. A fifth soldier—an officer by the insignia—waved the lead flatbed to a stop.

In the backseat of the trailing truck, Heller leaned forward. "Military. Not local police."

Frank's eyes narrowed as he studied the checkpoint, his jaw clenching slightly.

"Relax," Heller said, though his own posture remained rigid. "Our paperwork's solid. Wind farm maintenance crew, all above board."

The driver rolled down his window as a soldier approached. "Afternoon," the driver said, voice steady. "What's going on?"

"Routine checkpoint, sir," the soldier replied. "I'll need to see some identification and transport documents."

"Sure thing." The driver handed over a leather folder. "We're with Northwest Energy. Transporting wind turbine components to the Clearwater farm."

From the backseat, Frank watched as another soldier circled the first flatbed, inspecting the massive cylindrical turbine section. He seemed satisfied and moved to the second truck.

"Papers look in order," the soldier at the window said, handing back the folder. "We need to take a quick look at your cargo?"

"Go right ahead," the driver replied.

Frank and Heller exchanged a glance as the soldiers spread out, examining each flatbed. Two of them approached the third turbine.

Through the windshield, they watched as one soldier circled the turbine section while another climbed the small ladder attached to the flatbed. The soldier ran his hand along the turbine's surface, stopping at the rear cap.

"Hey, Miller," he called to his companion. "Come

look at this."

Miller climbed up beside him. "What is it?"

"This cap. Doesn't match the specs on the manifest. Different material."

The first soldier tapped the cap with his knuckles, producing a hollow sound. "Sounds off too."

Heller's hand slid inside his jacket, fingers wrapping around the grip of his pistol. Frank, sensing the movement, shot a sideways glance at Heller.

"Hold," Frank muttered, barely audible.

"They're going to find it," Heller whispered back, easing the weapon from its holster.

Without warning, Frank's hand clamped down on Heller's wrist like a steel trap. Heller tried to pull away, but Frank's grip only tightened, grinding the small bones beneath his skin.

Heller turned, finding Frank's cold stare fixed on him. Frank gave a single, deliberate shake of his head.

Outside, Miller was running his fingers along the seam of the cap. "Probably just a replacement part. Different manufacturer."

"Should we open it?" the first soldier asked.

"Nah," Miller replied after a moment's consideration. "Manifest says these are sealed units. Breaking the seal would void the warranty. Company would raise hell."

Frank maintained his vice-like grip on Heller's wrist, never breaking eye contact. A bead of sweat rolled down Heller's temple.

"Fine," Heller hissed through clenched teeth.

The soldiers climbed down from the flatbed. Frank slowly released his grip, and Heller quickly tucked the pistol under his thigh, out of sight.

"You just signed our death warrants if they find it," Heller whispered.

The officer approached the truck, peering in through

the driver's window. "And who do we have back here?"

"Technical specialists," the driver answered smoothly. "For the installation."

The officer leaned down, looking directly at Frank and Heller in the backseat. "Gentlemen."

Frank nodded once. Heller forced a professional smile. "Just eager to get to the site before dark, sir. Transporting these beasts can be tricky in low light."

The officer studied them for a long moment. "You look familiar," he said to Frank.

Frank stared back, expression unchanged, said nothing.

The officer's radio crackled. "Lieutenant, we've got another vehicle approaching from the north."

"Copy that." The officer straightened up. "You're clear to proceed. Stay on the designated route to the wind farm."

"Yes, sir. Thank you," the driver said, already putting the truck in gear.

As they pulled away, the convoy resuming its slow progress down the road, Heller turned to Frank, his face flushed with anger.

"Pull that again, and I'll kill you," he said, voice low but trembling with rage.

Frank glanced out the window at a ridgeline. "Sniper."

Heller blinked, then turned to look back. Sure enough, the glint of a scope was just visible on the rocky outcropping above the checkpoint.

"Next time," Heller said, adjusting his jacket, "let me handle it. That's what Walker pays me for."

Frank returned to staring at the river below, his expression giving away nothing of the calculation happening behind his eyes.

The convoy continued down the road, the afternoon sun at their backs, the NSA facility still miles ahead through the thick Idaho forest.

The Pentagon operations center hummed with controlled tension. Air Force General Carlton Hayes stood before a wall of screens displaying satellite imagery, each frame tagged with timestamps no more than eleven minutes old. Behind him three intelligence officers scanned readouts while a signals sergeant monitored communications traffic. Nobody spoke above necessity.

Lieutenant Abrams, the team leader approached General Hayes with tablet extended. His face suggesting information requiring immediate attention. "SIGINT intercept from NSA facility in Pahsimeroi Valley."

Hayes took the device without looking up from deployment schedules already consuming his attention.

"That facility's been decommissioned since the nineties."

"Yes, sir. That's why the transmissions were flagged priority."

Hayes studied the report. His expression hardening as implications registered. Communications traffic where none should exist. Power signatures from dormant generators suddenly active. Thermal blooms indicating human presence within abandoned government structure.

"Cross-reference with domestic terrorist watch list," Hayes ordered.

Abrams touched the tablet's screen, linking separate intelligence streams. "Multiple matches, General. License plates identified entering Pahsimeroi area last seventy-two hours. Vehicles registered to known militia members from Idaho, Montana, Wyoming, Oregon. Some with military backgrounds."

Hayes set aside scheduling conflicts that had occupied him for the previous hour. New priority emerging with clarity that eliminated competing concerns. "Any relation to the Patriot theft?"

"Analysis suggests seventy-three percent probability, sir. Timeline matches. Resource allocation consistent with securing a remote facility for weapons deployment."

Hayes stood. Crossed to wall map displaying western United States. His finger traced route from Colorado where the Patriots were taken to Pahsimeroi Valley, Idaho. The pattern emerging like constellations from seemingly random stars. "The Patriots aren't heading for border or coastal target."

"Sir?"

"They've found themselves a fortress," Hayes said, tapping Idaho location. "Remote. Defensible. Abandoned government facility with existing

infrastructure. Perfect staging ground."

Abrams added final confirmation. "Satellite thermal shows 500 plus human signatures at location. Consistent with multi-state militia convergence."

Hayes returned to command console. "Notify Mountain Home AFB. I want a platoon-sized assault team from Air Force Special Warfare on standby ASAP. They are to rendezvous with a AC-130J Ghostrider from

Cannon AFB as support element."

"General, if the militias don't surrender our forces would be attacking American citizens on American soil," said Abrams.

"Our troops have already been attacked when the Patriots were taken. Our troops are within their rights to defend themselves against these bastards."

"Of course, General. Do we need any further authority to approve the mission?"

"Negative. Air Force weapons were stolen. The Air

Force will get them back. I have all the authority I need." "Rules of engagement?"

Hayes considered response weighted with implications beyond tactical parameters. A potential constitutional crisis regardless of outcome. Congress would howl. But stolen military hardware represented line crossed beyond political debate.

"Recover the Patriots," he said. "Minimum force necessary but mission completion essential. Those missiles cannot remain under hostile control."

Abrams nodded. Orders transmitting toward men who would soon engage fellow citizens in armed conflict. The cycle repeating despite historical lessons suggesting futility of such confrontation. Americans killing Americans over different visions of America. The irony lost beneath operational necessity.

Hayes returned attention to map. The NSA facility illuminated in his mind beyond physical representation. Its isolated position both tactical advantage and vulnerability. Remote enough to establish defensive position. Inaccessible enough to complicate rapid response.

"Perfect location," he said to himself. "They know what they're doing."

The implications extended beyond immediate military response. Constitutional authority challenged by constitutional rebellion. Democratic processes replaced by force. The nation's founding principles interpreted through lens of violence rather than legislative deliberation. An old American story retold with modern weapons but ancient grievances.

Hayes issued final authorization with a voice betraying no doubt despite internal recognition of tragedy unfolding. Men would die today because of his decision. Men who considered themselves patriots regardless which side they served. The word claimed by both while neither maintained exclusive rights to its definition.

The operations center continued with electronic certainty while human affairs descended into ambiguity that technology could not resolve. The coordinates transmitted. The aircraft prepared. The confrontation scheduled despite moral questions that admitted no definitive answer.

Backdoor

The sun hung low in the Idaho wilderness, casting long shadows through the pine forest. Three militia technicians moved methodically along an overgrown service road, following what remained of a buried utility conduit. Decades of neglect had almost erased the path from existence, but the men knew what they were looking for. They had a map with GPS coordinates of the conduit and junction's location.

"Junction should be about fifty meters ahead," said Keller, a stocky man with a graying buzz cut.

Behind him, Martinez adjusted the heavy pack of equipment on his shoulders. "Hard to believe all this was just abandoned. State-of-the-art secure communications, left to rot in the ground."

"That's government for you," replied Brenner, the oldest of the three. His weathered face had seen decades in the Idaho wilderness. "When they shut down the facility, they didn't just turn off the lights. They made sure nobody could ever use the infrastructure again."

The men continued following their GPS tracking device until they reached a small clearing. Years of forest growth had nearly reclaimed the area, but the trained eye could still spot the man-made elements—a concrete pad mostly covered with moss, and the remnants of a protective housing now collapsed into rust.

"This is it," Keller confirmed, setting down his pack. "The primary junction node."

Brenner pulled out an old military entrenching tool and began clearing decades of accumulated soil and vegetation from the concrete pad. Underneath, they found a heavy metal access panel.

"NSA didn't skimp on materials," Martinez commented, running his hand over the corroded but still solid cover. "This was built to last a century."

Brenner wedged the entrenching tool into a seam and leveraged the cover up with a grunt. The rusted hinges protested but finally gave way, revealing a deep service vault below.

Martinez aimed his flashlight into the darkness. "There it is. The main conduit."

The three men stared at a thick pipe that entered the vault from one direction and exited toward the facility. The pipe itself was intact, but a section in the middle had been deliberately cut open. Inside, dozens of fiber optic cables had been severed—not hastily, but with thoroughness.

"Just like the archives said," Brenner murmured. "When the shutdown order came, they made sure the facility was truly isolated. Cut every optical line."

Keller climbed down into the vault for a closer inspection. "Look at this. They didn't just cut them." He pointed to the ends of the cables. "They fused the fiber ends with some kind of heat treatment. Made absolutely sure no one could easily splice them back together."

"Government paranoia at its finest," Martinez said. "Whatever they were doing in that facility, they wanted it buried for good."

Brenner unfolded a small camp stool and sat, pulling out a thermos of coffee. Keller pulled out a specialized testing device from his pack and attached it to one of the severed lines. "No signal degradation in the intact portions. Military-grade fiber doesn't deteriorate like the commercial stuff. If we can reconnect these lines, we'll probably have the original bandwidth capacity."

Martinez opened his equipment case, revealing a modern fiber splicing kit. "I brought enough materials to reconnect the entire primary trunk and two redundancies. That should be sufficient to reestablish full communication with the facility's internal network."

"Assuming the internal systems are still functional," Brenner added. "Those have been dormant even longer than these lines."

"Walker's team already confirmed the internal power grid is operational," Keller responded. "The facility was designed to maintain core systems in standby mode indefinitely. Military engineering from the Cold War era—built to survive anything."

The three men worked methodically for the next two hours. Martinez handled the delicate task of preparing and fusing the glass fibers, his hands steady despite the cold air. Keller continuously tested each connection, ensuring signal integrity. Brenner maintained lookout, his rifle resting across his knees.

"That's the last primary connection," Martinez announced, carefully sealing a protective sleeve around the newly fused fiber. "Moment of truth."

Keller connected his laptop to a junction port and

initiated a boot sequence. For several tense moments, nothing happened. Then a series of status indicators began to light up on his screen.

"We've got signal propagation," he said, his voice tight with anticipation. "The line is live all the way to the facility's main router."

Martinez and Brenner gathered around the laptop, watching as dormant systems began to respond one by one.

"Internal network is coming online," Keller continued, typing rapidly. "Security protocols initializing. Jesus, look at this—the facility's systems are picking up right where they left off when they cut the lines."

The three men made their way back down the overgrown service road, leaving behind the junction box with its newly blinking status lights—a piece of the past now connected to the present, pulsing with data for the first time in decades.

Deep within the NSA facility, decades of dust covered abandoned workstations and dormant equipment. Emergency lighting cast a dim glow across the main operations room where Walker and his team had established their presence after taking over the site. The militia had cleared only what they needed—power systems, basic environmental controls, and the central control terminals.

Walker stood behind Maddox, who worked at one of the few operational consoles they'd managed to revive. The vintage equipment hummed with new life, screens flickering with green text on black backgrounds—technology from another era now pressed back into service.

"How much longer until we know about the lines to Malmstrom?" Walker asked, his military boots crunching on the debris-strewn floor as he paced.

Larson, positioned at a communications station across the room, adjusted the settings on a tactical radio. "Field team should have reached the junction by now."

Walker nodded, his face betraying nothing. He moved to a large wall map showing the facility's connection to the outside world—including the critical fiber optic trunk lines running to western missile silos that had been deliberately severed when the NSA abandoned the site.

The radio on Larson's console crackled to life, the sound echoing in the cavernous room.

"Tech Team Four to Base, do you copy?"

Larson immediately grabbed the handset. "Base copies, Tech Team Four. Go ahead."

"Connection reestablished. Repeat, connection reestablished. We've successfully repaired the optical trunk line into Montana. Signal integrity holding at ninety-three percent—better than expected."

Walker moved quickly to the console, taking the handset from Larson. "This is Walker. Confirm you've established contact with the silos."

"Confirmed. We're getting handshake signals all the way to the Malmstrom Air Force Base."

A subtle tension released in Walker's shoulders—the only sign of his relief. "Good work. Return to base. We'll take it from here."

He handed the radio back to Larson and turned to Maddox. "Initialize the connection sequence. Let's see if these old circuits still remember how to talk."

Maddox, a former DARPA engineer with a perpetual five o'clock shadow, nodded and began typing on the antiquated keyboard. The screens around him filled with cascading command lines as he established a connection through the newly repaired fiber link.

"Initiating connection to Malmstrom," he announced.

"Negotiating encryption protocols..." He paused, waiting tensely. "Handshake accepted. We're in."

The main facility display—a massive screen that had gone dark decades ago—suddenly illuminated, showing a network diagram with green lines now connecting their position to the Montana relay station.

"Signal strength is solid," Maddox continued, genuine surprise in his voice. "Latency minimal. Cold War engineering at its finest."

Walker surveyed the awakening facility around them. "What's our status on internal systems?"

Larson moved to another console. "Main power grid is stable. Security protocols are initializing. Environmental systems coming online in sections three through seven."

"And the defense grid?" Walker asked, brushing dust from a nearby tactical display.

"Still dormant. Needs authentication to activate."

Walker reached into his jacket pocket and removed a black thumb drive, innocuous in appearance but carrying the culmination of years of planning. He handed it to Maddox. "Install it. Let's see if our investment paid off."

Maddox took the drive reverently, understanding its significance. "Once I insert this, there's no going back. The system will either accept it and give us full access, or it'll trigger the fail-safes and lock down completely."

"If it fails, we need to know immediately. There is no point in putting our men's lives at risk if we cannot accomplish our goal."

The room fell silent as Maddox plugged the thumb drive into a converted interface connected to the ancient system. His fingers moved deftly across the keyboard, navigating through layers of security to reach the system's core.

"Initializing backdoor deployment," he announced,

voice tight with concentration. "Bypassing primary authentication... injecting code package... establishing persistence within the kernel."

On the main display, a progress bar appeared, slowly filling as the backdoor program worked its way into the facility's systems.

"Subverting security protocols," Maddox continued. "Rerouting authentication queries... creating administrator access."

The progress bar reached seventy-five percent, then paused.

"What's happening?" Walker demanded.

"The system's detected the intrusion," Maddox replied, fingers flying across the keyboard. "It's trying to isolate and contain the code. Exactly as expected. Now comes the tricky part."

He activated a secondary program from the thumb drive. "Deploying the NSA skeleton key. Should work on any pre-2000 NSA security architecture… I hope."

The handful of militia members in the room collectively held their breath as the progress bar resumed its advance, creeping toward completion.

"Ninety percent," Maddox announced. "Ninety-five... and..."

The progress bar completed, and the screen flashed a simple message: "AUTHENTICATION ACCEPTED." Around them, the facility seemed to come to life. Dormant terminals activated, ventilation systems hummed louder, and additional lights flickered on throughout the operations room.

"We're in," Maddox said, unable to keep the disbelief from his voice. "Full administrator access. The facility is ours."

Walker leaned forward, studying the screens as various subsystems came online, their status indicators turning green one by one.

"Test the defense grid," he ordered. "But keep it in diagnostic mode. No active deployment yet."

Maddox navigated through the facility's systems, the ancient interfaces responding to his commands.

"Accessing perimeter security... initializing in diagnostic mode."

On the tactical display, a series of blue dots appeared around the facility's perimeter—sensor stations coming online for the first time in decades.

"Perimeter sensors operational," Maddox confirmed, checking diagnostic readouts. "Motion detection, thermal imaging, ground-penetration radar—all reading within normal parameters. The key works."

"What about the secure areas?" Walker asked, moving to a facility schematic displayed on another screen.

Larson checked readings from another terminal. "Airlocks responding. Environmental controls restoring optimal conditions. We can seal or open any section remotely."

Walker nodded, satisfaction evident in his usually impassive face. "And the main vault? The targeting chamber?"

Maddox navigated deeper into the system. "Vault security is... accessible. We have override capability for the targeting chamber. Whatever's still inside there, we can get to it now."

Walker straightened, taking in the transformed operations room. The facility that had been abandoned and sealed by the government decades ago was now awakening under their control.

"Send the confirmation to our people with the convoy," he ordered. "Tell them we have control of the facility. They are cleared to proceed with delivery of the

Patriot system."

As Larson relayed the message using their secure radio, Walker watched the black and white monitors showing the views of the security cameras monitoring the facility. Through layers of dirt and grime, he could make out the winding access road that led up to their position. "How long until they reach us?" he asked.

"At their current pace, about two hours," Larson replied.

Walker nodded. "And how long until we have full operational control of all facility systems?"

"According to these diagnostics," Maddox said, "the automated reboot sequence will complete in ninety minutes. After that, we'll have total control."

"Perfect," Walker said. He turned to address his team scattered around the operations room. "Twenty-seven years ago, the government buried this place and everything inside it. They tried to erase it from history because they feared what it could do." He paused, looking at each face in the room. "Today, we bring it back online. Today, we take back what belongs to the people. When that Patriot system arrives and is brought online, we'll have everything we need to ensure our success."

As the team returned to their tasks with renewed purpose, Walker moved to a dust-covered window, wiping away decades of grime to look out at the facility they'd reclaimed. The backdoor was open. The place was theirs. All that remained was the final piece—the Patriot system being transported in the wind turbines, currently making its way through the Idaho wilderness with Frank and Heller.

Walker checked his watch one last time. Everything was proceeding exactly according to plan.

The valley slept under moonlight as they approached. Three Blackhawks flying in tight formation, rotors synchronized to reduce acoustic signature. The AC-130J Ghostrider hung higher, circling like a patient vulture.

Inside the lead helicopter Staff Sergeant Wilson ran his final equipment check. Ten operators in full assault configuration. Each face blackened. Each weapon double-checked. The air thick with anticipation that preceded violence.

"Three minutes," called the pilot.

Wilson confirmed with hand signal passed through cabin. The men checked harnesses that would allow rapid descent from hover position. No landing zone on facility grounds. Just fast-rope insertion into a prepared killbox. Standard operation except targets were American citizens on American soil.

Arriving on station, the Ghostrider began its first orbit. Seven thousand feet above, its sensors gathering heat signatures and movement patterns at the NSA compound. The gunship pilot's voice cold as mountain air through the shared frequency. "Revenant has eyes on target. Multiple personnel. Defensive positions at perimeter rings. Engage on your mark."

Colonel Haversham's voice from command helicopter. "Weapons release authorized. Clear the perimeter."

From ground level it appeared as though judgment had descended without warning. The Revenant's minigun opened up first, its incredible rate of fire painting the compound in deadly tracers. One hundred rounds per second seeking human targets with mechanical indifference. Men caught in open ground disappeared in stuttered frame sequence. Bodies jerking as rounds found flesh, their existence converted to red mist before ears registered the sound. The smaller caliber shells ineffective against hardened positions but devastating to anything with blood and bone.

The gunship pivoted without pause. The Mk44 Bushmaster II chain gun joining the assault against reinforced positions. Thirty-millimeter shells penetrating sandbag emplacements and steel roofs. Watchtowers collapsed as support beams shattered. Defenders transformed from combatants to statistics in mid-breath. The gun's mechanical rhythm implacable as the tide.

Steady. Measured. Absolute.

Then the 105mm cannon spoke with voice that turned night to day. Concrete defensive positions that had required weeks to construct disappeared in single percussive moment. The main guns finding bunkers and command posts with first-round accuracy. Secondary explosions following as ammunition stores cooked off. The entire sequence unfolding faster than human comprehension could process. Death delivered in measured calibers according to target resistance. Mathematics of destruction reduced to a formula requiring only input coordinates.

Walker watched in disbelief from inside the command center. He had seen fearsome air assaults before, but nothing like this. Walker's defensive positions were eaten up by the hungry beast. His men reduced to component parts before radio could register their final screaming transmissions. Two minutes of concentrated violence had eliminated half of his perimeter defenses. Over 140 souls dead.

"Stinger teams deploy," he ordered. Voice steady despite witnessing extinction event rather than battle. "Fire at will."

On eastern ridge three men emerged from camouflaged position. Military training evident in their movement. One carrying launch tube balanced against shoulder. The other two providing security with practiced scans across surrounding terrain.

"Stinger team on ridge," called the Revenant's sensor operator. "Grid coordinate three-niner-alpha."

"Engaging," replied the pilot.

The gunship's Bushmaster traversed. Targeting solution calculated against moving hostiles. But the militia team had already achieved firing position. The Stinger's targeting system locked onto aircraft engine heat signature. Missile release sending smoke trail through cold mountain air.

"Missile launch detected," warned electronic countermeasure officer. "Deploying chaff."

The Revenant belched metallic confetti into night sky. Electromagnetic signature designed to confuse incoming projectiles. A race between technology and physics at supersonic velocity. The Stinger wavered, momentarily confused by suddenly multiplied targets. Then corrected course through terminal guidance system when chaff dispersed beyond effective range.

Second Stinger team emerged from western slope. Position calculated to eliminate chaff effectiveness through different attack angle. The launcher raised. Targeting system acquiring heat signature. Missile release leaving parallel smoke trail through cold mountain air. The dual attack precisely coordinated to overwhelm defensive capability.

The Revenant pilot fought physics with skill born from thousands of flight hours. Banking the aircraft away from incoming threat. Deploying remaining countermeasures. Reducing engine output to minimize thermal profile.

Insufficient.

The second missile struck starboard wing. Fuel ignited. The wing torn from the fuselage by the explosion. The aircraft transformed from predator to prey in single incandescent moment. Its descent no longer controlled by human intention but gravity's indifferent claim. The burning gunship carved a parabolic path from sky to earth. Its impact marked by secondary explosion as remaining fuel ignited. The forests claimed wreckage with hungry flame that spread through dry undergrowth. Enemy action transitioning to natural disaster with seamless efficiency.

The Blackhawks descended toward compound, rotors churning night air as assault teams prepared for fast-rope insertion. One helicopter maintained altitude, door gunner laying suppressive fire across militia positions. The minigun cutting swaths through remaining defenders, buying seconds for operators deploying from sister craft.

Ten men descended from the lead Blackhawk, their bodies silhouetted against aircraft's running lights. Professional soldiers suspended between sky and earth during transition that represented maximum vulnerability. Ropes hissing through gloved hands with controlled friction.

The fourth man still descending when AT4 team emerged from southeastern bunker. Launcher resting on operator's shoulder while second man called distance adjustment. Rocket release painting night with exhaust signature. Projectile traveling faster than warning shouts could reach those suspended.

Impact converted the aircraft into an expanding pressure wave. Metal fragments replacing air molecules in blast radius. The helicopter shuddered, losing lift as vital components separated. Its sudden descent driving it sideways into second Blackhawk where men still hung suspended on ropes. Aircraft collided with physics. Rotors intersecting with catastrophic results. Metal shards converting flesh to meat.

The third Blackhawk pilot witnessed the destruction. There were already operators on the ground under fire. He had little choice but to pursue the battle. The door gunner continued to fire as the third aircraft entered the compound's airspace. The assault team began its insertion. Small arms ground fire from the surviving militia was intense.

Six operators already on ground. Two suspended in transition. Two still inside cabin. The pilot's skill evident in aircraft control despite unpredictable environment. Professional dedication extending beyond reasonable expectation.

Walker's militia responded with crossfire calculated during defensive preparation. M27 rifles captured from Pendleton creating interlocking fields of death that allowed no safe movement. Tracers marking pathways through darkness where operators attempted to establish a perimeter. Terminal ballistics converting body armor from protection to fragmentation source. The rounds designed to penetrate ceramic plates performing according to specification.

A third Stinger team acquired the final Blackhawk. Missile release creating smoke trail connecting launcher to aircraft. Impact transforming night to temporary day. The helicopter disintegrating around remaining occupants. Component pieces scattered across compound in a pattern suggesting violent disassembly rather than controlled landing.

On compound ground, surviving operators established defensive position using wreckage as improvised cover. Their training evident in movement that prioritized tactical necessity over shock response. Weapons returning disciplined fire. Professional soldiers maintaining protocol despite outcome certainty.

Walker watched from the command center camera

monitors as militia closed distance. Staggered assault reducing operator numbers through attrition rather than direct confrontation. His men demonstrating training principles received during military service now applied against former comrades. The irony unrecognized beneath operational necessity. Americans killing Americans with American weapons designed to protect all equally.

In seven minutes the assault force was eliminated. The wreckage burning with chemical intensity that illuminated the compound more effectively than defensive lighting. With almost a third of his militia eliminated, Walker's expression revealed neither satisfaction nor regret. Only professional assessment of engagement concluded according to planning principles. The defensive positions rebuilt even as fires consumed evidence of destruction that had visited them.

The NSA facility continued preparations uninterrupted. Men moving with purpose that transcended conventional authority. Their actions now separated from legal justification by blood already spilled. The point of no return passed without ceremony or recognition. Just practical acknowledgment that certain decisions cannot be unmade once enacted.

Culper leaned against his desk when the secure line buzzed. Three in the morning by the clock on his Georgetown office wall. No good news arrived at such hour. Just confirmation of anticipations already forming in professional minds.

"Culper," he said.

The voice belonged to someone within Pentagon hierarchy but outside normal chain of command. A relationship built on information exchange rather than organizational requirement. "Air Force deployment failed. Complete loss."

Culper straightened. Operational timeline collapsed from theoretical to immediate. "What deployment?"

"General Hayes authorized strike package against NSA facility in Pahsimeroi Valley. Three Blackhawks with assault teams. One AC-130J gunship. All down."

His fingers tightened around receiver. The plastic creaking beneath pressure. "Casualties?"

"Complete. Thirty-two operators. Nineteen aircrew. No survivors confirmed."

The office air seemed suddenly insufficient. Molecules deserting atmosphere through some cosmic dismissal.

"When?"

"Ninety minutes ago. Wreckage still burning."

"Walker's status?"

"Facility intact. Operation continuing without apparent disruption."

"Who authorized the military strike?"

"Hayes. Pentagon oversight. POTUS briefed after deployment."

Culper calculated implications against operational framework that existed only in his mind and classified files. Walker's activities had triggered response chain not yet ready for execution. "Our intelligence confirmed missiles on site?"

"Affirmative. Stinger teams took down all aircraft. Professional deployment suggests military training."

The fool, he thought. Anger rising like groundwater after spring rains. Slow but inexorable. "Hayes underestimated."

Silence answered. Both men recognizing truth that required no confirmation. Military arrogance matched against militia preparation. The outcome determined before aircraft left ground.

"All channels locked," said the voice. "Official statements delayed pending confirmation."

"Understood."

The call ended without farewell. Words wasted when actions determined outcomes. Culper replaced receiver with deliberate motion that concealed internal calculation. The timeline now compressed beyond organizational capacity.

He crossed to the wall safe. Entered combination memorized decades prior. Inside waited contingency files designed for circumstances outside conventional authority. Contact numbers for men who operated beyond official acknowledgement. Resources available without paperwork or congressional oversight.

The selected folder contained a single page. A spreadsheet in a kind of military shorthand. Names. Locations. Capabilities. Men capable of addressing situations beyond legal resolution but beneath threshold requiring formal military deployment. The gray space between criminal activity and national security where statutory authority provided insufficient guidance for practical response.

Culper extracted a secure phone from his desk drawer. Direct connection to private military contractor maintaining standby force for government operations requiring deniability beyond standard covert protocols.

The bitter irony not lost on him—his response to Walker's militia would be men indistinguishable from Walker's own. Former soldiers operating outside official sanction. Men with specialized training and weapons operating in shadows constitutional framers never imagined. Both sides calling themselves patriots while killing fellow citizens. An eye for an eye justice.

Walker had forced escalation sequence not designed for domestic deployment. The stolen Patriots represented transition point between law enforcement jurisdiction and military authority. The casualties already inflicted demanding response beyond conventional parameters.

The phone connected on second ring. Voice answering with practiced efficiency that suggested expectation rather than surprise.

"Authorization code," it demanded.

"Broken Arrow Seven-Four-Niner. Authorization Culper."

Brief silence as verification protocols executed. Then: "Resources available?"

"Thirty-six operators. Three armored vehicles with support packages. Full tactical loadout."

"Timeline?"

"Immediate. Deployment location forwarded through primary channel."

"Authorization status?"

"Beyond standard protocol. Parallel universe administratively."

Another silence. The implications registering with professional assessment rather than emotional response. "Understood. Assets mobilizing. Confirmation through established channel."

The call ended. Arrangements initiated that would place men and equipment in motion without official documentation. The kind of operation that existed in shadow space between congressional authorization and executive necessity. The place where actual national security occurred despite constitutional restraint.

Culper returned the folder to safe. The wall clock showed progress of minutes that suddenly carried greater weight than hours prior. Somewhere in Idaho's mountains American servicemembers lay dead or dying. Aircraft wreckage marking transition from theoretical confrontation to actual bloodshed. The political implications extending beyond current administration regardless who claimed victory.

His desk phone buzzed again. Different line. Different security protocol. The office suddenly an insufficient container for events unfolding beyond its walls.

"Culper," he answered.

"The Pentagon is moving," said new voice. Different source but similar professional cadence. "Joint Chiefs in emergency session."

"Timeline?"

"Unknown. Military options under review. Paralysis while lawyers determine authorization parameters."

"Understood."

This call too ended without farewell. Just information transferred with economy that recognized time's sudden premium value. Events accelerating beyond bureaucratic capacity for response. The gap between official action and necessary intervention widening with each passing minute.

Culper gathered materials required for extended absence. The office would remain empty for the duration measured in days rather than hours. His authority temporarily self-vested rather than organizationally derived. The kind of operational independence that existed because certain functions required freedom from oversight to achieve objectives necessary for democracy's continuation.

The dead were beyond help. The living still requiring attention. Walker's operation was proceeding without apparent disruption despite military assets deployed against it. The situation deteriorating beyond conventional resolution parameters.

Outside his window dawn approached Washington

with methodical certainty. The city continuing normal patterns despite altered national circumstance. Citizens pursuing daily routines unaware that constitutional authority had confronted rebellion hours earlier. That theoretical debate had discovered practical consequence transcending courtrooms or legislative chambers. That Americans had killed fellow citizens for ideological difference rather than foreign threat.

Just like before. Just like before that. The national circle completing itself through violence that left no one untouched regardless which side claimed victory.

Culper lifted his secure briefcase. The weight appropriate to contents that determined life and death without judicial review. His mind already calculating operational parameters for a team not yet assembled against an opposition already proven lethal.

The four-door truck drove behind the third wind turbine providing support. The Idaho road paralleled a rushing river below as the vehicle made its way through the remote countryside. The NSA facility was still miles away, hidden somewhere in the thick pine forest ahead.

In the backseat, Frank stared out the window, watching the churning water. His weathered face betrayed nothing. Beside him, Heller shifted in his seat, his eyes constantly checking the mirrors.

"ETA twenty minutes," called the driver, a squarejawed man with military-cropped hair.

The front passenger, a younger man with a scar across his left cheek, nodded.

Frank grunted, still gazing at the river below.

Heller's hand moved slowly toward his jacket. "Frank."

Frank turned, his eyes immediately registering the

matte black 9mm now leveled at his chest.

"Walker's orders," Heller said, voice flat and emotionless. "Patriot system's being delivered. You're no longer needed."

Frank's eyes narrowed slightly. No surprise registered on his face, as if he'd been expecting this all along.

"Nothing personal. For what it's worth I thought you did a real good job." Heller added.

Frank grunted.

In one explosive motion, Frank lunged forward, his right-hand clamping around the barrel of the gun. He twisted the barrel upward and sideways, aiming it directly at the front passenger. The weapon discharged with a deafening crack inside the confined space of the cab.

The bullet caught the scarred passenger in the side of the head, spraying blood and tissue across the windshield.

The driver cursed, swerving the truck violently.

"Son of a—" Heller growled, fighting to regain control of the weapon.

With his free hand, Heller pulled a push dagger from his tactical harness and drove it through the back of Frank's hand still gripping the gun barrel.

Frank didn't scream. His face contorted in pain, but he maintained his grip for another crucial second before releasing. Blood dripped onto the floor of the cab.

The truck lurched as the driver struggled to control the vehicle with his dead companion slumped against him. Frank seized the moment, shouldering the back door open as the truck skidded dangerously close to the embankment.

Without hesitation, Frank threw himself out the door, tucking his body as he hit the steep slope. Rocks and brush tore at his clothes as he tumbled down toward the river, leaving a trail of blood from his wounded hand.

"Stop the truck!" Heller shouted.

The vehicle screeched to a halt at the edge of the embankment. Frank hit the cold water with a splash, the current immediately pulling at his body. He dove beneath the surface, pushing himself deeper into the river's flow.

Heller leapt from the backseat of the truck, gun in hand. He rushed to the edge of the slope, scanning the water for any sign of his target. Spotting a shadow beneath the surface, he squeezed off five shots in rapid succession. Water erupted in small geysers where the bullets hit.

The river swept Frank downstream, each stroke of his wounded hand leaving a faint trail of red in the churning waters. He stayed under as long as his lungs would allow, surfacing only when he'd rounded a bend that put him out of Heller's line of sight.

As Frank disappeared downriver, Heller lowered his weapon. He stood alone at the embankment's edge, the driver still dealing with the bloody aftermath in the truck.

When Heller returned to the truck, the driver asked, "Is he dead?"

"Yeah, he's dead," said Heller half believing that it was true.

Downstream, Frank pulled himself to the side of the river. Blood poured out of the wound on his hand. Frank knew that he had to reach Sarah before Walker had her assassinated. There wasn't much time. He tore the sleave off his shirt and wrapped it around his hand, then climbed to his feet and headed up the embankment.

The convoy appeared from tree line as it arrived at the NSA compound. Three massive flatbeds. Each bearing a turbine blade longer than any tree in any forest. The lead truck honked twice. Signal established days before. Men at perimeter fence opened the gate wider than designed.

Militia soldiers rose from defensive positions. Faces showing relief or triumph according to temperament. Weapons still trained outward watching mountain ridges for government response. For helicopters or gunships that might come same as before.

Walker stood at command building entrance. Hands clasped behind back. Posture military straight. The steel in his spine more evident now that his prize approached. Satisfaction held in check because good commanders never celebrate until the mission is complete.

The first truck eased forward. Tires crushed gravel beneath weight never intended. The driver leaned from cab window. Face streaked with road grime.

"You got someplace particular you want these?" he called.

Walker gestured toward cleared area inside inner perimeter. "There. All three."

Heller jumped from sign truck's passenger side. His boots hitting ground with force suggesting eagerness.

"No pursuit," Heller said. "Highway empty as a new grave. No air activity since we hit Forest Service road."

Walker nodded. Focused on trucks completing slow arc into position. The blades somehow more massive now they'd arrived.

"Cut the end caps," Walker ordered. "Deploy the system before the Intelex satellite makes its next pass."

Men moved with practiced efficiency. Welding torches fired up. Throwing sparks against composite shell. Cutting away end caps sealed days before. The metal glowing red then yellow then white beneath torch flame. The smell of chemicals and scorched paint filling the air.

The first cap fell away. Thud against packed earth. Inside turbine cavity revealed. The Patriot radar array nested in a cradle of support struts and packing foam. Men swarmed flatbed. Hands reaching into cavity. Supporting million-dollar equipment with muscle and will and greed for victory.

"Bring the crane," Walker called.

Heavy equipment operators started diesel engines. The construction crane rolled into position beside first flatbed. Men attached lifting straps. Connected cables. Coordinated movements like men accustomed to complex instructions.

The crane's engine growled. Hydraulics hissing protest. Cable tightened. The radar array rose from turbine cavity inch by careful inch. Suspended between earth and sky. Between intention and completion.

Swinging gently like promise not yet fulfilled.

"Pad three," Walker directed.

The crane operator nodded. Swung boom with care borne of practice. The radar settled onto concrete pad still showing marks from when government installation had been decommissioned. New purpose for old foundation.

Men attacked the second turbine with renewed intensity. Welders cutting. Militia soldiers securing the perimeter as the first turbine blade rolled away. Diesel engines rumbling against mountain quiet. The cap fell away. Revealed the Patriot's launch station. Missile tubes nested like deadly children in manufactured womb.

Walker approached Heller. Voice low beneath machinery noise. "Kane?"

Heller met his eyes. Then looked away. "Dead. Like you wanted."

"You're certain?"

"Put three rounds in him. Watched him fall into the river. No way anyone survives that."

Walker studied Heller's face. Looking for lie beneath

lie. For truth men try to hide sometimes even from themselves. Seemed satisfied with whatever he found. Squeezed Heller's shoulder.

"Good work getting the Patriots here. We're on schedule. The next phase begins as soon as the Patriots are online."

The crane lifted missile launching station. Metal gleaming dull. Carried upward like a perverse offering to sky that allowed such things.

"Power up the radar," Walker ordered. "Full system diagnostic before we connect to facility network."

Third turbine cap cut away. Final component extracted. The Patriot system control station with its displays and connections and computer core capable of tracking sixty targets simultaneously. Deciding which to kill first. Which to spare until last missile spent.

The technicians began assembling components. Connecting cables. Establishing power supply from the diesel generator brought for this purpose. Men who had studied manuals for years finally touching equipment they'd only dreamed of controlling. Fingers almost reverent against military-grade switches and hardened displays.

Walker watched. Face showing satisfaction denied until now. The acquisition complete. The deployment beginning. His plan transitioned from theory to iron reality surrounded by men who believed same as him. Who saw future written in missile tubes and targeting systems and revolution painted in familiar colors.

"Time to completion?" he asked chief technician.

"Two hours for full operational status."

Walker nodded. Checked his watch. Calculation visible in movements. "We have a window. No satellite overhead for ninety minutes. Work fast."

He turned to Heller. The lie between them now

foundation for what followed. "Prepare for visitors. Government won't stand idle once they know what we have."

Heller grinned. Expression showing teeth too eager for coming violence. "Stinger teams are redeployed. Defensive positions reinforced. Let them die trying to take this place."

The radar began to turn. A slow calibration sweep. The electronic eyes opening after transport darkness. Searching for targets in sky still empty of aircraft. Of threats. The Patriots waking into world that had no idea what their arrival meant. What change these men intended. What blood would flow before their purpose found completion.

Walker stood tall. Commander at moment of advantage. Of initiative. His plan transformed into hardware arrayed before him. Into men looking to him for next order.

Frank's boots scraped against the cracked asphalt of the narrow highway. His clothes were still damp from the river, his torn shirt still soaking up blood from the wound. He'd been walking for over an hour, putting distance between himself and the NSA facility where Walker's plan was unfolding. He knew that Walker's men would already be assembling the Patriot missile system making an air or missile assault to retake the facility almost impossible. Options would be few.

The late afternoon sun beat down on his shoulders as he trudged westward. Traffic was sparse on this remote stretch of road—just two logging trucks and a Forestry Service vehicle had passed in the last hour, none of them slowing. Frank preferred it that way. Anonymity kept him alive.

He paused at a bend in the road, checking the crude field dressing on his hand. The bleeding had slowed, but the pain remained sharp where Heller's push dagger had pierced through. His throat was parched, muscles aching from the river escape and hike that followed.

As Frank rounded the curve, a weathered wooden sign came into view: "U.S. FORESTRY SERVICE AIRFIELD - AUTHORIZED PERSONNEL ONLY." An arrow pointed down a narrow access road cutting through the pines.

Frank stopped, considering. Walker would have already secured the NSA facility by now. Once the Patriot system was installed, his next move would be tying up loose ends—including Sarah back in Oregon. She was insurance, leverage to ensure his cooperation. With his supposed death at the river, that insurance was no longer needed.

He checked his watch. Sarah had little time before Walker gave the order. The decision made itself. Frank turned onto the access road, his pace quickening despite his exhaustion. Two hundred yards in, the trees opened to reveal a small airstrip—little more than a paved runway with a hangar and a couple of outbuildings. A windsock hung limp in the still afternoon air.

Frank approached cautiously, scanning for movement. A white and green Cessna 414 with its twin engines sat outside the hangar, its wings catching the sunlight. Near it, a fuel truck was parked. The scene was quiet except for a radio playing country music from inside the hangar.

Frank entered a building that looked like an office. He picked up the phone on a desk and dialed from memory. He heard the clicks of secure connection establishing. A man answered and went through the authentication process before putting Frank through to another line.

Another voice answered, "Culper."

"Kane," Frank said, his parched throat making the words sound like rocks in a tumbler.

Culper's tone sharpened. "About damned time. Where the hell have you been?"

Frank ignored Culper's heated tone, "Patriots stolen. Inside wind turbines on trucks."

"We know about the damned Patriots. They've already arrived at the NSA compound and Walker's men are assembling them. You're too late, Frank." "Air assault. Now," said Frank.

"The Air Force already tried. Three Blackhawks and a Ghostrider gunship down. All aircrews and assault teams dead."

"Walker had Stingers."

"Yeah, well they didn't ask me before executing the assault."

"Spilled milk."

"Spilled milk? Shall I tell that to their families, Frank?"

"Try again. Ground assault."

"I'm working on it. It'll take time."

"Walker won't wait."

"What's his plan, Frank?"

"Secession. Western states."

"That's insane."

"Nuclear codes."

"How in the hell did he get nuclear codes?"

"Backdoor. Traitor."

"Holy shit. Are you sure?"

"Yes."

"Jesus Christ," Culper muttered, then his voice hardened again. "Listen to me. We need to move fast but smart. No more dead operators. You've been inside. You know the layout. I need you as a guide."

"Yes," said Frank. "When?"

"It's going to take time to finish assembling my team and equipment. But we can probably be there in eighteen hours."

"Maybe too late."

"I know, but it's the best we can do."

"Where are you now?"

"Close."

"Some advanced recon would help."

"Right."

Frank studied maps on the wall for a rendezvous point.

"Rendezvous Route 28 junction. Forest road 129."

"Got it. Eighteen hours from now. Hack."

Frank noted the time on his watch, then said, "Come heavy."

"We always do," said Culper.

Frank hung up. No goodbye needed between men accustomed to endings. He studied the wall map one more time. Burned locations into memory same way he'd burned Walker's death there. Calculated travel times.

Oregon and back. Possible. Just... with a little help.

General Hayes stood in the ops center at Mountain Home Air Force Base. Screens showed feeds from the MQ-9 Reaper drone circling Idaho mountains. The weathered face showed nothing beyond professional interest. Twenty-seven years of service carved discipline into features that revealed no emotion to subordinates watching for cue.

"Coming up on NSA facility perimeter now," said the drone operator.

Hayes nodded. The drone camera feed stabilized. In center of the compound three flatbed trucks. Massive turbine blades still mounted. End caps removed revealing contents.

"There," Hayes said pointing. "Enhance sector four."

The camera zoomed. Focus sharpening on activity surrounding one flatbed truck. Men gathering around white composite shells. Inside the hollowed turbine blade military hardware clearly visible. The distinctive shape of Patriot missile launcher unmistakable to anyone with Hayes' experience.

"They've got it," he said. Voice tight with confirmation of intelligence already provided. "They've got the Patriots."

The drone banked slightly. Camera shifting to another section of compound. Men working with obvious purpose. Equipment being positioned on concrete pads. The radar array already deployed. Tracking dish beginning slow rotation. Coming online before his eyes.

"Jesus Christ," the intelligence officer muttered. "They're setting up faster than we projected."

Hayes studied the scene with cold calculation. Men who should have been weekend warriors handling sophisticated military hardware with professional efficiency. Someone had trained them well. Provided technical expertise beyond backyard militia drills. The operation showing coordination bearing hallmarks of military planning.

"Keep the Reaper at maximum surveillance distance," Hayes ordered. "Continue monitoring."

The intelligence officer cleared his throat. "Sir, we're observing American citizens on American soil. This crosses jurisdictional—"

"Those are stolen military weapons," Hayes cut him off. "And forty-three of our operators died trying to recover them yesterday. This is military jurisdiction now."

The screens continued showing Walker's men assembling Patriot system components. Connecting power supply. Establishing command network.

Professional soldiers, not ragtag militia.

"Scan for survivors," Hayes ordered. "Our men from yesterday's operation."

The drone altered course. Camera sweeping mountain slopes surrounding compound. Searching for heat signatures that might indicate surviving helicopter crews or operators. For movement amid forest and rock.

"Continue monitoring that facility," Hayes told intelligence officer. "I want to know the minute those Patriots go operational or if any survivors are found."

The officer nodded. Hayes turned back to primary screen still showing drone feed. The implications settling like cold stone in gut. The situation evolving beyond political calculation. Beyond jurisdictional debate. War had started. Only question that remained was how the government would respond to challenge not faced since 1865.

At the Forest Service airfield, Frank exited the office. He crouched behind a stack of supply crates, watching as a man in Forestry Service khakis emerged from the hangar.

The pilot—mid-forties, medium build—walked toward the Cessna with a clipboard, beginning a pre-flight check.

Frank moved silently along the edge of the tarmac, keeping to the shadows. The pilot circled the aircraft, checking control surfaces and inspecting the landing gear. As he moved to the far side of the plane, Frank closed the distance between them.

Frank stepped into view without a word.

The pilot startled, turning quickly. "Jesus! You shouldn't be here. This is a restricted area." Frank simply nodded toward the plane.

"Fire spotting run." The pilot eyed Frank's disheveled appearance, noting the bloodied bandage. "You need medical attention? I can radio—"

Frank stepped closer, his expression hardening.

The pilot's hand moved slowly toward the radio clipped to his belt. "Look, buddy, I don't know what happened to you, but this is federal property. Why don't I give you a ride to the ranger station? They've got first aid—"

Frank moved with unexpected speed for a man in his condition. In one fluid motion, he closed the gap between them, twisted the pilot's arm behind his back, and pressed him against the Cessna's fuselage.

The pilot struggled briefly, then went still. "Okay, okay. I'm not going to fight you. You know how to fly this thing?"

Frank shook his head once.

"I ain't coming with you."

Frank increased the pressure on the man's arm, then released one hand long enough to point with his bloody hand westward.

The pilot's resistance wavered. "Oregon? That's where you need to go?"

Frank nodded.

"You're asking me to risk my career by flying you there."

Frank's steady gaze was his only response.

The pilot exhaled slowly. "I've got a full tank. Range of about 1500 miles." He paused. "Where exactly do you wanna go?"

Ten minutes later, the Cessna roared down the runway, lifting into the dark Idaho sky.

The pilot kept his eyes forward, hands steady on the controls. "Where exactly in Oregon?"

Frank searched through the pilot's maps until he found what he wanted. He pointed to a specific location, then traced his finger along what appeared to be a logging road.

The pilot laughed incredulously. "You want me to land this plane on a logging road in the dark?" "Yes," said Frank in his rasping voice.

The pilot shook his head in disbelief, "You must have one helluva death wish."

The plane banked westward, engines droning steadily as they raced against the setting sun. Frank calculated time and distance in his head. If they maintained speed and the weather held, they'd reach Oregon before sunrise—the perfect time to approach Walker's sawmill where he hoped Sarah was still held captive.

As the Patriot system became fully operational, the radar dish rotated. Full sweep every six seconds. Electronic pulse mapping sky invisible to human eye. The technicians hunched over displays showing nothing but mountain ridges and empty air. Then something changed. A small indicator. Yellow blip appearing at screen edge.

"Contact," the lead technician said. His voice tight. "Bearing zero-four-five. Range twenty-two miles. Altitude twenty-four thousand feet."

The room went quiet. Men looking toward Walker.

His decision alone what followed.

"Classification?" he asked.

The technician studied readings. Fingers dancing across keyboard bringing additional sensors online. "Small aircraft. No IFF transponder. Speed and flight pattern consistent with unmanned aerial vehicle."

"Reaper drone," said Heller. "Could be searching for survivors from the helicopter assault."

"Or it could be looking for the Patriots," said Walker.

Walker moved to the display. Studied the yellow dot making slow arcs over mountain valleys. Searching for heat signatures. For movement. For anything that might confirm presence of government men fallen from sky the night before.

"Perfect opportunity," Heller continued. "Clean test of the system."

Walker watched the dot continue its pattern. Mind calculating variables beyond technical. Political weights measured against tactical advantage. Against risk.

"If we engage, they'll know we have the Patriots operational," the technician said.

Walker nodded. "They already suspect. Confirmation serves our purpose. Shows capability. Intent. Resolve."

Men waited. The yellow dot completing another slow circle above distant ridgeline. The targeting computer already calculating intercept solution. Numbers appearing beside blip on screen. Range decreasing with each sweep.

"Engage," Walker said. "Single missile."

The order passed through command chain. Men at launch station responding with practiced movements. The missile selected. Targeting data transferred. Radar lock established against aircraft too distant for human sight.

"Target locked," the launch operator confirmed. "Missile armed."

Walker moved to the launch station. Stood beside operator. Hand resting on man's shoulder not for comfort but connection to what followed. To the consequence of his order.

"Fire," he said.

The launch officer pressed a sequence of buttons. No dramatic red switch. No movie moment. Just technical protocol executed according to procedure. Outside the launch tube door opened. Cold mountain air rushing in. The missile ignited. First stage propellant accelerating steel and circuitry and destruction skyward with a sound like the world was torn open.

Smoke filled perimeter. Men watched the missile climb toward the target still invisible to naked eye. The radar tracking both hunter and hunted now. Showing closing distance. The Reaper unaware of what approached from below. Still searching for fallen men. For wreckage among trees.

"On track. Impact in five seconds," the technician called.

Walker stood unmoving. Face hard as mountain stone. The seconds counted down silently in room full of men who'd crossed lines there was no returning from. The radar showed intercept. The yellow blip vanished from screen. The next battle in a conflict that would require a name soon enough.

"Direct hit," the technician confirmed. "Target destroyed."

No cheering came. No celebration. Just professional acknowledgement of system performing according to specification. Of weapon fulfilling design purpose. "Debris falling in quadrant seven," the technician continued. "No parachute deployment. No emergency transponder."

Walker nodded. "Scan for additional aircraft. They seldom fly drones alone."

General Hayes leaned forward. Eyes locked on screens arrayed before him. The Reaper drone's camera feed showing mountain landscape. Trees. Snow patches. Occasional rock outcropping. Then static. Electronic snow replacing image without warning. Without transition.

"What happened?" he demanded.

The operators exchanged glances. Fingers moving across keyboards with increasing urgency. Trying to recover signal. To reestablish connection severed without explanation.

"Drone isn't responding, sir," the mission controller said. "Last telemetry showed rapid altitude loss. Then nothing."

"Missile launch detected from target area," another operator called. "Radar station at Malmstrom picked it up. Consistent with Patriot missile profile."

Hayes straightened. The confirmation he'd feared written across blank screens before him. The stolen Patriots now operational. Deployed against American military assets on American soil. Simple drone today. What tomorrow?

"Get me satellite coverage," he ordered. "I want visual confirmation."

The screens changed. Satellite imagery replaced drone camera feed. Resolution lower but sufficient to show NSA facility nestled among Idaho mountains. Smoke rising from point within perimeter fence. The Patriot battery visible as arrangement of vehicles and equipment near facility center.

"They've gone operational faster than our analysts predicted," the intelligence officer said. "Full system deployment and integration. Whoever's handling the technical side knows what they're doing. They must be using our own veterans against us."

Hayes studied the image. Mind calculating response options already limited by political realities. By jurisdictional tangles. The nightmare scenario military planners dismissed as hypothetical now displayed in high resolution.

"Inform the Joint Chiefs," Hayes said. "And get me

full intelligence workup on that facility. Access points. Defensive positions. Personnel estimates."

"What about civilian oversight, sir?" the intelligence officer asked. "FBI has jurisdiction for domestic—"

"A military weapons system was just used to destroy Air Force property," Hayes interrupted. "While searching for our personnel likely killed in a previous engagement. This crossed into military jurisdiction the moment they stole military weapons."

The screens continued showing smoke rising from the facility. New configuration of a threat nobody had prepared for. American weapons turned against the American government. Not insurgents with rifles. Not protesters with Molotov cocktails. Professional soldiers with military hardware capable of denying airspace across three states.

Hayes said. "The militias have declared war against the United States. I doubt they know what that means. But they will soon."

The operators continued monitoring satellite feed. Smoke dispersing. Activity visible around Patriot battery as Walker's men secured system following successful engagement.

As the twin engine Cessna crossed into Oregon airspace, twilight began its slow ascent up the Cascade Range. Frank checked his watch again, a habit formed from decades of timing operations down to the second.

"We're about fifteen minutes out," the pilot announced.

Frank said nothing, his eyes fixed on the approaching mountains. The landscape had changed from Idaho's rugged wilderness to Oregon's dense forests and volcanic peaks. Somewhere ahead was the sawmill, and Sarah.

The Cessna descended, the pilot expertly navigating by landmarks rather than instruments. They skimmed treetops, following the contours of hills and valleys.

"There," Frank pointed as a clearing appeared in the forest.

The pilot surveyed the narrow strip visible in the dying light. "Christ. It's barely wide enough."

The pilot took a deep breath, beginning his approach. "One attempt. If it doesn't look right, I'm pulling up. I

didn't sign up to die today." Frank nodded.

The Cessna dropped lower, its landing lights illuminating the rough road surface. Trees loomed on either side, leaving precious little margin for error. The pilot's hands were steady on the controls, his concentration absolute.

The plane touched down with a jolt, bouncing once before settling onto the uneven surface. The pilot fought the controls as they rumbled down the logging road, slowing quickly.

The moment the plane had slowed enough, Frank unlatched the door and jumped out, landing in a crouch on the dirt road. Without a backward glance, he moved to the tree line, his eyes fixed on the distant lights of Walker's compound visible through a gap in the forest.

The pilot didn't waste a second. Before Frank had reached the trees, the pilot was already advancing the throttle. The Cessna lurched forward, turning in a tight half-circle on the narrow road. The engine roared as the pilot pushed it to full power, the plane gathering speed before lifting off into the darkening sky, disappearing over the treetops within seconds.

Frank stood at the edge of the forest, alone now. He checked his watch, calculating how much time Sarah had left. Then, with silent determination, unarmed, he moved into the shadows, making his way toward Walker's sawmill.

The last remnants of moonlight filtered through the trees as Frank moved silently toward the sawmill complex. The main gate stood unguarded—unusual for Walker's operation. Frank circled to the east side where a section of chain-link fence backed against a storage shed, creating a blind spot in the security cameras.

He scaled the fence with practiced efficiency despite his injured hand, dropping into shadow on the other side. The compound was eerily quiet. No patrol movement, no radio chatter. Only the distant hum of a generator broke the silence.

Frank crouched behind a stack of lumber, studying the layout. The main production floor was dark. The administration building showed a single light on the second floor. But his focus remained on the smaller structure to the north—the converted storage building where he and Sarah had been held.

No guards at the entrance. Not a good sign.

Frank crossed the open yard in short bursts, freezing between movements to scan for threats. Nothing. The absence of security made his pulse quicken. Walker never left assets unprotected.

At the detention building's entrance, Frank pressed his back against the wall and listened. Silence. He tested the door handle—unlocked. Another bad sign.

The door opened to a dimly lit corridor. Four cell doors lined the right wall, including the ones where he and Sarah had been kept. Frank moved to Sarah's cell, footsteps echoing softly on the concrete floor.

Unlocked, the door swung open to his touch.

Empty.

The cot where she'd slept showed signs of recent use—a blanket folded, a plastic cup of water still half-full on the floor. But Sarah was gone.

Frank checked his own former cell. Empty. He moved methodically through the building, checking each room, finding nothing but abandoned guard posts and vacant offices.

In the small break room at the end of the hall, a coffee pot was still warm. Someone had been here recently. Frank continued his search of the mill, every empty room increasing the tight knot in his stomach.

A noise from the supply closet near the back entrance stopped him. Frank approached silently, listening to the shuffle of movement inside. He positioned himself beside the door, waiting.

When the door opened, Frank struck with brutal efficiency. He grabbed the emerging figure, a stocky man in tactical pants and a black t-shirt, and slammed him against the wall. Before the guard could react, Frank's forearm was pressed against his throat, cutting off any shout for help.

The guard's eyes widened in recognition and fear. Frank increased the pressure on the man's throat just enough to make his intention clear, then eased back slightly to allow him to speak.

"Where is she?" Frank's voice was barely above a whisper.

The guard struggled briefly until Frank pressed harder. "Walker... took her," he gasped.

Frank eased the pressure again. "When?"

"Three days ago."

"Where?"

The guard hesitated. Frank shifted his grip to the man's right wrist, bending it at an angle that promised immediate pain.

"The facility," the guard whispered. "The one in Idaho."

Frank's expression didn't change, but something cold settled in his chest. "She's still alive?"

"Last I heard. Walker said he needed her there." The guard swallowed hard. "For leverage."

"Against who?"

"Don't know. Some government guy, I think."

Frank studied the man's face for any sign of deception. Finding none, he adjusted his grip.

"Who else is here?"

"Nobody. Walker pulled everyone except the perimeter team. Said we're shutting down operations here."

Frank released the guard just enough to create a false sense of relief, then struck him with his fist. The guard slumped unconscious to the floor. Frank dragged him into the supply closet, using the man's own belt to secure his hands behind his back.

Walker had taken Sarah right back to where Frank had escaped. Back to the NSA complex where the Patriot system was being delivered. Frank had no way of knowing if Sarah was still alive if Walker thought he was dead. Worrying about it wouldn't solve anything. Action might.

He slipped out of the building the same way he had entered, disappearing into the darkness with renewed purpose. Walker had made a critical mistake bringing Sarah to Idaho. He'd put all his pieces in one place.

And Frank was coming for them all.

The Imperial hugged the curves of the mountain highway, its powerful engine growling as Frank pushed it hard through the night. The headlights carved a tunnel through the darkness, illuminating the empty road ahead.

Dawn had broken. Two hours into the drive, he'd seen only two other vehicles—a logging truck and a state trooper who'd wisely chosen not to pursue the speeding black sedan.

Frank checked the dash clock: 6:37 AM. He'd made good time, but Idaho was still far. The Barrett and his body armor with the Colt Cobra revolver in its holster rested in the trunk. Frank wore the twin Redhawk revolvers in their shoulder holster and the Derringer tucked in his hidden boot holster.

The mountains loomed ahead, silhouettes against the early morning sky. Beyond them lay Idaho, the NSA facility, Walker—and hopefully Sarah still alive. Frank's injured hand tightened on the steering wheel, his focus absolute. Frank figured he had one shot at stopping Walker. One shot was all he'd ever needed.

Kicking The Door Down

In the half-light of the hangar elite men lined up in three rows before Culper. Black uniforms dark as oil against the concrete floor. Thirty-six faces wiped clean of identity by the flat black and green paint scored across cheekbones and eye sockets. Names replaced by numbers on their chests.

Culper moved down the line. His own face painted the same ritual black and green. A finger tugging at chest straps. Testing sidearm holsters. Checking safety switches. The only sound his boots against the floor and the occasional grunt of approval.

Behind the men three Stryker Dragoons waited. Black metal beasts crouched low on eight wheels each. Remote weapon stations raised like the heads of something ancient waiting to feed. The diesel engines cooled from their test runs.

The line of men stretched out like a living wall. Each carried an M4 carbine modified beyond factory design. Suppressors. Forward grips. Laser targeting modules. Each wore body armor with ceramic plates front and back. Each carried six magazines plus sidearm. Each face revealing nothing human beneath the camouflage.

Men who had done this before. Who understood odds. Who recognized that some would not return.

Culper ran a hand across the Stryker's hull. Felt the cold metal against his palm. The purpose of its design. A machine to deliver men and violence wherever needed.

"Load up," he said. His voice carrying no farther than necessary.

The C-17 Globemaster sat outside the hangar. Cargo ramp lowered like a mouth waiting to swallow men and machines. Pilot and crew already in their seats. Engines spooled. Navigation systems locked to coordinates that existed on no civilian map.

Three drivers and three gunner/commanders climbed into the Strykers. The vehicles awakening with mechanical growls that echoed across the concrete floor. The men filed into assigned seats with the economy of motion that came from repetition. No wasted movement. No unnecessary words.

Culper waited until they were loaded. Until the Strykers' engines settled into idle resonance that spoke of controlled power. Until every man had checked his gear one final time against the possibility of failure. Then he climbed aboard.

The team leader looked at him. A question without words.

"One minute," Culper said.

The cargo bay held the smell of diesel fuel and gun oil and sweat. The unmistakable scent of men preparing for war.

Culper moved to the center of the bay. Where men seated along metal benches could see him without strain. Where words would reach all equally. His eyes swept across them. Measuring what he saw against what he knew would be required.

"We go to do a necessary thing," he said. "Not a political thing. Not a legal thing. A necessary thing."

The men watched. Faces still. Eyes revealing nothing.

"When this country was young men like you secured its future. Without permission. Without recognition. Their names forgotten but their deeds remembered."

The cargo ramp began to rise. The sound of hydraulics joining the idle rumble of aircraft systems coming to life.

"These militias think themselves patriots. They speak of freedom while using stolen weapons to threaten their own nation. Today we answer that threat. Without hesitation. Without publicity. Without mercy."

Culper scanned their faces. Saw what he needed. The steel behind eyes that had seen worse places. Done harder things. The kind of men who formed the nation's last defense when all other options failed.

"We fly into mountains where normal approach is impossible. Toward men who have already killed federal troops. Who possess missiles capable of turning our aircraft to ash. Who believe their purpose justifies any action."

The ramp sealed with metallic finality. Locking them inside the mechanical beast that would carry them to violence.

"Remember what we are. Not government agents. Not soldiers. Not police. We are the consequence of choices when men place themselves above the nation they claim to serve."

Culper moved toward his seat. Said the final words

over his shoulder.

"The man who leads them is no amateur. He believes death can change a nation's course. Today we prove him right."

He strapped himself in. Felt the familiar tension in his gut that preceded all operations. The aircraft engines roared higher. His men waited in silence. The necessary weight of what they would do settled across them.

The C-17 began to move. Taking them toward mountains where men prepared to die for belief.

The Imperial devoured the highway. Frank's hands on the wheel like twin anchors holding the ancient metal to earth. Needle on the dash trembling past ninety-five despite mountain grades that would cripple lesser engines. The V8's growl a constant prayer to mechanical gods who favored the desperate.

Wind tore through the cracked window. Night air carrying pine and coming storm. Frank did not feel the cold. His body a furnace fueled by distance yet uncovered. By what waited at journey's end. By pure rage. The headlights carved a tunnel through darkness. Revealed yellow lines that vanished beneath the hood then reappeared in rearview like something born then consumed then forgotten. Frank's eyes never left the road. His mind calculating miles against minutes against the probability of Sarah still breathing when he arrived.

Towns appeared then surrendered to rearview darkness. Nameless collections of light where normal lives continued unaware of what approached in a steel coffin driven by giant with guns beneath his coat. Idaho border two hours back. The NSA facility perhaps three ahead if the car held together. If the road remained empty. If the gods who watched night highways favored the vengeful.

Mountains rose black against starscape. Ancient witnesses to human passage. To blood spilled on soil that would outlast both killer and killed. Frank pushed the engine harder. The car responded.

The road curved. Frank took it without slowing. Tires whining but holding against physics' insistence they surrender to momentum and gravity. The car's frame creaked. The engine snarled against demands that exceeded design parameters but not the will behind them.

Frank's damaged throat felt dry as canyon rock. His injured hand throbbed against the wheel. His head felt like it was splitting from too many concussions and simple dehydration. He needed to focus on the mission at hand. No time to stop and deal with the pain. He chewed a handful of extra strength aspirin retrieved from the glovebox. Bitter, but it took the edge off his pain.

The twin Redhawks hung against his ribs beneath the coat. The weapons waiting like witnesses to what would happen when distance between himself and Walker collapsed to killing range.

The Imperial drifted around another curve. Suspension groaning. Frank adjusted his path from years of pushing machines beyond breaking point. The car settled. Continued its consumption of miles.

A sign flashed in the headlights. Mountain pass elevation. Numbers meaningless against the singular calculation filling Frank's mind. Miles divided by minutes equaling Sarah alive or dead. The math absolute. Unforgiving as mountain stone. Clear as a bullet's purpose.

Frank drove through the night. The Imperial growling beneath him. The road unspooling before headlights' reach. The distance shrinking with each rotation of wheels that carried him toward violence as inevitable as sunrise.

In the command center the satellite phones arrived in plastic crates. Secure lines installed by technicians hunched over laptops with military encryption protocols flickering across their screens. The command center transformed hour by hour from abandoned facility to war room. Men moved with purpose that transcended individual belief. Their hands building something larger than themselves from remnants the government had left to rot.

Walker stood before the main display where satellite imagery showed a speck of land in turquoise water. Desecheo Island. Thirteen miles west of Puerto Rico's coast. Rock and scrub and bird colonies where nothing human survived beyond occasional research stations.

"Confirm coordinates," Walker said.

The targeting specialist hunched over keyboard and screen. His fingers entering numbers. The same fingers that had once guided similar systems for the government that now hunted them.

"Confirmed. Latitude 18.385 north. Longitude 67.480 west. Impact site eastern quadrant."

Walker studied the image. The island uninhabited except for lizards and nesting birds. The perfect demonstration of capability without human cost. A statement written in megatons that would require no translation.

"Yield setting?"

The weapons officer looked up from his terminal. "Minimum available. Twenty kiloton package. More than sufficient for an uninhabited target."

Walker nodded. His finger touching the screen where the island waited.

"Prepare launch authorization sequence."

The room stilled. Men at stations pausing to absorb the weight of what they heard. The theoretical becoming tangible with a speed that left some breathless. Others wore expressions carved from stone. They had crossed lines that permitted no return miles back. This was just another step toward a destination already chosen. Secession. Freedom.

The weapons officer entered codes received from sources no one questioned. His face revealed nothing as each authentication sequence cleared. As each failsafe disengaged. As each barrier between intention and nuclear fire dissolved beneath his fingers.

"Ready for launch authorization."

Walker produced a key from around his neck. Inserted it into the console designed for this specific purpose. The key that would transform protest into revolution. Words into deeds. Men into legends regardless of who prevailed. "On my order."

The communications officer raised his hand. "Notification package ready for transmission. White House. Pentagon. All major news networks." His voice betrayed nothing of the message's content. The manifesto explaining their action. The demands that would follow. The explicit warning that any attempt to assault the facility or tamper with the missile silos would trigger immediate launch of multiple ICBMs targeting the White House and Pentagon directly.

"Send notification," said Walker like it was nothing unusual. Like a walk in the park.

The communications officer pressed a sequence of buttons. The message already composed by men who understood the necessary of terror and concession. The optimal ratio of threat to demand. The document that would transform America regardless of whether government complied or resisted. The only question was if these men would be alive to see the transformation.

"Message sent. Delivery confirmation protocols engaged."

Walker's eyes moved to digital clock on the wall. The numbers advancing with the same certainty that had brought them to this moment.

"Ten minutes from notification to launch. As promised."

The men waited. Some standing straighter. Some finding reason to check equipment already verified. Some with eyes closed in what might have been prayer. All understanding transformation that had begun with a secure message moving through encrypted channels toward men in rooms much like this one but with different allegiances.

Walker turned to the targeting display. The island a green speck waiting for fire that would commute it to memory. "Confirm no ships within thirty-mile radius."

The radar technician consulted his screens. "Confirmed. Nearest large vessel is container ship sixty-two miles southwest. On course for Panama."

"Atmosphere clear of commercial and private aircraft over target area?"

"Confirmed clear."

Walker exhaled. Checked watch against wall clock. Found them synchronized as all elements in his plan had been for years preceding. He had the patience of a spider watching a web for inevitable vibration.

"Nine minutes until we change the world," he said.

No one spoke. The message traveling now through electronic channels toward men who would recognize true threat from false. Who would measure their remaining options against what approached Desecheo Island.

Walker looked at the men around him. Saw

commitment in their eyes. The certainty born from crossing lines that left no path backward. The discipline that came from understanding necessity beyond legality.

"Prepare secondary launch packages targeting the White House and Pentagon. In the event government response proves inadequate."

The targeting specialist entered new coordinates without hesitation. His eyes reflecting screen where the nation's capital appeared in overhead imagery. The Mall. The monuments. The buildings where power made decisions that had brought them to this moment. "Package ready for immediate deployment on your order."

"So we are clear, there will be no further warning should they choose to attack or disregard our demands. Retaliation will be automatic," said Walker so everyone in the room could hear.

Walker nodded. Turned back to the clock. The minutes advancing like judgment. With the certainty of what would follow.

They had declared war against the greatest military power on earth. The warning clear—any move against them would result in Washington itself vanishing beneath nuclear fire. They had committed themselves to a path that ended in either revolution or a footnote in history books written by the victors.

But victors had yet to be determined. The clock advanced. The beasts on the island unknowing of their sacrifice.

The monitor wall glowed electric blue, each screen a window to disaster. General Hayes stood motionless before them, hands clasped behind his back, spine military straight. The sudden blare of priority alert turned heads across the command center.

Major Reeves appeared at his side. "Message incoming, sir. Unknown origin."

"Put it up."

Text scrolled across the main screen. Hayes read without expression, only his eyes moving.

BY AUTHORITY OF THE CONSTITUTIONAL MILITIA OF THE WESTERN STATES: A DEMONSTRATION NUCLEAR LAUNCH WILL IMPACT DESECHEO ISLAND. COORDINATES: 18.385 NORTH, 67.480 WEST. UNINHABITED

TARGET. AFTER DEMONSTRATION, WASHINGTON WILL ACKNOWLEDGE OUR DEMANDS OR BECOME OUR NEXT TARGET. ANY MILITARY ACTION AGAINST THIS FACILITY OR ICBM MISSILE SILOS IN THE WESTERN STATES WILL TRIGGER IMMEDIATE LAUNCH AGAINST THE CAPITAL.

The room stilled. Twenty men and women frozen by words on a screen.

"Authentication?" Hayes asked.

"Signal traced to the NSA facility in Pahsimeroi Valley. Same facility where we lost contact with the Reaper." The communications officer's voice stayed steady. "Transmission carries classified signature codes. Someone with internal access."

Hayes checked his watch. "Eight minutes remaining." "Could be a bluff," Reeves offered.

"Satellite confirmation. I want eyes on that island now. And get a jet in the air for a flyover."

Screens shifted. Orbital view of the Caribbean appeared, a turquoise expanse speckled with islands. One highlighted in targeting box.

"Sir, we need to evacuate the White House," Colonel Mercer said from the back.

"Not yet. Call STRATCOM. I want verification of any

unauthorized missile activity from our silos."

Hayes moved to the secure phone. Picked it up with hands that betrayed no tremor. "This is General Hayes. Authorization Zulu-Seven-Bravo-Nine. I need immediate status on all ICBM installations in Montana,

Wyoming, North Dakota." He listened, face blank as stone.

"Unknown access detected at Malmstrom? When?" More listening. "And you're just reporting this now?"

He slammed the phone down. "Six minutes. STRATCOM confirms intrusion into the missile defense network. Some kind of backdoor breach at Malmstrom." The air in the room thinned. Breathing suddenly required intention.

"We need to scramble interceptors," Reeves said.

"Won't matter. Not if they've already seized control of the launch systems."

Hayes picked up the phone again. Punched in a different code. "This is Hayes. Get me the President." Pause. "I don't care if he's sleeping. Wake him."

Everyone watched the clock. Digital numbers falling toward zero.

Malmstrom Air Force Base

The silo doors parted, two massive slabs of reinforced concrete grinding sideways. Nothing moved in that Montana landscape. Just winter-dead grass and distant mountains standing sentinel.

Then fire erupted from earth itself. White-hot flame clawing skyward. The missile rose upon it, steel skin gleaming in morning light. Slow at first, defying gravity through sheer will and chemical rage.

A rancher five miles distant looked up from mending fence. Watched the thin white column stretching toward heaven. His horse spooked, snorting clouds in the cold air.

The missile climbed. Gathered speed. Its purpose simple as death.

Somewhere beneath that prairie, the empty silo steamed. Its concrete throat scorched black from birthing apocalypse. The doors remained open, mechanical jaws frozen in permanent scream.

Pentagon

"Sir," the satellite officer called. "Elevated heat signature from Malmstrom Air Force Base. Missile silo number four-seven showing activity."

"God help us," someone whispered.

"Mr. President," Hayes said into the phone. "We have a credible nuclear threat. Yes sir. Four minutes until potential launch." He listened. "No sir, I'm afraid this isn't a drill."

The conversation continued, Hayes's words clipped, precise. Information without emotion because emotion served no purpose now.

"Yes, sir. I understand."

He returned the phone to its cradle. Turned to the room where twenty pairs of eyes watched him for cue, for direction, for hope.

"Continue monitoring. Alert Caribbean Command.

Prepare statement for emergency broadcast system."
"Evacuation?" Reeves asked.

"Not enough time if they're serious. Three minutes." Hayes kept his voice level. "And if they're not serious, panic serves no purpose."

The satellite feed showed nothing but placid water around Desecheo Island. Sea birds circled its rocky shore. A research vessel floated twelve miles south, unaware it witnessed history's pivot.

"One minute, sir," the technician announced.

Hayes stood straighter. A man facing execution with dignity learned through decades in uniform. "Record everything. Whatever happens next, someone needs to know."

The countdown clock reached zero.

For five seconds, nothing changed. Then the satellite feed whited out. When picture returned, Desecheo Island no longer existed. Just churning water where land had been moments before. The shock wave spreading outward in perfect concentric circles.

The room remained silent. The impossibility of what they witnessed requiring more than words to process.

The phone rang. Hayes answered. Listened. Hung up. "NORAD confirms nuclear detonation," he said.

"Approximately twenty kilotons."

Someone made a sound like a wounded animal.

Hayes faced the room. "This is no longer a domestic terrorism incident. It's nuclear blackmail." He turned to communications. "Get me the Joint Chiefs. All of them.

And prepare the continuity of government protocols."

He looked once more at the satellite feed where water rushed to fill the void where an island had stood minutes before.

"It seems we're at war. With ourselves."

Desecheo Island, USA

The lizard paused on a sun-baked rock. Tongue tasting air that carried salt and heat. The iguana's ancient eyes blinked against the sun now climbing across eastern waters.

Nearby, a hutia emerged from undergrowth. Its nose

twitching against scents that announced safety or danger. Finding nothing threatening, it moved toward drought resistant plants. Its small paws worked with instinctual efficiency.

A Desecheo tree rat chittered from vine-wrapped branch above. Its body scarred from territorial disputes. It descended toward ground where fallen seeds offered morning sustenance.

Above, frigate birds circled. Their wings spread against thermals rising from rock that had never known human settlement. Their shadows passing over creatures who registered darkness without understanding its source.

None noticed first disruption of atmosphere far above. The air parting against object descending faster than evolution had prepared any creature to detect.

The ICBM pierced cloud layer at supersonic velocity. Its warhead separating from its delivery system. The targeting computer making final adjustments to ensure impact at the programmed coordinates.

The hutia paused in its feeding. Ears registering change in air pressure that preceded sound too massive for comprehension. The disruption existing outside all previous experience.

Impact transformed reality. The flash erasing distinction between creature and environment. The thermal pulse converting carbon to vapor. The pressure wave eliminating physical boundaries between objects.

The ocean rushed to fill void where island had existed. Water meeting superheated air creating steam cloud visible from Puerto Rico's western shore where humans with vocabulary for Armageddon watched with understanding no island creature could have comprehended.

Beneath waves that would remain radioactive beyond

human planning horizons, the island's bedrock glowed. The transformation witnessed by nothing that could record or communicate it.

Their ending required no comprehension to be complete.

Pahsimeroi Valley

The massive Globemaster aircraft threaded mountain passes like some steel-skinned serpent defying its own nature. Wings that spanned half a football field slipped between peaks with mere yards to spare. The veteran C17 pilot operated controls never designed for such maneuvers. No flight manual covered threading a military transport through valleys meant for hawks and small craft. The curve of earth and stone rising in periphery where only sky should exist.

Inside the cargo hold Culper felt each banking turn in his spine. The deck tilted at angles that sent loose equipment sliding. Thirty-six operators sat strapped against bulkheads watching the impossible unfold through small windows never meant to showcase a pilot's insanity.

"Fifteen minutes," Culper said.

No response necessary. Each man checked equipment already verified prior. Rifle magazines seated with palm strikes against body armor. Radios confirmed with minimal transmissions. Night vision secured for rapid deployment though dawn approached. These men understood preparation as religion. Violence as sacrament.

The three Stryker Dragoon drivers monitored systems designed for desert warfare now pressed into mountain operation. Remote turret gunners ran diagnostics on targeting computers that could paint a human silhouette at two miles distance. The vehicles themselves like mechanical beasts impatient for release. Their turbo diesel hearts dormant but ready.

Culper felt the satellite phone vibrate against his hip. Unfolded it with one motion.

"Confirmed launch from Malmstrom," came the voice, tinny through encryption protocols. "Impact on Desecheo Island in the Caribbean. Twenty kiloton yield.

Complete destruction."

Culper's face revealed nothing. "Understood."

He snapped the phone shut. Stood in the cargo bay where thirty-six operators waited strapped to benches bolted against fuselage. Men trained to move through chaos without becoming part of it.

"Gentlemen," he said. His voice carrying despite engine roar. "They've demonstrated nuclear capability. Desecheo Island in the Caribbean no longer exists."

No one spoke. Just the plane's metal skin groaning against physics.

"These aren't amateurs playing soldier," Culper continued. "They've crossed a line no American has crossed since the assault on Fort Sumter over 160 years ago." He looked at each man in turn. "Our window is closing. Either we cut their communication to those silos, or Washington becomes the next target."

The men's faces hardened. Not fear. Something colder.

Culper returned to his seat. Felt the plane bank toward a valley where no plane this size was meant to fly. The stakes rewritten in nuclear fire.

Inside the NSA command center, the technician leaned toward the screen as if proximity might clarify the anomaly. His finger traced the radar sweep where something substantial appeared then vanished like a ghost in the electric dark. The room hummed with machines breathing current through copper veins. The stolen Patriot system's heart beating steady beside men who'd breached oaths to operate it.

"There," he said. "Then gone."

Walker crossed the concrete floor. Boots silent against the industrial gray. The command center smelled of coffee and sweat and the metallic taste of anticipation. Men at stations salvaged from government storage watched their screens with the focus of converts to a new religion.

"Aircraft signature," the technician said. "Big. Transport class. Using terrain masking."

Walker studied the radar display. Watched the phantom bloom then disappear then reappear miles distant. A pilot threading mountain passes with a craft not designed for such maneuvers. Military approach without military subtlety.

"Lock status?" Walker asked.

The technician turned from the weapons console. His face lit blue from below. "No lock. Can't establish targeting solution with this flight pattern. We get milliseconds of signature then nothing."

The room grew quiet. Men watching Walker for reaction.

Walker's finger tapped the console edge. A metronome counting time without music.

"They're landing troops," he said. His voice carrying no emotion beneath the words. Just tactical assessment born from decades in distant trenches where other men had died for similar beliefs.

"We have eight missiles," Heller said. "We could saturate the approach corridor. Probability of hit—"

"No." Walker's voice cut through the room like a blade through meat. "The Patriots remain reserved for designated targets. The ones that matter."

"Sir—"

"Stinger teams will handle low-altitude craft if they enter engagement envelope. Our ground forces will engage whatever troops they're delivering."

Walker turned to Heller. The man's eyes carrying the fever of coming violence.

"Prepare all defensive positions. Full combat load. They'll come from multiple directions, hoping to split our attention."

Heller nodded. His hand already reaching for the radio that would carry the orders to men waiting in mountain darkness.

Walker moved to the tactical display. A board showing the facility and surrounding terrain in contour lines and elevation markers. His finger traced ravines where approach might come. Ridgelines where observers watched for exactly this movement.

"They'll use armor," he said. "Standard doctrine for assaulting fixed position."

The technician stared at the screen. The aircraft signature appearing once more before vanishing into mountain shadow. "Could be a C-17. Big enough to carry armored vehicles, including an Abrams MBT. But it can also carry two Bradleys or three Strykers."

"Agreed," Walker said. He pointed to the tactical display where the facility's three access roads met the perimeter fence. "Anti-armor teams here, here, and here. Claymore arrays wired for command detonation along all likely dismount paths."

The map became marked with defensive positions. With killing zones refined through days of preparation.

"They think us amateurs," Walker said. His eyes sweeping the room. "Weekend warriors playing soldier in the woods. They're wrong. Most of you served. Took the same oath they did. Honor it now by showing them the cost of underestimation."

Men straightened at their posts. Shoulders squaring against what approached.

"Move now," Walker said. "To your assigned positions. The defense of this facility was not an afterthought. It was the plan from the beginning. It's time to execute that plan."

The room emptied of all but essential personnel. Men flowing toward weapons and darkness and the chance to kill for belief. The radar continued its steady sweep. The aircraft's signature grown faint as it settled somewhere beyond the mountains.

Walker watched the screen a final moment. His face betraying nothing of the calculations behind it. The trap set. The bait taken.

"They've made their move," he said to no one in particular. "Now we make ours."

The technician adjusted parameters. Trying to clarify the vanishing signature now lost in ground clutter. His fingers moving across switches and dials designed by engineers who never imagined their creation in these hands.

Walker left the room without further word. The facility becoming a machine with single purpose. Men moving to assigned positions with weapons that had belonged to a government now turned against it. The inevitable confrontation between authority and its rejection approaching with the cold certainty of dawn.

Beyond the facility's concrete walls and chain-link fence and defensive emplacements the night waited. Men with guns on both sides. Each believing themselves necessary. Each willing to kill the other for conviction.

Each calling themselves patriot.

The Imperial settled into silence as Frank cut the engine. The mountain highway empty. Not even night creatures stirring across cracked asphalt where government maintenance had surrendered to wilderness years before. The mountains watching without judgment as they had watched all human passage. The stars hung motionless against void as dark clouds moved in. A storm was coming. No doubt.

Frank stepped from the car. Felt the mountain air cold against his face. His breath visible in predawn darkness. His injured hand ached where Heller's blade had pierced it, dried blood cracking when he flexed his fingers. The twin Redhawks hung over his armored vest beneath his coat. His KA-BAR in its sheath strapped around his waist. His eyes scanning ridgelines where others might hide. Found nothing but stone and pine and history indifferent to what approached. Before him the highway stretched empty in both directions, a black ribbon laid across the mountain's throat.

The first indication came as vibration. The air disturbed by something massive approaching from beyond mountain shadow. The sound following seconds later. Engines pushing against night. Metal cutting the atmosphere.

Frank did not move. His massive form still as the mountains against which it stood measured. Patient as death which had circled him for decades without finding purchase.

The aircraft appeared as shape against starfield and clouds. Four engines propelling mass never designed for terrain now navigated with professional disregard for safety margins. The C-17 Globemaster banking between peaks where altitude offered insufficient clearance for normal operation. The pilot executing maneuvers that spoke of skill and desperation in equal measure.

The landing lights swept the highway. Illuminated Frank stood beside the Imperial like a statue carved from human flesh. The aircraft descended. Landing gear extending from its metal belly. Its fourteen wheels touched the asphalt with squeals of rubber protesting against velocity and mass improperly managed.

Reverse thrusters engaged. The aircraft shuddering as brakes and engines fought physics. The mountain highway barely sufficient for operation never intended upon it. Cracks formed in the asphalt as the C-17 slowed. Stopped. The engines lowering to idle rumble that still filled night air with mechanical presence.

Frank waited. Watched as the cargo ramp descended from aircraft rear like a mouth opening to disgorge mechanical children. The first Stryker appeared. Eight wheels finding purchase against cracked asphalt. Remote weapons station swiveling as the gunner tested tracking mechanisms. Two more Strykers following. The vehicles taking protective formation around aircraft now vulnerable on the improvised landing zone.

Men flowed from the Globemaster's interior. Thirty-six operators moving with synchronized purpose born of repetition and necessity. Each carrying similar weapons. Each wearing similar gear. Each understanding the violence waiting beyond preparation now initiated.

A figure detached from the group. Approached Frank with direct purpose that denied hesitation. Culper's face painted ritual black across cheekbones and eye sockets. His uniform indistinguishable from those he commanded. Only his movement marking him as their leader. The weight carried visible in posture if not expression.

"You made it," Culper said.

Frank nodded.

"Did Pierce make contact?" said Culper.

"Mike Pierce?" rasped Frank.

"Yeah. He was our deep cover operative at the mill. I ordered him to back you up."

Frank seemed confused by the news, images of Pierce being shot by Sarah playing back in his mind. Trying to piece everything together, then… "Pierce is dead," said Frank.

"What?! How?"

Frank shook his head.

"Did Walker find out?"

Frank shrugged, offering no explanation.

"Look. We can't deal with that right now. Things have changed. Walker launched an ICBM. Twenty kilotons. He destroyed an island in the Caribbean as a demonstration. Nothing left but boiling water. Now, he's threatening to destroy Washington D.C. if we attack the NSA facility or the missile silos." Frank grunted.

"We've been ordered to standdown."

"Walker won't stop."

"I know. But I have my orders. They came from the White House. I am obliged to obey them." Frank grunted again, then considered.

"I'll cut the lines," said Frank.

"I believe you'd try," said Culper. "It's too risky." "I can do it," said Frank with eyes that held no doubt.

Culper considered long and hard, then said, "If you fail, Washington will have no choice but to submit to Walker's demands. It'll be the end of America as we know it."

"Won't fail."

"I want to believe you."

"Then do."

Another long pause as options were weighed and consequences considered, then…

"We'll wait for your signal before we attack," said Culper as he unholstered his sidearm. A Sig Sauer M17 with attached suppressor. He handed the weapon and two extra magazines to Frank. "Revolvers make noise." Frank nodded, checked the weapon's chamber.

He turned toward the treeline where the facility waited beyond darkness. He moved with strange fluidity for a man his size, shadow absorbing shadow until there was no division between Frank and the night that claimed him. Culper watched the emptiness where Frank had been and said to himself, "God speed, Frank Kane."

It started to rain. The first drops struck the asphalt like small bullets. Then the sky opened. Water fell not as rain but as judgment, sheeting down in biblical fury. The moon and the mountains disappeared behind curtains of gray. Pitch dark.

Walker leaned into the dim light of the monitors arrayed before him like empty windows. Gray screens drowning in pixels, stuttering images that watched the forest without judgment. The men around him stood or sat, faces blank as eggshell, waiting.

"There," said Heller, pointing to the northeast quadrant where something had moved among the pines. Rain slanted across the frame, a curtain of silver needles through which the world became smeared and uncertain.

Walker squinted at the screen. The movement had stopped or perhaps had never been. The corner of his mouth turned slightly, not quite a smile. "Nothing there. Just water playing tricks on the lens."

The security station smelled of coffee gone cold and men who had lived in their uniforms too long. Three days without proper sleep had hollowed their eyes into sunken pits. The stolen Patriots waited outside, their metal scales slick with rain, sensors blinking in the dark like the eyes of beasts from older times.

Heller shifted. His hand rested on the butt of his pistol, fingers drumming against the grip. "Maybe we should send out another perimeter team. Just to be safe."

"You want to pull men from defensive positions because the rain makes you nervous?"

"Not nervous. Just careful."

Walker studied the screens again, methodical as a doctor reviewing charts. "No air assault until morning at the earliest. Military still evaluating options. A ground approach with proper preparation would take days even if they had the men in position, which they don't."

"Unless they were already staged."

"They weren't."

Heller leaned closer to the monitor showing southeast, camera seven. "What's that?"

Walker followed his gaze. A shadow darker than the others, something not quite natural in its stillness. He tapped a key, zooming the image. Just forest. Just rain.

Just night.

"You're seeing ghosts," Walker said.

"Better ghosts than real threats we miss."

"Perimeter team reports nothing," said the radio operator, hand pressed to his headset. "All sectors accounted for. All guards on station."

Walker nodded once, satisfied. "Maintain current alert status."

The men settled back into watchfulness, attention divided between forest and facility. The cameras rolled on. Rain continued its assault, beating against earth and metal and men with a steady insistence.

Merciless

Washington D.C.

Rain slanted across the White House South Lawn, drops breaking against Marine One's idling rotors. The President hurried across wet grass, his wife's hand clasped in his. Secret Service formed a barrier of bodies against a threat no human shield could stop. Their faces set in professional masks that concealed nothing from those who knew where to look.

"Sir, we need to move now," said the lead agent, voice tight against his earpiece.

The President paused at the helicopter's steps, turning to look at the building he might never see again. White columns against a gray sky. Two centuries of democracy housed in mortar and stone that missiles could erase in seconds.

"History will call this our darkest day," he said.

"Only if we live to write it, sir," replied the agent,

ushering them inside.

Marine One lifted, banking south toward Andrews Air Force Base where Air Force One waited, engines already spooled. The President watched the city fall away beneath them, monuments reduced to miniatures, history made small by distance and perspective.

In the Capitol, the Speaker's Dining Room had become command central. Crystal chandeliers cast shadows across mahogany tables where democracy now bargained for its life. Papers scattered across surfaces, laptops glowed blue in the dimness. The fear in the room had physical presence, a thing that breathed and moved among them.

Governor Chapman from Georgia cleared his throat. "What if we just gave them what they want? Let the western states go?"

Eyes turned toward him, some angry, others considering.

"Treason," spat Senator Hargrove, pounding his fist on the table. "You're talking about dismembering the United States because terrorists told us to!"

"I'm talking about saving millions of lives," Chapman shot back. "My constituents didn't sign up to be

vaporized for your principles."

"Then get the hell out." The House Minority Leader stood, pointing toward the door. "Go. Run. This room is for people willing to defend the Constitution, not surrender it."

"The Constitution won't matter if Washington is a radioactive crater!" Chapman's face had gone scarlet. Two aides tried pulling him back to his seat.

Across the room, Representative Morris threw his phone against the wall. "The cellular networks are jammed. I can't reach my family. My children—" His voice broke, the last word dissolving into something primal.

"We need to leave now," said a congressional staffer, grabbing her purse. "There's still time to get clear of the blast radius." Three others followed her toward the door.

"Sit down!" Senator Malcolm's voice cracked through the chaos. "Everyone! This is exactly what they want—panic, division, surrender."

The room stilled momentarily. Outside, sirens wailed, their urgency carrying through centuries-old stone.

"How long do we have?" asked the Senate Minority Leader, her voice steady but thin.

"Eighty-three minutes." Malcolm spread papers across the table. "They want a constitutional amendment granting state sovereignty for eleven western states, with authority to form their own union outside federal jurisdiction."

"Constitutional amendments require two-thirds of both houses, then three-quarters of state legislatures," said the House speaker. "That process takes years, not hours."

Senator Whitman from Nebraska laughed, the sound brittle as ice cracking. "Ninety minutes? We couldn't get agreement on lunch orders in ninety minutes, let alone a constitutional amendment that would tear the country apart."

General Braddock, Chairman of the Joint Chiefs, stepped forward from the wall where he'd been standing. His uniform remained immaculate despite the hour, as if maintaining appearance might somehow preserve order itself.

"The Pentagon is locked out of missile authentication systems in Montana, Wyoming, and parts of North Dakota," he said. "The access codes have been altered. Our technicians are working to bypass them, but it will take days, not hours."

"How is that even possible?" demanded the Attorney General.

"Insider threat. We've identified a colonel with access who disappeared forty-eight hours ago." Braddock's jaw tightened. "The militias have been planning this for years."

A glass shattered as someone's hand trembled too severely to maintain grip. Water spread across classified documents no one bothered to save.

"This isn't about amendments," Braddock continued. "The militias know perfectly well we can't deliver what they're asking for in ninety minutes. They want to destroy or at least cripple the federal government so it cannot stand in the way of the states seceding from the union."

"Then why bother with demands at all?" asked a governor from the back.

"History," Braddock replied. "They need the record to show they gave us a chance. That we forced their hand."

Malcolm steadied himself against the table. "We need options. Now."

"I'm getting my family out," said a congressman, heading for the door. Two others followed. No one tried stopping them.

"You're abandoning your posts!" shouted the House Speaker.

"Our posts won't exist in eighty minutes!" came the reply as the door slammed shut.

The Chief Justice rose from his seat. "We could draft an executive proclamation acknowledging their demands, promise immediate congressional action. It wouldn't be legally binding but might buy time."

"Buy time for what?" asked the Secretary of Defense. "For more missiles to be aimed at other cities? For their movement to grow stronger while we look weak?"

"For our Special Forces to find and eliminate Walker," Braddock said quietly.

The room fell silent.

"Do we have assets in position?" Malcolm asked.

"No," said Braddock. "But we can get them in position… if we have more time."

"Jesus, we don't have more time," said Senator Hargrove as he wiped sweat from his forehead.

"We have seventy-six minutes," the Speaker of the House replied. "Best to prepare for all contingencies."

The Attorney General shook his head. "Draft the proclamation. Get the President to sign it electronically from Air Force One. We need options beyond prayer and vague military operations."

Morris, who had earlier thrown his phone, spoke through hands that covered his face. "What if we just launched first? Take out their facility before they can target us?"

"With what?" Braddock asked. "They control the missiles. We'd be targeting our own nuclear silos."

"So, target them. I'd rather lose a few missile silos than the White House and Congress."

"It wouldn't be a few. There are 120 ICBM silos at Maelstrom Air Base alone. We don't know which ones the militias control. Maybe all of them. Besides, we believe they can monitor the data streams from our satellites. If we launch they'll know it, then they'll launch. We lose either way."

"They could be bluffing."

"They obliterated an American island in the Caribbean. I doubt they're bluffing."

The room descended into fresh argument, voices climbing over each other in a cacophony of fear and desperate strategizing. Outside, evacuation sirens continued their mournful warning. Rain battered windows that had witnessed centuries of governance, now witnessing its potential end.

"Quiet!" Malcolm shouted. "Work the problem. Draft the proclamation. Continue evacuation protocols."

The aides who remained bent to their tasks, fingers flying across keyboards, voices dictating emergency provisions into recording devices for posterity. Democracy working against a countdown no election could reset.

"Sixty-eight minutes," called the timekeeper by the door.

Outside, Pennsylvania Avenue had been cleared of traffic. The rain washed across empty streets where power still flowed, lights still burned, but the people who gave those things meaning were moving away from the center, toward peripheries that might survive what approached.

In the drafting room, constitutional phrases centuries old were being restructured into sentences that might prevent their destruction. Words against warheads. The founders had prepared for many threats, but not this one. Not Americans with nuclear leverage against their own government.

"Transmission ready," called the communications director.

Malcolm looked at the document on his screen. A patchwork of concessions and promises wrapped in language dignified enough to disguise capitulation as negotiation.

"Will it work?" asked the Vice President, his face ashen beneath the room's unflattering light.

Malcolm closed his eyes briefly. "It buys time. After that, God help us all."

The rain continued its drumming, indifferent to the words crafted beneath its rhythm. The city waited, its monuments standing against a sky that might soon erase them. Democracy bartering for its tomorrow with promises it never thought it would need to make.

Pahsimeroi Valley

Frank appeared at the edge of the treeline, a darker shape against shadows. He watched the compound through the falling rain, counting seconds between camera sweeps. The mechanical eyes panned left to right, paused, then swung back in predictable rhythm. Guards moved along set paths, their patterns as regular as the rain. Frank timed their movements, waiting for the moment when blind spots aligned.

The militia guard outside the fence never heard him. Frank emerged from darkness like something born from it, moving beneath camera lines with the ease of long practice. The rain helped, its white noise drowning subtler sounds, droplets hitting the guard's hood with enough force to mask approaching footsteps. The man stamped his feet, trying to keep circulation going in the cold. He turned, sensing perhaps something in the air or the absence where it should have been filled.

The silenced pistol made a sound like a fist striking meat. The guard folded, a marionette with cut strings, his body knowing death before his mind had time to register the bullet that delivered it. Frank caught him before he hit the ground, lowering the corpse with gentleness.

He dragged the body into shadow where darkness would keep its secrets. The rain washed the blood into soil that had tasted worse things than one man's ending.

Frank crouched at the fence line, studying where metal met earth. Chain link stretched twelve feet high, topped with razor wire that caught raindrops like tiny diamonds before releasing them.

The KA-BAR slid from its sheath without sound. Frank dug where the ground stayed softest, the blade cutting through wet soil with practiced economy. No wasted movement. Just hands that understood work. He checked the hole's progress against his shoulders, measuring space against necessity. The ground beneath the fence reluctant but not impossible. Water gathered in the deepening depression, turning dirt to mud that smelled of pine and something older.

When the space proved sufficient, Frank flattened to earth. Soil stained his clothing as he slithered beneath metal teeth that would have seized a lesser man. His breath came slow and measured despite exertion. The ground showed only passing witness to his progress, rain already erasing evidence of disturbance.

Inside the compound, he rose to a crouch. The facility stood before him, concrete walls stained dark with water. Lights burned in scattered windows, yellow islands in the storm's vast sea. Men moved behind glass, unaware of what had crossed their boundary.

Frank scanned for patrols, for cameras, for anything that might register his presence where it wasn't welcome. Seeing nothing immediate, he moved toward the nearest building. Shadow claiming shadow until he and darkness became the same thing. Patient. Waiting. Inevitable.

Voices carried through the rain, two guards on patrol rounding the corner of a storage shed. They walked shoulder to shoulder, rifles slung across their chests, complaining about the weather.

Frank pressed against the wall, waiting. When they passed his position, he struck without hesitation. The silenced pistol coughed once, the first guard dropping without sound. The second turned, reaching for his weapon. Frank squeezed the trigger again, but the pistol failed to respond, mud from his crawl having fouled the action.

Without pause Frank dropped the jammed pistol in the mud and lunged forward, one massive hand covering the guard's mouth while the KA-BAR found the soft hollow beneath the jaw. The man's eyes widened then emptied. Frank lowered him to the ground, blood mingling with rainwater. He dragged both bodies behind the shed, arranging them in shadows where they wouldn't be found until morning. By then it wouldn't matter. He took a magnetic security card hanging from the shirt pocket of one of the guards. He moved back toward the building.

Frank paused at the maintenance entrance on the side of a building, rain sliding from his shoulders. He knew this part of the compound from his earlier reconnaissance with Sarah. The memory of her stirred something he thought he'd buried deeper. No time for that now. The door yielded to the security card taken from the guard. No alarm sounded.

The corridor stretched before him, silent. Frank knew what waited below—the fiber junction he'd found days ago, the vulnerable throat of Walker's operation. Cut it, and the missiles would go blind. But between him and that target lay a labyrinth of hallways and unknown guard positions. He considered his Redhawks. Too loud. It would be blade and hands from here.

Heller stood in the security office, face illuminated by the blue glow of monitor banks. The rain continued its assault outside, drumming against the roof in sheets that made radio communication staticky and uncertain. Militia men moved across screens like chess pieces, their positions mapped by cameras that watched with electronic indifference.

"Control to Echo Three. Report status." Heller leaned

toward the radio, fingers drumming against the console edge. Static answered. He tried again. "Echo Three, this is Control. Acknowledge." Nothing.

The radio operator glanced up. "Second missed check-in. Echo Four also failed to respond ten minutes ago."

Heller's jaw tightened. "Send Daniels and Martinez to Echo Three's last position. Tell them to maintain radio contact."

"Sir."

Heller moved to the tactical display where guard positions glowed as blue dots across the compound schematic. Two dots now flashed yellow for unconfirmed. The pattern bothered him. Not random. Sequential. Someone moving through his security grid with purpose.

Rain pounded the roof harder, the sound like distant gunfire. Heller touched the pistol at his hip, checking its presence from habit rather than conscious thought.

The radio crackled. "Control, this is Daniels. We're approaching Echo Three's position."

"Maintain open channel," Heller ordered.

For thirty seconds, only the sound of breathing came through the speaker. Men moving through rain, their footsteps squelching in mud. Then: "Jesus Christ." "Report," Heller barked.

"Echo Three is down." Daniels's voice had gone tight with controlled panic. "Wait. Found Echo Four. Same thing. He's cold. Been dead at least ten minutes."

Heller leaned closer to the microphone. "Secure position. Check perimeter. Weapons hot."

"Already on it. No sign of—" The transmission cut off suddenly.

"Daniels?" Heller's hand tightened on the radio.

Nothing but static.

Heller turned to the security team. "Full lockdown. I want two-man patrols, no exceptions. All non-security personnel to shelter in place."

The men scrambled to comply, checking weapons, activating emergency protocols that had been drilled but never expected. Heller strode from the room. He found Walker in the command center, bent over displays where missile telemetry data scrolled in constant green ribbons. "We have a breach," Heller said without preamble.

Walker looked up, face expressionless. "Show me."

They moved through corridors gone silent except for the distant drumming of rain. Armed men passed them, moving to defensive positions. Outside, the compound lay dark except for security floodlights casting harsh white pools across muddied ground. Rain fell in sheets that distorted vision and sound alike.

Heller led Walker to the northeast corner where Daniels and Martinez stood over two shapes beneath rain ponchos.

"When?" Walker asked, voice flat as stone.

"First missed radio check eighteen minutes ago. Second twelve minutes after. Found bodies six minutes ago." Heller peeled back one poncho. The guard stared skyward, eyes fixed on nothing, throat opened.

Walker studied the wound with clinical detachment. "Professional. Single cut. No hesitation." He looked up at Heller. "Where's the intruder's entry point?"

Daniels gestured toward the fence line where mud had been disturbed in a pattern not made by rain. Walker moved toward it, crouching despite the downpour, examining the ground with fingers that cared nothing for the blood and earth that stained them.

"Here," he said, pointing to a depression leading beneath the chainlink. "Someone dug under. Big man by the width. Came in quiet, took out the guards without alarm."

"Could be a team," Heller suggested.

Walker shook his head, rain streaming from his face like something washing away. "One man." He ran his hand along the fence post. "Kane."

Heller stiffened. "Impossible. He's dead."

"Apparently not." Walker rose, turning to face Heller with eyes gone winter cold. "You told me you killed him. Put three rounds in him and watched him fall into the river. That he couldn't have survived."

"He couldn't—"

Walker's hand shot out, grabbing Heller's jacket front with sudden violence. "Then who dug this hole? Who killed these men with a blade instead of a gun? Who moved through your security without detection?" Each question punctuated by a tightening grip.

Heller didn't flinch. "I'll find him."

"You'll kill him." Walker released Heller with a small shove. "He's here for the Patriots. For Sarah. For me. You find him before he completes any of those objectives."

Walker's eyes held nothing human. "If you fail this time I'll put you in the ground instead of him." He looked at the dead men, at the fence line, at the darkness beyond where Frank moved cold as the rain. "I want every man searching. Building by building. Room by room. Shoot on sight."

"Understood." Heller turned to Daniels, already issuing orders that sent men scrambling toward buildings where lights still burned behind windows gone black with rain.

Walker stood motionless, staring at the hole beneath the fence. His face betrayed nothing, but his hand had moved to the pistol at his side, fingers closing around the grip with something like anticipation. Like a man eager to reacquaint himself with an old adversary he thought lost forever.

The rain continued its assault. Somewhere in the compound, Frank moved through darkness like something born from it. Patient. Hunting. The distance between predator and prey shrinking with each passing heartbeat.

Walker returned to the command center, boots leaving muddy imprints across floors that had once housed government secrets. Now they carried different burdens. Men stood at stations watching screens where missile telemetry data continued its constant flow, unaware of the death that had breached their perimeter.

"Status report," Walker demanded.

The lead technician looked up, fingers pausing over keyboard. "Washington acknowledged receipt of our demands forty-eight minutes ago. No substantive response yet."

Walker's face hardened. "Prepare for immediate launch."

The room went still. The constant background hum of equipment suddenly louder in the absence of human sound.

"Sir?" The technician's voice had gone careful, a man testing ground that might collapse beneath him. "The ninety-minute deadline—"

"Is no longer operational." Walker moved to the main console, keying in access codes with fingers that never hesitated. "Kane is here. In the facility."

Men exchanged glances. Some reached for weapons holstered at hips.

The senior technician stood, his face pale in the blue light of screens. "That wasn't the plan. We give them time to consider. To see reason."

Walker turned, ice in his gaze. "Plans change. If we

lose the connection to the missile silos we are all dead.

We need to use the ICBMs while we still can."

"But Washington—"

"Will be ash within twenty minutes." Walker continued entering commands, screens responding with mechanical obedience. "Prepare for immediate launch sequence on all targeted warheads."

The technicians moved with less certainty now, the reality of what they prepared settling across shoulders suddenly burdened by history's weight. A country ending not with decades of decline but with minutes of fire.

"Launch sequence initializing," reported the weapons officer, voice steady despite what his hands enabled. "Arming codes accepted. Warhead yield confirmed at maximum capacity."

Walker nodded, satisfied. "Target acquisition?"

"Washington coordinates locked. Capitol Building as primary. White House and Pentagon as secondary. Estimated casualties seven-point-two million in immediate blast radius."

The room went silent again. Numbers that represented people had suddenly become real in ways abstract planning had never captured. Children. Families. Lives not yet touched by the politics that now threatened to erase them.

Walker seemed unburdened by such thoughts. "Proceed with countdown. T-minus ten minutes."

"Should we notify the western governors?" asked the communications officer. "They expected more time to prepare for the transition."

"No. They'll adapt." Walker moved to the tactical display where red circles marked blast radii across the capital region. "History remembers results, not methods."

Outside, rain continued beating against windows like

nature's own fists demanding entrance. Men moved through the compound searching for Frank, unaware their purpose had shifted from defending the future to enabling its premature arrival. The countdown began its implacable progression. Numbers falling toward zero with the certainty of gravity.

Walker watched the screens, face illuminated by digital glow that lent him spectral presence. A ghost already haunting history not yet written. "Eight minutes to launch. May God have mercy on those who forced our hand."

No one responded. Some bowed heads. Others stared at screens where their actions would soon be measured in megadeaths. The room filled with the silence of men who had crossed lines they had never expected to reach.

Inside the main building, it smelled of mildew and government neglect, decades of disuse hanging in the air. Shadows pooled in doorways like sentinels. Each corner promised discovery. Frank moved with patience. He paused at each intersection, listening for sounds that didn't belong in an abandoned facility brought back to life.

He moved through hallways gone colorless under emergency lighting. His footsteps made no sound against concrete floors worn smooth by years of bureaucratic passage. Signs in faded government typography directed toward departments long abandoned. SIGNALS ANALYSIS. CRYPTOGRAPHIC SERVICES. SECURE COMMUNICATION.

The stairwell door opened to darkness deeper than the night outside. Frank took a moment to let his eyes adjust. Concrete steps descended into the facility's bowels. Frank paused, listened. Only the building's mechanical heartbeat. The hum of ancient ventilation, the distant tick of water dropping from pipes never meant to last this long.

The stairwell swallowed light. Each step downward took him deeper into the shadow realm where government secrets had once lived. Five steps down, something changed in the air. A disturbance. The weight of presence. Frank stopped.

The metallic click of a safety disengaged. Frank felt it more than heard it, the sound traveling through air gone suddenly thick.

"You just refuse to die like some kind of God-sent savior," Heller said from behind him. His voice steady as the pistol now aimed at the back of Frank's skull.

"No," Frank said. "Not savior."

He lowered his head, tucking his chin to chest, his head lower than the collar of his body armor. The motion subtle but deliberate. From behind, Frank appeared headless, denying Heller the kill shot.

"Executioner," Frank said as he stepped backward up the stairs, moving upward toward Heller rather than away. His massive frame filling the narrow stairwell like something risen from depths where light never reached.

Heller fired. The sound bounced off concrete walls. Confined space turning single shot to thunderclap. The round struck Frank's backplate. Pain exploded across his shoulders. Ceramic taking punishment flesh could not survive.

Frank didn't stop. Another step backward, upward. Closer to the man who thought him already fallen.

Heller fired again. Second round impacting lower on the vest. Frank's breath left him. Ribs protesting impact even as the ceramic plate dispersed the killing energy. His leg found the next step. Reduced the distance.

The third shot struck between shoulders. Frank's knees buckled beneath pain's sudden weight. But backward momentum continued.

Heller aimed lower. The next round tore through Frank's thigh unprotected by his body armor. Muscle and sinew parting. Blood flowed spreading around the hole in his pants. Frank's leg dragged now but still he came. Unstoppable.

Heller's eyes widened. Space between them collapsed as Frank reached the landing on which Heller stood.

Frank swung around. His hand found the pistol. Closed around metal and the flesh that held it like a vice, pushing it upward toward the concrete ceiling. Both men used both hands in the struggle to control the gun. Heller fired. Frank pushed the weapon's slide lock up causing the pistol's slide to lock back, then pressed the magazine release button. The magazine fell to the landing with a clatter.

Cement dust from the bullet hole rained down on them both. Heller reached with his free hand toward the push dagger at his belt. The blade that had already marked Frank once.

Frank caught the second hand. Bone and tendon shifting beneath his grip. He redirected Heller's movement. The dagger's path altered. Steel finding Heller's abdomen with sound like canvas tearing.

Heller made a small noise. Not surrender. His fist drove into Frank's wounded side. Frank absorbed it like a mountain taking rain. Frank twisted Heller's gun hand. Bones surrendered with sound like green wood breaking.

Frank guided the pistol barrel higher. Past jaw. Past cheek. To eye socket where skull provided a ready hole. Frank pushed metal against yielding flesh. Heller understood what came next. He screamed in pain. His body tensed.

Heller's resistance ended. His body slumped against the stairwell wall, held upright by Frank's grip. Frank removed Heller's belt, then released him. The body folded onto itself. Frank wrapped Heller's belt above the wound in his thigh and cinched it tight slowing the bleeding.

He continued downward. The mission unchanged by his meeting with Heller. The junction room still waited. Cables still required severing. The pain in his leg registered as background noise against the duty that remained. Blood followed him down the stairs as he descended.

Frank reached a door marked SECURE COMMUNICATION and exited the stairwell into a hallway.

In the command center, Walker leaned over the console. His finger hovering above the final authorization key. Men around him stood frozen in the blue glow of screens. The missile control system displayed launch sequence initialized. Countdown timer reading three minutes seventeen seconds.

"Washington evacuations have begun," the communications officer reported. "Total panic in the streets."

Walker nodded. "Too late for them. Proceed with launch confirmation."

Frank found the junction room behind a steel door marked AUTHORIZED PERSONNEL ONLY. Inside, racks of equipment hummed with renewed life. Fiber optic cables ran along marked channels in the floor, bundled in river-like arteries that disappeared into the walls. Yellow emergency lighting cast everything in jaundiced tones.

"Targeting solutions locked," the weapons officer called.

His voice steady despite what his hands enabled. "Capitol Building primary target. White House secondary. Pentagon tertiary."

Walker's finger descended toward the key. "Two minutes to launch. May God forgive what men have forced us to do."

Frank traced the main trunk line with his eyes. Thicker than the others, it ran from floor to ceiling where it joined with government conduits still connected to missile silos beyond the mountains. The source of Walker's power. The connection to Armageddon.

Blood from his wounded thigh left dark footprints across the concrete floor. The KA-BAR would be insufficient against the hardened cable sheathing. Frank scanned the room, searching for anything that might serve.

"Launch sequence authentication accepted," called the technician. "One minute forty seconds remaining."

Walker's face reflected in the monitor's glow. No hesitation visible in eyes that had seen too much death to fear causing more. "Begin final countdown."

Against the far wall hung a fire axe behind shattered glass, preserved from some earlier iteration of the facility's purpose. Frank crossed to it, weight testing the handle's integrity. The blade showed surface rust, but the edge remained. It would do.

"Silos opening," the technician reported. Steel doors weighing thirty tons each sliding apart in Montana wilderness. "Missile pre-launch sequence initiated."

Walker turned to the strategic map where Washington appeared in satellite imagery. The capital unaware that its final moments had begun counting down. "We remake America today. Cleanse it with necessary fire."

Axe in hand, Frank moved toward the cable junction. "Frank."

Her voice came soft behind him. Too soft. He turned. Sarah stood in the doorway. Hair pulled back same as the first time he saw her at the mill. Same green eyes that had watched him across tangled sheets. Different now.

Harder. The Civil War era revolver in her hand aimed at his face with unwavering certainty.

"I know this doesn't seem fair. Mitchell's my father, Frank. I can't go against family. But I do care about you."

The gun barrel reflected the single bulb's light. A small sun aimed at his mortality.

She fired.

The bullet struck his cheekbone. Pain exploded white across his vision. His body followed physics, shoulders meeting concrete, skull cracking against floor. Blood warm against skin. Ceiling suddenly all he could see. His breath came shallow through damaged throat.

Sarah moved into his narrowing field of vision. Gun still aimed. Ready.

"I'm sorry, Frank."

The Redhawk appeared in his hand like conjurer's trick. His finger found the trigger before thought could form. The revolver's report filled the room with thunder. The .44 magnum round punched through her chest, tore past bone and organ and exited with flesh spray that painted the wall behind her. Her body lifted, thrown backward by force that defied her slight frame.

She landed broken. A small sound escaped her lips. Not words. Just air finding new passage through her ruined chest.

Frank lifted himself from concrete. Each heartbeat pushing pain deeper into bone. His cheek shattered where lead met calcium beneath skin. Blood dripping a steady rhythm onto floor. He crossed to where Sarah lay.

Her eyes found his. Confusion replacing certainty that had steadied her hand seconds before. Blood bubbled from mouth corners. Fingers twitched against cement seeking purchase in a world suddenly unmoored.

"No," he said, looking down at betrayal wearing a woman's face. "I'm sorry."

The light left her eyes the way it always did. Not dramatic. Not poetic. Just there then gone. Another ghost to walk beside him.

Frank turned back to the cables. The pain in his face nothing against what must be done. Blood dripped from his chin onto fiber lines that carried apocalypse beneath American soil. The axe rose in his hands. Vengeance and duty sharing the same motion.

Voices in the corridor outside. Frank heard them approach through the junction room's steel door. No time for stealth now. Only for action that might prevent millions of deaths.

The blade fell.

"One minute to launch. Point of no return in forty-seven seconds."

Walker inserted his key into the console. Turned it clockwise to final position. The screen before him changed from amber to red. The system now primed for his final command.

Frank swung the axe. The blade bit into the cable bundle with sound like bone breaking. Not deep enough. The outer sheathing split, but core lines remained intact. Data still flowing through glass veins toward missiles waiting in distant silos.

"First stage ignition sequence commencing. Thirty seconds to launch."

Walker stood straight. His hand resting on the terminal authorization switch. The red button Hollywood had made cliché now real beneath his palm. The room silent except for computers counting toward judgment.

Frank swung again. The axe blade sinking deeper. Fiber lines parting beneath force that came from desperation and rage equal measure. Blood from his cheek dripping onto severed cables. Still some strands remained. Still connecting Walker to the power of gods.

"Twenty seconds. Missile guidance systems online."

Walker looked at the men around him. At faces that had followed him into treason now transfigured as nationalism. "For the republic," he said, and pressed the button.

Frank's third swing came with everything remaining in him. The axe blade shearing through final strands of fiber. The cut complete. The connection severed.

In the command center, screens turned to static. Digital readouts displaying missile telemetry flatlined. Radar feeds stuttered then failed. Walker's hand still pressed against a button now connected to nothing.

"What happened?" His voice cut through sudden silence where machine hums had been constant companions.

The technician's fingers flew across keyboards, seeking answers from systems that no longer responded.

"Connection's lost. Complete termination of the fiber link."

"Restore it. Now!"

"I can't. It's physical, not digital."

Walker's fist slammed against the console, the sound startling men who had never seen his control waver. "Find the break. Now! We still have time to complete the launch."

"Sir, if the military—"

"They won't have time if we fix this. Send teams to check every junction point. Start with the lower levels where the main trunks meet."

Men scrambled to obey, pulling on tactical gear, checking weapons. The room buzzing with new urgency now that the impossible had happened.

Walker stood in the center, watching as his carefully constructed plan threatened to unravel. "Tell Heller to double the perimeter guards. They've penetrated the facility."

The technician hesitated. "Who has?"

Walker's eyes were winter cold. "It doesn't matter who. Just that they die before they reach us."

Frank dropped the axe. The tool having served its purpose, now just dead weight. The wooden handle clattered against concrete.

He reached into his pocket for the satellite phone. Thumbed the power button. Screen glowed blue in the dim room. His thick fingers pressed the message function. Typed single word to Culper: GO. He sent it. Waited. No connection. The underground room blocking signal that needed clear sky to reach orbiting satellites.

Frank tucked the phone away. He had to reach higher ground. Needed a signal to confirm mission completion.

But something else pulled at him. Unfinished business. Walker remained somewhere above. The man who'd orchestrated all this. Who'd nearly burned down a nation to remake it in his image.

He drew the Redhawks from their holsters. The matched revolvers settled in his palms like old friends returning. He checked each cylinder from habit. Rounds waiting in their chambers. Six shots in each hand.

The corridor outside filled with voices. Radio chatter. The sound of men. With anger. No time to find better position. The junction room offered little cover. Just equipment racks and shadow. Frank moved to the wall beside the door where he'd be hidden from immediate sight. His breathing slowed. The pain in his leg and face retreating behind resolve that had carried him through worse.

The door swung open. First man entered with rifle leading. Military stance. Eyes sweeping the room like searchlights. He spotted the severed cable immediately.

"Junction's been cut," he said into his radio.

Two more men followed. Weapons high and ready. They spread into the room, maintaining distance from each other. Tactical dispersion.

The first man approached the cable. Bent to examine the clean cut. "Looks fresh. Within the last—"

Frank stepped from shadow. The Redhawks extended. One targeting the man at the cable. The other covering the two by the door. There was a moment of perfect stillness. Of recognition. Of calculation too late to matter.

The Redhawks roared. Their voices filling the small room with thunder. Muzzle flash turning darkness to strobing day. The first man fell backward. Center mass shot leaving perfect hole where life had just been. The second round caught the next man in the throat. His hands rising too late to staunch what couldn't be stopped.

The third man fired his rifle from the hip. Rounds sparking against equipment racks beside Frank's head. Frank's left Redhawk answered. The .44 round striking just below the man's sternum. Lifting him backward through the doorway he'd just entered.

More voices in the corridor. More boots approaching. Frank moved to the door. The Redhawks still hot in his hands. Three men down. More coming. But somewhere in this facility waited the man who'd orchestrated everything. The head Frank needed to cut off.

Frank stepped over the fallen man. Checked the corridor. Four more approaching from the left. Elevator access. They spotted him immediately. Rifles came up. Frank ducked back as rounds stitched the wall where he'd just been. Concrete dust filling the air like pale smoke.

No route to Walker in that direction. He glanced right. Emergency exit sign glowed at corridor's end. The stairwell would lead upward. Toward command center where Walker would be managing the crisis Frank had created. Toward roof where satellite signal might reach. Two purposes aligned on same path.

He fired both Redhawks around the door frame. Not aiming now. Just covering fire. Keeping heads down while he moved. The revolvers bucking in his hands as rounds tore through the corridor.

Frank ran toward the exit. His wounded leg a dull fire with each step. Behind him shouting. Men organizing pursuit. More boots on stairs somewhere ahead. He reached the emergency door. Threw his weight against the push bar while firing his Redhawks. Remaining rounds low. The door reluctant then surrendering to mass and momentum.

Stairwell stretched upward. No time for hesitation. Frank took stairs two at a time. Pain protesting but ignored. His breath coming harder now. Blood loss and exertion extracting cost that mind could deny but body still paid.

Door above opened. Two men appeared on landing. Their rifles finding him in the narrow space. Frank fired upward. The first Redhawk's round catching the lead man in the chest. He toppled backward into his companion. Both falling in tangle of limbs and weapons.

Frank didn't slow. Pushed past them at the landing. The surviving man's hands reaching for him. Finding only air as Frank continued upward. Past doors marked with level designations. Each one potentially leading to Walker. But Frank needed higher ground first. Needed confirmation that outside world knew what he'd done. Knew the threat was neutralized.

Behind him pursuit grew. Men calling positions through radios. Coordinating to cut off his escape. Frank reached a door marked LEVEL ONE. Command center level according to blueprints memorized before mission start. He paused. Weighed options. Walker would be there. So would dozens of armed men. First the signal. Then Walker.

He continued upward toward roof access. The final landing. Door with push bar and warning about alarm. Frank hit it with shoulder already resigned to pain. Bright light momentarily blinded him. Fresh air against his face. He stood on the facility roof. Gravel crunching beneath his boots. The sun hanging low in western sky.

Frank pulled the satellite phone from his pocket. Powered it on again. Signal bars appeared. Connection established with orbiting technology miles above. He sent the message again. GO. Confirmation that would tell Culper that the fiber lines were cut. That nuclear launch was prevented. That ground assault could commence.

Message sent. The screen displayed confirmation.

Done. One mission complete. But Frank wasn't finished. He had to go back down. Had to find Walker. Had to end the man whose vision had nearly ended millions.

Frank approached the exit door on the roof. He heard a multitude of footfalls coming up the stairs. In just a few moments he would soon be outnumbered. His Redhawks were almost empty. He snapped open the cylinders and emptied the shells and casings. He pulled two Speedloaders from his tactical vest and loaded the revolvers. He snapped them shut just as the door burst open and the men hunting him poured onto the rooftop.

He was out of time. Time to fight.

The roof offered little cover. Just ventilation ducts. HVAC units. Utility shed twenty feet to his left. The men spotted him and opened fire without warning, without demand for surrender. He dove to the gravel. Bullets whizzed past him and chewed tar paper at his feet.

He returned fire with deadly accuracy. One of the men was hit in the shoulder, spun around, fell with a groan, his collar bone fractured.

Frank scrambled to his feet as he continued to fire. Another man was hit in the forehead. He crumbled to the rooftop. Dead.

Frank dove behind the nearest air handler. Rounds sparked against metal where his body had been a heartbeat before. The steel housing wouldn't stop rifle rounds for long.

He reloaded, ejecting the spent casings along with several unspent bullets. He pulled two more Speedloaders from his harness. He was getting low on ammunition. He reloaded the Redhawks and snapped them shut.

Walker was below. Just one floor down. Command center on level one. Frank couldn't afford retreat. Couldn't allow the man to escape.

The firing intensified. Rounds punching through the air handler's thin metal housing. Frank kept low. Felt a bullet pass through sheet metal inches above his head. He gauged distances. Angles. Firing lanes. The staccato rhythm of the rifles told him their positions. Their discipline revealed in how they maintained covering fire while maneuvering for clearer shots.

He waited for pattern in their fire. For the microsecond when rifles emptied and reloaded. When covering fire faltered. It came. Brief hesitation in lead storm. Frank moved.

He came around right side of air handler. The Redhawks extending with arms that never trembled regardless of what waited. First man spotted him. Tried bringing rifle to bear. Too slow. The Redhawk roared. Heavy .44 round struck militia man center chest. Force lifted him backward like the hand of God.

The other men shifted fire toward Frank's new position. He was already moving. Three strides across open roof to maintenance shed. Bullets tracing path behind boots that didn't slow despite leg wound still leaking blood.

Two men left if no more arrived. He was never that lucky. From the shed's corner Frank fired again. The left Redhawk finding another militiaman who'd exposed himself seeking better angle. Round caught him in the throat. Man dropped like a puppet with cut strings gasping for air.

Two more militiamen joined the fight running form the rooftop doorway.

The three militiamen still in the fight adjusted their tactics. Two providing suppressive fire while third circled toward Frank's position. Flanking maneuver.

Frank waited. Counted their rounds. The rhythm telling him magazine capacity. When next pause came he rolled from cover. Prone position offering smallest target. Both Redhawks found third man attempting to flank. Two rounds struck his pelvis where body armor ended. Man collapsed screaming.

Remaining militia concentrated fire on Frank's position. Concrete chips stinging his face as rounds impacted inches from skull. The shed disintegrating around him with each bullet's passage. No sustainable position.

Frank moved again. No cover this time. Just speed and determination carrying him across the open rooftop toward men who realized too late what approached. First Redhawk emptied at closer range. Heavy slugs punching through chest and neck of another man who managed one wild shot before momentum carried him backward over roof edge. His body disappearing into space.

Last militiaman standing. His rifle tracking Frank's movement. Finger tightening on trigger that would end what stared at him across narrowing gap. The rifle spoke. Round catching Frank's shoulder. The ceramic plate held, but the impact spun him halfway. Pain flared white across vision. He didn't fall.

The final militiaman's rifle jammed. He worked rifle bolt trying to clear it. Too slow. The Redhawks barked. Two rounds struck militiaman between eyes that showed only surprise. Nice grouping.

Seven down. Roof secured. Frank reloaded and holstered the Redhawks. He was out of Speedloaders. He had twelve bullets in the two revolvers and that was it for the big guns. He still had his Colt Cobra and the Derringer, but neither carried the power of the Redhawks.

Frank needed to find Walker before he escaped. Frank knew that if Walker was killed or captured the militiamen would lose heart and flee or surrender. Walker was the priority.

Reckoning

They came through the darkness, three men in ghillie suits the color of wet earth. The fabric moved like dying grass in the rain that fell without pause or mercy. The first man stopped, hand raised in signal understood without words. Through night vision goggles he saw the militiamen on the ridge, four of them spread-out. Their rifles propped against rock, faces turned toward the compound below, smoke from cigarette trailing upward before rain destroyed it.

The first sniper eased a suppressed Glock from its holster. He moved across ground made silent by water's constant work. His boots finding purchase in mud that accepted his weight without protest that might betray his passage. The second sniper circled right. The third left. Each man understanding their role in what would follow without need for communication that might reach ears not meant to hear it.

The first militiaman never registered the shadow that materialized behind him. The suppressed pistol made sound no louder than a man spitting. The 9mm subsonic round entered skull just behind the ear, its passage transforming the man from sentry to memorial. The sniper caught the body before it struck ground that would have announced his work to those not yet rendered irrelevant.

The second militiaman turned at sound too faint to be recognized but sufficient to trigger instincts. The suppressed pistol spoke again. Another body lowered to earth with care.

The third and fourth militiamen fell without witnessing what killed them. The three snipers working with coordination born from years operating together in places where official reports would never acknowledge their presence.

"Ridge secured," the first sniper said, voice barely audible in microphone positioned against throat that carried words without need for volume that might reach those who waited below.

"Confirmed," came reply from Culper, still hidden in the treeline.

The first sniper assembled the Barrett from components carried in backpack designed for exactly this sequence. The suppressor extending the barrel's already considerable length by fourteen inches, the black metal dulled to prevent reflection that might betray position to watchers below. He settled against stone made slick by rain that continued its work.

The second and third snipers positioned themselves along the ridge, feet braced against mud that shifted beneath them, Barrett rifle stocks pressed against shoulders. The scopes adjusted for distance made variable by night's interference in calculations designed for sunlight's more measurable behavior.

"Target acquisition," the first sniper said. Through his scope the compound spread beneath him.

"North tower," Culper's voice came through communication device no larger than a seed positioned in the sniper's ear. "Priority target."

The Barrett's trigger broke with precise pressure. The suppressor diminished the sound, rendering mechanical thunder to something approximating branch breaking beneath heavy snow. The man in the north tower disappeared in red mist briefly illuminated by security lights before the rain erased evidence of his existence. The body remained standing three seconds, nervous system not yet informed of death's arrival, then toppled from the tower.

The second sniper fired. The round traveled distance between ridge and compound with indifference to rain that tried and failed to alter its trajectory. The man at the eastern gate fell without sound that reached those still operating the mortar position that formed next target in sequence already agreed upon without need for verbal confirmation.

"Mortar team at southwest wall," the spotter said from position beside the third sniper.

The Barrett spoke again. The first militiaman at the mortar position transformed to memory. His companions turned toward sound sufficient to register despite rain and distance. The second sniper fired. Another militiaman fell. The third tried running. The first sniper's round caught him between shoulders that would never again shrug against fate.

"AT4 team behind west barricade," Culper called watching through his binoculars. The anti-tank weapon capable of destroying the Strykers. Culper's men within them preparing for a ground assault that would follow once the snipers finished their work.

The three Barretts fired in sequence so rapid the sound merged into what witnesses might have mistaken for single event. The AT4 team fell without opportunity to employ weapon that might have altered what would follow. Their bodies cooling in mud made liquid by the rain's constant work.

"Second AT4 team at south entrance," Culper said over the radio.

The snipers shifted position, the mud accepting their movement without complaint that might have reached those still unaware of their presence. The Barrett's worked in sequence. More militiamen added to the tally that would never appear in official reports.

"Southeast guard tower," Culper identified. The snipers fired. Another militia position rendered uninhabited.

"All primary defensive positions neutralized," the first sniper reported.

"Maintain overwatch," Culper replied. "Engage any target that threatens the assault vehicles."

The snipers settled deeper into mud that held them like lovers reluctant to surrender embrace. The rain fell across the Barrett's metal skin. Steam rose.

Below them the militiamen continued their patrol, unaware that many of their defensive positions now stood empty of all but corpses.

Walker stood at the wall map of the NSA facility, the paper gone transparent at fold lines. Behind him the command center hummed. Men moved between stations in choreography made automatic by military habit none had surrendered despite discharge papers held in drawers far from this mountain outpost.

"Sir," said Ellis, the radio operator. His fingers tapping

against the console with nervousness beyond his ability to disguise. "Tower three not responding to scheduled check."

Walker turned from the map. His eyes found Ellis across the room made dim by emergency lighting still straining against years unused. "Try again," he said.

Ellis pressed the transmit button. "Tower three, tower three, radio check, over." Static answered, white noise filling the space where human voice should have responded. "No response, sir."

Walker's face revealed nothing despite growing suspicion that prickled at neck hairs military cut kept high and tight against skin gone pale from winter's dominance of these mountains. "Tower one?"

Ellis tried. More static. "Negative."

Walker moved across the command center, boots silent against the elevated false floor covering the room's cable runs. He took the handset from Ellis, turning dial to different frequency not monitored by those in the room.

"Heller, position check."

Three seconds passed. Four. Nothing. Walker kept his emotions in check. He knew everyone was watching him.

"Run a physical check on tower three and tower one," said Walker.

"Understood," said Ellis.

The men moved with renewed purpose, prior boredom erased by orders that confirmed what they'd prepared for without fully expecting. Someone had found them. Someone had breached their perimeter. The revolution now threatened.

Walker studied the security monitors, their grainy black and white images showing nothing beyond empty towers where men should have stood watch but no longer did. Empty mortar positions where tools of war remained, but those trained in their operation did not. The darkness and rain conspiring to hide whatever approached.

The men around Walker checking weapons, checking systems, checking each other for resolve. Walker knew what approached without seeing it. Knew what came for them with purpose born from same devotion to principle that drove him but directed toward outcome precisely opposite.

In the trees Culper raised his fist. The Strykers halted at forest's edge, diesel engines idling. Dawn's first gray light filtered through rain still falling across valley floor stretching between trees and compound. Thirty-six men crouched behind armor, faces painted with patterns that broke human features into something the eye refused to recognize.

"Phase one complete," Culper said into radio. "Snipers maintain overwatch. Call targets of opportunity."

"Confirmed," came reply from ridge where the Barrett rifles waited.

Culper turned to his men, their eyes finding his without need for words that rain might drown anyway. "Three teams. Alpha takes north entrance. Bravo east. Charlie with me through main gate. The Strykers clear path ahead. Patriots are primary objective, command center secondary."

The men nodded, muscle memory replacing conscious thought. Each understood their role, their position, the sequence requiring no rehearsal.

"Execute," Culper said.

The men moved like water finding lowest points in terrain, flowing around trees and across muddy ground that tried holding them but failed. The Strykers followed, their engines growing louder as drivers engaged gears that propelled sixteen tons of steel toward the compound's perimeter. The main cannon on the lead vehicle traversed, finding target selected through thermal imaging that painted the world in heat signatures rather than mere reflection.

Inside the compound Walker's men moved from recognition that this moment had always waited beneath their preparations like bones beneath skin. They took positions behind barriers constructed for exactly this contingency, their rifles held ready by hands steadied through belief that made fear irrelevant to its execution.

"Incoming. North, east, and west," called the spotter from a tower still standing at compound's northwest corner.

Walker stood in the command center, watching screens where camera feeds showed black dots emerging from treeline, their approach measured in yards that vanished too quickly.

"All defensive positions engage at will," he said into the facility-wide channel. "Hold the perimeter at all costs."

The first cannon spoke. The 105mm shell traveling distance between Stryker and defensive position. The concrete bunker exploded from a direct hit, fragments slicing through air briefly visible where floodlights still functioned. The men behind it rendered component parts no longer recognizable as human.

Walker's militia answered. An AT4 anti-tank rocket launched with sound like a giant catching breath. The projectile crossed the open ground in eye-blink, smashing into the lead Stryker. The explosion momentarily brighter than any light yet invented by man. The armor held, its surface merely scarred where lesser vehicles would have surrendered structural integrity.

The second Stryker trained its 30mm autocannon on the AT4 position. The autoloader cycled with mechanical efficiency. The shells finding the target that disappeared in fountain of earth and blood thrown skyward before rain could wash it from the air.

On the ridge the Barrett rifles continued their methodical work. The first sniper finding militia machine gunner who thought himself protected behind sandbagged position overlooking the compound's eastern approach. The heavy .50 caliber round disabused him of this misconception, the man's existence converted to past tense before sound of the shot reached his ears.

Culper's men advanced in formation, using terrain and smoke grenades to mask their approach. When militia fire found them they answered with controlled bursts rather than the panic-fire of amateurs. Three-round groups seeking center mass where body armor might delay but not deny their purpose.

"Bravo team, contact front," came terse report from the eastern approach.

The first Stryker pivoted, its 105mm main gun traversing with deliberation born from electronic calculation rather than human urgency. It fired once. The reinforced guard post at eastern gate ceased to exist.

The militia fought with determination inseparable from desperation. Their defensive positions reduced one by one beneath Stryker cannons and Barrett rifles working opposite ends of same equation. Men fell where they stood or crawled wounded across ground made slick with blood.

"Patriots located," called Culper's point man. "Northeastern corner. Heavily guarded."

The third Stryker changed course, its wheels finding purchase in mud that might have stopped vehicles of lesser weight or determination. The 30mm cannon fired with mechanical regularity. The militia who had formed a protective circle around the stolen missile systems discovered difference between bravery and mathematics.

The first Stryker reached the compound's main gate. Concrete barriers placed by men who believed their foresight sufficient against whatever might approach.

The sixteen-ton vehicle disagreed, its mass converting them to rubble soon indistinguishable from the mud. The gate itself fared no better, steel links briefly visible before the Stryker's passage erased evidence of their existence.

Walker stood in the command center, watching screens where his revolution collapsed in pixels. The men with him checking weapons with hands no longer steady despite discipline's insistence. It won't be long now.

"They've breached the perimeter," said the security officer. "Teams seven and twelve no longer responding."

Walker nodded, face betraying nothing despite knowledge that men he'd recruited and trained now lay cooling on soil. "Initiate evacuation sequence. Main drive purge. Hardcopy destruction."

On the ridge the third sniper found a militia commander directing mortar team behind the command bunker's protective wall. The Barrett fired with authority. The commander fell, the men with him momentarily frozen by the shell's unexpected intrusion.

The second Barrett took advantage of their hesitation.

Another man down. Then another. The mortar abandoned by men whose enthusiasm for revolution suddenly diminished.

Culper moved with Alpha team behind the first Stryker, using its bulk as shield against militia fire growing increasingly desperate as the compound's defenses failed.

The third Stryker reached the Patriot battery, its cannon suddenly silent in deference to ordinance value. The commandos moved from behind it, engaging militia still defending the missiles with desperate recognition that their loss represented failure.

The 105mm cannon on first Stryker remained operational, its voice speaking with authority taking out defensive positions with ease. The remaining militiamen fought back but to little avail. They were simply outgunned by the Strykers.

Walker watched video feeds still functioning despite the compound's systematic dismantlement. The Patriots now surrounded by men in black fatigues. The defensive positions reduced to rubble beneath which men who had followed him now lay dead.

"Sir," said his radio operator. "Team three at Patriots is gone. Team five at eastern bunker not responding."

Walker nodded, face composed despite recognition that plans made over years had found their dissolution in hours. "We move to contingency Omega. Secure the tunnel."

The Strykers continued their destruction of anything that opposed their progress, the 30mm cannons cycling with mechanical indifference to human concerns. The 105mm speaking only when targets presented sufficient resistance to justify its particular application.

Culper moved through the compound, men flowing around him with rifles finding those who had chosen poor defensive positions.

"Patriots secured," came report through radio. "All missile systems intact. Warheads secure."

Militiamen threw down their weapons and surrendered in droves. They were willing to die for their cause, but when the fiber cable link was severed, their cause was lost. They would not sacrifice their lives for nothing. Not even their loyalty to Walker and their fellow militiamen.

The Strykers completed their circuit of the

compound's perimeter, ensuring no defensive position remained capable of offering resistance that might delay the operation's completion.

The rain continued falling. The soil drank blood made indistinguishable from water yet distinct in meaning assigned by those who had shed it willingly if not eagerly.

Frank exited the stairwell. The hallway stretched before him, lit by emergency bulbs strung along ceiling gone yellow with age. Frank moved without sound, the twin Redhawks held up, barrels still warm from work already completed on men who had stood between him and his purpose. Blood marked his passage, some his own, more belonging to those who had chosen poorly their positions relative to his.

Voices ahead. Men shouting coordinates, positions, orders that revealed discipline despite situation collapsing around them. The command center door hung ajar, light spilling through gap where steel had warped against frame never designed for decades of neglect followed by hasty resurrection.

Frank positioned himself against the wall, weight balanced on balls of feet worn hard through years of walking.

The door exploded outward, wood and metal disintegrating against something heavier than human intention. Three men emerged with rifles already tracking toward where Frank had stood milliseconds before. But he had moved, the Redhawk in his right hand firing once. The man on left fell, face gone concave where hollowpoint had restructured features beyond recognition. The second Redhawk answered. Another man down.

The third man fired, rounds stitching plaster where Frank's head had been before he moved again, the big revolvers somehow keeping pace with his motion despite their weight. The Redhawks fired again, using up precious ammunition. The man's chest opened, white bone visible briefly before blood filled the gap.

Frank stepped toward the doorway. Movement inside, men taking positions behind computer stations and improvised barriers. Low on ammunition, Frank was in the gunfight he had hoped to avoid.

The first man charged, weapon raised. A Redhawk's report ended discussion before it began. Frank holstered the empty revolver. The second Redhawk remained in his left hand, single round waiting for circumstance demanding its expenditure.

"He's here," someone shouted inside.

Frank recognized the voice. Walker. The man he had crossed mountains and conscience to find.

"The tunnel," Walker continued. "Secure the exit."

One of the Redhawks found its final target, a man who appeared in doorway with shotgun that would have erased Frank's presence had reaction time proven insufficient. The man was dead and the revolver was empty. He slid it back into its holster.

The Colt Cobra was in his hand, smaller than the Redhawks but no less lethal at distances now collapsed to feet instead of yards.

The command center door now stood fully open, the room beyond visible in static snapshots provided by muzzle flashes. Two men down, caught by Frank's initial entry. Three more moving toward a door in the far corner, disappearing through.

The last man through turned, rifle raised. Frank's Colt answered, two rounds finding center mass despite movement and distance. The man fell back through the door, legs still visible as final twitches transferred nervous system's last commands to muscles no longer receiving proper blood supply.

Frank moved through the command center, stepping over bodies still bleeding. The door in the rear wall stood open, darkness beyond, passageway leading down rather than out. An escape tunnel planned for exactly this contingency.

He paused only long enough to verify what the room contained. Computer stations gone dark. System monitors showing missile launch systems disconnected.

Papers scattered across floor. The revolution abandoned mid-sentence. Its practitioners now fleeing through passages beneath earth that promised outlet beyond this facility's boundaries. No sign of Walker or his corpse. He was gone with the remaining technicians.

Frank followed, the Cobra held ready against an unknown number of men walking the path ahead. His boots finding steps worn smooth by passage of workers who had built this place when the Cold War made such construction seem necessary rather than absurd. The darkness wrapping around him like an old companion.

Ahead Walker moved through darkness. Two men with him, their weapons held ready for pursuit that felt inevitable despite hope that perhaps this final contingency might prove unnecessary. The tunnel stretched before them, a concrete throat leading toward an exit outside the compound perimeter.

"How many followers?" asked Manning, the youngest of those still with him. The man's rifle held across chest still rising and falling with exertion born from adrenaline rather than physical strain.

"Just one," Walker said. "Kane."

"We find a place to ambush him," said Manning.

"You do that. Both of you," said Walker. "There's a turn in the tunnel up ahead. That'd be a good place. Give you some cover."

Behind them Frank moved through darkness made navigable by emergency lights that painted everything the color of blood not yet spilled but promised.

The two men crouched at the tunnel's bend, rifles aimed at the darkness from which Frank would emerge. Walker had already moved on. Water leaked through concrete overhead, droplets marking time like a broken clock. Their breath clouded in the cold underground air.

"You hear anything?" whispered Manning, finger tight against the trigger.

Reeves, older by a decade, held his hand up for silence. The tunnel amplified every sound. The drip of water. The scrape of boot against grit. Their own heartbeats like drums in their ears.

"He'll come," Reeves said.

Frank moved through the tunnel like a creature born to darkness. His boots made little sound against the concrete floor wet with decades of seepage. He paused at each junction of pipe and conduit, listening.

He knew they waited ahead. Men always waited. Men who believed in causes worth dying for.

Manning and Reeves breathed in the darkness, rifles sighted on empty space, eyes straining for movement where light failed.

Something changed in the air. A shift in pressure. A scent not belonging to mold and concrete and stale time.

"There," whispered Reeves, sighting down his rifle barrel.

Frank crouched low, pressed against the tunnel wall. The tunnel smelled of cordite and copper and fear gone cold. He saw the faint outline of rifle barrels extending beyond the bend. Saw the subtle movement of men trying to remain still. Neither invisible nor silent to senses honed through decades of finding men who didn't wish to be found.

He reached down, picked up a chunk of concrete no bigger than his thumb. Threw it twenty feet ahead where the tunnel bent. The small rock clattered against the floor, echoing in the enclosed space.

"That him?" Manning whispered, aiming toward the sound.

Reeves fired three rounds into the empty darkness. The muzzle flash blinded them both momentarily. Frank charged, diving to the floor as he rounded the corner. The concrete scraped his forearm raw. He rolled once and came up firing.

The Colt fired twice in rapid succession. Its crack filled the tunnel like trapped thunder. Manning took the first round center mass, dead before his body understood what happened. Reeves managed to squeeze off a wild shot that ricocheted off the ceiling before the second bullet caught him in the throat. He dropped to his knees, hands clutching at the wound as if to hold life inside where it belonged.

Frank rose to his feet, approached the dying man. Their eyes met in the dim emergency light. Reeves tried to speak but only bubbles of blood escaped his lips. Frank unsheathed his KA-BAR and finished off Reeves with a quick strike into his chest. A mercy neither asked for nor required.

Frank moved on. Only two bullets left in the Colt. He would make them count. The pain in his cheek had become background noise against purpose that pulled him forward. Blood still seeped from the wound Sarah had gifted him with her betrayal. Frank touched it without thought. Fingers coming away red and wet.

The maintenance tunnel ended at a steel door. Walker emerged into a clearing where the rain had turned soil to black muck that sucked at boots. A metal shed stood thirty yards distant.

The Ram's engine caught on the first try. Walker pulled out of the shed. The truck's tires found purchase against mud that would have trapped lesser vehicles.

He drove without looking back. The rain-slick mountain road descending through forest that had witnessed conflict before America claimed it for history books. The wipers worked against the deluge with steady rhythm like a metronome counting down. The truck's engine growled through gears.

Frank reached the end of the tunnel. He pushed through the exit into rain that struck like small caliber rounds. The clearing spread before him. Fresh tire tracks in mud showing passage of a heavy vehicle heading east. He knew it was Walker.

The Imperial waited where he'd left it beyond the compound's perimeter. The storm intensifying as he moved through forest. His shadow followed, black upon black, ghost behind ghost.

The Imperial's door groaned against frame. The engine coughed then caught like a living thing answering to a voice it recognized. Frank pulled away as smoke rose from the facility behind him.

He followed the tire tracks onto the mountain highway that twisted through wilderness. The V8 roared through tunnels of pine that crowded road on both sides. The speedometer trembling past ninety. Each turn taken precisely because mistakes at this velocity meant a conclusion he wasn't prepared to accept.

The rain painted the Imperial's windshield faster than wipers could clear it. Frank hunched forward, eyes narrowed against the deluge.

He spotted the truck's taillights through a curtain of water and darkness. The Ram fought the incline that slowed even modified engines. Frank pushed the

Imperial harder. Metal protesting beneath his hands. The gap narrowed with each turn. Each straightaway. The hunt approaching its inevitable conclusion.

Walker's face appeared in rearview mirror. Eyes narrowed in recognition of the black shape that materialized from the rain behind him. The Imperial's headlights cut through the darkness. He pressed harder on the accelerator. The Ram surged forward. The Imperial matched his speed then gained.

The Imperial slammed into the Ram's rear bumper, steel meeting steel with a sound like the world splitting in two. Walker's truck fishtailed, tires fighting mud and momentum. Frank pressed the accelerator harder. The engine roared. He pulled alongside the Ram, matched its speed on the rain-slick asphalt.

Frank squeezed the Colt's trigger. Glass exploded inward as the first round shattered the truck's driver side window. The second round found Walker's shoulder, tore through cloth and flesh. Blood sprayed across the Ram's interior. Walker fought the wheel, face twisted in pain and rage.

The Imperial struck the truck's side panel. Metal screamed against metal. Walker's truck crashed through the guardrail, steel posts snapping like matchsticks. Frank tried to correct but physics had claimed them both. The Imperial slid sideways on the wet asphalt. The world tilted.

The car plunged down the embankment. Frank braced against the steering wheel as the Imperial carved a path through saplings and brush. The ancient tree appeared in the windshield like judgment made of wood. Impact threw him against the dash. Metal folded around the tree trunk. The frame bent. The engine block cracked. Steam rose into rain-soaked air.

Frank pushed the door with his shoulder. Metal

groaned then surrendered. He fell to the wet earth, pulled himself upright. Fresh cuts marked his face and forearms. Blood mixed with rain, dripped from his chin. He stood swaying like a tree in high wind.

Below him Walker's truck lay on its side, steam rising from the hood. Empty. Frank scanned the forest floor. Boot prints in the mud led downhill toward the river that cut through the valley.

He followed, each step driving shards of pain through his ribs. His breath came short and sharp. He crossed the clearing where Walker's prints disappeared into a pine thicket. The river appeared through the trees. Gray water rushing over stone worn smooth by centuries.

Frank stepped into the current. Cold shocked his system. The water reached his waist, pulled at him with hungry hands. He crossed, found Walker's tracks on the far bank leading into forest grown thick with undergrowth.

Walker watched from behind an ancient cedar, breath held in lungs burning for release. He checked his pistol. Two rounds remained. He thumbed the safety off, pressed his shoulder against wet bark.

Frank stopped at the tree line. Rain lessened to steady drizzle. Silence descended like a physical weight. He scanned the forest, eyes moving from trunk to trunk. Somewhere among the ancient trees Walker waited. Frank reached down into his boot and withdrew the Derringer. He cocked the trigger. The Derringer was hard as hell to aim with its short barrel and small grip. It felt like a toy in his massive hand.

Walker tensed. He heard Frank approaching. Slow deliberate steps crushing wet leaves. He counted to three then swung around the trunk, pistol extended in both hands. He fired. The round split air where Frank had been a moment before.

Frank hit the ground and fired the Derringer. The bullet struck Walker in the right chest. Stunned, he dropped his pistol and watched it slide down the embankment. He turned to see Frank cocking the Derringer to fire the second round.

Walker dove down the embankment scrambling on his belly like some primeval creature trying to reach his pistol. Frank fired the last round in the Derringer. It missed. Frank could see Walker's pistol just a few feet away from Walker's hand. No time.

Frank spotted a fallen pine trunk, diameter thick as his thigh. He lifted it with arms gone beyond pain and hurled it.

The log struck Walker across the lower back with sound like axe meeting wood. Walker screamed. His legs stopped moving. Useless flesh below the waist where his spine had given way.

Frank stood over him, breath coming in clouds visible in the cooling air. Walker stared up through rain dripping from pine boughs overhead. His hand clawed mud as if searching for a weapon that wasn't there.

"I won't surrender," snarled Walker.

"Never," said Frank. He knew this about the man.

Had always known it.

"Give me my gun. Let me finish this." Frank shook his head once.

"Your knife then. For old times." Walker's voice steadier than a dying man's had right to be.

Frank considered, then nodded. He drew the KABAR from its sheath. Offered it hilt first.

"Be my second," Walker said. "Like we did for Rodriguez in Tunisia." Frank nodded once more.

Walker positioned the blade beneath his chin. The steel cold against skin gone pale with shock and blood loss. He took a breath. Started the thrust upward. Pain greater than his resolve flared white-hot behind his eyes. He faltered. The blade penetrated skin, drew blood, but stopped short of the brain stem that would end his suffering.

Frank waited for a long moment. Pain was what Walker deserved. Then, Frank's boot found the knife hilt. One swift kick drove the blade upward through bone and tissue into the brain that had conceived revolution and brought them both to this moment in a forest older than the nation they'd fought to destroy and preserve.

Walker's body relaxed. Rain washed blood from the knife hilt still protruding from his jaw. Frank stood watching as life departed eyes that had seen the same things his had. That had drawn different conclusions. The sky continued weeping. The river continued flowing. Time passed unmarked by anything but the increasing cold.

Frank knelt beside the body. Closed Walker's eyes with fingers calloused from building lighthouses and taking lives in equal measure. He retrieved his knife. Wiped it clean on Walker's jacket. Blood so familiar it barely registered anymore.

He left the body where it lay. Forest creatures would come. Forest seasons would pass. What was left of Walker would rot. Nature had its own justice.

The Imperial sat at the base of the C-17's loading ramp, a broken warrior awaiting final transport. Rain fell in scattered drops like the last thoughts of a storm too tired to continue. The massive cargo aircraft loomed above, its hold a cavernous mouth ready to swallow whatever men deemed worth transporting.

The Imperial's once-proud body bore witness to its

final battle—frame bent where it had embraced the ancient tree, driver's side crumpled inward like a crushed tin can, headlight dangling by wires like a gouged eye, hood warped and split where the engine block had nearly pushed through upon impact—yet it ascended the ramp with a dignity that suggested even in destruction it remained something built to endure what lesser machines could not survive.

Frank stood apart, shoulders hunched against weather that matched his mood. The medic had done what he could with limited supplies, his practiced hands had moved across Frank's weathered landscape of old and new damage. The wound in Frank's shattered cheek where Sarah's bullet had been extracted now lay clean and sutured, skin pulled together with neat black stitches that would add one more scar to a collection beyond counting. The flattened slug rested in a metal specimen jar, a souvenir Frank wanted. Purple bruises mapped the impact points where his body had met the Imperial's interior during the crash. His left hand was wrapped in gauze where glass had opened three fingers to bone. Dried blood still clung to his hairline despite attempts to wash it away. His limp more pronounced from the thigh wound that had received fresh bandages. He moved like something held together by will rather than sinew, a man whose body had learned to carry pain as others carried wallets or watches—a constant presence acknowledged but not requiring comment.

Frank watched without expression as the winch motor groaned. Cables tight, pulling the Imperial up the ramp inch by laborious inch. The tires, one flat from impact, dragged across metal like something reluctant to leave earth behind.

The loadmaster directed the operation with hand signals universally understood by men who moved heavy things through spaces never meant to accommodate them. The Imperial settled onto the cargo bay floor with a sound like finality.

Frank approached as they disconnected cables from the car's frame. He ran scarred fingers along the hood, tracing damage done.

The loadmaster appeared beside him, clipboard in hand. Rain spotted the papers he carried. He assessed the damage with eyes that had seen worse things transported across continents.

"Hell of a car," he said. "Don't build 'em like that anymore."

Frank nodded once.

The loadmaster handed Frank the clipboard and pen. "If you give me your brother's address I'll make sure your car... or what's left of it gets dropped off. He must be one helluva mechanic if he's gonna fix it for ya." "No. Hedge fund manager," said Frank.

"Well, I suppose that's good. Probably gonna cost more to fix it than it's worth."

Frank grunted like he didn't care.

Culper approached, boots ringing against the metal ramp. His face scrubbed clean of night's work, only the eyes still carrying evidence of what had transpired on the mountain slopes now miles behind them.

"Are you sure there's nothing else a grateful nation can do for you, Frank?" Culper asked.

Frank shook his head, handed the clipboard back to the loadmaster, then walked up the ramp and disappeared into the cargo hold along with the Imperial.

"That guy is one weird duck," said the loadmaster, watching Frank's massive frame vanish into shadow.

"Yeah, but thank God he's our duck," said Culper.

He turned away as the ramp began closing with hydraulic certainty. The sound of machinery overwhelmed the diminishing rain. The aircraft prepared for departure from a place that would remember nothing of what had happened in the darkness now lifted.

The little boat's engine coughed then died. Frank tied off at the weathered pier, rope biting into palms still calloused from work laid aside weeks before. The lighthouse stood against a sky threatening rain.

He climbed stone steps worn smooth by passage of men now dust. The door opened to familiar smell gone wrong. The feral cat had left messages in every corner.

The scarred Tom appeared on the staircase. Yellow eyes narrowed upon the giant who had abandoned what was now its domain. Frank stood in the doorway, rucksack heavy against his shoulder. The cat's back arched. Its tail straight as a rifle barrel.

"Pisshead," Frank said. His damaged throat making the word sound like stone dragged across metal.

The cat hissed. Teeth yellowed by age and diet of mice. It stood its ground on stairs that Frank had rebuilt with hands.

Frank moved toward the cat. His bulk blocking light falling through the single window. He reached toward it. The cat swatted with claws extended. Drew blood across knuckles scarred by years of placing such marks on others. Frank looked at the red beads forming. Something shifted in his face. The suggestion of what another might recognize as smile.

"Thanks," Frank said. "Good to be back."

He moved to the cupboard where he kept supplies meant for just such homecomings. Frank placed a can of tuna on the counter. The cat's attention shifted. Its suspicion momentarily suspended in favor of hunger.

Frank opened the can. Set it on the floor. The animal

ate with concentration ignoring Frank as he moved to the window. Ocean spread before him. Waves constant as violence he couldn't escape. Rain began falling. The cat continued eating. Frank continued watching. Each accepting the other's presence in space that would never belong to either.

Letter to Reader

Dear Reader:

I hope you enjoyed *The Defiant*. I enjoyed writing all the twists and turns in the story, then again… I enjoy rollercoasters.

The next book in The Frank Kane Series is *The Unbroken*. Frank's back and ornerier than ever. Culper, Frank's cat, the Imperial, and the Redhawks are also back. Like all the books in the series, the Unbroken is a fast-paced thriller filled with suspense and action.

Sharing my books with your friends and reviews are always welcome. Thank you for supporting my work.

Regards,

David Lee Corley, Author

Author's Biography

Born in 1958, David grew up on a horse ranch in Northern California, breeding and training appaloosas. He has had all his toes broken at least once and survived numerous falls and kicks from ornery colts and fillies. David started writing professionally as a copywriter in his early 20's. At thirty-two, he packed up his family and moved to Malibu, California, to live his dream of writing and directing motion pictures. He has four motion picture screenwriting credits and two directing credits. His movies have been viewed by over fifty million movie-goers worldwide and won a multitude of awards, including the Malibu, Palm Springs, and San Jose Film Festivals. In addition to his twenty-four screenplays, he has written twenty-nine novels. He developed his simplistic writing style after rereading his two favorite books, Ernest Hemingway's *The Old Man and the Sea* and Cormac McCarthy's *No Country For Old Men*. An avid student of world culture, David lived as an expat in both Thailand and Mexico. At fifty-six, he sold all his possessions and became a nomad for four years. He circumnavigated the globe three times and visited fifty-six countries. Known for his detailed descriptions, his stories often include actual experiences and characters from his journeys.